Frequency Studios

presents

Bad Kitty:

Haley's World

Bad Kitty Book 2

by Ethan Sasportas

ISBN (Paperback): 978-1-7378949-3-3
ISBN (Hardcover): 978-1-7378949-4-0
ISBN (eBook): 978-1-7378949-5-7

Published by Frequency Studios

TABLE OF CONTENTS

Purple Dawn

Omniwatch Data Entry:

Multiversal Cluster 77. Designation: Frequency
Universe 9, Timeline 1-C1-C13
Earth: 6000 BC

The world looked very different. If people from modern-day appeared and looked up, they would have thought that this was an alien planet, but it was not. The sky was purple instead of blue and always remained the same. There was no difference between day and night; the weather was comfortable and unchanging around the entirety of the lush world, and the peoples of Earth were thriving.

Things were unrecognizable compared to the present, but the most striking difference was in the sky to the north. A large yellow sphere hung in place, and in the center was a circle of white and a smaller circle of red. This was what the world once referred to as the Sun. The gas giant Saturn dominated the northern sky, with Venus and Mars between it and the Earth in a polar alignment. It was a golden age for the world, and the Humans were starting to advance in their mystical and technological prowess.

Populations had spread throughout the world, and one nation in particular was on the cutting edge. Antarctica, at that time, was a paradise, and the leading minds from around the world would regularly meet there to exchange ideas. This was the place where Humans discovered that reality was not just one realm but a spectrum of energetic densities. A reality upon a reality upon a reality.

Some were populated, others were not, some were beautiful, and others were harsh, but all were a part of each other. A part of the same world. They met other species of people, much like themselves, in some of these densities and began friendships and trades with their fellow Terrans. Things were great for the people of Earth throughout many densities, and Antarctica, known then as Atlantis, was at the center of it all. The Human's realm became known as the First Density. The Second Density, though thriving with life, was found to be unpopulated, while the Third and Fourth Densities were populated by multiple species, such as the Alfan and the Dvwargarians.

5200 BC

The sky had done something that no one had ever seen before. It started to change. All that the Earthlings had ever seen was a constant purple glow, but something was now different. Although the sky remained purple, it started to brighten. It wasn't a startling difference. In fact, it was so subtle that most people didn't even notice at first. The sky would brighten, then it dimmed back down. This pattern continued and, as it did, became more pronounced.

Then it happened.

A flash erupted from the polar alignment, and long, comet-like tails extended out from Venus toward the core of the system, toward Saturn. The purple plasma sheath that surrounded the Saturnian worlds was disrupted as its magnetosphere contacted one from another star, a bright yellow dwarf. The sky became brighter than anyone had seen before as it took on a more bluish hue, and a new feature appeared on their original sun. A crescent of light that rotated counterclockwise.

As the crescent rotated, the light dimmed, and, for the first time, the people could look up to a dark sky and see the cosmos. More stars than they could possibly count, and the cometary tails of Venus shone brightly. The rotation continued and the sky became bright once more, dazzling the eyes of the people. This was when timekeeping, as it is understood today, began.

4300 BC

The tails of Venus took on different forms and shapes over the centuries. Three tails became four. They shifted through various patterns and presented a beautiful display, especially at night. But then the red spot in the middle of their Sun grew larger as Mars began to move closer to the Earth. The neighboring planet took up much of the sky, and a tail of red dust extended down toward the northern horizon. Some people described it as the World Mountain, and others as Mars growing a beard. The red planet then pulled away as it moved toward Venus and settled back to its usual place for a short period of time.

The people of Earth talked about the moving heavenly bodies and began recounting the events, personifying the planets and describing the scenario as a conflict amongst godly beings. But the shifting of the planetary alignment was far from over. Mars began his approach once more, and this time, Venus also left her perch. The cometary tails converged into one as it shifted toward Mars and struck him hard, sending him closer to the Earth. Closer than the red planet had ever been.

Tails of dust from both Mars and Earth extended out toward each other when their electrical fields mixed. The Hero of the Sky fell and rocked the Earth as storms manifested on a planet-wide scale. People desperately sought shelter as meteors slammed the ground and cosmic lightning bolts arched between the two planets. After much loss of life, the skies began to clear, and Mars was making his way back up toward the beautiful, angry Venus.

Her cometary tails spread out like serpents, giving her the appearance of long, wild hair. The red tail of Mars pulled away from the Earth and extended out toward Venus. Venus's tails converged into one and met the tail of Mars, forming a twisting ribbon of dust and plasma as the two gods in the sky did battle.

The catastrophe had wiped away much of Earth's population, and technological knowledge was lost. Atlantis's destruction was total, and there were no known survivors. But many Atlanteans did escape. They ported into the Second Density, where a good number of them managed to find some shelter and rode out the rest of the cosmic storm. They, too, observed as the skies cleared and Mars made his approach to Venus. They battled, then made their peace as they fell back into their axial positions once more. A short period of time later, they left their positions and began to wander off across the sky.

With the dueling magnetospheres of Saturn and the yellow dwarf star, there was a sudden flash when Saturn ejected several planet-sized spheres from within itself to reach electromagnetic equilibrium and then began to move from its northern throne.

As it moved away from the center of the sky, another world became visible. Jupiter. The new planetary bodies fell back into Saturn, but a massive electrical arch discharged from Jupiter, striking Saturn and releasing the bodies back into the sky. Saturn and its new moons fell away into the distance as Jupiter took the throne, but this would not last. Venus and Mars were now shrinking in the sky, and Jupiter also started to retreat while a smaller and brighter yellow sphere worked its way from the east to the west.

The planets settled into their new orbits around the yellow dwarf star. The people would tell the story of when the gods did battle in the sky, unaware of what their continued, collective focus could produce. Around the world and through the generations, these stories were told. The populations grew, and the names changed, but the stories were about the same cataclysmic event. And with the energy of so many people focused on the same personified concepts…

The gods manifested.

Created by the combined imagination of mortals. These stories had become religious practices, and with the continued focus of so many people, the energy of these manifestations individualized and became self-sustaining. The gods became real people, individuals with free will.

In the Second Density, the surviving people retained their scientific knowledge, and they had some gear and equipment in the bunkers of the research facilities. Starting from almost scratch, they were diligent and industrious people who went to work, recording all data and knowledge they had as others began building. Bit by bit, they worked in an effort to make contact with the other densities, hoping to find that the rest of Earth's peoples had fared better than they.

2350 BC

The people of Earth had taken a different path than their previous civilizations. Corruption had spread, and malicious practices had become commonplace. But the time came when they looked up, watching with a mix of awe and dread as Venus grew larger in the sky. They had heard the stories of old, told down through the generations, about when the beautiful Maiden of the Sky became angry, and now, Earth's orbit would bring the two worlds close to each other once again.

Quakes and storms became frequent and with increased intensity as the planets drew closer together. Venus's cometary activity began to display as it once did in the stories, arching plasma toward the Earth. The storms raged, and the rain fell like never before. Massive flooding occurred in all densities, again devastating the populations.

From the Mediterranean area, Venus herself watched in horror as the planet that was her namesake initiated the cataclysm. Even the gods, with all their abilities to command the elements, were powerless to prevent the deluge. Many of them combined their efforts, but what should have worked simply did not.

Some of the more empathic gods, such as Bastet, while hovering high in the sky and attempting to calm the deluge, noticed the Universal Sentience. And then she felt it rolling over her…grief. Like that of a parent losing their child, except this was magnified to an intensity beyond anything the goddess could bear. Overwhelmed, Bast instantly passed out, but her best friend Artemis, by her side, caught the Egyptian goddess before she fell.

"Bast, wake up!" she shouted in fear for her friend as lightning cracked through the wind-driven rain. After a moment, she regained consciousness, crying hysterically. "Bast, look at me! Look at my eyes!"

Focusing in on Artemis, Bast choked with sorrow as she said, "The Creator's heart is breaking, but this must happen." She grabbed Artemis and pulled her in, hugging her tight while the tears flowed down Bast's cheeks. "We can do nothing," she sobbed.

Over a month later, the skies finally cleared, and the planet Venus appeared much smaller. Over the next few months, she shrank to the size of a far-away star in the night sky as the two planets settled into their permanent orbits.

0033 AD, First Density

The sky had become unnaturally dark, like night had occurred in the middle of the afternoon. Struggling to exhale, Yeshua had endured torture that few could ever comprehend. The nails through His wrists and ankles held Him in place against the Roman cross, and He had to pull Himself up to release His breath. After a painful exhale, the crucified man slumped back down, the physical position forcing Him to inhale again.

Despite the trauma, pain and exhaustion, He was still mentally clear and coherent. His words for the last few hours had been labored and strained, but the man gathered His strength one last time. He pulled Himself up, allowing the air to escape His lungs as He managed a shout, "It is finished!" and with that, Yeshua released His spirit.

The energy pulsed outward, unseen but not unnoticed. In all densities, the wave of peace was felt by mortal and immortal alike, and many dropped to their knees, shedding tears in a state of catharsis. The pulse continued outward, permeating all of existence, felt by sentient beings across the entirety of the universe.

He looked like a normal man, save the fact that he was in the sky. It had been three days since the Son had died, but he looked to Yeshua's tomb on the ground with gratitude. The earth beneath him trembled when the Seraph touched down, and he, with strength beyond that of the mortals, rolled the stone away from the tomb's entrance.

Inside, he could see the cloth with which Yeshua had been wrapped and laid to rest, but there was no body. The Seraph couldn't even begin to hide his smile as a tear of joy rolled down his cheek. He jumped on top of the stone, sat down and waited. Feeling both honored and excited, the Seraph was ready to tell mortals about the good news. Moments like this were when he loved his job.

Second Density. Canaan

Tasi was five foot eight, barrel-chested and had thick, muscular arms. He had two complexions. His face, like most of his body, was pale, but from the top of his head and down his neck and back, the skin was a grayish-blue. The two tones met and formed a line down the sides of his neck, which continued behind his shoulders and down the sides of his torso. This two-toned complexion was normal amongst the people of the second density. The only thing different about Tasi's complexion was that it was pale when compared to most others in the region.

The man opened his eyes and, a couple of blinks later, could see the landscape clearly. He pushed himself up from the ground, grunting as he twisted and sat upright, leaning back against a large boulder. Every muscle hurt and the blood from his split lip was dried. It was unusually warm today, but at least he was dumped on the shaded side of the rock, and the cool feeling against his back soothed some of the discomfort.

Tasi had been betrayed. His band was desperate and falling apart after their leader had been killed, and every job they planned ended in failure. The merchant travelers had been hiring more protection as of late and the group of brigands, more disorganized. The attempt on a convoy two weeks ago cost two of the men their lives, leaving the rest more disheartened than ever.

But Tasi, just sixteen years of age, had paid attention as he grew up with this band and could easily see that it did not have to be this way. So, he did what the rest didn't seem willing to do: he took control. When they were sitting around the fire, chewing on what little scraps they had, he stood up and practically shouted, "We can do better than this!" The others all looked at him with surprise. Although no one here doubted his intelligence, Tasi had always been meek around his peers, so to see him speaking up and demanding attention certainly piqued their interest. "We've done this same thing countless times, with great success! But now we fall apart easily before the simplest of convoys ever since we lost Abner."

He began walking around the fire, looking his peers in the eye as he passed, "Abner taught us how to succeed and succeed we did. Now, with him gone, we have all veered off the path, doing things during a job we normally wouldn't have. We've lost our discipline. But," he said as he hoisted his finger into the air, "I believe we can get that back. I suggest we bring his methods and training back into practice, redetermine who plays what role and proceed with an actual plan." A slight, confident smile made its way onto Tasi's face as he said, "We have talent here. With proper coordination, we could become unstoppable."

The words were convincing and gave everyone a sense of confidence as they all began to discuss how to proceed. Tasi was surprised by how readily the others listened to his directions, but it paid off. Two weeks later, the brigands hit a large caravan. They quickly decimated the hired guards and tore through the feeble opposition that the merchants themselves could muster. On their way back to camp from the successful raid, they decided, for reasons unknown, that they no longer needed Tasi.

Now, he sat against a rock with nothing but his worn-out clothing. They even took his waterskin. Tasi stared off into the distance, wondering why the betrayal. Wondering why he failed when he did as Abner would have. Wondering if he would die here. The more he analyzed the dynamics in his head, the more he could not deny a major difference between how he and Abner led. Tasi focused on the merits of the ideas. The efficacy of how they could all function as a cohesive group. Abner, on the other hand, blended that with fear and intimidation. The man could be just as ruthless as he was inspiring. Most dared not question him, and those who did sometimes lost their tongs. Or more.

"If I survive this," Tasi shouted to the open air, "I will make sure everyone fears me!"

First Density

Peering across the deserted, rocky landscape, the man had much on his mind as he stood there and waited. Molech was concerned about the events from three days ago. Events that may have adverse effects on his efforts. In a flash of orange light, another man manifested next to the troubled god. Turning toward the new arrival, Molech saw that Baphomet looked a little haggard. Cocking his head to the side in confusion, Molech asked, "What happened to you?"

Baphomet began to shake his head in irritation but then let out a chuckle and shrugged. "I was in another land and noticed a farmer struggling to push his cart to the top of a hill." The malicious god smirked as he continued, "So I decided to have a bit of fun. I cast a driving rain upon him, slickening the grassy hill." Baphomet laughed a bit when he said, "You should have seen him struggling. He just would not give up. He even slipped and hit his head on the corner of his cart!"

Molech also chuckled while listening to the story but then waited for Baphomet to compose himself.

After a couple of breaths, he continued, "It was a nasty gash, and he was so frustrated that I started harvesting some of his energy. But then I got bored, so I stopped the rain and watched as he again neared the top." Baphomet blew out a sigh, and then the irritation became evident on his face. "It was time to come here, and the man finally got to the top. So, I called down a bolt of lightning to end him, but it struck me instead."

Eyes and mouth widening with surprise and confusion, Molech asked, "How did that happen?"

"Cernunnos," Baphomet spat as if speaking the name left a foul taste on his tongue.

Molech scoffed and rolled his eyes. "I grow weary of him. Was Ares there, too?"

"No," Baphomet replied.

"Good, we do not need their meddling right now."

"I don't understand why they bother," Baphomet stated. "They never even associate with the mortals anymore. So, why do they care what we do with them?"

Molech shook his head and said, "That doesn't matter right now. We have bigger problems."

"Such as?"

"You must have noticed that wave of energy three days ago," Molech said.

"I did," Baphomet replied. "It was the purest magick I've ever felt. But it was nothing I could use."

"But now it's inevitable. The mortals' consciousness will start to expand," Molech paused to make sure that Baphomet was paying attention, "And that does not bode well for us. If we fail to have this sphere ready when Lucifer is freed, he'll do to us far worse than anything we've done to the mortals."

Few things could bring a chill to Baphomet's spine, but the mention of an angry Lucifer was one of them. "Have you spoken to Set?"

"Yes," Molech said with a sigh, "He cares not for the schemes of either Lucifer or the mortals. We'll have no help from him."

"Unfortunate, but not unexpected," Baphomet replied. "I'll gather the others and have them meet us at…oo! Do you sense that?"

"Yes," Molech said with an air of intrigue.

"Now that's an energy that I can use," Baphomet said enthusiastically.

The two gods shifted their vibration, phasing themselves into the Second Density, to find an empty landscape much like the one from which they had departed. But there was something radiating from the other side of the boulder. The emotional energy was so intense that they noticed it from another density, and Baphomet started to siphon it for himself.

"Wait," Molech said, and then he heard a man shout, "If I survive this, I will make sure everyone fears me!"

Molech turned to Baphomet with a sinister grin and telepathically said, "This might be the opportunity that we've been searching for." As Baphomet thought about it, a slow nod became more pronounced while a smile spread across his face. Molech smirked, then walked around the boulder and introduced himself to Tasi.

CHAPTER 1
Reset

First Density. Upstate New York. Saturday. August 13, 1977

Akira Watanabe pulled the curtain just a bit to the side and peeked out the window into the wooded landscape. A squirrel, the source of the sound Akira was investigating, sat on a tree branch just beyond the glass.

A brilliant mind reared in the Second Density's Japan, Akira had two passions besides his family: his studies and computers. He stood at five feet eleven inches tall, was of medium build with dark brown hair parted in the middle and his bangs dangled around the frame of his glasses.

The skin on the back of his neck was a darker tan color, and it mixed with his pale front pigment in a speckled pattern down the sides of his neck. He breathed a sigh of relief, turning for the sofa where his wife, Brenda, and son, Derek, were seated. They had fled to upstate New

York in the First Density and were laying low in an old post and beam house, secluded deep in the woods.

Akira and his wife Brenda were psychologists and had spent the last few years studying body language. The technology in the Second Density was more advanced than the First, and after writing a facial recognition program that detected deception, the couple gained attention from the Podman in their district. Five days earlier, an enthusiastic demonstration had been presented, impressing the governing official with the accuracy of the program, but a moment later, this amazing accomplishment became Dr. Watanabe's undoing.

The Podman, who suspected disloyalty in one of Kone's personal guards, had played a video of the Cetatian leader giving a speech. He was watching to see if the program would indicate any deceptive behavior from one of the guards, but Akira was still in the room, and the only thing that the program displayed was Kone himself, with repeated hits on potential displays of falsehood.

He had tried to act like he did not notice, but as soon as he got home, Akira took his family and fled. Having no doubt that they would be among the next to disappear. Akira knew that the life they had known was at an end and that the best thing which he could hope for was that they would never be found, so that they could start a new life.

When the Cetatian State decided that one must disappear, all evidence of one having ever existed was erased. The name was removed from all records, and any work that was left behind, if ever made available, was credited to "anonymous." He looked to his son and vowed that Derek would not suffer this fate.

Perched on a tree limb, Vedant Sahmbo lowered his spyglass after Akira pulled the curtain closed. The Cetatian Hunters were amongst the best trackers in the world, and Sahmbo was the Hunter-Ralt. As such, all other Hunters were subordinate to him. Kone himself had assigned Sahmbo to find Akira Watanabe after he disappeared, and the

Proctors' best detectives could not find the man. It wasn't easy, especially since he had somehow found a way to leave the Second Density, but the Hunter-Ralt does not become so without good reason. Sahmbo had, once again, found the unfindable and contacted the Proctors to come and detain Watanabe.

The Hunter moved with grace and agility as he made his way back to the ground. Standing at five-foot seven, Vedant's skin was a dark brown color in front and dark green on his back. The two pigments mixed into a spotted color-line down the sides of his neck. His long salt and pepper hair was tied back into a tail, and he had a neatly trimmed mustache.

Sahmbo wasn't on the ground for more than a minute when seven bright white lights flashed before him. The lights were gone as quick as they appeared, and in their places were seven Cetatian men. Five Proctors, a Commando and the wizard who had ported them.

Surprised by the larger-than-expected group, Sahmbo said, "Don't be careless. His wife and child are with him."

"Acknowledged," said the Commando as he and the Proctors started for the cabin. While the team walked away, Sahmbo heard the Commando say to the sergeant. "Removing their names will be your job."

In desperation, Akira dove between the Proctors and the sofa, shielding his wife and their son from the pistol bolts. He was dead before his body hit the floor, and the next blast was a direct hit on Brenda. As she lifelessly collapsed away, a proctor took aim at the final Watanabe but hesitated.

"It must be done," stated the Commando, and the Proctor steadied his aim once more.

Although terrified, the young Derek Watanabe could tell from the way this man stood that he didn't want to pull the trigger yet was still undecided on whether he would follow through.

"Stop!" they all heard the voice of the Hunter-Ralt demand. The team looked to the door as Vedant strode into the room and stood between the boy and the others. "I claim my right. Spoils of the Hunt," he stated firmly and pointed toward the boy behind him. "He comes with me."

"He cannot," the Commando said. "They have been marked for full deletion. By Cetatian law, it must be as if they never existed."

"My right of Spoils is also law," Vedant reminded as he locked eyes with the Commando.

The tension in the room increased as the Proctors, whose job was to enforce Cetatian law, stood by, unsure of what to do. The boy read the room and could tell that the Hunter meant business, would not budge, and the Commando was not happy with the current impasse.

After a moment, the Commando said, "His name must be removed."

"This claim makes me his guardian," Vedant said, "His last name is now Sahmbo." The Hunter-Ralt narrowed his eyes. "You *will* leave him be."

First Density. Montana. Friday. October 30, 1998

Deep in a wooded area of foothills was a simple and secluded log cabin. Inside the living room, there was no furniture, but along the walls was a variety of swords, daggers, sticks, staffs and guns. A mat covered the floor, and in one corner was a circular object. Silver in color and two inches thick with a three-foot diameter, other than the fact that it was placed in the corner, it seemed unremarkable. Until the spark appeared a couple of feet above its surface. Little blue-white arcs spread out from this spark, forming what looked like a horizontally spinning ball of electricity. It opened at the vortex, growing wider and moving sideways above the disk.

As it moved, the opening followed the shape of a person kneeling. The vortex continued across the disk, depositing a woman as it shut and disappeared, all in under a second. She was on her knees and had her arms crossed in front of her, fingers wrapped around her shoulders. The woman was leaning forward and sobbing heavily as large teardrops splashed down to the port pad on which she kneeled.

She was wearing a black one-piece tactical jumper. A harness, woven into the fabric, ran over the shoulders and down the front and back as well as around the waist and the mid-thighs with small metal disks embedded throughout. In one of the two scabbards on her back was a katana, multiple knives were strapped in various spots to the jumper, and a bolt pistol was in a magnetic holster on her left hip. But on her right hip was the most eye-catching weapon that she carried. A metallic whip.

Hyperventilating and ready to choke, the woman tried to snap herself out of this inexcusable panic. She was a Hunter! Sharp mind, sharp skills, discipline and a code of honor, Hunters were capable and in control. And few had the self-control and mental discipline of Sabrina Carmen. She was one of the best, yet turned into a quivering mound of fear and sorrow by the simple touch of a ten-year-old girl. Utterly defeated by a lesser opponent.

Sabrina focused and, after a moment, managed to steady herself, regaining control of her breath. She rose to her feet, stepped from the port pad and walked to the middle of the room. Deliberate and intentional breathing, precise movement and form, mental and emotional discipline, Sabrina called on her training and forced herself into a practice routine to regain ownership of herself…

But then suddenly, she collapsed to her knees in another bout of heavy sobs.

First Density. Columbia, Connecticut. Sunday. November 1, 1998

With a furrowed brow and blue eyes locked upon her opponent, Haley was hunched with a slight bend in her knees, ready to spring into action. Her long blonde pigtails swayed slightly in the breeze as a mischievous smirk, bit by bit, revealed itself to the other girl staring back.

Standing tall and confident, Elizabeth raised her right arm to the side, palm up. Her brunette ponytail also swayed in the gentle breeze as light became visible above her palm. Bringing up her other arm, light began to coalesce above her left palm as well, a glowing orb of sparkling amber and indigo in each hand.

Haley was now sporting a huge grin as she wondered how much longer her best friend could keep a straight face. She was an empath and could feel another's emotions as if they were her own. And Haley knew that Elizabeth was giddy enough to pop.

An amber light flashed in Elizabeth's hazel eyes, and she drew her right arm back for a throw.

"Don't laugh!" Haley called out.

Elizabeth stopped short of the throw as she burst into giggles, and her orbs diffused to nothing. "No fair!" she laughed as her empathic friend also chuckled.

"Okay, okay," Haley said, "we'll do it right this time."

The two girls regained their composure, and Haley got back into position while Elizabeth again readied her mystical bolts.

"Okay," Haley said, and Elizabeth wound back for a throw.

The young mystic's arm shot forward, and the orb zipped straight for her friend. Haley dashed to the right, avoiding the shot as the second bolt came her way.

Haley, with an abrupt stop, leaned to her left, and the mystical bolt buzzed by her ear. She ducked when a third bolt came her way, allowing it to pass overtop her head. Feeling good about the successful dodges, Haley started to stand back up straight when a fourth bolt thudded into the front pocket of her coveralls. "Hey, I wasn't expecting that! You usually do only three."

A chuckle escaped from Elizabeth's lips as she shook her head. "That's the point," she said with that gotcha-grin, "we need to be ready if those Archons come back. They're total a…"

"Hey!" Haley shouted, preempting the foul language.

Elizabeth held her hand up in front of her, and another orb appeared. "What are ya gonna do about it?" she asked with a playful grin.

Haley smiled back and held up her hands, gathering energy into orbs of blue and purple light. "This!" she gleefully shouted with a throw. The orb elongated slightly as it flew forward, taking on a shape that resembled a kitten.

The ethereal feline rocketed toward Elizabeth as the mystic leaned to the side and threw a blast of her own. Haley was quick and nimble, and Elizabeth more so, making it difficult for each other to land a hit. That didn't matter for long because, after a few moments, there was no more dodging and weaving but hysterical laughter as the ten-year-old girls were just pelting each other with orbs of light.

"What are y'all doing?"

The girls stopped and looked to see Haley's dad, Harry, standing on the back patio.

A big smile on her face, Haley said, "We didn't want to wait until winter."

"Winter?" Harry asked.

"Yeah," Elizabeth said, "for a snowball fight!"

After a quick chuckle, Harry said, "Neil, Sandra and Junior are on their way. They'll probably be here any time now."

"Cool!" both girls said in unison.

Harry then smiled, "And I've got some cider on the stove top."

Ten minutes later, steam rose from two large glass mugs as the girls, with wide and eager eyes, watched Harry scoop the vanilla ice cream from the tub on the kitchen table. He placed a scoop in each mug, and the ice cream began melting into the hot cider. Since they were out of caramel, he drizzled maple syrup overtop the floating scoops and said, "Have at it."

"Thanks, Dad!" said Haley.

"Thank you," said Elizabeth.

Sliding his four fingers through the handle and thumb against the other side, Harry picked his mug up from the counter and took a sip. He turned around and leaned against the counter as Neil and Sandra, also seated at the kitchen table, sipped from their mugs.

"How long will Junior be asleep?" Haley asked.

Sandra, with a tired grin, said, "Hopefully a while. He's been cranky today."

"He takes after his mother," Neil stated flatly, and Sandra smacked him on the side of the arm but couldn't hide her smile. Neil didn't even flinch, but he lifted his arm and put it around Sandra's shoulders as she leaned in and kissed his cheek.

Looking at Harry, Sandra asked, "How long do you think before word gets out?" Another species of people, called Cetatians, shared the planet with Humans.

Two days ago, they had worked with a reptilian people from a parallel universe called Archons to discreetly take the area. A small, out-of-the-way town like Columbia was the perfect location to establish operations without drawing too much attention, so they captured the townsfolk and used copies of them to prepare for the arrival of the remaining Archon population, but Haley, Elizabeth and Neil, with the help of some United States Marshals from the Archon's universe, stopped them from succeeding. Now everyone in town knew that Cetatians, Archons and parallel universes existed. All subjects that were classified information, but Sandra's true concern was that everyone saw Haley and Elizabeth use their energetic abilities.

Thankfully, the entire town wanted to keep this to themselves, as no one liked the idea of news crews and curiosity seekers turning their peaceful corner of the world into a tourist hot spot. But people talk, and some will discuss it with trusted friends. Though folks may be selective, it was only a matter of time before word and rumor would spread.

"I haven't got the slightest idea," Harry said with his southern accent and a shrug. "Too many possibilities on that one," he finished as the phone rang.

Harry answered the phone, and Elizabeth asked, "So, why is Junior cranky?"

"He's teething," Neil replied while glancing toward the living room where the infant was sleeping.

"Elizabeth," Harry said as he hung the phone back on the wall, "that was your mom. She's on her way.

Montana

Walking along the wall, Sabrina looked amongst the weapons and stopped in front of the nun-chucks. Although better than nothing, she always saw them as an impractical weapon, so she never brought them into the field. Yet twice a week, the Hunter would practice, considering it to be an excellent proprioceptive exercise.

She removed them from the wall and went to the center of the room, searching for that focus. Sabrina began moving her hands in a blur as the nun-chucks whooshed through the air around her. Her form was near flawless, and she immersed herself in the moment when she felt the wooden handles in her grasp, felt the fast-paced tension and release in her muscles as she moved with the utmost accuracy.

After five minutes of intense practice, she placed the nun-chucks back on the wall and then returned to the center of the room to cool down and meditate, but instead, she stood there as her mind wandered.

Why? Sabrina wondered in silent thought. *It was years ago and should no longer bother me.* She took a deep breath and blew it out in a sigh…

Then her eyes widened as she sensed a presence. In a blur, the Hunter pivoted with a lightning-fast strike and her right fist thudded to a stop in the left palm of Derek Sahmbo.

Shocked, Sabrina stared into the Hunter-Ralt's eyes as he calmly looked back into hers. They stood there in silence for about twenty seconds before she started to break, the tears welling up as she started to breathe erratically. Sobbing, Sabrina collapsed into Sahmbo. He slid his arms around her shoulders and pulled her in tight, already deducing what had happened to her. Sahmbo hadn't seen her fall apart like this since they first met as children, and her trauma was fresh. But now, that trauma had come back to haunt her.

Columbia

Turning off the burner, Harry set another mug on the table for Maggie. Moments later, they could hear a car pulling into the driveway.

"She's here," Elizabeth said with a smile. Haley was glad to see her best friend finally getting along with her mother. The farmgirl understood Elizabeth's frustrations, but having lost her own mother to hypothermia in January, she had hoped that Elizabeth would understand what she had while she had it. And, after the events of Friday, she certainly did.

Harry filled the mug on the table with cider as the shutting of a car door was heard. Then he set a coffee mug down next to it, which immediately caught Elizabeth's attention. The young mystic looked at the second mug with confusion, then heard another car door shut. Her eyes shot open so wide that they could have rolled out of her head as Harry, with a big smile, started pouring coffee into the mug.

Haley, too, snapped her eyes wide as she felt the excitement and anticipation radiating from outside. The two girls looked at each other with shocked smiles and then turned their heads when they heard the front door open. There stood a man, 5'10, in a Navy working uniform. He had short brown hair, glasses, a mustache and a giant smile.

"Dad!" Elizabeth shouted as she jumped out of her chair and ran for him. Ryan Guerrerio had his arms out wide, ready to hug his daughter when she dove into him, wrapping her arms around his waist and burying her face in his chest. "Dad," she sobbed as tears flowed down her smiling cheeks. They held their embrace for a while and then looked each other in the eyes.

"I've missed my Dynamite," he said with a smile and kissed her on the forehead.

Elizabeth wiped her eyes, grabbed him in another hug and said, "I've missed you too."

After she let go, Haley hugged him next. "Welcome home," she said with a warm smile and misty eyes.

Ryan said, "Wow! You've both gotten a lot stronger since last month."

Montana

They were in another room of the sparsely furnished cabin where Sabrina sat cross-legged on a mat with her arms folded across her torso and her fingers around her shoulders. Her eyes fixated on the floor about three feet ahead. Sahmbo sat on a bench, facing her with his palms in his lap.

After a deep breath, Sabrina finally broke the silence. "How long have you known about his place?" she asked in a hushed voice.

"Awhile," he said, then asked, "So, are you an empath?"

Still looking at the floor, Sabrina began a slow nod and answered, "I think so," her tone subdued. "I don't know how else our emotions got so easily mixed." After letting out a sigh, Sabrina added, "She felt like music."

"Music?"

She nodded and continued. "A beautiful melody," her eyes began to water. "Sad...but sweet."

Sahmbo stood up. "And this wouldn't have likely happened if it wasn't already bothering you at that moment." He walked over to Sabrina and held out his hand. She took it in hers and stood to her feet, looking into the Hunter-Ralt's eyes as he asked, "What brought it to mind?"

Tears started to well up as she softly said, "Elizabeth, she...she reminded me...of who I used to be." She closed her eyes tight and composed herself. After another deep breath, she said, "Please tell me that Kone did not give them to the Archons."

"As I promised, no. They weren't even captured," Sahmbo answered as Sabrina looked to him in surprise, yet quite relieved. "And Ahnk-Hume is in the custody of the United States Air Force."

Sabrina's jaw dropped with this news. Sahmbo paused briefly to let that sink in and then continued, "The other six Archons are still here, but the connection between universes was lost and can't be reestablished. So, they are all that remain."

After a deep inhale, Sabrina blew out a sigh of relief at this bit of news. She, like many of the other Cetatians, was not at all fond of the sadistic people. "That is probably for the best, but what happened?"

Sahmbo said, "Somebody turned off the portgate." An unexpected sense of satisfaction and accomplishment came over Sabrina as he delivered the news.

"Take some time, as much as you need," Sahmbo said, his concern genuine. "Now that your empathic senses are opened up, it could take a while for you to sort out your own feelings from others, and I've heard that this tends to be overwhelming." He hugged her one more time and said, "I've got work to do." They kissed and released their embrace, "I'll be back to check on you in a couple of days."

Columbia

From one end of the table, Haley watched Elizabeth and Ryan take seats across from each other. They both placed their right elbows on the surface and reached forward with their left hands. They hooked their fingers and pressed their right palms together, ready for the arm-wrestling match.

Upon arrival at the New London Sub Base, Ryan was briefed on everything that had happened about Friday's events by the Base Admiral and an Air Force Colonel. But here, he got to hear it firsthand as the girls enthusiastically told him about their adventures beneath the town. They waved their arms around while making whooshing and zipping sounds as they described one of the battles. Ryan had been hearing them talk about their abilities, but his jaw still dropped when they conjured orbs of light in their hands.

"I thought that yours were supposed to look like kittens," Ryan said to Haley.

Haley looked to Elizabeth, who smiled as she gathered her energy. Haley sensed the protective field, so she threw the blast toward Elizabeth, and it took on its usual kittenish shape as it sped toward her friend. The ethereal feline softly burst against Elizabeth's field, where amber and indigo light rippled out across the spherical surface of the otherwise invisible barrier.

"Wow!" Ryan exclaimed as Elizabeth threw one at Haley, resulting in blue and purple light rippling across the farmgirl's protective field.

"You might want to restrict the light show to outside," Harry said, knowing the kind of oomph that the girls could pack into those orbs.

Haley and Elizabeth began to tell Ryan about their nanotech com-systems, which they called PJs and then demonstrated. Haley held her arms out wide, and her red flannel shirt began to ripple like it was made from liquid. The tiny bots reconfigured themselves, and her flannel became the orange and yellow striped shirt she had worn on Friday. Then her coveralls changed into the pair of jeans she wore Saturday, and her shirt changed into a gray sweatshirt. The nanobots also supported their movements, further enhancing their already considerable strength.

Haley watched in surprise as her best friend cycled through a variety of outfits and dresses. Elizabeth wasn't really tired when she first tried to sleep the previous night, so she began putting on all her clothes until the entire wardrobe was programmed into her PJs. Handing a phone to her dad, Elizabeth said, "This is part of it too."

Ryan flipped the phone open and looked at the screen, which displayed the word "SCANNING." A second later, it read, "IDENTIFIED: Guerrerio, Ryan A." The next words displayed were "PARENTAL ACCESS GRANTED."

"Awe," Elizabeth said in mock disappointment. Of course, she knew he would have access, just as Maggie, Harry and Neil did. And Colonel Decker.

Ryan watched the screen in amazement as it responded to his thoughts, and then, his jaw dropped. A video began playing as he thought of the battle that the girls had just described. The Cetatian woman on the screen moved with incredible dexterity, dodging every shot that the girls threw at her. Ryan saw, from his daughter's point of view, a lightning-fast punch directly toward the screen, and then he saw the room's ceiling. The woman stood above Elizabeth and aimed her gun.

His head tilted a bit in confusion when Haley grabbed the woman's wrist, causing the shot to go high, and they both collapsed on the decking in tears.

"What happened here?" Ryan asked.

"We entangled," Haley said.

Maggie clarified, "They're both empaths. Haley seemed to find what was bugging her."

"I don't know what was bugging her," Haley said, her eyes misting a bit, "Just how she felt."

Ryan looked at his daughter's forehead to see the last hint of a faded bruise in the center. The remnant of the woman's wallop that knocked Elizabeth to the decking. He began to steam over this woman attacking his daughter with such force but then became more curious than angry as he watched the clip again.

"This was less than forty-eight hours ago," he said with surprise written all over his face. "You barely have a bruise."

With a shrug, Elizabeth said, "We don't get hurt as easily now."

"And you can fly in these things?"

"No," Haley answered. "I was using Logan's PJs then and his can fly. Gus did put thrusters in ours before they left, but we can't use them until we're eighteen."

"Unless we're under water," Elizabeth reminded.

Haley crossed her arms, turning her head the other way as she muttered, "I'm not going swimming."

After the conversation, they went into the kitchen, where Elizabeth, looking into her father's eyes with determination, wanted to test her new strength. With a mental command, she deactivated the strength enhancements of her PJs, leaving only her own. They were both grinning, ready for the challenge.

"Go!" Haley shouted, and the Guerrerios's arms tensed.

Their hands wobbled back and forth a bit, and then Elizabeth's hand started to be forced back. Ryan couldn't believe how much resistance his daughter was able to muster, but he was slowly moving his hand forward.

She grunted through her words, "What did you teach me about cards?"

Also grunting, Ryan said, "Never play them all at once."

Elizabeth grinned through the struggle as an amber glow appeared in her eyes, and she began pushing harder. Ryan started losing inches as his daughter's face went red with the effort.

"Remember who you learned that from," Ryan said through gritted teeth and then pushed harder.

Their hands went back and forth a couple more times, but after another moment, Elizabeth's knuckles touched the tabletop.

They both blew out a long sigh and looked as if they were deflating in their seats, a little winded but laughing.

"You guys were almost as close as me and my dad," Haley said. She and Harry had tried the same thing the day before with pretty much the same result.

"I can't believe," Ryan said, still a little winded, "that this might be the last time I can beat my daughter at arm wrestling."

CHAPTER 2
This Just In

First Density. Location: Unknown

Two men stood, one on either side of the large elevator door. Deep underground, this facility was one of the most secretive places in the world. The Airmen standing guard both held rifles and turned toward the door as it slid to the side.

Five men, all armed, stepped out from the car and into the hallway; two lined up along each wall, and the fifth stepped out ahead and then turned around. "Step out from the lift," the man in front ordered, and Ahnk-Hume entered the hallway.

At ten feet and four inches tall, Ahnk-Hume was an intimidating sight. Most Archons varied in height anywhere between five and eight feet, but seven and a half was the average. They have the typical humanoid shape of a head, torso, with two arms and two legs, although they have proportionately longer limbs relative to Humans and Cetatians. They have no earlobes and only a pair of nostrils where a nose would be expected, and scaley skin which added to their durability.

But Ahnk-Hume was not like most Archons. He was a Drakel. Like all Archons, Drakels possessed six digits on their hands and feet, had innate psychic abilities and were natural mystics. A Drakel is usually larger than the common Archon as all were above seven feet tall, have four arms and long, powerful tails. Many were nearly ten feet! Some, like Ahnk-Hume, were also blessed with large leathery wings, allowing them to glide. Ahnk-Hume's wings were rested against his back and upper shoulders, draping down his body like a cloak.

Both pairs of wrists, bound behind his back, were in cuffs made from a mineral called fordriva that prevented the Drakel from phasing out of the First Density. The physiology of the Archons did not allow them to remain on the Human's plane of existence unaided for more than about fifteen minutes. The density's energy was too intense and would push the reptilian beings back into the Second Density.

Using a set of arm bands made from the same mineral as the cuffs, Ahnk-Hume had entered the First Density to personally deal with Haley Starr and got more than he bargained for. Now, he was being led by the United States government to a cell that the rest of the world didn't know existed.

The Drakel made his way forward as five more armed men walked out of the elevator behind him. The group walked in silence down the long hallway lined with large metal doors, finally stopping at one with four men standing by.

The door slid open, and four of the men in front entered as the point-man turned toward Ahnk-Hume and motioned to the door. "Step inside," the Airman ordered.

Ahnk-Hume hunched to avoid bumping into the header and walked through the door to see his new home. The room was a forty by forty-foot square with a ceiling of twenty feet. To the Drakel's right was the southern metal wall, and ten feet from the wall to his left was a row of vertical bars, behind which was the remaining thirty feet of the room that would be his cell. There was a desk, some sort of control panel and a chair on the outside of the bars, where a guard was already posted. The man pushed a button on the panel, and a five-foot section of the bars shifted into the cell and then slid to the side.

Sneering as he walked into the cell, Ahnk-Hume heard the cell door slide shut and click into place. "Step backward to the bars," one of the men ordered, and when he did, the guard unlocked and removed his cuffs.

The Drakel turned around to see the men leaving the room. The guard was seated at the desk, and the security team leader remained, waiting until the rest of the men had left the room.

Once the door shut, the man turned to Ahnk-Hume and said, "The guards will be rotating at frequent and irregular intervals, and they will not speak with you. There are active disruption emitters preventing the use of magick and there are multiple cameras, which are constantly monitored from a remote location. There are also more guards posted outside this door at all times."

When the man finished speaking, he abruptly turned and left the room. Only the guard remained and, true to the man's words, would not engage with Ahnk-Hume. With nothing to be done, the Drakel walked to the back corner of the room and sat on the large cot.

Second Density. Location: Unknown

Sitting around the ornate wooden table, the four Podmen were reporting the latest geopolitical situation to their leader, Kone.

"…and the tensions are escalating between the two nations as quickly as you predicted," one of them said.

"Excellent! Have the narrative pushed by the media in these countries," Kone began as he pointed at the map, "and then in those countries a week from today. Once the general populations believe that the threats are imminent, they'll demand that their governments intercede."

Kone controlled most of the media in the First Density, and they only reported what Kone wanted everyone to believe. And believe it, the people did. They could switch among the various news channels and find the same story being reported. The multiple sources repeating the same information was good enough confirmation for most of the unsuspecting people.

"Motivate the crowd, and they'll do our work for us," Kone said. He stated it often enough that the others began to call it his motto, but they couldn't deny its effectiveness.

First Density. Hartford, Connecticut

"What do you mean it'll ruin our credibility?" Drew dared to ask. Andrew Bean was an investigative reporter who worked for The CT Up-Date, a small independent newspaper in Hartford. Twenty-three years of age, he was five-foot-eight, slender in build, with short red hair and glasses.

With frustration on his face, the editor-in-chief threw his arms out wide, "Because it would look like a political hit-piece! That information would make us look biased." Mark Zanders's irritability was becoming more frequent as of late. This was expected as the newspaper industry was struggling from the internet's rise in popularity, but he had less patience than ever and seemed to always be on edge. He was in his mid-forties, and journalism had been his entire life. Lately, he had made some odd choices. Choices that the bullpen often couldn't believe.

The story in question was about Larry Waller, a prominent politician. Drew had followed some paper trails and found that Waller may have been using his position to prop up some insurance companies in which he owned stock. "If you're worried about that, then why'd you greenlight the story on Sam Winston?" Drew asked in exasperation. "The accusations against him were completely debunked, yet you pushed it through to the front page. Twice!"

Zanders's face went red. "Congratulations, you're writing gossip articles for the next month!" He managed to keep his volume reasonable, but no one in the room doubted that he wanted to scream.

"Are you serious? I actually have solid eviden—"

"Eh, eh, eh…" Zanders interrupted while holding up his finger, a stern look on his face. "One more word, and you don't have a job. Now, go find a non-political story. Maybe a forgotten urban legend or something."

Drew stood there for a moment, dumbfounded.

"Go!" Zanders almost shouted, snapping Bean from his stupor.

Drew made his way across the bullpen as Mark stomped into his office and slammed the door shut. Irma, one of the gossip columnists, ran up alongside him. "I can't believe this! He's never been this bad before."

"It is what it is," Drew huffed. "Maybe I can help you with your article until I find a story to write."

"Yeah! That's the spirit!" Irma beamed with her usual bubbly demeanor returning. "Forget about grouchy, and we'll have fun working together." Her head snapped to the side when she heard her name called, followed by, "Fan mail!"

"Yes!" she exclaimed, followed by a high-pitched "Eeeeeeee…" as she trotted to the cart.

Pulling open the office door, Zanders shouted, "Miss Gurd!" She spun and froze, looking like a deer caught in headlights. "Inside volume, please." He calmly closed the door.

Holding still another few seconds, Irma finally relaxed a little, looked at Drew with a sheepish smile and said, "That could've gone worse."

Columbia, Connecticut

The large screen had a sharper picture than any high-definition monitor that he had seen before. The town's Resident State Trooper, Ed Weathers, had spent Friday with the rest of the townsfolk, stuck in a cell. The Archons had used teleportation to replace the earth and rock beneath their town with an underground complex. After capturing the people in town, the reptilian invaders replaced them with cloned bodies called shells and projected their consciousness' into these avatars, intending to continue their business unnoticed. Until Haley and Elizabeth ruined their plans.

Now, this facility that had held Ed and the rest of the town as prisoners was under the control of the Air Force, working in cooperation with the Connecticut State Police. They had scoured the facility from top to bottom, and the scientists and engineers assigned here were as excited as children on Christmas morning.

They had an excellent map of the entire facility and were in the process of setting up equipment in the underground structure's command center. The group marveled at the clarity of the giant screen mounted into the eastern wall. The images displayed were from the surveillance cameras throughout the many labyrinth-like corridors, and most systems could be operated from this terminal, including the portgates.

With a stone-like monolithic appearance, the portgates had an archway through the center and were connected to each other in a network, allowing people to step into one and out of another. Colonel Decker, who already had knowledge of this kind of tech before the incident, now had control of all the gates in this facility. When the facility's main operations had been hacked during the "incident," they momentarily had access to portgates on this system into the Second Density, but the Cetatians quickly deactivated those gates manually, disconnecting them from the network.

In the command center stood one of these gates. Ten feet tall and eight feet wide, the archway inside was about the size of a set of double doors and a control panel was mounted to the left side. The monolith appeared to be made from polished stone and had intricate aquatic-themed carvings along the surface.

Ed, an airman and a couple of scientists looked over to the gate as a vortex manifested. It opened and expanded to fill the archway, and Colonel Decker stepped out, followed by Colonel Suarez and Lieutenant Colonel Parker of the Connecticut State Police.

"Ahnk-Hume is behind bars," Suarez informed Ed.

"Good," Ed replied. "Six more to go."

Parker mentioned, "The Archons are probably not in our jurisdiction at the moment, but if they hold a grudge, then they might come looking for the girls."

"Which is why we're going to keep some undercover officers in town at all times," Suarez said.

"I'll have some extra men assigned to this post on standby should you need them," Colonel Decker told them.

Haley was sporting her rig, which consisted of four parts. She wore a gauntlet on her right forearm, to which her custom-made potato gun was attached. A flexible tube ran from the back of the gun to a wooden backpack that held potatoes. When the gun was attached to the gauntlet, Haley's palm rested on the trigger mechanism, allowing her to squeeze the handle. Once to load a potato and then again to launch it.

When she rolled her shoulder back, the potato gun would contact the cradle on the side of her pack, triggering one set of clips to disengage from her gauntlet as another set locked onto the cradle, leaving her arm free. She raised her arm, leveling the barrel with one of her wooden targets, at which she often launched potatoes. She gathered her energy into the potato gun and released it.

The kitten-shaped blast launched from the gun at the target, splintering the wood from the concussive burst of the orb's impact. Staring blank-faced at the obliterated target, she muttered, "We should probably find something else." So, they took the bales of hay from the Halloween decorations and set up empty soda cans and other *disposable* items.

Ryan stood at the window watching the two girls playing in the backyard. The Seaman took another sip from his mug as Harry came and stood beside him. "So, we're raising superheroes now," he commented.

"Yup," Harry replied. "And they've already made some enemies."

"We need to train them. Make sure they're prepared if the lizard-people come after them again," Ryan said.

Nodding, Harry replied, "I've been thinking the same thing. We're going to need to set up a regular schedule. Maybe Maggie and Neil could work with them together to hone their…" he held his hands up and wiggled his fingers, "…special abilities."

Ryan chuckled, "They don't call Maggie the 'crazy crystal lady' for nothing."

"Am I being summoned?" Maggie asked as she walked into the room.

"We were talking about training the girls," Harry said.

Ryan looked to his wife and asked, "What do you think about you and Neil working together to coach the girls with their abilities?"

Maggie said, "We were just discussing that until Junior woke up and stole our attention." She then squealed a bit and added, "You should have seen that little smile."

Windsor Locks, Connecticut

Sitting behind the wheel of his Chevy Lumina, Drew stared at his cup of coffee, looking very unsatisfied.

"Did they make your coffee wrong?" the man in the passenger seat asked. Larry Cromwell was one of Drew's contacts and had always brought him good information. He was six-foot-one with short brown hair and large muscles from his time well spent in the gym. The brother of a State Trooper, Larry, was able to point Drew in the right direction to dig up substantial information without saying the things that he shouldn't. Never had he betrayed his brother's confidence until today.

Now, they both sat in Drew's car, parked at a Dunkin' Donuts across from Bradley International Airport.

"No," Drew responded. "I'm just waiting for the punchline."

Larry gave him an incredulous look, "Have I steered you wrong before?"

"Your info has always been good," Drew replied, "but do you really expect me to believe that an entire town was kidnapped by aliens? That's ridiculous! Why did you really call me out here?"

"This comes straight from my brother," Larry said. "He's been in the underground base. Seen the teleportation technology and laser guns." Larry shook his head, knowing that it sounded unbelievable. "Look, I thought he was pulling my leg at first, but he was both shaken and excited. He's seen a lot, but he's never been like this. I believe him, and I think you should check it out."

"C'mon, you can't be serious," Drew snapped. "Columbia had a gas leak. These things happen."

Larry looked at Drew with a bit of confusion, "You alright? You're not usually this testy."

With a sigh, Drew said, "I almost lost my job today." He explained to Larry about the unpleasant exchange with Zanders.

After Drew finished his recounting of the argument, Larry said, "Wow! Zanders has always been a stand-up guy; I wonder what's got him acting like…not him. And everybody knows that Waller is crooked. Bummer that he's also named Larry." Drew nodded, and Larry continued, "But since you can't do any political stories right now, that's all the more reason you should check this town out."

"It was a gas leak," Drew insisted with obvious irritation.

"Then why is there a heavier police presence now? And more importantly, why is the Air Force hanging around?"

The conversation was interrupted by a knock on the driver's side window, and the pair looked over to see Mark Zanders standing beside the car. With a sigh, Drew turned his key and rolled down the window.

"Hi, Larry," Zanders said.

Larry tilted his head back and said, "Hey, Mark."

Zanders then looked to Drew, "We need to talk after you guys are done."

Larry said, "No problem, I've got to get going anyway." He then gripped Drew's shoulder and whispered, "Good luck."

"I can hear you," Zanders said.

Larry opened the car door and stepped out of the vehicle. When Drew started to open the door to go with his boss, Zanders stopped him, "Your car, not mine."

Columbia, Connecticut

Sandra was carrying a fussy Junior, and Neil had the diaper bag. They were preparing to head back home as Harry grabbed his truck keys. Harry, Haley and Elizabeth were about to head to Joey's coffee shop while Ryan and Maggie planned to pick up some groceries, but then there was a knock at the front door.

Harry made his way to the door and turned the handle, being cautious due to Friday's events. He opened the door just a bit, smiled and pulled it wide open as he said, "Hi." There stood a woman, 5'10, with long black hair. She had dark skin, yellow eyes with specs of green and was dressed in a black pair of slacks and a vibrant blue silk blouse.

"Bast!" Haley and Elizabeth shouted in unison, and they rushed to the door to give her a hug.

The Egyptian goddess, with a warm smile, wrapped an arm around each of them and pulled the girls in tight. "Hello, girls," she said.

They released their embrace, and Bast stood up, looking at everyone else. "Hello, everybody."

Maggie smiled and returned her greeting as Neil nodded and said, "Bastet."

They introduced her to Ryan and Sandra, who were not present on Friday, and then to Junior. Bast's eyes softened further upon seeing the infant. "Hello, Little One," the goddess gushed.

"So, to what do we owe the pleasure of this visit?" Harry asked.

"Nomad," Bast replied. As she said his name, the orange cat came walking in the door and sat beside her feet.

"Meow," Nomad said with a downward inflection. This cat was old and had walked with a limp for years, but his limp was now gone, as well as the crooked bend in his tail. He looked young again.

"Nomad was at the end of his years, so I asked him if he'd like to be…" She turned toward the girls and continued, "…your familiar. And he said yes."

"Familiar?" Haley asked.

"Mom's mentioned something like that before," Elizabeth said.

Maggie smiled, "An animal companion to a practitioner of magick."

The girls, as usual, were already petting Nomad as he brushed himself against their shins. Haley and Elizabeth had known this cat longer than they had known each other and were always happy to see him.

"Should I add cat food to the shopping list?" Ryan asked Maggie as Hayseed walked up to Nomad, and they began to sniff each other.

Windsor Locks, Connecticut

"So, you were following me?" Drew asked as they drove past the fast-food restaurants, heading to the highway.

"No," Zanders replied, "I was just stopping for a coffee, and you happened to be there."

The blue Lumina turned onto the highway entrance ramp as Zanders said, "First, I want to apologize. You're right about what you said."

"Then why did you berate me in front of the entire bullpen like that?" Drew asked, his irritation still obvious. "And where are we driving to?"

"Right back to Dunkin' Donuts after this conversation. As for yelling at you, I'm at the end of my rope, and I snapped. I'm sorry."

"What's got you stressed, other than the World Wide Web?"

After taking a deep breath, Zanders said, "My family's being threatened. I still don't know who they are, but if I don't play ball and run the right stories, these people say that I'll suddenly be a widower with no kids."

"You think its Waller's people?" Drew asked.

"Probably," Zanders said, "But I can't prove it. I'm sure you know by now that at least half of these politicians are somebody else's puppet. I've found a couple of bugs at the paper and one in my car."

They merged into the highway traffic heading toward Interstate 91 as Drew asked, "Do you want me to investi…"

"Absolutely not!" Zanders sighed and said, "I appreciate the offer, but it's too risky. You're the only one I've told so far, and I need to keep it that way for a while."

With a nod, Drew said, "I could have Larry drop a hint to his brother. If Chet looks into it on his own…" He stopped his suggestion as he saw Mark shaking his head.

Not wanting to discuss the nerve-racking topic any further, Zanders asked, "What did Larry have to say? Anything interesting?"

"Yes…and no," Drew replied and then gave him the gist of what the informant had told him.

"Did this involve the fish-people, too?" Zanders asked with a genuine chuckle, the first time he had laughed in a while. Drew snickered a bit as well until Zanders said, "I want you to go check it out."

As he pulled off an exit ramp, Drew laughed again. But then he noticed that Zanders looked serious. "You're not kidding. You believe him!?"

"Of course not," Zanders said. "But he's always been reliable, so there's probably something going on out there. Besides, if these kinds of rumors start to fly around, you'll be able to counter them with facts. That's what you do best."

Columbia, Connecticut

The sign on the door said that they were closed on Sundays, but Drew found the place to be busy. The small shop, simply called The Coffee Shop, had seventeen customers inside the dining room with only two open tables remaining. The journalist could see through the window that everybody was animated with conversation, talking back and forth between tables. He checked around to see if there was any indication of a private party, but there was not. So, he opened the door and entered.

The entire place was hushed when he set foot inside as the patrons turned their heads in his direction. After a quick look, they all went back to their talking, but at subdued levels. Some of them stood up and switched tables to continue a conversation in a quiet manner.

Drew walked up to the counter where an athletic-looking man was working. He was five-foot-nine, with shaggy black hair and brown eyes. "What can I do for you?" Joey asked with a pleasant smile.

"Can I get a coffee with cream and sugar?"

"No problem," Joey replied as he grabbed a mug.

A moment later, Drew went to the open table against the wall, set a manilla folder down and took a seat, positioning himself for a good view of the room. The way everyone was quietly speaking, Drew had the sense that he was intruding, so he opened the folder and began to rummage through the papers. Most of them were blank, and he looked intently at one as if he were reading while he tried to listen to what the other patrons were saying. It wasn't more than a minute when he rolled his eyes at someone's mention of the fish-people, which was followed by a quick shushing sound from another.

Within five minutes, the conversations returned to normal speaking levels, but nothing of note was said. People spoke of their jobs, getting cars fixed and plans for Thanksgiving. All mundane. Flipping through papers, Drew sipped his coffee and continued to listen for a while until four more people entered the shop.

A six-foot man with a buzz-cut wearing a flannel shirt tucked into his blue jeans. Two preteen girls, one blonde with long pigtails, wearing coveralls and a purple bandana. The other was a brunette with a ponytail, wearing a gray zip-up hoodie and a small wooden cross on a twine necklace. Last through the door was an absolutely stunning woman, five-foot-ten, with a blue blouse and long black hair. Everybody looked at the door and began clapping as Harry, Haley, Elizabeth and Bast entered the dining room. Haley gave a sheepish grin as she waved to everybody, and Elizabeth took a sweeping bow.

"What would you like?" Harry asked Bast.

"I'd love a black tea," she replied.

As Harry went to the counter, the girls and Bast took a seat at the final table and began chatting with the others around them.

CHAPTER 3
Do A Little Digging

Second Density. Location: Unknown

The wooden conference table was three inches thick and had aquatic carvings around the outer edge. The surface was polished with a clear coating, and holographic lighting was displayed within the finish. A red light glowed on the surface at the head of the table, and Kone tapped it with his finger. "Stand by," he said.

After Kone motioned to Podman Bach to continue, the man said, "The traitors seemed to all but disappear until recently. They've broken into the archives twice. We need to put a permanent stop to them before they become a real problem."

Kone nodded and said, "I agree." He then stood up, "Fortuitous timing for you to bring that up." The Cetatian leader tapped the surface of the table and said, "Bring them."

The door opened, and two Commandos walked a restrained Cetatian man into the room, followed by two more Commandos escorting a restrained Alfan man.

"Perhaps these two might shed some light on the subject," Kone said to the Podmen. The Cetatian was 6'1 with dark hair, light skin and green eyes. His secondary pigment was orange with a speckled color-line. He was wearing cargo pants and a black polo shirt. The Alfan man, wearing blue jeans and a tan tunic, was five-foot-three. His eyes, slightly larger than Cetatian or Human eyes, were blue. He had an angular face, which was framed by his shoulder-length blond hair and long pointed ears.

"So," Kone began, "your little club seems to be up to their old tricks. You would have been better off remaining in the Fourth Density." Clasping his hands behind his back, Kone walked around the table and approached the two prisoners. "Tell me, what were you looking for." The two men glared at Kone, making it obvious they were in no mood to cooperate. Turning toward the Alfan man, Kone said, "If you won't answer that, then perhaps you'll tell me this. Why are your people joining the traitors of the Cetatian State?"

"Because," the man replied in a melodic voice, "we know you won't stop with the First Density. It's only a matter of time before you come for my home. I know what you once tried to do to my people."

"You know your history," Kone said.

"No. I was there," the Alfan man replied and sternly reminded, "We live for five-hundred years."

"No…" Kone responded calmly as he waved his hand and unleashed a mystical bolt. It hit the Alfan, and his body slumped in the restraining harness. "…*you* don't."

"No!" the Cetatian man screamed as Kone turned toward him.

"What were you looking for?" the Uniralt asked.

The Cetatian man spat in Kone's face and shouted, "Cetatians and Humans are…"

His words were cut off when Kone grabbed him by the throat and jacked him against the wall. The man choked and gagged as Kone, his face still bearing an expression of calm, reached up with his left hand and placed his fingers against the man's right temple and his thumb against the left. Kone squeezed, and a sickening crack sound was heard. He released his grasp, and the Cetatian's dead body slumped in the harness, his forehead deformed from Kone's crushing grip.

One of the Podmen handed Kone a handkerchief. He took it and wiped away the spittle while returning to the head of the table. Kone then tapped the table's surface, and everyone heard a woman's voice. "Yes?"

"I had two traitors in the conference room," Kone said.

"When would you like the cleaning crew to arrive?"

"About twenty minutes."

The woman then asked, "Do you need maintenance as well?"

Kone looked to the wall where he had held the Cetatian and saw no damage. "Not this time. Thank you," and tapped the table, closing the channel.

First Density. Columbia, Connecticut

Harry first set the basket of cheese fries down on the table between Haley and Elizabeth, next the tea in front of Bast, then his coffee and took a seat.

"Bast was just telling us about Ptah," Haley said to her father. "He likes to build things, too."

Looking to Harry, Bast said, "He's all about craftsmanship and attention to detail. You two would probably get along well."

"Sounds like he should meet Yesh Goldman," Harry replied, referring to the owner of Goldman's Woodworking Studio. "His work is incredible! He even helped me design Haley's rig."

Bast smiled and said, "I once came across a wood figurine of a leopard. It was exquisite, and Ptah was very impressed. As it happens, the piece was one of Goldman's."

"Hey Bast," Haley said, "Were the pyramids built by aliens?"

With a slight chuckle, Bast replied, "No. They were built by the mortals."

"What about crop circles?" Elizabeth asked.

She again shook her head. "No." After a couple seconds of thought, she decided to divulge, "They're made by the Seraphs."

Elizabeth tilted her head in curiosity, and Haley asked, "What's a Seraph?"

"Cosmic beings," Bast answered. "But you would know them as…"

"Angels," Elizabeth interjected, and Bast smiled while nodding.

"Wow," Haley whispered as she let the thought sink in. Then she mentally shifted back to extra-terrestrials and asked, "Have aliens been here?"

"Yes, but not in a while. Most tend to stay away from our sphere due to the Cetatians. Except for a select few with whom they make trade."

Elizabeth was getting excited over the thought of the universe beyond Earth. "Have you been to space?"

Nodding, Bast said, "No."

"Why not?" Haley asked, looking confused. "With your power, can't you just go?"

"Actually, I can't," Bast answered to looks of surprise from both girls and Harry. "I don't know why, but we, with the exception of Odin and a few others, can't leave a sphere under our own power. Mercury once snuck onto a space shuttle, though. He said it was amazing. Once he was beyond Earth's atmosphere, he could travel anywhere in the universe through an interconnected web of flowing energy in an instant. I think scientists refer to these as some kind of currents."

"Birkeland currents," Harry said.

"That's it!" The goddess continued, "Mercury also warned about touching down to a world without space travel, lest we be trapped there. He came back about a month later because he quickly became homesick."

Haley noticed a sense of curiosity that was not from them. She looked over her shoulder to a slender red-haired man at a table near the wall, who was thumbing through some documents. She knew it was coming from him and likely had nothing to do with the folder in his hands. When she turned toward Bast, Haley could tell that the goddess had also picked up on the potential eavesdropping.

Finishing her tea, Bast said, "I must be going now, but I'll stop in again soon to say hi."

The girls got out of their chairs and gave Bast a hug, then she waved goodbye to everybody and walked out the door.

Second Density. Location: Unknown

Derek Sahmbo walked into the conference room to see Kone standing near the head of the table, with several Podmen seated around it. Four Commandos stood along the wall near the other door, and two dead bodies hovered in restraining disks next to them.

"Thank you for coming so quickly," Kone said and then pointed to the suspended bodies at the other end of the room. "Do you recognize them?"

Sahmbo walked around the end of the table and approached to see one Cetatian and one Alfan. He pointed to the Cetatian man, "That's Stanek Marta, one of the traitors. I have an entire file on him. I'm unfamiliar with the Elf."

"Well, the traitors' meddling has become more frequent as of late. Even though most of them have taken refuge in the Fourth Density, I believe they have a few centers of operation here in ours. I want you to find them."

With a nod, Sahmbo pulled a thin, rectangular device from his pocket and took some photo captures of the dead men. He turned to Kone and said, "I'll keep you updated," and then made his way toward the door.

"How is Hunter Carmen?" Podman Bach asked before Derek reached the door handle.

"Recovering," Sahmbo replied. He had no trouble reading the accusatory undertones of Bach's body language.

"Tell me," Bach continued, "how did two ten-year-old girls manage to get past her?"

Knowing that Kone detested empaths, Sahmbo didn't want to reveal Sabrina's newly discovered senses. "They had help."

"From whom?" Bach pressed. "Two of the Marshals were in your custody at the time, and another went with a local after the wizards in the fire station. The last one entered the town hall from the surface shortly after. Who was left to help them?"

"Alexander O'Connor was here as well. And he too has abilities."

"Such as…?"

"Electrokinesis," Sahmbo said, and sympathetic groans were heard from some of the other Podmen. Sabrina was well known for her electric whip, and such an ability would turn that asset against her in an instant.

Podman Bach slowly nodded his head as he said, "That does make sense now." He looked up at Sahmbo and said, "Tell her that I wish her a speedy recovery."

"I will," Sahmbo said with a nod and turned to leave when he saw Commando Conrad enter the room. The two locked eyes, faces remaining stoic. Derek nodded and said, "Commando."

"Hunter-Ralt," Peter Conrad replied.

Without another word, Sahmbo left the conference room. Everybody knew that these two men did not care for each other, but being professionals meant putting differences aside to focus on the tasks at hand, and whenever these two men worked together, success was practically a guarantee. Despite their distaste for each other's methods, they had a mutual respect, but the idea of a confrontation between these two has sparked many a hot debate.

First Density. Newington, Connecticut

The apartment door opened, and Drew walked in to see his roommate, Ian, watching television. He was still in his restaurant uniform and eating a burger from work. Ian looked over with a smile and waved, then turned back to the TV, held out his arms and asked, "What do you think?"

He finally did it. Ian had been saving for a new television, and now a fifty-inch flatscreen was in place of the old tube TV that had been there just this morning. He had always been a bit of a hippie, but unlike the reputation that comes with the territory, Ian had an excellent work ethic.

"Nice," Drew replied. He walked over and sat on the couch as he let out a long, dissatisfied sigh.

"Was your day that bad?" Ian asked.

Shaking his head, Drew answered, "No. Just…actually, yeah. Today could have gone much better."

Ian looked at Drew, expecting further elaboration.

"Not getting into it," Drew said, looking toward the new TV. He pointed to the flatscreen and said, "Tell me about it."

Not saying a word, Ian continued to look directly at Drew. Waiting for an explanation.

After another uncomfortable minute, Drew said, "Fine," and turned toward Ian. "I almost got fired this morning, then Zanders apologizes for snapping at me, then he gives me a special assignment chasing wild geese." With an exasperated sigh, Drew leaned forward and placed his face into his palms. "I am so sick of conspiracy theories." He then sat up and looked at his roommate. "No offense," he quickly added.

With a chuckle, Ian said, "None taken. I get it. You're a journalist. You need verification for everything." Ian tended to believe in the fantastical rather than the mundane.

"Yeah, well, now I'm supposed to dig into that gas leak in Columbia the other day. Crazy rumors starting to circulate around that one." Drew sat up and became a little more animated, mostly from irritation, as he described the story he was supposed to be chasing.

"Sounds to me like he wants you to debunk it and show everyone what really happened," Ian said, attempting to encourage his friend.

"Yeah, but that's easier said than done when the townsfolk are talking about aliens, gods and fish-people." With a smirk, Drew added, "You'd fit right in there."

"I like these people already," Ian replied.

"You should have seen the woman that was there," Drew told him. "She was absolutely gorgeous. She looked Middle Eastern and had a unique name. Bast."

"I'm gonna guess that she's Egyptian," Ian said. "Bast is the name of an Egyptian goddess."

"Because this," he made quote signs with his fingers, "'story' isn't weird enough on its own. The only thing that added any credence to Larry's version of events was that there were some Humvees at the warehouse."

"So, what was the military doing there?" Ian inquired.

Drew shook his head, "Don't know that it was the military. Civilians buy Hummers." He took a breath. "Here's what I'm gonna do. I'll call the gas company tomorrow and then see if I can get a statement from anybody at the warehouse. That should put this whole waste of time to bed."

The next morning, Drew woke up feeling certain that he could wrap up this wild goose chase in about an hour. When he got to the office, he looked up a real estate listing for a house on the market in Columbia near the warehouse and then called the gas company and inquired about getting service to that address. He first was confused, then frustrated with what they had to say; but the frustration changed into curiosity and intrigue after the gas company insisted that there was no service in that area.

Drew hung up the phone. He needed to go back to Columbia. While the thought of aliens and fish-people was still absurd to the journalist, it was now obvious that the gas leak narrative was false. Drew immediately ran to Zanders and told him about what he had found.

"That is interesting," Zanders said. "But we're going to have to put that on the back burner for now. There's an event going on in Podunk, and I need you on it." After a pause, he added, "I know, I know. It was finally getting interesting, but I can't *really* leave one of my best investigative journalists on a gossip column."

Second Density. The Ozarks. Monday. November 2, 1998

He danced to the music while dressing the turkey. The upbeat tunes matched his mood as he pre-heated the oven. He stepped up the pace, and the small pouch that hung on twine around his neck began bouncing around, but he quickly reached up, caught it, and tucked it under his shirt without skipping a beat. The man was usually found tinkering with his inventions, but he had spent the last two weeks in the house alone, and his wife would soon be home.

Manny Suarez grew up in the Second Density's Spanish Harlem. Standing at 5'10, he was fit and had dark brown skin with a bluish secondary pigment and black hair. Though his hair was thinning, not one of them was gray. He was a genius technician, and those who knew him believed that he could build almost anything. With his inventive talent, he could have easily gained state attention, an aspiration of many inventors, but he never put himself out there.

As smart as Manny was, he considered his most brilliant achievement to be staying off Kone's radar. He had known other scientists who had received commissions from the Cetatian State. They had gained access to resources and materials that allowed them to fully demonstrate their ideas. But when they were on the verge of a new discovery, they suddenly and quietly disappeared. Manny understood that state access came with a price. The price of eventually knowing too much.

He managed to stumble across another path. By happenstance, he had made the acquaintance of Vedant Sahmbo, the Hunter-Ralt at that time, who began providing Manny with what he needed, and in exchange, he would develop gear for the Hunters. Through this working relationship, the two had come to trust each other.

Then, one day, Vedant came to him with an eleven-year-old orphan. "You're the only one in the area that I trust," he explained as a young Sabrina Carmen stared off into the distance, her trauma and the wound on her forehead still fresh.

Manny tried to refuse, but Vedant insisted that it would only be for a month until he found her a new home. Sabrina barely spoke a word for a week and a half. She just stared at the floor, numb. At two weeks, she suddenly fell apart, melting into a puddle of sobs. Manny came and sat next to her but did not say anything. He placed his hand on her shoulder and let her cry. After a few moments, Sabrina turned toward Manny and grabbed him in a hug. Now no longer numb, she finally felt safe enough to talk.

Their new bond grew and strengthened; Sabrina started calling him Papi, and he raised her as his own. She and Derek grew up together, training under the Hunters, learning their code and way of life. As Sabrina became an adult, Manny met Darcey Wells, a Hunter who would eventually become his wife. They now live on a homestead in the Ozarks of the Second Density.

Once a year, Darcey would walk into the woods with nothing but her clothes and remain there for two weeks. It's a traditional practice called Remembrance that most Hunters still observe. She was due back in a couple of hours, and Manny was looking forward to her return. The oven beeped, and he opened it, placing the turkey inside. He closed the oven, set the timer and then heard a knock at the front door.

"Papi?" Sabrina called out as she entered the house.

"Sabrina!" Manny responded with glee as he ran to the front hall. He saw his daughter holding a bag and closing the door. "Sabrina," he said again and practically crushed her in a hug. "How do you always get past the sensors? Even Darcey hasn't figured out how, and she helped me install them."

"I've missed you, Papi."

Manny released the hug, placed his hands on her shoulders and looked at her face. "There's that smile that could light up a room." He let go of her shoulders and sighed as he turned back toward the kitchen. "Such a shame that you rarely let anyone see it."

"I smile for you, Papi."

He motioned for Sabrina to follow him while he asked, "How did the new grapple harness work?"

"Perfectly," She answered. "I didn't need to use my hands at all."

The Hunters usually wore a black one-piece utility suit of Manny's design, with a magnetic grappling harness woven into the outfit. Along the harness were small metal discs every few inches that worked with a cylindrical handle. The handle was five inches long with a slim metal disc called the anchor on one end. A Hunter would point the handle at a wall or ceiling and launch the anchor. Once attached to a surface, the Hunter would hold the base of the grapple handle to one of the metal discs in the harness, causing it to activate and pull the Hunter up toward the anchor on an invisible magnetic zip-line.

Manny made all the Hunters' suits, upgrading and improving the design over the years. He had a bit of a challenge making one to properly fit Sabrina as she matured. In contrast to her natural agility, Sabrina had a slightly thick build and was well-endowed. Manny stiffened the material in the chest, firmly holding her ample bosom in place to prevent issues during acrobatic maneuvers. It took some trial and error, but Manny had finally gotten the suit tailored to where Sabrina was comfortable and could move without worry.

And then there was the Great Zipper Incident of '94. Sabrina had been tasked with locating a rogue Commando and, if able, detaining him. Eager for this particular assignment, she had tracked him to an apartment building in the Second Density's San Diego and, seeing a slim window of opportunity, made the choice to take him on directly.

Like all Commandos, he was an elite fighter and equaled Sabrina's skill. He couldn't match her speed, but the Commando held a comfortable strength advantage over the Hunter. Items were knocked around the apartment as they exchanged attacks and counters while Sabrina kept him on his toes. But he could take strikes better than she and accepted a couple blows to move in and gain the upper hand.

Then it happened. The struggle caused too much strain, and the teeth of the zipper separated with a pop. The Commando's eyes dropped down briefly but he was a disciplined warrior and immediately ripped his focus away, putting it back where it belonged. But it was too late.

That fraction of a second was all Sabrina needed to land a solid blow to the side of his neck, impacting the nerve for an instant knock-out. Using her right of spoils, Sabrina claimed a jacket to cover up, along with the reason for her eagerness, the Commando's special-issue blade made of mayum, a rare and unbreakable metal.

Sabrina hated her wardrobe malfunction but had to admit that if it hadn't happened, she would have lost the fight…and her life. She didn't like to leave things to chance, so she was quite hard on herself for making such a bad choice, biting off more than she could chew. But it was Derek who helped her put things in perspective. "It wasn't entirely luck," he said.

Sabrina looked at him with confusion. "How do you figure?"

"You were engaged in combat, and something unexpected happened. You didn't let that something become a distraction, but your opponent did. It wasn't entirely luck. It was you." Derek pointed to her and said, "You were better mentally prepared than your opponent. And that's why you won the fight."

That helped relieve a bit of Sabrina's self-doubt, but she spent many a night thinking, trying to wrap her mind around the idea that her vulnerability was what saved her.

Now, Manny had made his daughter a new utility suit that used sensors in her collar to detect her neural patterns, allowing Sabrina to activate the magnetics by thought without the use of a grapple handle. The other day, Sabrina had placed anchors on the walls and ceiling of a large room that housed a generator and was able to zip through the air in any direction she chose without letting go of her weapons.

"Good, because I already made one for Derek, too. I'll update the assembly gear to make these for everybody, but I'm running low on graphene, and I'm going to need more to produce them. They need power, and you can't do your job with an extension cord." He led her through the kitchen toward a door, the incredible smell of turkey filling the room.

Manny had found a method of absorbing ambient energy for power but needed a graphene-copper composite to make it work. He had even devised an electrical grid that would solve many energy problems but knew it would never be accepted. An absorption unit would be placed every few blocks, drawing in energy and providing power to the grid and a single unit could be replaced without interrupting the grid's service, which was still fed by all other functioning units. But, because a unit couldn't scale up, the method could not be centralized, preventing a single person from having full control. That would not fly with Kone.

Opening the door, they descended the stairs to the basement, which was Manny's workshop. What's in the bag?"

"My whip," She answered. "It was crushed under falling cement. I was hoping you could repair it."

Looking in the bag, Manny sighed. "That's…going to be a while. Do you still have the other?"

"Yes," she answered as her eyes dropped down to a small box in the center of Manny's workbench.

Noticing that the box caught her attention, he smiled and said, "I've finally gotten it right."

"What's that?"

"An anchor wallet. Not sure if that's what I'm calling it yet," he said with a smile. Sabrina could hear the echos of excitement reverberating from his heart. "I figured it out a couple of weeks ago," he continued as their eyes lingered on the bench. "Wait until you see this!" His Spanish accent seemed to thicken with his enthusiasm.

Reaching for the box, he opened it and removed a small square object. It was two inches wide and a quarter inch thick with a magnetic anchor disk on one side. Manny held it up for Sabrina to see as he flipped the top layer open to reveal another anchor disk inside. Another layer opened in the opposite direction, uncovering another, then again and once more. "It holds five disks," he proudly stated, but Sabrina stared at him in confusion. "What?"

"How did it take a genius like you so long to figure this out?" she asked.

"Because," he began as the smile returned to his face, "it can finally do this." Manny folded the wallet shut and tossed it like a frisbee. The wallet spun through the air and then burst in the middle of the room, launching one disk to the ceiling and the other four onto the walls.

With a dangling jaw, Sabrina looked at the anchors, amazed. "That…could come in handy," she said softly.

"Mira," he said as he picked up the wallet from the floor and held it up. The anchors dislodged from the walls and ceiling as they magnetically returned to the wallet, which then folded itself shut. He handed the wallet to his daughter and said, "I figured this could save you some time in a pinch. And as usual, it'll attach to the suit's belt and harness."

"Thank you, Papi. This is incredible!"

"I've made a bunch. Figured Derek would want a couple of these, too. I hope the Commandos don't copy this one as quick as they did the grapple harnesses." He launched into an explanation about the sensors properly detecting the room and devising a functional deployment system. He was in mid-sentence when he looked back at his daughter and stopped talking. Sabrina's face was difficult to read, but he knew her well enough to tell when something wasn't right. "What is it?"

Sabrina, looking back at him, said nothing, but a few seconds later, mist began to collect in her eyes.

"What happened?" he asked in a gentle tone.

The moisture in her eyes collected and began running down her cheeks, followed by some sniffles. Sabrina began to shudder a bit as her breathing became more erratic, and she buried her face in her palms. "Papi," she sobbed as Manny reached out and hugged her tight. "It's been so long…and I still can't shake it."

It took a few moments, but Sabrina composed herself. They went upstairs, sat down at the kitchen table and she told her father about the encounter with Haley.

And their empathic entanglement.

CHAPTER 4
Practice Makes Perfect

First Density. Columbia, Connecticut. Late Spring, 1999

"Oof!" Haley blurted as she landed on her back.

"Sorry!" shouted Elizabeth and offered a hand, helping the farmgirl back to her feet. "I just really get into it."

"I know. I felt it empathically," Haley then smirked, adding, "And physically."

Ryan chuckled at Haley's quip. They sparred under the observation of their fathers three times a week. Twice a week, Maggie or Neil worked with the girls in controlling their energy. Even though they couldn't do things anywhere near the girl's level, they could guide them through meditations and exercises, helping them become more accustomed to their abilities and learn their limits. Limits that they continued to overcome. The girls' strength continued to slowly increase as well. Haley finally won her first arm wrestling match against her father. A week and a half later, Elizabeth beat her dad. A week after that, both girls were winning consistently.

While training, they would deactivate the strength assist in their PJs while also activating the binders, which prevented the girls from being able to use their powers. No super strength or durability for the first half of the session. Haley didn't like practicing techniques over and over again, although she sometimes enjoyed sparring if her mood was right. What she liked the best was the target practice.

Elizabeth looked forward to her training, and it showed. She would even practice her techniques in her room first thing in the morning. While Haley was content to practice the abilities that she naturally manifested, Elizabeth wanted to expand past that.

Haley and Elizabeth went a few more rounds before they decided to call it a day. The protective headgear and gloves began to ripple and flowed in a liquid-like manner as the nanobots merged back in with the rest of their clothing.

"Ready to go blast stuff?" Haley asked Elizabeth with a smile.

"Oh yeah!"

They turned off their binders. The girls could program clothing and some accessories into their PJs. Haley discovered that the com-system accepted her gauntlet and wooden backpack for her potato gun without issue, but it wouldn't accept the gun itself. That was recognized as a weapon that required authorization from Gus Decker, the inventor of the PJs, who was kind enough to give it right before he and the other Marshals left to explore the multiverse. He also set Elizabeth's to do the same on only one occasion, pending authorization from her parents.

With a mental command, the nanobots rippled out from Haley's clothing, forming the gauntlet and potato gun onto her right forearm as the pair headed further into the backyard with Maggie, who would be supervising their practice this day.

Across the potato field was another one of Columbia's wooded hills. The bottom of this hill had a large sheer rock face, which provided a good barrier that could withstand their blasts. Here, they couldn't be seen from the road, so, naturally, it was where they set up targets to practice their aim.

After successfully hitting all her targets, Haley conjured the backpack portion of her rig from the PJs. She rolled her arm back and touched the potato gun to the cradle on the side of the pack, causing the clips to disengage from her gauntlet as the other clips clicked into the cradle. Haley set up more targets as Elizabeth prepared for her round.

Some of the blasts hit hard, and some dissipated upon impact. Maggie had them working to fine-tune how much punch they packed into their mystical bolts, and these exercises paid off as they gained more control and precision with their shots.

"Do the big one," Elizabeth said to Haley with a confident grin, referring to the farmer's sustained beam of energy.

Haley could sense Elizabeth's excitement. Her best friend had been trying to replicate this for the last few months. The way she eagerly said it this time made Haley think that she may have broken that barrier. "You mean the Cat-Tastrophe?"

"Are you really going to call it that?" Elizabeth asked.

Haley just shrugged. Clearing her mind, she reached deep within herself, gathering and concentrating energy to an extreme intensity. A fierce blue glow appeared in her eyes, and arches of blue and purple light began to crackle from her skin to the ground. She mounted her potato gun to her gauntlet and raised her arm toward the rock face.

Unleashing her energy, a wide, sustained beam of blue light shot out of her arm cannon at the hillside, filled with purple lights in the shape of various types of cats, all rocketing forward within the beam. It hit the rock wall and continued as a slight trembling could be felt beneath their feet.

"Whoa," Elizabeth whispered. She turned toward Haley and said, "I think it was stronger than last time."

"Well?" Haley asked, looking at Elizabeth.

"Well, what?"

Haley smirked and said, "I feel your excitement. You can do it now, can't you?"

A smile appeared on Elizabeth's face. "I think so, but I didn't want to let it loose until we were here. I was afraid that if it worked, I would accidentally break a lot of stuff."

Haley cradled her potato gun, smiled and motioned with both hands toward the rock face. The empath could also feel the anxious anticipation from Maggie, who had been waiting to see her daughter achieve this feat. Elizabeth took a deep breath. She was very good when it came to focusing her mind and could often slip into what she called 'the sweet spot,' the same state that many athletes described as being 'in the zone.'

Haley sensed the intense energy Elizabeth was gathering. An amber glow appeared in her eyes, and a moment later, arches of amber and indigo light began to crackle from the young mystic. Her eyes were fixated on the spot where she intended to land her blast, and she held her hands up, palms out, before her.

Elizabeth released her energy; a beam of sparkling amber with swirls of indigo shot forward, hitting the stone-faced hill. She sustained the beam for about four seconds. It wasn't as big or as powerful as Haley's, but it was the first time she had pulled it off.

"Way to go, Beth!" Haley shouted, jumping up and down in celebration.

Staring at the hillside, Elizabeth's eyes were open wide, as was her smile. "It finally worked!" The young mystic threw her fists into the air. "Yes!" she exclaimed. She joined Haley in the jumping and twirling, celebrating the new breakthrough. The two girls hugged and were still cheering when Maggie wrapped her arms around them both.

First Density. Location: Unknown

The very sight of the walls was grating on him. Day after day, month after month, it was the same view, the same bars, and the lowly Humans would not speak to him. Other than the food and change of clothes that was brought to him every day, Ahnk-Hume had nothing but his own thoughts that echoed over and over again in his head. At first, they replayed the events that led him here. He thought about how Haley, in another universe during the year 2019, landed that nasty blow to his head, cutting him off from the Archon hive mind. Oh, how he hated the mental loneliness!

Then he thought about how they happened to come to this universe while trying to solve a different issue and found a new, great opportunity. Along with a chance to get revenge on a ten-year-old version of the woman he hated more than anything. It was a pleasing prospect that he would have never expected, and Ahnk-Hume had intended to not let this bonus pass him by.

Next, he thought about how he let his own emotions, which had become more unstable and intense since being severed from The Hive, get the better of him. The young empath sensed this and taunted Ahnk-Hume, coercing him into reacting as an unthinking, angry child throwing a fit. *I am a warrior! And I lunged like a filthy wild animal!* He dove at her, telegraphing his moves and fell right into this wretched girl's trap. He played these events repeatedly in his mind to the point where he was slowly driving himself insane.

Ahnk-Hume clenched all four fists. *How could I be so foolish?* He was a genius battle tactician and an elite fighter. He had tortured and maimed his enemies, feeding on the negative energy to boost his own mystical powers and enjoyed the euphoric feeling, the high from his foes' agony. Oh, how good it felt to hurt others. He dominated powerful opponents and took part in defeating entire civilizations.

But then lost it all to a little Human empath. Outside of other members of The Hive, he cared nothing for the feelings of another. In fact, the concept of being empathic seemed utterly ridiculous to him. The Archons sensed emotions mystically, but when Haley felt another's emotions, it was a shared experience. And she used this against him, robbing him of his opportunity.

He replayed these events yet again, for there was nothing else to do. He sat in his cell, reliving his own defeat.

Second Density. Location: Unknown

Kone was discussing events with a wizard in his office when the tone sounded. He tapped the surface of his desk, and what was once a painting on the wall now displayed the image of one of his Generals.

"The Hunter-Ralt has found another," the General informed Kone. "And this time, they're still there."

Sahmbo had found three of the traitors' bases, but each time, they were already vacated. It was becoming clear that the traitors had no intention of staying put for very long. Little was left behind besides a destroyed portgate at one and some files containing already-known information at the others. But everyone knew that Derek Sahmbo was relentless, and it was only a matter of time before he had caught up with them.

"Excellent," Kone said. "Be sure to leave a couple alive for questioning."

"Yes, sir," replied the General. "There are Hunters, Commandos, Soldiers and Proctors surrounding the building now. The traitors aren't even aware of our presence yet. We're about to begin."

"Proceed," Replied Kone.

"Yes, sir. I'll report back shortly."

The General ended the transmission and said over everyone's earpieces, "Initiate the operation."

A steel building, this abandoned warehouse was in the badlands of the Second Density's California. All at once, the surrounding people came overtop the rocky hills and began moving in. Two of the traitors standing outside the building's main entry saw the force coming over the hills and ran in the door, shouting, "They've found us!"

Sahmbo was the first through the door, firearm up. He confirmed the entryway was clear, and a Commando, some Proctors and Sabrina came in behind him.

Inside, they saw four men carrying small computers run through a doorway near the back, followed by a fifth man shouting, "Move, move, move!"

Sahmbo moved as fast as his feet would take him and followed through the door. The back room contained an active portgate, through which all but one man had entered. "Hold it!" the Hunter-Ralt ordered.

The traitor knew that he would be shot before he made it through the gate. So, he slowly held his hands out to the sides and turned around. Two Proctors entered and stood on either side of Derek with pistols drawn. The Proctor to his left, a sergeant, said, "We await the Hunter's orders," as a Commando entered the room with his sidearm trained on their target.

The traitor made a slow sweeping motion with his left hand, indicating for the others to look around. They did so and saw the cables running along the walls to charges embedded throughout the structure. Then, they heard a beeping sound.

"Evacuate immediately!" Derek ordered through the earpieces. The traitor turned and dove through the portgate as the forces of the Cetatian State made a hasty retreat. They all ran up and back over the rocky hills surrounding the warehouse. After a moment went by, the charges detonated, and the building buckled as flames spewed out from the doorways.

"Headcount!" Sahmbo demanded.

Everyone was accounted for, and a firefighting crew arrived. Once the building was cleared, Sahmbo and the other Hunters went back inside and began looking through the rubble for anything that could indicate where they may have gone.

Sabrina couldn't help but notice something. She could hear the song of frustration coming from everyone because they wanted this traitor debacle to be done, but Sahmbo and a couple other Hunters, weren't frustrated like the others. They were relieved.

Probably because nobody got hurt, she thought.

First Density. Columbia, Connecticut

Haley, Elizabeth and Maggie entered the house through the back door. When they got to the kitchen, Harry and Colonel Decker were seen looking over some large sheets of paper. The colonel looked up and smiled. "Hello," he said in his gruff, baritone voice.

Haley waved with a smile, and Elizabeth said, "Hi."

Decker rolled the papers and placed an elastic band around them. "Sorry I can't stick around and chat, but I have to return to the base." He shook Harry's hand, waved to everyone else and walked out the front door.

Looking up at Maggie, Haley asked, "Are you guys staying for dinner tonight?"

"No," Maggie answered. "Ryan should be home from work soon, and there are some things we need to do around the house." She then looked to Elizabeth. "If we get them done soon enough, maybe we can work a little more on your pyrokinesis."

Elizabeth held her hands up to her mouth as she tried not to squeal. She hadn't done anything with this ability for the last two weeks. Maggie instead decided to focus on her hydrokinesis, which took a lot of the young mystic's concentration.

She had taken well to manipulating fire and air, but water was a struggle. So Maggie had her daughter working with the element, helping her advance her connection to it. At first, Elizabeth was only able to make small ripples in a bowl of water. After some frustrating practice, she could now make a small container of water slosh around any way she wanted. She even made the water that splashed outside of the bowl roll across the plastic-covered table and collect into a puddle. Then, she made it flow upward like the stem of a wineglass and over the edge of the bowl, returning to the rest. As excited as she was with her progress, Elizabeth was eager to work with the other elements again.

As time went on, Elizabeth continued to excel in her martial training. While Haley wasn't bad at it, she just couldn't keep up with the young mystic, and it sparked feelings of inadequacy. Even when the dexterous farmgirl gave it her all, she couldn't match Elizabeth in hand-to-hand combat. The mystic was too fast and nimble. Though Haley didn't expect to match Elizabeth's fighting skill, she thought that she should be doing better than she was. Elizabeth was a natural, and Haley was not. She had more punch in her energy blasts but also knew that there were ways that energetic abilities could be nullified and wanted to be able to hold her own should that happen again.

After a little while, Harry noticed Haley's non-verbal hints of worry and sat down to talk with her. When she told him her concerns, Harry suggested, "We try a little extra training a couple times a week. And don't be afraid to come to me when you're worried about things. That's what I'm here for. Don't be afraid to speak up."

Haley's heart usually wasn't in it, but even when it was, the improvement was minimal. One day, Harry walked into the barn to see Haley had finished her chores, and she was twirling a broomstick as she often did when the realization hit the former Marine like a ton of bricks. *Why didn't I think of this before?*

Calling a colleague who was an expert in bojutsu, Harry arranged for Haley to train with a staff. She wasn't confident when they began, but as time went on, the farmgirl took to it almost as well as Elizabeth took to empty-hand fighting. It wasn't long before Haley discovered that she could channel her energy through the staff to add some extra punch.

Newington, Connecticut. September 25, 1999

Work had been crazy. Just one thing after another, but there was finally a lull, and Drew had a chance to breathe a bit. Because he had been running so hard for the last few months, Zanders had given him the next week off, and he intended to enjoy it. Due to Drew's workaholic tendencies, many of his co-workers had a pool going on whether or not he would still show up on Sunday morning.

He wasn't home for more than an hour before thoughts of the story from Columbia started creeping back into his mind. A few rumors about the town still circulated, but nobody took them seriously. Although Drew didn't buy into any of the stories, he knew that things didn't add up, and curiosity was Drew's primary motivator.

He had made a couple of calls the week after he had spoken to the gas company. He also contacted the State Police and tried to get ahold of someone from the warehouse. Everything dead-ended with, "No comment." After that, he had been busy with more pressing investigations. "Maybe now would be a good time to revisit it," he said aloud. "But where to begin?"

"Revisit what?" Ian asked as he walked into the living room.

With a self-deprecating chuckle, Drew said, "I'm thinking about that not gas leak from Columbia again."

Ian smiled and said, "I'm off tomorrow. Why don't we take a ride in the morning? You said I'd like the place."

Columbia, Connecticut. September 26

Haley had spent the morning in the field, helping her dad with some post-harvest cleanup, and Elizabeth had come over after church to lend a hand. After lunch, they filled some five-gallon pales with water and headed to the back of the potato field near the rock-faced hill, the surface of which was becoming worn from the constant blasts.

The water was there for Elizabeth to practice her hydrokinesis. Harry and Ryan had built a firepit near the rocky cliffside, and the girls began setting up kindling and sticks, but they had to wait for Harry before they were allowed to start the fire.

They typically didn't train on Sundays, but this was more playing than practice. Although she did well with her bojutsu and enjoyed the sparring now and then, Haley found the practice utterly boring. Her mind would start to wander before the low block's third repetition.

Elizabeth's efforts had paid dividends with the expansion of her abilities. She was consistently producing a large, sustained blast like Haley's, just still not quite as powerful. Her hydrokinesis had improved to where she could move water through the air with a wave of her hand, making water flow out from one pail and into another.

Her pyrokinetic abilities had grown as well. Elizabeth would hold her hand out before her and close her fingers, snuffing out the flames in the pit. Then, with a wave of her hand, water would flow from one of the buckets and onto the smoldering wood.

Once Harry had arrived, Elizabeth flicked a lighter and pulled on the flame, combining it with her own energy until she held an orb of fire in her hand. With a throw, the flame shot toward the fire pit, igniting the wood.

Unlike the last time, Drew found that the Coffee Shop was closed this Sunday, so they went to a gas station and picked up some sandwiches instead. Ian was looking through the small sandwich selection when he noticed an attractive woman browsing drinks by the cooler. So he approached with a smile to strike up a conversation.

Drew was filling his tank when Ian and the young lady came walking out of the store while sharing a laugh. *How does he do that so easily?* Drew silently wondered. The pump handle clicked and stopped as Ian returned to the car with some food.

"Got you a sandwich and some cheese curls."

"Thanks."

"And you're right, I do like this place."

"Yeah," Drew said as he glanced at the woman getting into her car, then back to Ian with a smirk, "I can tell."

"Uh-huh. She's pretty cool," Ian returned Drew's smirk when he added, "And informative."

Drew raised an eyebrow, "Oh?"

"Yeah. Do you like potatoes?"

It was only a few moments before they arrived at a place called StarrLight Farms.

Drew scrutinized the farmstead. "I can't tell if this is a business open to the public or just somebody's house." The place was a single floor with a covered wrap-around porch and two dormers that popped out from the roof. Maybe there was a second floor or at least a small upstairs room.

"Either way, they're probably not open on Sunday." Ian was thinking out loud more than making a statement.

"Well, after coming all this way, it couldn't hurt to knock." Drew and Ian both exited the vehicle and walked onto the porch. Drew gave a couple of solid knocks and waited.

After a moment of no answer, Drew raised his hand to give one more knock when he heard a girl's voice shout, "Yes!"

The pair walked around the side of the house and saw the potato field and three people at the other end: two standing on the ground and one climbing up a rock cliff on the side of a large hill.

Haley was near the top of the rock face when she jumped away from the cliff wall and began to crackle with energy. Her beam was unleashed toward a marked spot on the cliff wall, and she maintained her aim while dropping to the ground. She landed on her feet, and Elizabeth said, "You did it this time!"

Turning to respond to Elizabeth, Haley's jaw suddenly dropped, matching the stunned expressions of the two men standing on the other side of the field.

CHAPTER 5
Echos

Elizabeth, with a mental command to her com-system, sent Colonel Decker a message as soon as she saw Drew and Ian. He was already in town at the underground facility, which they were now calling Camp Yeoman, and had arrived within minutes. Now, Drew and Ian were seated at the kitchen table across from Harry and Colonel Decker while the girls were upstairs in Haley's room.

With a sigh, Drew said, "Don't worry, I'm not going to run this story. I didn't come here looking to make a public spectacle of two minors."

"Bummer that the world can't know about their heroics," Ian added.

Decker placed some papers, non-disclosure agreements, in front of them. "Perhaps someday," he said, "But not anytime soon."

Drew looked over the verbiage on the form, nodded, and reached for his pen.

"At least you don't have to admit to aliens," Ian said with a grin.

"I've never said that there's no such thing as aliens. It's just that extraordinary claims require extraordinary proof, and now," he signed the document, "we have no proof to make such a claim."

"You said that you were sick of all that alien and fish-people talk."

"Yes, not because it's impossible, but because it's ridiculous to jump to such conclusions," Drew shot back.

"But this time, it was the case."

"True, but it doesn't matter. Journalistic integrity requires minimizing harm, and turning two girls' lives upside down would be as irresponsible as it gets," He handed his pen to Ian, who also signed the NDA.

While Drew and Ian were having their discussion, Colonel Decker was looking at the screen of his phone. He had come to appreciate the com-system that Gus had designed. With a thought, it pulled all their records from the internet. There wasn't much about Ian, but Drew had published many articles over the last couple of years, and everything indicated that he was all about integrity. Decker was becoming more confident by the moment that he would honor the agreement.

A knock was heard at the front door, and Harry excused himself to answer. He opened the door to find that it was Ryan, Maggie and Admiral Book from the New London Submarine Base, carrying a backpack. "Come in," Harry said.

They came into the kitchen to see Decker, Drew and Ian all standing while Decker shook their hands. "If there comes a time when this can be discussed publicly, you'll probably be the first one I call, but honestly, don't hold your breath on this becoming declassified."

"Understood," Drew replied, returning the firm handshake.

"Not to worry," Ian put in, "Drew loves to *not* talk about this stuff."

Decker motioned to the others, "These are Elizabeth's parents, and this is Admiral Book. Should you break the agreement, he's the one that you'll have to deal with."

Drew and Ian turned to see a very stern look on Book's face. He was downright intimidating when he offered his hand for a shake, which was one of the firmest the two young men had ever experienced.

"Wow!" Ian commented. "That's one heck of a grip."

"Probably from all those years as a SEAL," Decker mentioned.

The intense gaze from Book let both men know that he meant business, so they quickly bid everyone farewell and left to return to their normal lives.

As soon as the Chevy Lumina pulled out of the driveway, Book's expression softened considerably, and he gave a warm hello to Harry and the colonel. "So, do you think we can trust them?"

"I do," Colonel Decker replied. "Even without the bad-cop routine, I think they intend to honor the agreement." Decker had a reputation for accurately judging character, and many thought that he had missed his calling. It was often said that he should have worked for the FBI as a profiler.

Walking down the stairs from Haley's room, the girls were followed by Hayseed and Nomad, who were eagerly awaiting supper. They stepped out of the stairwell and turned the corner to find her father sitting at the table with Ryan, Maggie, Colonel Decker and another man in military dress who they didn't recognize.

Harry turned his head to see them and smiled. "C'mere, girls, and see this."

Haley and Elizabeth said "Hi" to Colonel Decker.

"Hello, Haley. Elizabeth." The colonel motioned to the other man. "This is Admiral Book."

"Hello," Book said with a friendly smile. He motioned to the table, "What do you think?"

They approached to see a backpack sitting on the table. It was blue in color, dome-shaped, with a cradle space on the right side featuring clips that matched the ones on Haley's potato gun. It was made of a sturdy material that was fitted on a strong frame. "Is that what I think it is?" Haley asked.

"Yes, it is!" Harry picked it up off the table, saying, "I know you like to tumble when shooting spuds, but your wooden rig just doesn't cut it. And since they," he motioned to Colonel Decker and Admiral Book, "had access to better materials than just wood, they took another design I made and built it."

"Consider it a thank you for stopping Ahnk-Hume," Colonel Decker said.

"And I hope to see you both at the New Year's Eve Ball on the Sub Base," the admiral added, then motioned to the new rig and said, "Would you like to test it?"

With a grin, Haley picked up the new pack and slipped her arms through the straps. She clipped the waist belt together, adjusting the strappings to fit, and the nanobots swarmed onto and through the new pack. The rippling stopped, so Haley removed the new pack and handed it to Elizabeth, who did the same and then set it back onto the table.

Now programmed into their PJs, the nanobots began moving again to form a perfect replica of the new pack. Haley conjured the gauntlet and potato gun on her arm, removed the gun and handed it to Elizabeth so she could attach it to the gauntlet forming on her arm.

"I'll be right back," Haley said and ran into the front hall to grab a couple of bricks by the door.

She came back into the kitchen, cradling the bricks in her arms as tiny bots broke them down for mass, allowing her to conjure another potato gun and the flexible tube that connected the gun to her pack. Now, both girls were sporting a fully functioning rig. Haley rolled her arm back, and the clips on her gauntlet disengaged as the ones on the pack took hold, leaving the gun cradled on the side of the pack.

She did it again, and the gun was released from the cradle and was now mounted on her gauntlet. "Nice!"

Admiral Book was aware of what the PJs could do and had seen Decker alter his clothing with a thought, but it still impressed him to see the pack replicated twice in a matter of seconds. "Imagine what that could do for mass production."

Harry held up a sack of potatoes and said, "Shall we take a few shots before the sun goes down?" He felt a brush against his leg, looked down, smirked, and said, "After we feed the cats."

Second Density. New York City, New York. October

She walked along the busy sidewalk, trying not to become overwhelmed by the chorus of emotions from the people around her. The sun had just dipped below the horizon as a chilly breeze intermittently whooshed between the buildings. Sabrina tightened the waistband to her coat and continued following the man twenty feet ahead of her. This was not her typical hunt. In fact, it wasn't a hunt at all but protection for a man that she, at one time, never would have never considered protecting. A man that her father suggested she should speak with a long time ago.

Randy continued along the sidewalk with his wife and their thirteen-year-old son. He was once a Proctor and once had the potential to make Sergeant. Mean, blunt and relentless, most feared being on his bad side, and Randy loved the power trip. And with those power trips, his ego grew, and he began to get careless. Then, one day, Randy and his squad strapped an eleven-year-old girl to an interrogation table, teasing and scaring her. They thought it would teach the young one to grow up respecting state authority, and they also thought it was hilarious.

They zapped her with low-level tasers to make sure she knew who was in charge. But Randy grabbed a horsewhip for the mounted Proctors and thought he'd give her one last good scare. He didn't mean to actually cause an injury, but when he gave it a good snap, the skin above her left eyebrow split.

He didn't care much…at first. A couple of nights later, he got into bed for a good night's sleep, but every time he closed his eyes, he saw her face. Night after night, the girl's face haunted him and it was driving the Proctor crazy. He couldn't figure out why it was bothering him so much, and the two from his squad, who had been part of the bully session, said to forget about it, that she was just a random kid, and that it didn't matter.

But this was not sitting well with him, and his conscience would not let this go. He asked some other Proctors who were working that night about her, and one of them recognized the description. Randy's heart sank further, and he became consumed by guilt when the Proctor told him that she was orphaned that same day, but a Hunter had taken custody of her, and nobody knew where she had gone from there.

If you think the image of that girl had haunted him before, it was nothing compared to what it became after this news. It was less than a month before he resigned from his position and left the Proctors. He took on a job as a common laborer and began seeking psychological help.

As she grew and trained, Sabrina kept a close eye on him and the two others. As teenagers, she and Derek snuck into the psychologist's office and took copies of Randy's records. Sabrina herself read about his nightmares. How her face haunted the former Proctor and how he was now helping other people with their problems. Probably as some sort of penance. He even used his connection with the Proctors a time or two, preventing others from being on the receiving end of the kind of treatment that he had once been so famous for dealing with.

Manny had been told of all these findings and had been encouraging Sabrina to speak with him, believing it would be beneficial for them both and maybe, just maybe, they could put this trauma to rest. Even years later, Sabrina still had not taken that advice. But she would not stop monitoring Randy's activities.

In his efforts to do good, Randy had become a pillar of the community. And that's what brought Sabrina to him now. Community was not something that the Cetatian State could let grow. The more cohesive and bonded a community became, the harder they were to control. And Randy was the center of that growth. The state had ways to deal with such people without showing their hand. A desperate thug, or "useful idiot" as the State often referred to them, would be hired for cheap to eliminate the problem. If caught, they appeared to be a random lunatic.

Because Sabrina had been monitoring Randy all this time, she had learned what was coming and intended to prevent it. She minded her empathic senses, hearing the echoes of what everyone was experiencing. It was loud! A variety of feelings all at once. It was too overwhelming with so many people, so she tried focusing on a particular range of emotions.

Five people nearby caught her attention. Sabrina concentrated on them, and one rang out! She turned to glance at this man, who looked pretty much how he felt. He was wearing a pullover hoodie and tattered blue jeans. The hood was up, but she could still see his face. The man was haggard from the withdrawals of substance abuse, desperate and staring hard at Randy.

The man began to move and increased his pace with every step. He knocked a couple of other people out of the way and pulled out a knife, lifting it above his head while he stepped in front of Randy. He started to hack down when his wrist was grabbed from behind. One of that hand's fingers pressed into the man's wrist, causing him to drop the knife, and before he could react, his arm was twisted behind him. He felt something slap into his back, and then metallic tendrils wrapped around his body, ensnaring his legs and trapping his arms to the side. The next thing he knew, he was hovering six inches off the ground.

"It's not what you think! It's not what you think!" he shouted.

Spinning him around, Sabrina said, "I'm not a Proctor…But they are."

Two uniformed Proctors were hurrying through the crowd, and Sabrina had her credentials displayed when they arrived.

"Good evening, Hunter," the sergeant said.

"Was he a contract?" the officer asked.

Shaking her head, Sabrina replied, "No." She motioned toward Randy. "He just tried to kill this man."

"No, no!" the thug shouted, "I'm working for The State!"

"Oh," the sergeant began sarcastically. "We haven't heard that one before."

"You stupid cops! I really am!" He squirmed in a fruitless effort to wriggle out of the restraining disk while the Proctors took statements from Randy and his family, but Sabrina kept from facing Randy directly.

Once finished, the officer handed Sabrina his restraining disk to replace the one holding the junkie, said, "Thank you, Hunter," grabbed the hovering man by the shoulder, and the Proctors walked the thug away.

"Thank you," Randy said. Sabrina took a deep breath, sighed and turned around to face him. Even though years had passed, Randy instantly recognized her face, and his turned pale. "You're…you're…"

She fought against the mist that wanted to form in her eyes with success and then lifted her left hand, pulling her bangs to the side to reveal the vertical scar.

Randy was not nearly as successful at keeping his eyes dry, and the empath could sense his gut dropping and the reverberating guilt.

His wife, with a pleading look in her eyes, spoke up right away. "He's not who he used to be!"

Sabrina Looked into her eyes and then back to Randy's. "None of us are."

"I…I…there's no amount of 'I'm sorry' that can…" His voice trailed off as he reached for words that just were not there. For years, he had thought over what he could say to convey his remorse, and now that the opportunity was in front of him, all he could do was stammer.

Sabrina lowered her head with a sigh, looked back up to Randy's eyes and said, "I've…I've seen who you've become since then." She looked to his wife, "He's become a good man," looked to his son, "a good example." And back to Randy. "You help those you can, support those who need it, and the community is better off because of you." The mist started to build in her eyes. "I know you've changed. You've become someone I respect. Someone that I…" She shut her eyes tight for a second to regain control, opened them and said, "I forgive you."

Tears of shame flowed down Randy's cheeks as he heard the words that he thought he would never hear or deserve.

"But you have to keep your head down for a while," Sabrina went on. "Your efforts have gained the attention of those who do not like to see strength in the populace. I suggest you all go visit family in another district for the time being because this junkie won't be the only attempt on your life."

"You mean, he really was working for The State?"

"No. But he was manipulated by them to do this. You've created discord between people and The State of Cetatia. And they cannot have that. So please, go home, pack some things and go visit family. Get out of Podman Bach's district for a little while."

"We could go visit my brother," Randy's wife said to him.

Sabrina nodded, "You won't see me, but I'll keep watch over you until you get home, and then I should be leaving as well. Podman Bach is already not fond of me."

They parted company, and Sabrina made sure that Randy and his family got home safely. She sat atop a building in the chill breeze, thinking about the conversation. It felt like a weight was lifted for them both, but this was only part of healing. There were two other Proctors that were involved. One was already dead from a violent altercation of his own making. The other lived in this city but had become a miserable and belligerent drunk. Randy was the easy one to speak to, but the other…the Hunter shook her head. *I'm not ready to talk to him.*

First Density. Location: Unknown

As a hive mind, the Archons were able to use their unified mental power to suppress emotional reactions. The more members of the Hive, the easier the emotional control. They all retained their individuality yet could draw upon each other's knowledge and experience at any time. Being severed from his Hive, Ahnk-hume's emotional range expanded, making self-control more difficult.

But over the past few months, Ahnk-Hume had learned. His emotions were still continuing to expand alongside his mastery of self.

He had wanted to scream. He had wanted to punch things, but he sat there and presented nothing but calm, hiding the turmoil that raged within. The weakness that he did not want others, especially Humans, to see.

The sorrow. The loneliness. Oh, how he longed for companionship. The mere presence of one of his own kind. The mental community of the Hive. The presence of Nokitahm. This solitude was what had been weighing on him most of all. This empty feeling that he could not stand made him wonder if any of the other Archons had ever felt this. *Of course not. I would have known.* He was at least thankful that none of his kin would have to experience such deep and painful feelings. The kind of feelings that he and his kin often inflicted on others. The Drakel winced as he thought about that.

What was that? He physically twitched from the thought, another new experience for him. *What is this wretched feeling?* he wondered in both fear and distress as his heart rate increased slightly. He couldn't identify the turning in his stomach because the Archon had never felt guilt before.

CHAPTER 6
But Those Who Are Sick

Final Density, AKA, The Astral Plane

Thirty-one people were present, amazed by the glowing and translucent appearance of everything around them. An hour ago, they were aboard a small ship, but they all now stood as spirits without bodies after the vessel sank. Most of them were here because they were followers of Hel, who appeared before them.

"Welcome, my people," she said in a stern and stately manner. "Follow me to your new home." Hel waved her hand, and a gray stone gateway appeared. The hinges of the metal bars creaked as they swung open, and Hel said, "Let's go."

A blinding light flashed in front of the open gateway, and a man was standing there, blocking Hel. The expression on his face was a mix of anger and disbelief, and his gaze bore into Hel's eyes when he pointed out toward the crowd and said, "They do not belong here."

Hel looked over her shoulder at the crowd of ghosts toward the three people to whom the man pointed. Two Humans and an Alfan who were prisoners on that ship. She turned back to the man and said, "They all came in at once. I didn't notice."

Turning to the crowd, the man took a step toward the three in question and the other spirits moved out of the way. The man approached, and the three spirits trembled in terror, but his visage softened, and he said, "Fear not! I am Michael." He waved his hand, and the air itself seemed to pull back like a couple of curtains, revealing another existence. "We can make proper introductions later. Through here and straight ahead to the Gates of Pearl. Your loved ones are waiting."

"Thank you," one of them said. They stepped through, and the spatial rift sealed itself closed.

Turning around to look directly at Hel, a white light appeared in Michael's eyes when he took a step toward the Goddess of Death. With his next step, the glow of ethereal translucent wings became visible as Michael raised his right hand. Flames appeared in his palm and billowed outward into the shape of a large sword. He continued toward her and said, "You have crossed a line that must never be crossed. And now, you must pay the price for your transgression."

"And you know that I don't want anyone coming here who did not choose to be here. I am not trying to claim unwilling spirits."

The flaming sword was lifted high, and Michael was about to swing when he stopped and tilted his head, listening to something that no one else could hear. Lowering his arm, Michael opened his palm, and the flames of his sword dissipated into nothing as the light of his eyes and wings faded.

"I know not why, but The Father has decided to show you mercy." Turning to look at the crowd and then back to Hel, Michael said, "You've lived a long, long time and have led many people astray. Tell me, how do you live with yourself? Do you even sleep anymore?"

Looking unimpressed, Hel said, "It's easier than you think."

Michael's expression remained firm but also became earnest when he said, "Please, Hel, repent. Accept Yeshua's gift and come back to us while you still can. Because as the saying from your world goes, you are on very thin ice."

A blinding light flashed, and the Goddess of Death made a quick motion with her arm. The Seraph was gone. Hel turned to look toward the others, rolled her eyes and scoffed, "Angels. They take themselves so seriously." With a wave of her hand, she said, "Let's go." The goddess watched the spirits as they all filed through the portal and, before following behind them, opened her hand to look down at the object she was holding with a smirk. A white glowing feather from the wing of an Archangel.

Second Density. Location: Unknown

Seated at the head of the table, Kone had his elbows propped on the surface, and the tips of his fingers pressed together while he listened to the reports about the progression of their plans.

Podman Kruduck was gaining enthusiasm as he told of the many politicians that had been replaced with shells in nations all around the First Density, piloted remotely by their own people. Next, the General-Ralt reported the same success, replacing the military personnel in those same countries.

These shells were clone-like copies of the people that were replaced. Putting on a pair of high-tech goggles, someone could pilot the shell as if it were their own body. They thoroughly researched the political and authority figures before abducting them so that a Cetatian actor could fill that person's role and, when the time came, give the orders to police and military personnel that would facilitate a quick and smooth takeover of the First Density.

Most of the abducted targets, and in some cases their entire family, were either killed or sacrificed to Molech, which was overseen by the Archons, but some were kept alive in order to glean more information.

"Between our plants and the Illuminati, we have enough people to seize control of the First Density now," Podman-Ralt Gates said. "We can proceed sooner than planned if you like."

Commando Conrad cleared his throat, and everyone looked at him. "I'd advise against that." Peter Conrad was the best strategist among them, and Kone knew it. The Commando could have become a General by now, but that would take him out of the field, and he was all about the action. Despite remaining a Commando, Kone recognized Peter's tremendous talent. For this reason, Kone always welcomed him to the table with the Podmen and Generals. As a Commando, he was subordinate to the Generals, but at this table, Conrad was addressed as an equal.

"This is a long game," Peter stated. "We could take control with little effort, but that would create much resentment from the people of the First Density. And that would be counterproductive for our plans further down the line."

"Which is why," Kone began as he stood up, "we will be waiting until New Year's Eve." The Uniralt clasped his hands behind his back and strolled around the table while he spoke, making eye contact with all in attendance as he passed. "That will give us enough time to push the tensions in some of these nations to the point of attack. That's when we make our move. No, not everyone will believe what we have to say when we reveal ourselves, but we can convince most that it was we, the Cetatians, who stopped the wars right before they became nuclear. That will earn us some good faith, enough to gain their trust over the next couple of years, and then we will have them join forces with us to stop the Dvwargarian and Alfan threats."

The Generals were aware of these longer-term plans, but this was new information to the Podmen.

"We can keep control over the Humans once they've fallen in line," Conrad stated, "but we must convince them to do so first." The Podmen, considering the new informaton, began slowly nodding while looking at each other.

"I do like this idea," Podman Bach said. "But I have one issue, a possibility of failure from within."

"And what would that be?" Kone asked.

"The Hunters," Bach spat. "They've become more unreliable of late. They cling to their precious code like an American to the Constitution and that code conflicts with many of our upcoming plans. Did they ever even stop the traitors? No! They either need to be stripped of their excessive autonomy or be removed entirely!" Even though the Podman delivered his words calmly, everyone knew of his dislike for the Hunters, so they were not surprised when his face turned red from anger as he spoke.

"There has been no activity from the traitors since Sahmbo found them in California. With a call that close, they've all probably retreated to the Fourth Density," Kone stated while approaching Podman Bach. The Uniralt looked Bach directly in the eyes. "But you bring up a valid point. I'm sure you've noticed that none of them are here for this meeting, and that is because of the very reasons you've just mentioned."

Despite his best efforts over the centuries, Kone was unable to get the Hunters to forsake their code. As time went on, this code prevented them from taking part in more of Kone's plans, and now it was reaching the point of liability. "The Hunters have been invaluable, but things are changing, and our upcoming plans will certainly bring us to an impasse. We can still use them for some of our current operations, but after we take control of the First Density," Kone looked to Commando Conrad, "you can oversee their deletions."

Peter nodded, and Bach smiled.

First Density. Columbia, Connecticut. Thanksgiving

The potato smacked into the empty soda can and crunched it against the rock. The next can in line received the same treatment. It had been cold lately, but today was clear without much breeze, so the girls were taking the opportunity to launch some spuds. Elizabeth took out a row of cans and set up the next for Haley.

Five cans went down, then Haley aimed at the next, but the shot made a different puff sound with a pop, and the can remained. "I'm out," the farmgirl said, looking down at the burlap sack. It, too, was empty. She sighed, raised her arm back up, and a blue glow appeared in the barrel. She concentrated more energy into this shot, and the charged orb sped forward, taking on the shape of a bobcat's head. It hit the can, releasing a concussive burst on contact, taking out the other cans with it.

Elizabeth raised her arm and focused, trying to funnel her energy into the potato gun the way Haley did, but was not able to do so. "I don't understand," she said. "Why can't I blast through the gun like you do?"

"Dunno," Haley replied with a shrug. "Took me a while to make my eyes glow, but you could do that right away."

"It helps that she feels the gun as an extension of herself."

Recognizing the voice, both girls turned with a smile on their faces to greet the Egyptian goddess. "Hi, Bast!" they said in unison.

"Hi. And happy Thanksgiving."

"Happy Thanksgiving," they both replied.

"So, you both have potato guns now? Fun!"

"Yeah!" Haley exclaimed. "It's nice to have somebody to shoot with."

Elizabeth asked, "What do you mean by feeling the gun as an extension of ourselves?" She looked past Bastet to see Hayseed and Nomad trotting across the potato field.

"This is more than just a potato gun for Haley. It holds great emotional attachment. Not only has she been using it longer, but it was a gift from her father and bears her mother's badge number. It has, in a sense, become her wand."

"But why am I able to do it with my staff too?" Haley asked. "Elizabeth tried, but that won't work for her either."

"Yeah," Elizabeth said. "It doesn't make sense. I can put my energy into something, so why can't I run it through?"

"Well, even though enchanting and channeling are similar, they are not quite the same. It takes some getting used to. Have you tried making an actual wand?" Bast asked the young mystic. "Not that either of you really need one, but some find it advantageous to use an object as a focal point."

Elizabeth shrugged. "Hadn't thought of it. I just think it looks cool to shoot blasts out of the gun, and I wanted to do it, too."

"You'll most certainly learn to in time." Both Nomad and Hayseed were nuzzling against her legs when Snow, an all-white cat, came trotting out from the woods.

"Hi, Snow!" Haley said when he arrived.

Haley used her com-system to call the landline. She could hear the phone ringing through the tiny speakers in her bandana when her dad picked up. "Hello?"

"Hey, Dad! Bast is here, alright if we light the fire?"

"Sure, we'll all be out to say hi in a few minutes."

"Okay, thanks, Dad. Bye."

"Bye."

Haley smirked. "Go for it, Beth!"

With a smile, Elizabeth flicked the lighter and tugged on the flame, expanding it until she had a stream of fire swirling around her arm. She reached out to the fire pit, and a fireball shot forward, setting it ablaze.

"And you think you need to gun barrel to make that look cool?" Bast asked Elizabeth.

"Well..." Elizabeth couldn't think of what to say, so she just laughed. The three of them sat down on the ground next to the firepit, and Bast started telling them a story as Snow climbed into her lap. Nomad nuzzled against Elizabeth and Hayseed with Haley. A few moments later, Harry, Ryan and Maggie came out with some marshmallows.

"Hi," Maggie said.

"Hello," Bastet replied. "Happy Thanksgiving."

"Thanks."

"We've got plenty of turkey if you're interested. Neil and Sandra are coming over soon, too."

"Great!" exclaimed Bast. "I haven't seen them in weeks."

Second Density. Location: Unknown

Kone tapped the glowing light in the polished surface of his desk. "Yes?"

"There's two people here to see you," a woman's voice said.

"Send them…" A flash of orange alongside a burst of black mist, and the two of whom the voice spoke were in front of him. A man wearing a hooded sweatshirt with blue jeans and sneakers and a thin woman wearing black strips of cloth wrapped around her body. Kone cut off the call. "This is unexpected. What brings you two here today?"

The woman smiled, "We have a surprise for Molech."

"You know that he is not fond of surprises and…what happened to you?" Kone asked, looking at the large bruise on the left side of Baphomet's face.

"I had…a disagreement with…never mind that. We need to talk to Molech."

Kone nodded and closed his eyes. When he opened them, they had become two swirling pools of black and red. When he spoke, it was a different voice. "So, what happened to you?"

Baphomet sighed, "Does it even matter which one of you I'm speaking to anymore?"

"Not really," Molech replied with a smirk.

"Tell them," Hel said.

"Fine," Baphomet huffed. "I got some cultists to make some sacrifices for me. Got me good and juiced up! So, when I came across Cernunnos and Quetzalcoatl, you know I couldn't let that opportunity pass by." He grinned, "I was doing pretty good, too, considering I was fighting both of them at once!" Baphomet's expression became a snarl, "I had no idea that they were waiting for Thor. I found that part out when Mjolnir hit me in the face."

"I see," Molech said dryly while looking at the large bruise.

"Tell him the rest," Hel insisted.

"What more is there to tell?"

"The part where I found you unconscious."

"They…" He sighed again. "They must have given me a swirly while I was out."

"He was face down in the toilet of a gas station bathroom," Hel explained.

Molech barely suppressed his chuckle while shaking his head. "Baphomet, Baphomet, Baphomet…Why must you always use up your extra power as soon as you get it? If the other gods catch on to what we're doing, we'll need it."

"Some might believe you to be dead, but most think you're in hiding and fear your schemes."

"They know I'm in hiding, and they're right to fear my schemes. When Artemis and Cernunnos couldn't find me, and these links disappeared." He glanced down at the cufflinks on Kone's sports coat and smirked. "They knew what happened. Why do you think they keep such a close eye on you?" The gemstones that were fashioned into cufflinks were enchanted and could conceal one's presence from anybody, even gods of hunting. They were swiped from Olympus at the same time Molech's trail went cold.

Kone thought about the man who made these links. The concentration necessary, the energy it must have consumed to create such an artifact. The man was a master of magick and oh-so-clever, but an artifact like this must have drained him severely. The man had a talent unlike anything else Kone had ever seen in his nearly two thousand years, and no one has been able to make a magickal item like this man could. Each one that he produced was extraordinary and must have been just as taxing, which is why there are so few.

"Yeah, yeah, I know. But we've got something you gotta see!" Baphomet smirked and gestured to Hel, more than happy to change the subject.

With a smile, Hel held out her hand and opened her fingers to reveal in her palm a translucent, ethereal feather.

The face of Kone bore an expression of shock. "Is that what I think it is?" Molech asked.

"Yes," Hel replied with a smug smile. "A feather from an Archangel's wing." Her smile widened just before saying, "Michael's."

Molech reached out with Kone's arm and picked the feather out of Hel's hand, "How did you…? This is incredible!" The cufflinks might shield him from a god's detection, but Seraphs were a little different. With this now in Molech's possession, he could avoid their detection entirely, allowing the malicious god more freedom of movement. It also could facilitate teleportation beyond almost any barrier, perfect for surprise attacks.

"With New Year's fast approaching, you might need it," Hel said.

A smug smirk dominated his face as he replied. "Indeed."

First Density. Location: Unknown

Ahnk-Hume was sitting on the edge of the cot. His lower arms were folded across his abdomen, supporting the elbows of his upper arms as his chin rested in his palms. There was a part of him that wanted to no longer be the thing that he had been, but there was another part that longed and craved to revel in the ways he had known. *I can't go back to what I was…*he thought, *but I cannot resist being what I am.*

Ahnk-Hume's lower fists clenched tight with his frustration and inner turmoil. *How can I be anything if I can't be what I am…but…*His mind came to a halt, too emotionally overwhelmed to process anything further, so he just sighed. *I am a defiled thing, and there's nothing or no one who can change that. But how would it be possible to save the next generation from the corruption that we have become from this…*

"Addiction," he muttered under his breath while tensing all his muscles in frustration, thinking about how once an Archon hatches, the Hive will imprint onto their mind within an hour. And with that will come all the sick and twisted desires that go with it.

Ahnk-Hume was hatched into this way of life, and so all other hatchlings would be too. *How could I possibly spare our descendants from such an existence?* That's when there was a spark from the breaker box, and a set of bars dropped down from the ceiling, keeping him confined to the cot.

The guard picked up the phone and pressed a button. "The inner bars malfunctioned…Yes, it sparked…He's on the cot." The guard nodded, said, "Thank you, sir," and hung up the phone. It wasn't long before the main door to the room slid open, and a maintenance man walked in.

That was incredibly fast, Ahnk-Hume thought. *It had not even been a moment since the guard made the call.*

Confined to the corner where he sat on his cot, Ahnk-Hume watched as the maintenance man opened an electrical panel and took up his tools. He looked toward the guard and paused.

Ahnk-Hume followed the maintenance man's gaze to see that the guard was sitting in the chair with his arms folded and his eyes closed. Sleeping.

The maintenance man looked at Ahnk-Hume and said, "Can't say I blame him. I've seen him around the last couple of days, and he's been pushing hard." He smiled and then turned back toward the panel, continuing to work and said, "I'll wake him up before I leave. Hope you don't mind, but this will take me a couple of minutes." He turned back toward Ahnk-Hume and said, "I'm very good with electrical but a little out of practice." Turning back to the panel, the repair man explained, "I'm usually working with wood."

"You're…you're talking to me," Ahnk-Hume said in confusion and demanded, "Why?"

"Because you're the reason I'm here. Why wouldn't I?"

"You dare quip with me?" the Drakel snarled. "Do you know what I am?"

"Yes." the man replied with a smile. "You…are the one with whom I am speaking."

"I am not one to be trifled with!" Ahnk-Hume growled. "Look at me. Take a good look and tell me, what do you see?"

The maintenance man put the tools down and walked up to the cell door. He put a finger on one of the bars, pushed and the cell gate slid to the side. This shocked Ahnk-Hume as the maintenance man walked right up to the barrier, but the Drakel would not drop the facade. "What do you see, Little Man?"

He looked up at Ahnk-Hume's face and deep into his slit pupils. "I see the eyes of a man desperately seeking redemption." He held the eye contact, and Ahnk-Hume knew that there was no fear within the maintenance man. A few seconds later, the Drakel dropped his eyes to the side as this strange visitor walked out of the cell and back to the electrical panel while the cell door slid shut.

He picked up a screwdriver and began to turn a fastener in the panel. "Tell me, Ahnk-Hume, Hatchling of Thurduun…" The man turned his head back toward Ahnk-Hume to see the Drakel, his jaw hanging slack from hearing his proper name. "…Do you believe in redemption?"

Ahnk-Hume dropped his head and tried to process this entire conversation. He wondered if he was hallucinating. The Drakel looked back to the man, who was again working on the panel and wondered, *Who is this man that messes with my mind?* He sneered as he shook his head. "No, I don't," Ahnk-Hume said, answering the man's question. Then, with a smirk, he added, "Not for things like me."

The man closed the panel, turned to face Ahnk-Hume directly and, with a smile, said, "I once knew a thief who thought the same thing. But he also learned that when you think all is lost, believe in me, and I'll be there to help you."

The guard lifted his head while slowly blinking his eyes.

"Just in time," the maintenance man said while turning on the control board, and the inner-cell barrier retracted back to the ceiling. "It's all set. Have a great day."

"You too," said the guard, unaware that he had even dozed off. But then he turned his head back toward the maintenance man and called, "Hey, Goldman!"

He turned back to look at the guard.

"Thanks for the talk earlier. It really helped."

With a warm smile and a nod, Goldman turned and left the room.

CHAPTER 7
Auld Long Syne

First Density. Columbia, Connecticut. December 31, 1999

"…and after the latest skirmish, there's talk of possible nuclear retaliation." The news anchor was looking directly into the camera when she delivered the line, a grave look of concern on her face. Harry lifted the remote with a sigh, pressed the button, and the screen went dark.

Haley's eyes shot open from worry, and she turned toward her dad. "If it gets really bad, will they send Uncle Ryan over there?"

"It's possible," Harry shrugged. "But we shouldn't worry about that right now. They'll be over here soon, and I want you girls to enjoy the night."

Propping her left elbow on the table, Haley muttered, "Not if I have to wear that dress." The New Year's Eve Ball on the New London Submarine Base was a formal event, which meant the farmgirl had to wear something appropriate. So, they went looking for a dress. Haley found one that was royal blue with some fancy lines of purple and fell in love with it. The dress was beautiful, displayed her favorite colors, and she couldn't wait to try it on, so she ducked into the dressing room.

The door flew back open, and she threw her arms wide as she called out, "Ta-da!"

"Is this the one?" Harry asked.

"Yes!"

"Alright. Go change back into your regular clothes. We still got to pick up some chow."

"Okay." Haley went into the dressing room, and the PJ nanobots rippled through the dress, programming it into her com-system. She took the original off while her coveralls reformed underneath and carried it out to the shopkeeper. She loved the colors. She loved the way it looked on her.

But after they had gotten home, Haley conjured it from her PJs and walked around wearing it. It was only five minutes before she realized just how uncomfortable it was. Wearing the dress felt fine if she was standing still, but moving around in it quickly became a chore. At least the version conjured from the PJs automatically shifted for a tailored fit, but it didn't stop it from feeling cumbersome.

"You chose it," Harry said. "And look on the bright side. Changing your clothes afterward is easier for you than anybody else."

"I hope I don't knock anything over," she sighed.

After Ryan, Maggie and Elizabeth arrived, they all got into Harry's truck. A club cab pickup, Harry and Ryan got into the front seats while Maggie and the girls slid into the back. Traffic wasn't too bad considering the holiday, and they arrived at the base in forty-five minutes. After parking the truck, they opened the doors and stepped out when they suddenly heard "Meow."

"Uh-oh," Haley said, looking under the seat to see Nomad curled up. "How did you...?" She sighed.

"Again!? Oh, great," Harry said. "Nomad, you sneaky little..." He sighed. "What am I supposed I do with you?"

"We can't just leave him in the truck. It's too cold," Haley said.

"He can handle the cold better than we can," Harry said, "but no, we can't leave him stuck in the vehicle. Come on out, Nomad."

The cat hopped out of the truck and into the parking lot.

Haley knelt and petted him. "We can't bring you inside, so be careful until we get back, okay?"

"Meow," Nomad replied with a nod of his head.

"Why'd you bring your cat?" a gruff voice asked, and they turned to see Colonel Decker.

"We didn't know that he was in the truck until just now," Elizabeth said.

"Good thing he's not your average cat," Decker replied. He turned to Harry and Ryan, "Admiral Book wants to see you. He has something to discuss."

"Stay out of trouble until we come back," Haley said once more to Nomad, and the cat trotted off to explore.

Harry and Ryan both signed the paperwork. Between their service records and recent events, Admiral Book trusted them and was about to show them a classified submersible; made possible due to information obtained by a certain Air Force Colonel. Decker had been digging into the limited intel on the Cetatians and had managed to uncover some design plans, which he provided to the Navy through carefully selected channels.

Colonel Decker was grateful to have met Admiral Book, as there were rifts becoming apparent in the governing system. Things seemed fine to the casual observer, but behind the scenes, everything was splitting into two factions. One wanted more control, and the other wanted to preserve the Constitutional Republic. It was a cold, quiet civil war.

Admiral Book, also coming to the same conclusions as Decker, was always keeping his eye open for trustworthy patriots who would defend their country. He knew he could trust the two men before him and wanted them onboard should things heat up.

Looking around the room, the girls saw many Naval Officers in full-dress uniforms, most of them discussing the current events happening overseas. Maggie led the girls to a table, where they sat to have some snacks while the band continued to play. She noticed Haley looking around with an air of discomfort. "Is the dress still bothering you, sweetie?"

The farmer shrugged. "Kind of, but that's not the problem."

"What's up?" Elizabeth asked.

"Some of them are looking at us weird," Haley replied.

Maggie smiled. "Some of the people here know what happened last year. They probably recognize you two."

"It's not that," Haley shook her head. "They're looking at us like…like," she shrugged, "It feels like they're out to get us."

An expression of concern crossed Maggie's face. "Is this something you're feeling empathically?"

Haley glanced down, then back up to Maggie and let out a long, slow "Yeah."

Typically, Colonel Decker would not be on a Naval base for New Year's Eve, but Captain Delwin, an old and trusted friend of his, was here this year, and Decker needed to touch base with any potential ally when it came to the cloak and dagger politics happening behind the scenes. He walked through the room and saw Haley and Elizabeth sitting with Maggie at a table. The colonel was about to go speak to them when he saw Captain Delwin speaking to some officers on the floor.

He approached Delwin, and the officers noticed the captain's eyes fixated. Following his gaze, they saw the approaching colonel and stepped aside to allow him into the conversational circle. With a smile, Colonel Decker said, "It's been too long, Good Captain. How have you been?"

Delwin smiled back. "Good to see you too, Colonel. How are the skies treating you?"

"Well, thank you." Decker couldn't help but notice something was off, but he couldn't put his finger on it. Delwin's mannerisms and expressions were just like he remembered, and the captain, by all appearances, was the same old Delwin. What was bugging him? Decker's eyes dropped to Delwin's wristwatch, which was digital instead of analog, and then back up to the captain's face with a smile. "The music that the band's playing reminds me of that time we worked in Maine."

"I was thinking the same thing," Delwin replied with his usual smirk.

Decker glanced over toward the girls at the table and said, "I've got something I need to see to, but I'll be here all night. We need to catch up."

"Certainly. I'm not going anywhere."

"Excellent, I'll talk to you shortly." Decker excused himself and made his way toward the table. As he did, he wondered who he actually had just spoken to. Decker and Delwin had never worked in Maine.

The three ladies looked up to the colonel when he arrived at the table. "Hello," Maggie greeted.

He could tell from their demeanor that they were growing uncomfortable and may have already come to the same conclusion as he.

"Happy New Year. How are you tonight?"

Haley tried to be discrete when she said, "I think some of the people here are shells."

Decker nodded, "We should all take a walk."

A brisk wind whipped down the Thames River, making the choppy water slap against the docks where Admiral Book had led Harry and

Ryan. Subs were seen along most of them, but they continued past them all to an open pier and followed the admiral out to the end.

Book turned to face the other two. "Gentlemen, this is the next step for us in undersea operations. It has been dubbed the Otter." He waved his hand to the side of the dock as a small ship broke the surface. The smooth hull emerged with a hatch on the top. Only thirty-five feet long, the sub had a sleek design and resembled the shape of a pufferfish. "This vehicle is faster, far more maneuverable and can dive deeper than any other design so far."

The hatch opened, and a SEAL climbed out and saluted. "Everything is set, Admiral."

Book turned back to Harry and Ryan. "Time for the tour. We'll—" The admiral was interrupted by a ringing in his pocket and pulled the phone out to see that the call was coming from Colonel Decker. "Excuse me," he said and answered the phone. "Yes?"

"Admiral, we have shells on the base. Many of them. I'm on my way to your office now."

"I'm not there. Meet me by the new car."

"Understood." Decker ended the call and said to the ladies, "Follow me," and they left the building.

On the other side of the world, two countries prepared to eliminate each other with their greatest weapons. Launch codes were entered, and keys were turned, but much to the soldiers' surprise…and relief, nothing happened. New orders suddenly came in. "Stand down."

The same thing happened on the opposing side as some political leaders were unexpectedly detained by military personnel. These were not isolated incidents, but in every country around the world, orders were given to detain leaders from apparently legal channels.

Politicians, military commanders, even police officers, many were blindsided by those who were supposed to be their own allies. What they did not know was that these allies had been replaced with shells piloted by Cetatian military actors. Those in positions of significant power who were not detained were either a shell replacement of the original or were already in league with the Cetatian State. There were some skirmishes as small pockets of resistance pushed back, but with little understanding of what was happening and no idea who to trust, the small-scale battles ended as quickly as they started.

As Decker led Maggie and the girls outside, they felt the chill breeze assault their skin. Elizabeth conjured a jacket, removed it and handed it to her mother. With a thought, both girls altered their clothing to something more comfortable and didn't have to worry much about the cold due to their PJs. Haley didn't mind one bit, happy to be back in a pair of coveralls.

They continued toward the docs when personnel carriers sped by, much faster than permitted, carrying armed men. Three of them passed, but the fourth screeched to a halt twenty feet away.

Decker said, "Keep moving."

Men jumped out from the back of the truck and raised their firearms. "Stay where you are!" one of them ordered. Another said into a comm, "We have them."

The nanobots of Decker's sleeve rippled, flowing forward to form a gun in his hand, and he fired. The bullet hit his target between the eyes. The man staggered back a couple of steps, and the bullet was lodged into the skull, but catching his balance, the man showed no discomfort as he returned fire.

A full-face helmet quickly formed over Decker's head. The PJs were bulletproof and blast-resistant, but Maggie did not have the same protection. Haley and Elizabeth threw out their protective fields, shielding all four of them as a hail of bullets and bolts of yellow light flew in.

The potato gun formed on Haley's right arm, and she sent a mental command to her com-system, hijacking the base's public address speakers, and they began to play a song called Dare by Stan Bush. She dropped her field while raising her arm, a blue glow in the barrel of her potato gun. She fired four blasts, blue and purple kitten-shaped orbs sped forward toward the armed men.

Just as fast, Elizabeth was throwing sparkling orbs of amber and indigo light at their assailants. The first volley finished off the man that Decker shot, turning him into a gel-like substance that dropped into a puddle and started dissolving, leaving only the clothing behind.

The shells returned fire, but their shots were deflected again by the girls' energy fields. Haley concentrated more energy into her next shot and released a charged blast, turning two more of them into gel.

Echoing across the base, the song was distorted from the placement of the PA speakers and was more irritating than inspiring, but with another thought, Haley's com-system made the adjustment, delaying the song a bit in the closer speakers so the soundwaves from different spots would reach her location at the same time, making the music clear to her while sounding like a distorted and irritating echo everywhere else.

After making quick work of the shells, Decker said, "This way!" and they ran for the lower base.

Struggles erupted all over the base as those who were not under Cetatian control were being detained or eliminated. Haley, Elizabeth and Maggie followed Colonel Decker toward the docks but were met with more opposition.

They came under fire from shells on top of a building. The girls threw up their shielding as Decker said, "I'll take care of them." He activated the thrusters in his PJs and flew into the sky once the girls dropped their fields. On his way up, he switched his gun from conventional to blast mode as he rose higher than the rooftops and rained down zipping bolts of yellow energy. The bullets didn't affect him too much, but Decker took a shot from a bolt pistol, which did sting. He gritted his teeth and continued firing, taking out more of the shells.

More assailants showed up on the ground, firing bolts of yellow energy. They made a zipping sound as they shot through the air. Haley erected her field again, shielding Maggie as Elizabeth dodged to the side, hurling another mystical bolt in return.

When the music started blaring across the base, Harry immediately knew that it was Haley's doing and became worried. "What's going on?" he asked Admiral Book.

"We've got shells. Lots of them. Colonel Decker is bringing your daughters here now."

As soon as the words were spoken, they could see lights of yellow, blue and amber flying back and forth near the buildings.

"That's them!" Ryan started to move, but Admiral Book stopped him.

"You're unarmed." He looked to the SEAL, who nodded and hopped onto the dock, running for the buildings.

Decker dropped all but one of the shells on the rooftops and flew down toward the last. Many of them were a little uncoordinated from being in bodies that were not their own, but this one did not seem to have that problem. He was a Commando, and this shell was a replica of his own body, allowing him to use the full extent of his skills.

Shot after shot was fired by Decker, and the Commando dodged them all, firing back as he moved. Decker took another shot and dropped down to the other side of the rooftop, using an HVAC unit for cover.

Elizabeth threw some charged orbs at the Cetatian soldiers, and the larger blasts took them down quickly. She saw Colonel Decker drop to the rooftop. "Haley!" she called, pointing to Decker's location.

"I got it!" she shouted back and ran toward the building. With a powerful leap, she cleared the first story as ethereal claws of purple light extended from her fingernails, and she clung to the side of the wall, scaling up the second story and onto the rooftop.

Decker was a well-trained, disciplined warrior from the United States Air Force, but the Commando was an elite fighter whose training was on par with a Navy SEAL. Though he put up a good fight, the colonel was in over his head. The Commando swept his leg, dropped him to the tar and pulled a knife.

"Hey, fish-face!"

The Commando looked to see a blonde pig-tailed girl crackling with blue and purple energy. Haley released the blast through her arm cannon, and a stream of energy blew the Commando off the rooftop, gelling him in an instant.

Another vehicle was speeding toward Elizabeth and Maggie. Elizabeth grabbed her mother and jumped over a jersey barrier right before the car scrapped against the concrete and stopped. They could both feel the unnatural vibes radiating from the vehicle in an instant.

The doors were flung open, and three people stepped out. Standing at seven feet, they had lanky builds, with longer limbs than that of Humans, six fingers on each hand. Their ears were holes with no lobes and no discernable nose, but instead, two slits for nostrils.

"Archons," Elizabeth spat as an amber glow flashed in her eyes. She gathered her energy and held an orb in each hand.

"We've missed you," one of them said with a sinister smile. He started chanting, and the two ladies could feel the mystical energies coalesce.

"Nope!" Elizabeth shouted and threw an orb at the chanting Archon's mouth, interrupting his spell. She threw a few more, but they could cast protective fields of their own, blocking the young mystic's shots.

One of them dropped his field and spoke a word as he swung his arm, throwing sharp, red-glowing shards of hard energy. Elizabeth dove, grabbing and pulling her mother down as she went. One of the shards grazed Maggie's cheek, leaving a slice between her nose and ear.

"Ow!"

"That's it!" Elizabeth growled. She pulled a lighter from her pocket and gave it a flick. Fire began to swirl around her arms and torso as she stood up and unleashed a stream of flame.

The Archons shielded themselves from the mystic's fire, and Elizabeth kept it up, trying to wear them down, but she was exerting herself as well and felt her energy draining.

Then a man came in from behind, ran past them and leaped the jersey barrier as Elizabeth ran out of steam. The flames subsided and the Archons dropped their fields to return fire but were met instead by a Navy SEAL diving in, knife first.

He sank his blade into the neck of one Archon while he drew his sidearm, firing a bullet through the eye of another, turning them both to gel. He turned toward the third, who fired a blast at the newcomer, but the SEAL dodged and thrust his knife forward. The Archon brought his arm up, catching his wrist and reached out for his other to keep the gun pointed elsewhere.

"Drop me," Haley said to Decker as she gathered her energy. The colonel let go and the farmer unleashed a pounce, propelling herself down faster than terminal velocity and slammed feet first into the top of the Archon. The energy released gelled the Archon and knocked the SEAL to the side as Haley rebounded upward and then dropped back to the ground. "Are you okay?" Haley asked the SEAL.

He climbed back to his feet with a smile, saying, "You must be Haley."

Decker touched down to the ground alongside the group, and they sprinted for the docks.

"C'mon," Harry shouted as they made their way onto the pier. He took Haley's hand and led her into the Otter.

Ryan did the same with Maggie and Elizabeth. Colonel Decker and Admiral Book followed them while the SEAL watched for any more enemies.

Another shell came running onto the pier, shooting as he went. When the SEAL raised his firearm, an orange and white blur of fur jumped into the back of the shell's knee, causing him to stumble. Nomad continued running down the pier toward the Otter while the SEAL squeezed off a few rounds, turning the attacker to gel. Nomad dove into the hatch of the submersible. The SEAL shrugged, saying,

"I guess the cat's coming too," while climbing into the submersible. He closed the hatch and said, "Good to go!"

The Otter sank into the river and disappeared, speeding out to sea.

CHAPTER 8
Not So Silent Service

The inside of the Otter was well-lit and had twelve seats. Two at the front for piloting the vehicle, and the other ten placed evenly behind them. The front was a large display screen, allowing them to see ahead as they continued downriver and out into Long Island Sound.

There were three members of a SEAL team present. Two were at the helm, and the other who had assisted on the docs. Admiral Book had everyone take a seat and buckle in as they increased speed across the sound.

Haley and Elizabeth were taking in the sight. It was like a craft out of a sci-fi show, and the display allowed them a detailed view of the sound's floor. Schools of bluefish were plentiful, as were several striped bass and other manners of sea life. "This is so cool!" Haley exclaimed. "Where are we going?"

Book answered, "An undersea base. Hopefully, the Cetatians don't know about it, but with everything going on right now, I don't know how many secrets, if any at this point, that we've managed to keep from them." He turned toward the SEAL, Senior Chief Petty Officer

Williams, at the helm. "Contact the rest of your team and have them meet us there."

"Aye, Admiral," he responded and began tapping the surface of the control panel."

"So, I take it that this isn't the only Otter," Harry stated.

"No." He stood up to address everybody. "We are heading out to the continental shelf. The base was built into a cavern in the side of the shelf break, and once we're there, we can contact others and take a better assessment of the situation."

As their journey continued, Haley's expression changed from one of wonder to one of worry mixed with sorrow, which did not go unnoticed by Harry. As she crossed her arms and hunched, her father leaned over and asked, "Are you okay?"

She answered with a long, slow, sad "Yeah." She looked up at the monitor ahead. "It's just that…it's a lot of water." Harry reached over and placed his hand on her shoulder, giving her a reaffirming squeeze and a sad smile. They were both missing Haley's mother, Heather, and she couldn't help but wonder what this latest adventure would be like if she were here.

It was less than an hour before they were diving. The display showed a steepening slope, and then it dropped like a cliff. Shortly after that, they came to an opening in the side of the shelf break, and the Otter entered a cavern, rising to break the surface of the water in a docking pool.

"There's no response from anyone on the comm," Williams said. He turned to Oldman and Elrod, "Check it out."

"Aye, Skipper," they both replied, grabbed some equipment from the back and climbed the ladder. Elrod opened the hatch and waited a couple of seconds, listening. He climbed out, firearm at the ready, and scanned the area with his eyes. Nothing.

After Elrod climbed out of the hatch, Oldman followed and they scouted the docking area; not a soul in sight.

The Otter's comm crackled to life with Oldman's voice, "There's no one here, sir. Want us to scout the rest?"

"Affirmative," Williams said, not happy about remaining behind. But he couldn't leave the admiral unguarded. "The base has clearly been compromised, so don't use its communication system. Just assess and return."

"Aye, Skipper," they heard Elrod's voice respond.

Feeling their emotional state, Haley realized just how brave these men were. They were walking into a potentially deadly unknown yet kept their feelings in check and pressed on like the professionals that they were. "How'd they learn to control their feelings like that?"

"What do you mean?" Williams asked with a look of confusion.

"You're doing it too. You're scared, but it doesn't stop you."

Admiral Book explained to Williams, "Haley is an empath and can feel your emotions like they were her own."

"But I don't sense anybody else out there right now. Just them."

"How far can you sense?" asked Williams.

"Not sure, let me try..." Haley closed her eyes and focused completely on her empathic senses. She tried to block out the others in the sub and concentrated on the two SEALS scouting. She pushed out a little further in the direction they were headed, nothing. Concentrating harder, she tried to feel if there was anything more.

Her eyes popped open. "Fear! I feel fear. Way off that way," she pointed in the direction that the scouts were heading.

"We have people deeper inside," Williams stated over the radio. "Scared people, but that's all we know so far."

"Acknowledged," was Oldman's response.

Elizabeth stood up. "We should go with them."

"No," every adult present said in unison.

"We have movement," Elrod reported. He left the comm open, and the others could hear a snarl or growl. Whatever was making the noise sounded like it was congested with mucus, and it intensified with the tapping sounds of large claws scrambling across the floor. Both Haley and Elizabeth recognized those sounds, which were followed by copious gunfire.

"Report," Williams ordered when the shots ended.

Elrod responded, "There was…it…it looked like some kind of lizard-like canine."

"They turned to gel after we shot them, but they can take a lot of fire before going down," Oldman added.

Decker pulled up some footage from his com-system of the mindless beasts that Haley and Elizabeth faced last year in what was now Camp Yeoman and cast it onto the view screen.

"Um, how did this get on our screen?" Williams asked.

"I did that," Decker said. "These are what they just killed."

"They have no mind," Haley added. "They're made to kill anything that isn't a shell. They're kinda like…robots, but not made of metal."

The viewscreen switched to a sensor display. "We have incoming," Williams said.

"Is it the rest of your team?" Book asked.

The screen displayed two dots, incoming vessels, that were similar in make to the Otter but not the same. "Negative," Williams said. "They're Cetaitian craft."

"Guerrerio, Starr, there are firearms stored in the back. Everybody out! We need to move," Book ordered.

Ryan and Harry each took a rifle and two sidearms while the others climbed up the ladder and out of the hatch. Williams went first and hopped down to the dry surface and watched the water while the others all followed. Once everybody was on the ground, they headed into the tunnel where Elrod and Oldman had gone while Williams took up the rear.

Two submersibles broke the water's surface. They were the models after which the Otter had been designed. After their hatches were thrown open, Cetatian soldiers began to exit the vehicle. The first one out took a bullet to the face from Williams, but these shells could handle more damage than a natural body. Also, it did not harm the actual soldier, who was safely in the second density wearing a pair of control goggles. A second shot went into his eye, which was not as bullet-resistant as the rest of the body, and he collapsed, turning into gel.

"Move!" Williams called out, and they ran down the corridor. The area transitioned into a man-made structure as the tunnel opened to a wide natural cavern in which the base was built. They continued running as the hallway became a large clear tube with a flat floor that continued into the main structure. The bottom half of which was submerged in the seawater below. The group neared the end of the entry tunnel as their pursuers entered the dock end.

Williams pivoted and fired to cover everyone else's escape, doing serious damage to one of them as they returned fire. He could have dodged when the yellow bolts zipped down the tunnel, but he didn't want to leave the others exposed, so Williams took a hit to the torso and went down. Hurting, Williams tried to get back up but could only lift his head to see more bolts of yellow speeding his way. The bolts came to an abrupt halt in front of him while ripples of amber and indigo light waved out from the points of impact against Elizabeth's field.

"Can you stand?" she asked.

"I think so."

She reached down and grabbed his belt, hoisting him up to his feet. Williams was aware of her enhanced strength but was still surprised by how easily she did that. Haley and Harry were by their side in an instant.

Harry supported Williams and said, "Let's go," while Haley raised her arm and conjured her potato gun, whisps of blue light flowing on the surface.

Elizabeth dropped her field, and Haley released the charged blast. The large blue and purple orb rocketed forward, taking on the shape of a bobcat's head. It hit the lead soldier, releasing a concussive burst that gelled three of them. Elizabeth threw her own charged orb of mystical energy, taking out one more soldier right before Haley threw out her protective field to block the return fire.

The field dropped, Elizabeth hurled another charged orb, and Haley let loose with four regular blasts, finishing off the remaining shells in the tunnel entrance. They turned to run with the others as Haley called out, "More are coming!"

Newington, Connecticut

"Aren't you supposed to be covering an event tonight?" Ian asked when Drew walked into the apartment.

The reporter dropped onto the couch, "Already did. Mark gave me the rest of the evening off after I turned in my piece." He smiled while removing his glasses. "I'm out of steam anyway. You know, I just might join you for that drink tonight."

"Then let's get started." Ian poured Drew some rum. "Another hour to go. Wanna watch the ball drop?"

"Sure," Drew answered while reaching up to accept the glass.

The television displayed a live broadcast of Times Square and the crowds that had gathered to celebrate the New Year.

Ian smirked, "So, any worries about the Y2K bug?"

Drew shot Ian a look, saw his roommate's smirk and couldn't suppress his own chuckle. "Shut up."

The picture on the television went fuzzy and began to glitch.

"What's this?" Ian asked and stood back up to go check the wires, but before he got to the set, the screen changed to display a man's face. He looked to be in his late twenties or early thirties, with pale skin and brown eyes. His head was shaved, revealing a blue secondary pigment that covered the top of his head and came to a widow's peak where his hairline would be.

"People of the world. My name is Kone, and I am the leader of the Cetatian people in the Second Density. We have been watching your society for generations, and unfortunately, it has become too volatile. War is the rule rather than the exception, and while we tried to keep to ourselves, you have forced our hands. You have developed weapons that, when used, would affect our existence as well.

Kone's face was stern as he continued. "We can no longer afford to remain silent and have used our greater technology to stop the launch of your nuclear weapons. If they were to be detonated in the

First Density, they would also cause severe damage in the Second Density. Therefore, we have taken control, not only to preserve our home, but yours as well. Things do not need to be the way they have been. A brighter future is possible for all of us."

Kone sat up a little straighter. "So, now we have an opportunity for true progress! We are not here to disrupt your way of life but to enhance it. For now, go to work, pay your bills, visit with friends and family. Live your lives."

"We will begin introducing new concepts and technologies to you in small steps, giving you the time to understand and adjust to the new concepts, and you will soon see the better future we can all share. For tonight, continue your celebrations, and I bid you all a happy New Year."

The screen turned to fuzz, and the regular broadcast returned. The crowd in New York were all standing still, looking up to the Mega Screen in stunned silence. A moment later, they became animated in discussion of what they just saw.

"Is this a joke?"

"We're being invaded!"

"This can't be real. It's a bit."

Ian switched the channel to a local news station.

"…claiming to be the leader of the Cetatians. They overrode all frequencies, and the message was broadcast on all channels and radio stations. Our White House correspondents are checking with government officials now…"

Ian muted the television. "This isn't good."

Undersea Base, The Atlantic

They hurried down a corridor to see the body of another serviceman mangled on the floor, and the snarling of another mindless beast was heard coming around the corner. The claws tapped on the floor as it went. Haley jumped up and clung to the ceiling with her hands, swinging her feet forward and letting go, flinging herself above the unnatural creature and pouncing. Her feet slammed into the beast, releasing a wave of blue energy, gelling it with one shot.

More of them charged down the corridor from behind. Ryan and Decker started unloading bullets into one of the charging creatures, and the concentrated fire took down the threat, but more came in behind it.

Elizabeth crackled with amber and indigo light, raised her palm and unleashed a sustained beam of energy into the three others, taking them all down.

They continued through the base, finding the bodies of more servicemen. "This way," Haley said, pointing in the direction of the fear. Harry and Ryan both put an arm around Williams to help him run as they hurried toward the base's med bays.

Coming upon two intersecting corridors, more beasts and Cetatian soldiers arrived and began firing. Haley, Elizabeth and Nomad ducted into the left corridor while the others dove to the right.

The soldiers charged down to the intersection and split, forcing the two groups further down and away from each other. The girls ran down and around the next corner and readied some blasts for the oncoming Cetatians.

Harry and the others dealt with more soldiers and a beast as they were forced further down their corridor.

After shrugging off a couple of rounds, a soldier reached out with both hands to grab Harry, but the marine, with a longer reach, had no problem landing and following through with a solid blow from his left.

The Cetatian twisted with the punch and was bending over to his left but then slowly and deliberately stood back up and turned his face back toward Harry. The skin between the right side of the shell's nose and cheek was split open with a nasty yellow fluid oozing out, but he showed no discomfort. In fact, a smile began to expand across his face, and he suddenly reached out and grabbed Harry by the throat and with one hand, easily hoisted him into the air. The soldier began to squeeze. Harry, hardly able to breathe, decided to return the favor with a good swift kick to the solar plexus.

The soldier dropped Harry while doubling over, and Harry grabbed the man's hair on the way down. The marine guided his opponent's face into his knee as they landed. The Cetatian's face cracked off the kneecap, he rolled onto the floor, and then his entire body began to turn to gel.

Ryan fired with his rifle, dropping a soldier when another creature came leaping for his throat. But before it got there, a shot was fired from elsewhere, and the beast turned to gel, splashing into him. Another shot fired; another soldier dropped. Oldman and Elrod had found them.

Haley gelled another soldier, "I need some mood music!" She sent a mental command to her phone, hijacking anything that would function as a speaker, and the lower strings of an electric guitar could be heard throughout the base. The rift played again, then the guitar was joined by other instruments and a powerful voice from the band Heart, singing Barracuda. They continued through the base, taking out more Cetatian soldiers and shell beasts.

Ducking through a door, they ran through the kitchen and were already out the other side before Elizabeth noticed that Haley had grabbed a sack of potatoes. Coming up to a locked door, their PJs had no problem tapping in and undoing the mechanism. They fired a few more blasts and ducked into the room, closing the door behind them.

"Portgates!" Elizabeth exclaimed. "Maybe we can find everybody else and get out of here."

Haley started scanning the gate with her phone in hopes of finding where it could connect when a loud and sudden bang was heard from the door.

Pivoting back toward the door, Elizabeth held a sparkling orb in each hand, and a light flashed in her eyes as she asked, "What now?"

Another sudden noise rang out from the door while Haley tried to sort out the gate. "It's active, but I can't tell where it goes." She started dumping the potatoes into her pack and as she put it on, there was one more loud bang, and the door was blasted out of its frame; Cetatian soldiers rushing in from the corridor.

Haley and Elizabeth dashed to opposite sides of the room, but the Cetatians were bottlenecked in the doorway, allowing the girls to gel them as they entered.

The portgate formed a vortex and began to open. Elizabeth shouted, "Not yet. We gotta get the others first."

"I didn't turn it on!" Haley replied while firing at the door.

"Uh-oh." Elizabeth turned around to see an Archon step through the gate. "No, you don't!" she shouted, charging and throwing blasts at the reptilian.

He blocked her shots with his own field as the young mystic approached and was surprised when she didn't stop her charge. Elizabeth leaped forward, funneling her energy into her fist and swung at the sadistic being. The Archon sidestepped, grabbed her wrist and twisted, flipping the young mystic to the floor.

Having just dropped another soldier, Haley spun around and let loose with a volley of blasts. Laughing, the Archon threw up his protective field, stopping her blasts, but was surprised when a mystical bolt hit him in the face. Elizabeth was still inside his field.

From the floor, Elizabeth threw a couple more blasts, forcing the Archon to focus on her more than his shielding. So, when a bobcat-shaped orb slammed against his weakening shield, it dropped, and he was assaulted by a volley of kittens.

The Archon stumbled backward a couple of steps, and Elizabeth jumped up, funneling energy into her fist. The mystic punched him in the solar plexus, releasing her energy with the impact, causing him to double over as he fell back. Nomad jumped onto his face and clawed at his eyes. He landed on his side in the fetal position, and as Nomad jumped away, both girls unleashed a charged blast, turning the reptilian to gel.

They heard footsteps, accompanied by snarling, in the corridor coming their way and a hoard of mindless beasts came charging into the room. Blasts were hurled toward the oncoming creatures while more soldiers came in behind them. "There's too many," Elizabeth said. "Open it!"

The portgate activated again and the girls kept blasting while falling back, stepping through the gate. As soon as they were through, Haley closed it and shut it down to prevent them from following.

"Phew, that was close," Haley said as they turned around to see a room full of people looking at them with expressions of confusion and shock. "Oh, spuds!" she muttered when they realized that they were at a Cetatian military facility in the Second Density.

Slack-jawed, both girls were staring back at the crowd of Cetatian military personnel, who were matching their shocked expressions when Elizabeth nudged her elbow against Haley's arm. "Hey," she said quietly.

"Yeah?" Haley asked, her voice just as soft, not averting her eyes from the personnel.

"Run," Elizabeth whispered.

"What?" Haley asked.

"Run!" she shouted, and they took off for the nearest door.

"Hey, stop!" one man bellowed, and everybody began running after them.

First Density. Undersea Base, The Atlantic

Harry fired the rifle, dropping another solder with the round. "It's out." He pulled the sidearm and a bolt pistol to continue firing. They all now had bolt pistols, which they had been taking from the defeated Cetaitian soldiers but were becoming overrun by sheer numbers. After squeezing off a few more rounds, Harry's firearm was empty. That was the last of their ammo.

Williams had some white around the edge of his vision. It hurt to breathe, and he had to lean against the wall to stay upright with his injury. He grunted and continued to fire with the bolt pistol, but despite his training and willpower, he was only Human, and his strength was quickly waning. More Cetatians appeared at the other end of the corridor as Williams collapsed.

"Cease fire!" came the command from behind the lines. The blasting stopped and the one who gave the order stepped to the front of the line. "I see you have wounded," he stated. "Lay down your arms and surrender, or you will be killed."

Harry tried to think of another option, but he had nothing. Running the scenarios through his mind, there wasn't one that wouldn't end in their own slaughter. The SEALs were making the same calculations when there was a commotion from behind the enemy soldiers.

Guns fired from the other end of the corridor, and when the closer Cetatians turned to see what was happening, Harry, Ryan, and the SEALs opened fire, taking many of them down. It all happened fast, and only a moment later, they could see who had thinned out their enemies from behind. The rest of the SEAL team had arrived.

Second Density. Location: Unknown

Her com-system scanned the control pad, and the door slid to the side, allowing Elizabeth through and shutting right before Soldiers came around the corner. She was now standing at the end of a large hallway, which intersected with another eighty feet ahead. The wide intersection is where a large square-shaped counter was located and desks were set up on the inside. There were three women working at these desks, and they were all wearing scrubs.

Ducking behind a cart in the hallway, Elizabeth realized that she had entered a medical facility. *Great,* she thought. *Now what do I do?* She looked around and saw no patient rooms in this section of the hallway and hoped that that meant they would be less likely to come her way. There was what looked like a maintenance closet and a large metal door across the hall with a control pad.

Elizabeth tried to listen to what the nurses were saying, but they were too far away for her to make out the words. Her collar rippled and extended up in the shape of an earbud while she used the com-system's scanners to hear what they were saying. As it happened, they were discussing their lunch break, making Elizabeth's stomach rumble.

A couple moments later, two of the women left, heading to the cafeteria while the other stayed behind. Elizabeth spent the next five minutes trying to figure out a course of action, but the remaining nurse stood up from her desk and came out from behind the counter, entering the bathroom door next to her station.

This is my chance, Elizabeth thought and started walking softly down the hallway. She tuned her senses to the energy around her as she walked, but before she could take five steps, she felt a presence behind her. With a sudden burst of speed, Elizabeth pivoted one hundred and eighty degrees, swinging with her right, but the person behind the young mystic caught her by the wrist with a firm grip.

Sabrina glanced down at Elizabeth's knuckles, seeing those same scars as before and then back up to the girl's eyes. "At least now you make a proper fist," she said, smacking the palm of her hand over the mystic's knuckles and then releasing her grip. Stunned with both fear and confusion, Elizabeth just stood there, slack-jawed. "And you actually have good form now, too," Sabrina added. "Though there are forms better suited to how you move."

Elizabeth stared for two more seconds and then asked, "So…you're not gonna beat the snot out of me?"

Footsteps and voices began to echo from the other end of the hallway, and Sabrina glanced around, then turned to the large door with the control pad. She punched in a code, and the lock disengaged.

"Hurry," Sabrina said as she opened the door, and they both ducked into the room. Sabrina shut and secured the door as Elizabeth's attention fell upon the shelves in the room. They were fully stocked with cases of syringes.

Elizabeth turned and looked to Sabrina, the confusion still written on her face. "Are you…helping me?"

Sabrina shrugged, not exactly sure what she was doing. "I…I'm getting you and Starr out of here."

It was Elizabeth's turn to shrug. "I don't know where she is. We got separated." She then glanced at the shelves and asked, "What're all these for?"

"It's a serum that everyone who goes to the First Density takes. If our DNA is tested, it will read as Human," Sabrina said.

"How does that work?" Elizabeth asked.

Not knowing, Sabrina just shrugged.

From her PJs, Elizabeth conjured her phone. She flipped it open and began scanning the syringes. A couple of seconds later, the information appeared on the screen. "What's saline solution?"

"¿Que?"

Holding up the phone for Sabrina to see the screen, she said, "Saline solution. What does that do?"

"Nothing," Sabrina answered with a confused expression on her usually stoic face. "It's a placebo." There was a vibration in Sabrina's pocket, and she pulled out her phone. Looking at the screen, she said, "It's Sahmbo." She held a finger in front of her mouth and made a shushing sound, then answered the phone. "Yes?"

"Starr has been captured," Derek said. Elizabeth covered her mouth as she gasped. Sabrina turned toward the young mystic, saw the ear bud and shot her an incredulous look. "And unfortunately, Kone has handed her over to the Archons. Have you seen the other girl?" he asked.

Looking directly into Elizabeth's eyes, Sabrina answered, "No."

Derek noticed a faint stress in Sabrina's voice that normally was not present. "I'm sorry," he said.

"For what?" Sabrina asked.

"For putting you in a tight spot," Derek replied. "I know what you're likely to do after I tell you this."

Sabrina remained silent as she waited for Sahmbo to elaborate.

"They took her to the interrogation room on level six. Just do me one favor," he said.

"I'm listening."

"Try to keep your new friend out of sight." With that, Sahmbo ended the call.

Elizabeth looked at Sabrina with shock while the Hunter, just as stunned, mouthed the words, "How does he do that?"

"Where's level six?" Elizabeth asked.

"One floor down," Sabrina answered.

"What do we do?"

"Not we," Sabrina said sternly. "Me. You need to hide until I get her. Then all three of us will port out of here."

Glancing around the room, Elizabeth asked, "Where do you want me to hide?"

"Meow," they both heard from above.

"Nomad!" Elizabeth said while looking along the upper walls. Her eyes settled on a vent cover, and she ran over to the wall.

"Meow," Nomad said again as Elizabeth reached up.

"It's too high," the young mystic said.

"We can't worry about a cat right now. We need to hide you so I can go get Starr."

"I'll hide in the vent," Elizabeth replied. "It worked last year."

Without any better ideas and no time to waste, Sabrina let Elizabeth stand on her shoulders to reach the vent cover. "It's stuck," Elizabeth said, and Sabrina handed her a knife. Elizabeth used the blade to pry open the cover and then crawled into the vent with Nomad.

Elizabeth reached out to hand back Sabrina's knife, but the Hunter said, "Hold onto that until I come back."

After pulling the cover shut, Elizabeth watched Sabrina leave the room and heard the locking mechanism engage. The young mystic sighed and turned toward Nomad. "What do you think…can I really trust her?"

"Meow," Nomad said, then turned around and started walking away.

"Where are you going?" Elizabeth asked as the cat disappeared into the dark. Her collar rippled, and the nanobots began to run up her neck. They streamed around her ears and to the front of her face, forming into what looked like a pair of safety glasses but with night vision, and she could now see Nomad standing a little farther down, waiting.

She started to crawl in his direction but needed to go slow to keep the noise to a minimum. When she got close, Nomad moved further down the vent, stopping at an intersection, and waited. After Elizabeth caught up, Nomad turned and walked through the vent to the right. She continued following until he led her to a vertical shaft.

After a noisier-than-intended descent, Elizabeth followed Nomad through the vents for another couple of minutes until he stopped at a vent cover. She caught up, looked out through the slotted cap and gasped. Grabbing and holding the cross hanging on her necklace, Elizabeth prayed, "Father, please help."

She let go of the cross, pulled the knife and kicked the vent cover open, dropping into the room.

CHAPTER 9
Shinobi

As Haley was coming to, she opened her eyes to see the world as a blur and had the sensation of falling. The farmer thudded to a stop on her back as she gained her bearings and realized that she had just been dropped onto a metal table. Haley felt the straps tightening around her wrists and ankles as one of the Archons made an unnerving giggle. Her head was suddenly slammed back to the table's surface when Haley tried to look at her surroundings. Then another Archon was securing a head strap in place, preventing the farmgirl from turning her neck.

While Haley didn't get a good look at the room, she did confirm that all six Archons were there, in person. Another strap was tightened around her waist, allowing her no wiggle room. She couldn't move, and her stomach was sinking, yet the archons seemed to feel giddy, almost euphoric, with the events about to unfold.

They tilted the table upright, and Haley could now clearly see the large room and all six Archons standing before her. Almost the size of a high school gymnasium, the walls were bare concrete, and she was positioned at one end of the room, facing the door at the other, which had a large landing step between the threshold and the floor.

Cells lined the wall to her left, two of which housed mangled bodies, prisoners who had succumbed to their wounds. It was obvious that they had been propped against the bars to be seen by the next victim to help boost the anxiety and terror. Around the room, there were a few stainless-steel cabinets on casters, and Haley shuddered to think what instruments of pain might be contained within. The farmer's breathing started to increase as one of them rolled a cart full of sharp, metal tools in front of her, gleefully displaying what they intended to use.

Haley started to feel lightheaded as the terror built. Cold ran down her spine, and she began to hyperventilate. One of the reptilians did a strange-looking happy dance as he radiated joy. Her sense of horror was fueling them as they tauntingly held a serrated blade up in front of her face, letting her get a good view of the wicked-looking edge.

Shuddering as her terror increased further, she became dizzy, and the edges of her vision started to fade. Then, there was a jab in her arm, bringing her senses back into a clear focus. The Archon that was holding the needle stepped in front of Haley with a sadistic grin, which displayed the many sharp teeth behind those thin and scaly lips. His skin was like that of a python's, and his breath was as foul as a dog's halitosis. The yellow, silted pupils of his eyes widened as his gaze bored into Haley's eyes.

"No falling asleep," Nokitahm said with eager enthusiasm, "You must fully experience our craft."

Haley couldn't believe the total bliss they seemed to be experiencing from her terror. One of them leaned toward her with the serrated blade. He slowly moved the tip close to one of Haley's blue eyes, and she began to whimper in horror. The tip came right up near her lens as she started to scream but then was pulled back.

"Not yet," the Archon said teasingly, "We're going to use that first," he finished, pointing to Nokitahm holding what looked like a short whip with nine tails. "We're going to start small and work our way up," he said with a sick grin as Haley, once again, began to hyperventilate.

The two Proctors, a sergeant and an officer, were standing guard outside the door when they heard Haley scream. They were assigned to this post by Hunter-Ralt Sahmbo, and their orders were to prevent any interruptions, regardless of what they may hear. They glanced at each other, and the sergeant nodded as the officer dropped a hand to his holster. "Proctors," they heard a woman's voice say.

Nearing the two guards, Sabrina heard their emotions and knew what they were most likely about to do. The average Proctor would be outmatched by one of these Archons, and there were six inside that room. If they chose this course of action, the Proctors would probably find themselves strapped to tables right alongside Haley within a minute's time. Even if they managed to survive, they would be traitors to their post and marked for deletion.

"Leave!" Sabrina said flatly. The officer looked to the sergeant, who nodded, and they complied. As soon as they left, Sabrina tapped the keypad on the wall, and the door slid to the side.

Nokitahm was holding his arm high in the air, about to bring down the first lash, when Sabrina stepped into the room. Everybody looked to the woman standing there on the landing as the door slid shut behind her. The Hunter didn't need to see her fellow empath's face. She could feel Haley's fear, and, considering their last meeting, the farmer was not comforted one bit by Sabrina's sudden appearance. None of the Archons had seen this woman in over a year. "What are you doing here," one of them asked with obvious irritation.

Looking at Haley strapped to a table, much like the one back when she was abused, Sabrina's blood boiled, and her eyes began to water as she looked back to the Archons, reaching for the coil on her right hip. "You like to feed on negative emotions?" Sabrina unrolled and electrified the whip as she narrowed her eyes. Her next words were dripping with venom, "Toma un poco de la mia."

As soon as they were away from Sabrina, the sergeant keyed his comm. "Officers Jenkins, Shamus and Fontane. This is Sergeant Redding. I've authorized your comms for channel two. Switch over and respond."

A few seconds later, all three officers acknowledged his call. "Get your plasma rifles," he ordered, "and meet me on level six ASAP!"

A sadistic grin spread across Nokitahm's face when all of them, as a Hive, thought, *Another toy!* An Archon launched an orb at the Hunter, but the whip rolled and cracked forward, snapping the missile from the air. More mystical bolts followed, all snapped aside by the electric whip. The six reptilians unleashed a barrage of bolts and shards, too many for Sabrina to snap away, so she dodged to the side while drawing her pistol with her left hand.

When Sabrina opened fire, the Archons threw their hands forward, erecting energetic barriers to shield them from her attack, which gave Sabrina the opportunity she wanted. She let go of the whip, which depowered and coiled upon itself, magnetically attaching to her right hip. She pulled out the wallet and tossed it toward the middle of the room as she dove behind one of the stainless-steel containers. The device activated and five anchor disks shot outward. Four lodged themselves on the walls, and the fifth on the ceiling.

Engaging the grapple harness as the Archons charged toward her, the Hunter levitated out from behind the cabinet into the air as the Archons dropped their fields to unleash another attack, but Sabrina was ready and began firing her bolt pistol. The Archons scrambled, and Sabrina zipped across the top of the room, firing along the way and dropped down between them and Haley while grabbing her whip.

Bolts and shards flew toward them, but Sabrina began snapping them away while returning fire with her pistol. They were raising and dropping their fields, returning fire and raising them again as Sabrina picked her shots, not wanting them to have another chance for a unified attack. The Hunter knew she couldn't hold this spot for long, so she tossed her pistol into the air.

With a quick and fluid motion, she drew a blade with her left hand, threw it behind her toward Haley and caught her pistol to resume fire as Haley's eyes popped wide, startled by the mayum blade punching through the leather strap around her right wrist and into the metal table. Her hand was free! Haley wasted no time in undoing the other straps, and as soon as she hopped off the table, her PJs came back online, jamming the cameras as she felt the connection to her energy field again.

The Archons were closing on Sabrina, who tossed her pistol again, grabbing a handful of pellets from one of her pouches and throwing them to the floor. Catching her gun as smoke filled the room, she rushed forward, coiled her whip, slid between an Archon's legs, and popped right back up behind their line.

As the Archon nearest to her turned around, Sabrina launched upward with her grapple harness, kicking one in the face. She dropped back down and dodged to the left, avoiding a mystical bolt and punched another one in the solar plexus.

With visibility obscured, Sabrina shot straight up toward the ceiling, taking the Archons' full attention with her as Haley, who now had her potato gun mounted to her gauntlet, took aim. A squeal of feedback was heard from all speakers as she fired a charged blast. The Archons were close enough together that when an ethereal bobcat hit the floor at their feet, it released a concussive burst on impact, which pushed away some of the smoke with the pressure waves and the reptilians were knocked over like bowling pins as the 1998 version of Blue Monday began to play.

Then they saw the farmgirl, a blue glow in her angry eyes, stepping forward from the haze. They made haste to erect their protective fields and sprung back to their feet as Sabrina was firing shots on her way back down to the floor. Haley also began firing; two of the Archons focused on her while Sabrina engaged with the other four.

Dodging and countering, Sabrina never held still. The Archons being much stronger and very durable, the Hunter knew she could not outlast them, and most of her strikes would be little more than a feint discomfort. She stuck to one fighting style and landed some punches when she could. Punches that she pulled. Having to roll with a couple herself, she continued until the Archons began to anticipate her movements.

She tumbled into a summersault between the two of them and sprung back up with a pivot as an Archon turned toward her, his left hand glowing with red energy. Sabrina drew her sword with a slash, and the glow faded when the severed hand dropped to the floor. With an abrupt change to another fighting form, Sabrina landed a powerful kick to the stomach of the Archon on her left. The unanticipated move knocked him off balance, and he fell onto his back.

One of the two reptilians to Sabrina's right hurled mystical shards at the Hunter, forcing her to dash backward, while the Archon, who had just lost his hand, was gripping his forearm in shock. With her left, Sabrina drew and fired her pistol at the one getting up from the floor, knocking him back down while sheathing her blade and shifting her aim to the two charging at her.

Nokitahm and his fellow Archon both ran at Haley, who pulled the tray of sharp blades in front of her and kicked it forward. An ethereal kitten rushed in behind the rolling tray and burst on impact, scattering the blades like shrapnel. The Archons put up their fields as Haley turned and ran to the back wall, jumped up and clung onto it.

She was making her way toward the ceiling when Nokitahm said, "No pouncing. Shrarkraku-Flumkor!"

He reached out as he spoke, closed his fingers and twisted his wrist as he pulled his arm back in, and Haley felt energy envelop her before being yanked off the wall, bits of concrete still stuck in her claws. She was spun around as she flew to Nokitahm, and he caught her by the throat in his right hand, looking into her eyes with a smirk.

"No pouncing." He started to squeeze, so he was surprised when Haley smirked back.

The words were strained and raspy but easily understood when she said, "Thanks for making it easy for me." And then she pounced. Nokitahm lost his grip as he was pushed back by some sort of field when she shot down. Her feet hit the floor, and she rebounded back up with the energy burst that knocked them both over. She charged a shot on her way up, intending to unleash it on one of the two below her, but saw two Archons rushing at Sabrina and, instead, fired at a new target as she began to drop. She released the blast and pounced again, slamming her feet to the floor and releasing a blue energy wave that knocked the two Archons over as they were attempting to stand back up.

Sabrina was about to fire at her two assailants, but one was knocked to the floor in a daze by a bobcat from Haley to the face, while the other stumbled from the concussive burst. The Hunter pulled her whip while she fired her pistol at the second Archon, trying again to get back up.

Recovering from his stumble, the fourth Archon resumed his charge. Sabrina's lips snarled with disgust at the sadistic being hurtling toward her, and she moved her arm with a twist of her wrist. The electrified whip rolled forward and snapped against the Archon's arms, splitting his skin through the sleeves, accompanied by a searing jolt. A blood-curdling shriek echoed from the reptilian as Sabrina lashed again and again while the Archon was disoriented.

After the initial shock, the Archon who lost his hand became angry and charged at Sabrina while she was lashing the other with the whip. Sabrina could hear the rage from behind her and let go of the coiling whip as she pivoted toward her attacker. The other was swaying in a stupor from the lashes and shocks.

The Hunter switched to another fighting style as she dodged and countered, no longer pulling her punches but now aiming for pressure points and landing a few solid hits on the nerves, coaxing a few winces from him, then she shot upward while the Archon was having trouble controlling his twinging and partially numbed arms and right leg.

On her ascent, Sabrina grabbed her whip and passed it to her left hand, then drew the katana with her right. She dropped her feet down onto the left shoulder of the Archon, plunging her blade into his left peck while snapping the whip out to her side, ensnaring the neck of the one she had lashed and turned on the current.

A gurgling groan escaped from the Archon beneath her as the other convulsed, and she rode the shoulder down to the floor. Both reptilians hit the ground at the same time, and Sabrina launched back into the air before the other two could reach her.

Realizing that they had underestimated the Hunter, the remaining four Archons banded back together, three of them erecting fields, protecting the fourth while he chanted. Even though this was a battle of attrition that favored the Archons, they now understood that continuing this fight as they had would come with an increasing price that they were not willing to pay. So, they decided to tilt the scales further in their favor with a summoning spell.

Haley and Sabrina began firing in an attempt to wear down their shielding, but with just a couple of spoken words, a vortex appeared before them. It opened to the same location in another density, where a being stood who was happy to heed the call.

Standing at eight and a half feet tall, the demon had the appearance of a lanky gargoyle with brown leathery skin covering a muscular frame and a pair of wings to match. His bare feet had talons, his fingernails looked like claws, and a pair of horns protruded out from the thick dark hair on his head. The only article of clothing he wore was a tattered loincloth. The demon looked upon Haley and Sabrina with a yellowish-orange glow in his eyes, flashed a wicked grin that revealed large, sharp canines and raised his arms above his head as they erupted with flames.

As the two ladies were about to open fire, the vent near the ceiling kicked open, and Elizabeth slid out, feet first and raising her arms. She had the knife grasped in both hands above her head as she dropped. The blade began to glow with white light, and the demon howled in pain when she plunged it into the crook of his neck as she dropped.

The young mystic siphoned some flames from the demon and expanded them around her arms as she touched down to the floor, launching fiery attacks at the Archons.

The demon, confused as to how such a simple blade so easily pierced his durable skin, pulled it from his neck right before a concussive burst from a bobcat knocked him back a couple of steps. Haley then turned her aim toward the Archons, who were closing on Elizabeth and launched a volley of kittens.

Sabrina launched into the air, firing at the demon as she went. The demon shrugged off the pistol bolts, turning instead toward the girl who had hurt him, but as he began moving toward Elizabeth, he felt the sting of an electric whip cracking against the tip of one of his wings and turned his attention up toward the ceiling as Sabrina felt his anger rise. The demon spread his wings, and they began to glow with the first flap, lifting him up toward the Hunter. With a swing of his arm, a wave of hellfire shot toward Sabrina. She dashed to the side while firing back.

Another flame forced Sabrina to dash the other way as the demon came closer, backing her toward the corner. She fired again, but this time at his wings. A bolt hit, and the demon's flight faltered a bit, giving Sabrina an opening to escape from the corner. The Hunter zipped by the demon as he tried to right himself and slashed with her katana as she went, but it did no damage to the resilient skin of his forearm.

Raising her pistol, Sabrina again fired for the wings. But the demon shot forward, bursting into flames while spinning like a corkscrew. She dropped down as he came in fast, hitting the wall in her absence. She looked up to see him, the talons of his feet and the claws of one hand clinging to a damaged wall and holding one arm out toward her, flames manifesting in his palm.

They kept their eyes locked as Sabrina touched down to the floor behind an Archon who was throwing shards at Elizabeth. She launched back upward as the stream of hellfire blasted the reptilian, grabbed the whip in her right hand and fired for the wings with her left. The demon launched into his corkscrew attack as the whip rolled forward. With a loud snap, the end of the whip hit his right eye, and he dropped to the floor with a shriek.

An other-worldly growl reverberated from the demon's throat. He snapped his arm to the side, and the three ladies were all thrown into the air, slammed, and held against the wall. "Play time's over," the demon sneered, and he began closing his fingers. All three could feel the telekinetic force slowly crushing in on them as the demon closed his hand. Haley and Elizabeth tried to counter by pushing out their own protective fields, but the demon's grip was too strong.

The Archons gathered around him, thoroughly enjoying the demonic display. So much so that they didn't notice the door slide open. All four of them took a plasma bolt to the back of the head and dropped to the ground, unconscious. Sergeant Redding cranked his plasma rifle up to full power, and the other four Proctors did the same. The demon looked toward the door as the sergeant pulled the trigger.

When the first bolt hit him in the face, Haley, Elizabeth and Sabrina all slid to the floor. The five proctors blasted away, and the three ladies followed suit. Half blind and with a barrage of mystical and plasmatic bolts, the demon was so overwhelmed that he couldn't even tell which way to retaliate. The assault being too much, the demon began to fade from view and disappear, banished back to his realm.

Sabrina turned toward the Proctors and saw the sergeant standing tall and looking quite pleased with himself.

"We await the Hunter's orders," he announced with a smile.

"Detain them," Sabrina replied.

"Yes, ma'am!" he said as they all reached for their restraining disks. The sergeant slapped a disk on the back of an Archon, and four metallic tendrils extended out, wrapping around the limbs and cinching tight. It emitted a magnetic field, causing it to levitate, and the reptilian hung in the air, feet dangling just off the floor. The field also disrupted the Archon's conscious connection to his energy, preventing him from using his magick.

"This one's dead," Shamus called out. Sabrina looked over to see the Archon, who had perished at the end of her blade.

The other five were lined up along the wall. Sabrina walked up to one of them and sneered. "They are the last of their kind. They should consider themselves lucky that genocide is forbidden to Hunters because today…" She drew her katana and held it up, using the flat of her blade to lift the Archon's chin and get a good look at his face. "I would not be so noble on my own." She withdrew her sword, and the Archon's chin dropped back down to his chest. Turning toward the sergeant, she said, "Thank you, Sergeant. But…" She motioned toward the cameras. "…do you realize the position this puts you in with the State?"

"I don't care," the sergeant replied. "I heard one of them scream," he said while pointing toward the girls. "I have a daughter about their age, and I couldn't live with myself if I let this continue." He looked toward the girls and then back to Sabrina, "We need to get them out of here."

"The cameras aren't working," Haley informed them. "They didn't see anything you did in here."

"You jammed them?" Sabrina asked.

"Yep."

"I have a port-out," Sabrina said as she walked to the table where Haley was restrained. "But first, we need to put on a show for the cameras in the hallway," she added while pulling her mayum blade from the table.

First Density. Montana. December 31, 1999

When the vortex shut, Haley found herself standing on a metal disk in the corner of a room. As they let go of each other's hands, Nomad hopped down to the floor from Haley's shoulders. Various weapons lined the walls, and the rest of the room was empty, save for the mat on the floor.

To her left, Elizabeth was taking in the sight of crossbows, swords, staffs, various firearms, and some items with which she was unfamiliar. "Do you know how to use all of these?" she asked while stepping off from the pad.

"Yes," Sabrina answered.

Moving toward the center of the room, Haley slowly turned around, wondering how much practice it took Sabrina to learn all of this. The farmer then thought about how Elizabeth practiced honing her skills, which made Haley start to feel some guilt. People work hard to acquire their skills, yet Haley would absorb hers. The empath felt the experience of a cat and energetically replicated it as a new power, or more accurately, a new way to use her power. She felt like she was cheating.

Sabrina noticed the odd feeling from Haley but did not address it. "Welcome to what I guess is now my home."

"It feels peaceful here," Haley commented and then realized how strange it was that she said that in a room full of weapons.

As Elizabeth walked along one of the walls, she was about to ask about why Sabrina was helping them when her eyes fell upon a pair of sai. Fixating on them in an instant, they were simple yet beautiful, and Sabrina could hear the young mystic being drawn in by their song.

Sensing Elizabeth's state, Haley walked over to see what had her friend so fascinated. Haley came to Elizabeth's right side as Sabrina approached her left.

The mystic looked up to the Hunter and asked, "So, you really are a ninja?"

"In the colloquial sense," Sabrina replied, "I suppose so."

"Well, what do you think of as a real ninja?" Haley asked.

"They worked in the service of a shogunate. Scouting, espionage, blending in and mingling with people to collect information that their shogun could use." Sabrina explained.

"Wow!" Haley exclaimed. "They were secret agents!"

A hint of a smile appeared on Sabrina's face and disappeared just as quickly when she answered, "Yes."

In her mind, Haley began to hear the James Bond theme song, except it was how she thought it would sound if it were played on traditional Japanese instruments, not realizing that the sounds conjured in her head were that of a Chinese pipa. The mental tune continued to play as her imagination unfolded, and she visualized a Japanese man. Tall, handsome and, for whatever reason, wearing a tuxedo. He suddenly spun around in a cartoonish whirlwind like the Tasmanian Devil and when he stopped, was wearing appropriate period clothing. He left the building and mingled amongst the people of a rival shogunate, hiding in plain sight.

Making his way through the area, the man ducked between a couple of buildings and, in another whirlwind, changed his clothes to that of a stereotypical ninja outfit. It was all black, had a hood that covered his face and a katana strapped to his back. The secret ninja agent scaled up the building, hopped across a couple of rooftops and climbed into a window without making a sound.

With impossible stealth, he made his way to a secure door, picked the lock and entered the room. Many scrolls were on the shelves in this room, but he was here for one. The ninja quickly identified the proper scroll, pulled it from the shelf and began to make his exit. He climbed outside the window and utilized an obscene amount of unnecessary acrobatics as he flipped, twisted and tumbled silently across the rooftops.

After getting to the woods, the ninja made haste for his shogunate, where he was met by the Shogun himself. The ninja presented his master with the scroll, and the Shogun immediately opened it. Eyes widening with the information, the Shogun now knew exactly what to do. One of his men handed him a blank scroll with an inked quill, and the Shogun penned, "D7." He handed it to a man on horseback, who took off like a shot, accompanied by the sound of a revving engine and squealing tires. He disappeared over the horizon with unrealistic speed and, a few seconds later, reappeared, riding back to his Shogun with another scroll. The Shogun took the scroll and opened it, a victorious smile on his face as he read the words, "You sank my battleship!"

Elizabeth noticed the far-away stare and slight, but goofy grin on her friend's face and knew that she was knee-deep in another one of her daydreams. "Haley!"

The farmgirl snapped back to the real world with a slight startle, looked to Elizabeth and got a big smile on her face as she clenched her right fist and exclaimed, "Ninjas are awesome!" She looked at Sabrina, "What's your finishing move?"

"Finishing move? What's that?"

"You know, the move that you always use to finish off the bad guy! Your signature move!"

"I…why would I use the same move?" Sabrina asked, finding the idea foolish. "That would make it too easy for my opponent to anticipate."

"But Ryu has the Dragon Punch. Stone Cold Steve Austin has the Stunner. What do you have?"

"I have whatever ends the conflict quickest," Sabrina answered. "I see no reason to have a signature move."

"But it would make you look even cooler!" Haley exclaimed.

Sabrina shook her head. "This isn't a tournament. If I stopped to do things like that, it could get me killed."

"Well, I don't want that to happen. But you gotta have a little fun now and then."

"When the time is appropriate. But right now, we need to rest while we can. And I need to figure out how to get you two back to your parents."

CHAPTER 10
This Ain't the North Pole

Second Density. Location Unknown

The phone rang, and Sahmbo pulled it from his harness. "Yes," he answered to hear Kone's voice, sounding rather unhappy for someone who had just conquered the world.

"Go to your nearest com-terminal. There is some surveillance footage you must see," the Uniralt instructed.

There was a terminal at the end of the hallway in which Sahmbo walked. He immediately went to it and punched in his personal code. Upon hitting enter, the clip instantly popped up and began to play. It was Sabrina ordering away the Proctors from their guard duty and then a clip from inside the interrogation room.

As soon as Haley was freed from the table, the cameras went fuzzy and then were set to a repeating loop that made the room appear empty. The video then switched back to the hallway, showing Sabrina along with Haley, Elizabeth and a cat running from the room.

The Proctors from earlier had returned, fired a few shots at the retreating ladies, and the sergeant managed to nick Sabrina's shoulder. The next clip was around the corner, where they had a moment away from the line of fire to use a port-out.

The Proctors came around the corner as the vortex closed, and the sergeant called in, "We've got a rouge Hunter!"

The monitor then changed to a live display of Kone's unhappy face. Derek perfectly feigned an expression of surprise as Kone said, "You know what this means."

With a nervous nod, Derek said, "Please, give the Hunters an opportunity to fix this."

"And how do you plan to 'fix it?'" Kone asked, using his fingers to gesture quotation marks.

Sahmbo sighed. "I don't know yet."

"You have accomplished much for the Cetatian State over the years, and I know what Hunter Carmen means to you. That is why I contacted you right away. I have not yet put out the deletion order. I will give you twenty-four hours to bring her in and convince me to give her another chance. A chance that I've afforded very few throughout the centuries. But if she's not standing in front of me by this time tomorrow, Hunter Sabrina Carmen *will* be deleted." Kone cut the transmission, and Derek's monitor returned to the main screen.

Second Density. The Ozarks. January 1, 2000

The New Year celebrations may have come to a screeching halt for many in the First Density, but for most of the Second Density's population, things continued as normal. In a secluded homestead, two glasses clinked together as Manny and Darcy exclaimed, "Happy New Year!" They both tilted their glasses up to drain the champagne when Darcy's phone began vibrating. The buzzing followed a unique pattern for a notification, increasing in intensity and then back down, producing a sound like a soft buzzer trying to imitate a siren. Darcy almost choked when she heard the buzzing, and her eyes popped wide with fear.

"What?" Manny asked in confusion. Darcy's shaking hand almost spilled what was left in the glass when she set it on the coffee table. Although advancing in age, the retired Hunter had kept herself fit, and Darcy, channeling that fear into action, stood up and leaped over the back of the couch. Her feet hit the floor, and she ran into the kitchen, where the phone vibrated so furiously that she thought it might fall off the counter. Picking it up, she saw a message on the screen that she hoped would never come.

"Harsh winters!"

Darcy turned around to see Manny approaching, still confused. "We have to go! Now!"

There were one hundred and twelve Hunters across the globe, and they all received the same message, prompting them to gather their families with haste. For most of the Second Density's population, things continued as normal. But for the Hunters, everything was about to change.

First Density. Montana

It was two thirty in the morning. Sabrina, making no noise so as not to wake the girls, gathered up some equipment and headed out into the freezing cold woods. Four hours later, Haley and Elizabeth woke up to the smell of deer steaks and eggs.

"Oh, man. That smells so good!" Elizabeth said to a sleep-addled Haley, who did not wake up as quickly as the enthusiastic mystic. The farmer slowly nodded her agreement. They were both starving after the crazy events of the night before.

Haley stumbled to her feet as Elizabeth jumped up, but they both thought mostly about their parents, wondering if they were okay. They walked into the kitchen to see Sabrina cooking at the stove. The Hunter looked over her shoulder at the two girls.

"Good morning," she said, sounding awkward as she was not used to greeting guests. She then got a look on her face as if she suddenly realized something and walked to the front door. Haley could sense what the Hunter sensed and smiled a bit when Sabrina opened the door, letting Nomad back into the cabin. "He really had to pee. It made me uncomfortable."

"The joys of being an empath," Haley said while rubbing her eyes.

They sat around the small table in the kitchen to eat breakfast, and Sabrina set a plate on the floor for Nomad. As they were finishing, both Haley and Sabrina perked up, sensing someone's approach.

Noticing the empaths' shift in facial expressions, Elizabeth tuned her energetic senses outward and was also able to sense someone's presence. The girls looked at Sabrina, wondering if she knew who this was. Then they noticed Sabrina's head turn, looking past the two girls. Haley and Elizabeth looked over their shoulders to see a man standing behind them. They recognized him as the Hunter who had defeated the Marshals last year.

"Uh…hi?" Haley said in a sheepish manner.

"It's okay," Sabrina said. "This is who told me where you were last night." She noted an intense anxiety in his stomach that was unusual for the Hunter-Ralt.

"And Kone is quite upset about that," Derek informed them. "I need to move all three of you to somewhere safer."

"Meow," Nomad said.

"Four," Sabrina corrected.

"Four," Sahmbo said and held up a port-out. "I have some friends that have offered shelter. They are expecting you." He placed the port-out on the table and said, "They're in the Fourth Density."

With a stunned expression, Sabrina looked at Derek. "Are they who I think they are?"

After an uncomfortable silence, Derek nodded. "Yes."

"And you never told me?" she asked, looking truly hurt.

He nodded again.

"Why don't you trust me?!" Sabrina practically shouted as she shot to her feet.

"I do. More than anyone. I kept you out of it so if I made a mistake, you wouldn't suffer the consequences."

The two Hunters stared at each other for a moment. Haley could sense the strange combination of appreciation and anger from Sabrina while Sahmbo was experiencing a combination of remorse with the satisfaction of keeping a loved one safe.

"Now, all the Hunters know. We've evacuated from the Second Density because Kone was planning to eliminate us all. He didn't think that I knew. We can discuss the merits of my decision later. Right now, we need to get you all to safety."

He walked around the table and up to Sabrina, looking into her brown eyes while placing his left palm gently on her right cheek. "I'm not perfect, but I'll always do what I think is right when protecting the people that I love." He turned toward the girls. "I'll find out how your parents are and let you know, though it could be a bit."

Turning back to Sabrina, he continued, "The rift had been growing for some time, and now the Hunters are considered enemies of the Cetatia. Gather your things and be ready to go in ten minutes."

Sabrina leaned in and gave him a quick peck on the lips, pulled back and said, "I'm still mad at you, though."

A few moments later, they all gathered in a circle, joined their hands in the center, and Nomad hopped up on Haley's shoulder. "I hope to see you in a few days," Sahmbo said. Sabrina nodded, and the girls said, "Bye." Sabrina activated the port-out, and the vortex opened, engulfing them.

It closed, and they were standing under the arch of a portgate in a new location. Haley and Elizabeth saw three people standing before them. Two were about four feet tall, built like fireplugs and sported full, long beards. The other one was five foot seven, slender build, with eyes slightly larger than usual, and long, pointed ears.

He spoke with a melodic voice in a Gaelic-sounding accent when he said, "Welcome to Tír na nOg."

Second Density. West Antarctica

A storm blew across the frozen tundra, and visibility was nearly nonexistent. Atop the ice was a large dome-shaped tent, anchored with metal stakes, which sheltered four smaller tents inside. The team taking shelter from the storm had trekked across the polar ice cap making impressive progress, until the storm had brought them to a halt. But the team was prepared and had plenty of supplies; they would not be deterred.

Fourth Density. Og Palace, Tir na nOg

Several Alfan and a few Dvwargarians occupied the long and spacious hall. Part of a larger cliffside complex, the walls of this area were carved from the stone and lengths of wooden roots ran through them like veins, which were adorned with healthy green leaves. In the center of most leaf bunches was a blossom. Tiny vines held a translucent globe with a flower inside, which glowed with soft yellow light. The combined glow of all the blossoms provided plenty of light for people to see.

Along the eastern wall was a series of portgates. Many of them were constructed, appearing to be made of stone and standing ten feet tall and twenty feet wide with a large archway through the center of the three-foot-thick structure. They were beautifully crafted and decorated with woodland-themed carvings.

However, not all the portgates were man-made. Many of them were large geodes between eight and ten feet tall. The spherical egg-shaped stones were sliced in half, revealing the purple crystals that covered the inside surface. When the crystals receive a surge of energy, a vortex forms and opens, allowing one to step through and out from the geode's other half.

Nomad hopped off Haley's shoulder as she, Elizabeth and Sabrina took in the sights around them. The most interesting of which were the three men standing in front of them.

"Are you guys bikers?" Haley asked the two Dwarves, who looked at each other and started laughing hysterically as the Elf joined in.

"I guess not," Elizabeth said dryly while Haley, feeling the mirth from the three men, tried very hard not to start laughing herself.

Sabrina, also experiencing their humor, had a much better time maintaining a straight face.

"Nah," the Dwarf to their right said as he caught his breath. "I'm a Dvwargarian. Or a Dwarf, if you'd like." He spoke with the same accent as the Elf, whom he pointed past to the other Dwarf and added, "But he's a biker."

"And also, a Dwarf," the other quickly responded with a rough voice and a different accent.

The man in the middle said, "And I'm an Alfan. More commonly known as an Elf."

The eyes of Haley and Elizabeth were wide open, as were their mouths in an expression of shock. Sabrina was aware of their existence but had never met any of them before.

"My name is Gwening," the Elf said. Motioning to his left, "This is Staggeth." The Dwarf waved, and Gwening motioned to his right. "And this is Dunks."

"How ya doing?" Dunks asked with a welcoming smile big enough to be seen through his beard.

"You guys are real?" Elizabeth said, the shock still on her face.

"Absolutely!" Dunks exclaimed, enthusiastic to meet people from another realm.

All three extended their hands, and the ladies stepped forward, accepting their handshakes. Haley noticed right away that Staggeth's ears, though normal in length, were pointed like Gwening's, but Dunks were not.

"I assume you three have had a bit of a journey," Gwening said. "Follow us, and we'll show you to your room."

"Room?" Elizabeth asked.

"Yes, ma'am," Dunks said. "The Hunter-Ralt had it arranged."

Sabrina didn't know how to feel. She wanted to slap Derek and hug him at the same time. *How did he manage to make such connections without me having the slightest idea?* She silently wondered.

Dunks remained at the post while the ladies followed Gwening and Staggeth toward the southern end of the port depot, where there was a large arched opening in the eastern wall. Getting closer, Haley and Elizabeth could see the stairs that led up to another level within the earthen complex. Though made of stone and earth, the walls were perfectly smooth, and Haley could see a silhouette of her reflection in them.

The group climbed to the top of the stairs and entered a large room. Cavern was more like it. The floorspace looked to be the same as the port depot, but upon looking up, the ceiling was hundreds of feet above them and appeared to be made from a knotted mass of giant tree roots.

"Whoa…" Haley was looking straight up to the root-ceiling where there were glowing specs of yellow, floating like dust suspended on a breeze. Spread throughout the room on the floor were large tree stumps that stood no more than a foot high, ten feet in diameter and perfectly flat. A single large mushroom grew out from the side of every stump.

"This one," Staggeth was pointing to a stump ahead of them, where another Alfan was standing by and holding a staff.

Haley could not hold her curiosity, "Can I ask something?"

Staggeth turned back with a playful grin that was easy to see through his well-groomed beard and said, "You just did. But what's the question you want to ask."

After a quick chuckle, Haley asked, "Why are your ears pointed, but Dunks's were not?"

"Because I was born here in the Fourth Density. Dunks is from the Third."

"So, everybody born here would have pointed ears?" Elizabeth inquired.

"That's right."

"I want pointed ears!" Haley said, getting a bit of that daydream grin. Turning to Gwening, she asked, "Do Elves from the Third Density have round ears?"

"No," he answered as they arrived at the stump. "Elves always have pointed ears. And so do the Gnomes."

"Gnomes?!" both girls blurted.

He turned to the man standing at the stump. "How are you today, Row?"

"Doing well," he responded with a pleasant smile and a voice as melodic as Gwening's. Row took his wooden staff and lightly smacked it against the mushroom cap, causing it to release spores. The puff of spores settled on the stump, and Row pointed toward the ceiling.

The three ladies looked up to see one of the giant roots dislodge and uncurl like a tentacle and what appeared to be some kind of cage-like object hanging from its end. The animated root lowered the object down to the stump, and the girls could see that this cage-like object was made up of intertwined vines. Row opened the gate and motioned for them to step in, which Gwening did.

The ladies followed, and Staggeth said to Gwening, "I'll see you in a bit."

With a nod, Gwening closed the gate. Row gave the mushroom another tap, and the vine-like root flexed, lifting them upward toward the ceiling. Haley and Elizabeth were riveted as they watched the ceiling become larger in their view. When they got close, a tangle of vines started to separate from one another, opening a passage to the floor above.

They rose, and the root tendril held the cage up past the glowing pollen, through the hole and to the palace's bottom floor, setting it down on a stump next to the opening. The vines flowed back in, closing and sealing the gap around the root, and Gwening opened the gate.

First Density. Willimantic, Connecticut

A pounding on the door was heard, snapping Neil awake. *Who could that be?* He had tried calling Harry or Ryan, but nobody was answering their phone. Even with his PJs, Neil was unable to contact Haley and Elizabeth or even Colonel Decker. He tried calling again and again until he had fallen asleep in his living room chair.

Rubbing his face while walking toward the door, Neil hoped it would be them, but another round of loud knocking commenced, followed by a man's voice. "Police! Open up!"

What could they want with me?

He unlocked and opened the door to see two officers standing on the porch. One was wearing a Willimantic Police uniform. The other was wearing a Cetatian Proctor's uniform. *This isn't good.*

"Neil Portman?" The Cetatian cop asked. He was five feet and eleven inches tall, with neatly trimmed brown hair and brown eyes. Other than the secondary pigment down the back of his neck, he didn't look any different than a Human.

"Yes?"

"We have some questions and need you to come down to the station," the Willimantic officer said.

"Regarding what?"

"You were involved with the incident in Columbia last year," the Cetatian officer said. "The others involved are now missing."

"Yeah, I've been trying to reach them since the big propaganda message last night," Neil responded with obvious contempt. "And so far, I've got nothing...just like you." He slammed the door in their faces.

He turned to walk back toward the kitchen when the door was kicked in. "You don't have a warrant," Neil shouted.

"New set of rules." the Cetatian officer said and slapped a restraining disk on Neil. The tendrils wrapped around him, cinching down snugly, and Neil was levitated a couple of inches off the floor.

Sandra came running into the hallway, "What are you doing?" she demanded.

"Ma'am, stay out of it," one of them said. "Tend to your child before we detain you, too, and he goes into state custody."

Sandra stood there, absolutely stunned, but she knew that trying anything would be foolish. "But...but...he's done nothing wrong. Don't take him from me!" she pleaded.

Sorry, ma'am, but this is how things run now and…" Metallic tendrils wrapped around both officers, and they were hoisted a few inches off the floor.

"Sorry, officers, but this is how I run things now," Derek said as he walked into the door. He went up to Neil and deactivated the restraining disk. "I'm getting you and your family out of here." Turning back to the officers, he said, "And tell Kone to tread carefully, or he will become my next hunt."

"Are you crazy?! Nobody threatens Kone! A threat to Kone is a threat against The State."

Sahmbo pulled the Proctor close and looked him in the eye, "Kone *is* the threat to The Cetatian State. And when men like us continue to cooperate with him, we ourselves are part of the problem." He pulled on the Proctor again, bringing their noses to touch. "I will no longer be part of that problem." The Hunter-Ralt shoved the Proctor away, and he floated down the hall. "I will be part of the solution."

First Density. Location Unknown

Many of those stationed on this base were relieved of duty and dismissed, replaced by Cetatian soldiers. A general, accompanied by a Commando, walked down the corridor to a large set of metal doors. They now had all the access codes and opened the door to find a Human still seated at the desk. He looked up, seeing that these men were not of the United States Air Force. "Who are…" A bolt of yellow light struck him, knocking him out. They would have had no problem killing the man, but they were trying to keep up optics for the long game and were ordered to spare as many as possible.

Sitting on a cot inside the cell, Ahnk-Hume looked on to see the General go to the control desk and punch in some commands, which made the cell gate slide open. "Archon," the General said, "it is time for your release."

Ahnk-Hume smiled.

CHAPTER 11
Sanctuary

Fourth Density. Og Palace, Tir na nOg

Everything was a light wooden color. The walls, the ceiling, it was all curving and flowing wood, covered with the same vines that had the light flowers down below. The entire palace was the inside of a giant tree. Hollow limbs stretched up and out, housing stairwells to the higher levels. The ladies stepped out of the cage and looked up, taking in the sight.

"This way," Gwening said with a gesture toward a set of stairs. They followed him up to another level and were greeted by someone Sabrina recognized.

Hunter Reggie Stewart smiled and walked up to Sabrina, reached out and placed his hand on her right shoulder while she placed her hand on his. A Hunter's greeting. "Glad to see you've made it," he said in his thick Maine accent.

"This is a pleasant surprise."

"All the Hunters are here," he replied. "Well, most of us." He looked to the girls, "Haley and Elizabeth!" His smile was genuine. "Glad to see you two here as well." He leaned down with a sheepish grin, "Sorry about all the chasing you around last year. Didn't want to do it, but if we stayed out of it, the Commandos would have been there instead, and they don't hold back."

"How did all the Hunters get here?" Sabrina asked.

"When the call went out, we all went to the lodge. Sahmbo had portgates set up in the lower levels that came here. We came through, and then he destroyed the gates so the Commandos couldn't follow."

"Commandos?"

"Yeah," Stewart answered. "Wasn't long after we got there that they showed up. Looks like we all made the deletion list. I was one of the last ones through. And since you're here, Sahmbo must have made it out."

"Yes, he came to me a half hour ago. I don't know where he is right now." She looked around the palace. "How did he get this all arranged?"

"I'm just as surprised by it, but he's not the one who made the original arrangements."

"Who did?"

Stewart smiled. "It was Vedant."

"Vedant?! Is he here? I haven't seen him in a couple of years."

Gwening shook his head. "No, he's out on a hunt. But if you would come this way, there is someone who would like to meet you."

"I'll see you later," Stewart said.

As they followed Gwening, Elizabeth noticed a slide switch next to the zipper on Sabrina's jumper and asked, "Do you all wear the same outfits?"

"Customized, but yes. Why do you ask?"

"I was wondering what that switch is. I don't see the other Hunters with one."

"It's just an extra clasp to make sure my zipper stays together," she said.

They continued through a series of passageways to an upper level and down a hallway, all just as beautiful and alive. Other people passed them by. Some were Elves, some were Dwarves and even a few Humans, but there were a few people of another race that neither Haley nor Elizabeth recognized. They were around three feet tall with large noses, spindly limbs and long, pointed ears, looking almost cartoonish in proportions.

Haley asked Gwening, "Who are they?"

"Gnomes," he replied.

"Wow! So that's them. This is really cool," Haley said, sighed, and added, "But I'm worried about our parents."

"Me too," Elizabeth replied. I don't know what we can do, though."

Sabrina could hear their concerns in their voice and could also feel it in her gut as well. "Derek said he'd find them. So, he will find them." She sighed. "I understand your worry, but we can do nothing about it right now. We must deal with what's in front of us."

They came to a large arched doorway on the side of the hall, and Gwening stepped through. Following him in, they entered a large room with a dome-shaped ceiling that was open on one side. The floor extended past the ceiling to form a large balcony that was enclosed by what they first thought to be glass, allowing plenty of light.

A man wearing a slim crown stood up from a chair at the head of a table. He had shoulder-length brown hair, large blue eyes and elongated pointed ears. The Alfan man gave them a warm smile and said, "Greetings. You must be Hunter Sabrina Carmen. Vedant has spoken so much about you. I am Larriforn, King of Tir na nOg."

First Density. Undersea Base, The Atlantic

The large room was full of control panels and workstations. The metallic frames of the walls held large, thick windows, giving them a clear view of the cavern outside. The Command Center was built into the structure, right above the water level. The floor was also made of thick transparent panels, allowing them to see down into the water.

After the rest of the SEAL team arrived, they cleared the base of shells and found the rest of the base's surviving crew. Williams was brought to the med bay, and a doctor was tending to his injuries. But they all knew that they could not remain here for long because more Cetatian forces would soon be on their way.

"Activate it," Admiral Book ordered, and a seaman punched a code into one of the panels.

As the base's communications array powered back on, a message came through: bits of data from multiple channels, and it all came together, like pieces of a puzzle, as soon as it reached its intended target. Colonel Decker's phone rang. Admiral Book began working on a communication while Decker looked at his phone screen. Seeing who it was, he answered immediately. "Neil, are you okay?"

"Yeah, um…the cops tried to arrest me for last year, and that Hunter guy who caught the Marshals…he showed up and saved me."

"Are you talking about Derek Sahmbo?"

"So, you've heard of me?" Derek said.

Hearing the voice, Decker said, "Put him on!"

Neil handed the phone to the Hunter, who said, "Colonel Decker, this is Hunter-Ralt Derek Sahmbo. Starr and Guerreiro are safe. They have escaped to the Fourth Density and are currently under the protection of the Alfan people until they can be reunited with their parents."

"Am I supposed to just believe that you've had a change of heart?" Decker asked.

"No, that would be foolish. What you need to know is that the Cetatian Hunters are not your enemy, but what the Cetatian State has become is. We have left the Second Density and are not allies of Kone. I plan to take Neil and his family to the Fourth Density as well. Starr and Guerreiro would like to know the status of their parents. Are they okay?"

"Yes. But I have some questions."

The admiral closed his comm, turned to Decker and silently mouthed, "The President is secure!"

Decker and Sahmbo took a couple of minutes sizing each other up before Decker determined that this was not a setup. With a mental command, Decker's PJs cast video of the call onto the Command Center's main monitor. They could see both Neil and Derek on the screen, but only audio made its way back to Neil's phone. Everyone listened as Sahmbo talked about Kone and what he knew of his future plans.

Fourth Density. Og Palace, Tir na nOg

One of the gates of the port depot activated, and Derek came through with Neil, Sandra and Junior.

"Hunter-Ralt!" Dunks exclaimed.

While the two of them greeted, Neil and Sandra were taking in the view. But for Neil, there was something more. He could feel the energy around him. Everywhere!

For years, Neil had practiced mysticism, but due to the diminisher's frequencies working into the First Density's broadcast infrastructure, he was never able to truly connect with his field. But now, here in Tir na nOg, there were no such signals in the air, nothing to prevent him from fully connecting. His senses came alive, he felt lighter on his feet, and the ambient energies became as significant to his senses as soundwaves were to his ears. He felt…lightheaded.

And he fell over.

One of the Elves ran to him. "Are you okay?"

"I'm dizzy…I feel…everything."

The Elf immediately knew what had happened, "Get him some apples!" he called.

Nomad's ears perked up, and he turned his head toward the balcony. He walked out to the edge and hopped onto the railing against the glass-like transparent leaves that formed the awning. "Meow." His voice echoed, and everyone could feel an energy emanating from the cat.

"What was that?" Gwening asked. As soon as he did, Bast appeared before them.

"Bastet. It has been some time," King Larriforn said.

"Yes, it has," she replied. "I hope all is well." She turned toward the girls. "I just heard about what has happened in your realm and called out to Nomad. I'm relieved to see that you two are safe, but how did you come to be here?"

The girls launched into an enthusiastic story about their run from one Naval base to another, the Cetatian facility and Sabrina helping them escape. As they were coming to the end, both Haley and Elizabeth heard notification tones from their PJs. They looked at their phones to find unexpected but welcome news. Haley looked to Bast and exclaimed, "Neil's here!"

He had chewed through three apples like he was starving to death while he adapted to the overwhelming rush of his mystical senses. Feeling more stable, Neil stood up and was surprised at how easy the movement was. Like he weighed nothing. "Does this happen often here?" he asked.

"Sometimes," one of the Elves answered. "But only with people from the First Density. When one suddenly finds themselves beyond the influence of Kone's diminishers, it can all come flooding in at once."

Neil's PJs sounded with a notification, and as he was pulling out his phone to see what it was, the phone rang. "Huh. Didn't think I'd have any signal here." He saw the call was from Elizabeth. "Hello?"

"Hi. Haley and I are here, and we're safe," she said. "Are you okay?"

"Yeah. And I spoke to your dad. He's okay for the moment, but I have to talk to somebody about opening a gate for them."

"Are they still at that water base?"

"Yes, and we need to give them a viable gate to link with before more of Kone's goons show up."

A few moments later, they were standing before King Larriforn, explaining the situation. After hearing Sahmbo out, the king allowed them to access one of the gates in their depot, and soon, Book, Decker and the others from the underwater base were stepping through to the Fourth Density.

"Dad!" Haley exclaimed when Harry came through, practically tackled by his daughter's hug.

Maggie and Ryan both took hold of Elizabeth and squeezed her tight.

Two of the seamen brought Williams through on a gurney, and an Elf shouted, "Bring him here!"

They rolled over to the Alfan man, who held up his hands and began a soft hum. His hands started glowing with yellow light, and the Elf transitioned from a hum to an ah. He increased his volume, and the light intensified while the swelling on William's torso reduced. The Elf finished his song, and Williams regained consciousness, sitting up on the gurney and looking first at the Alfan healer with his large eyes and long pointed ears, then around at the area, confused.

"Where…where are we?" He looked down at his own torso and said, "It doesn't hurt to breathe anymore."

"We need more apples!" Dunks shouted when Maggie stumbled.

As Maggie was acclimating to her energetic senses, another portgate activated, and a group of Gnomes stepped through. Haley looked over and couldn't help but notice their facial features. The eyes, the cheekbones, skin tone and even their style of dress. Other than the large noses and ears, they looked Native American, and curiosity drew her closer.

One of the Elves looked at the leader of the Gnomish group and said, "Ambassador Tisquantum! It's good to see you!"

"And you as well, Dannon!" the Gnome said, returning the Alfan's greeting with equal enthusiasm. Tisquantum turned his head and noticed a blonde-haired, pigtailed Human girl staring at him. "Can I help you?"

"Oh, umm," Haley stammered at first and reached up to scratch the back of her head. "It's just that…I've never met Gnomes before."

He smiled and said, "Well, my name is Tisquantum of the Pukwudgie Tribe, from the land of the same name. Where are you from?" he asked, extending his hand.

She reached out and grasped his hand for a shake. "I'm Haley from Connecticut."

"First Density?"

"Uh-huh," she replied, nodding her head.

"Then you would know Pukwudgie as Delaware."

"Cool!"

"I heard about what happened to your realm. My condolences. Kone is a problem to all densities."

The Starrs, Guerreiros and Portmans were in the conference room with Sahmbo and Sabrina, as King Larriforn took a little time getting to know them while considering possible living arrangements. The Hunters had quarters ready for them beforehand, but three families and nearly thirty US servicemen were not something that they had anticipated. King Larriforn was enjoying the rare opportunity to actually speak with some folks from the First Density. Having been charmed by Haley, Ambassador Tisquantum was also there, interested in meeting the others from the Human realm. Bast appeared, holding Hayseed and Trinket.

"Hayseed!" Haley exclaimed, running over to snuggle her cat. Bast smiled at the happy reunion while handing Trinket to Sandra.

Book, Decker and the US servicemen were gathered in the training grounds with the Hunters, where they were meeting some Guardsmen who had offered to open their homes to some of the refugees.

"Seeing all of this must be quite the culture shock, but Glaid is mostly Humans," Larriforn explained, "and you'll find it to be much like the towns you're familiar with in the First Density."

Harry and Dunks had seemed to hit it off. The Dwarf nudged him with his elbow and said, "I live there too. You can stay at my place for now. Do you like to ride?"

"Horses?" Harry asked.

With a laugh, Dunks replied, "No. Motorcycles."

The soft yellow light from the flowers throughout the palace all shifted to a deep red color, and the Elves suddenly bore expressions of concern. A dwarven guard rushed into the room, followed by another Dwarf and an Elf. "Your Majesty! Powries are coming! The Guardsmen are prepared to engage, and word has been sent to Glaid."

"Those disgusting goblins," Tisquantum muttered. The Powries were a group of worshipers of Hel, who were comprised mostly of Gnomes, although there were some people of other races who joined them. Goblin was a derogatory term reserved for Gnomes of criminal behavior.

"Send them," King Larriforn commanded.

Bast stood up, "Wait! There is no need. I will deal with them."

With a look of shock, Larriforn said, "But you are not to involve yourself with the conflicts of mortals. Won't you be taken to a tribunal in Asgard?"

"They are attacking a place where I already am." The goddess gave a knowing smirk, "The Powries are interfering with my dealings now. Consider it a loophole." With that, she vanished from sight.

An army of Gnomes charged at the palace. Some of them were dead bodies animated by a possessing spirit, a few of them were true undead, and the rest were still living. Many had maces and clubs, some had guns, a few had bolt pistols, and all had their eyes set on the palace structure, eager to spill Elven blood for the pleasure of their goddess. How they got so close undetected was anybody's guess. As they neared Og palace, an Egyptian woman suddenly appeared.

A golden light glowed in Bastet's eyes, and the entire army was hoisted ten feet into the air. The living people squirmed and flailed with confusion, but the reanimated corpses stopped moving and stared at the goddess with contempt because the spirits within recognized her.

The glow in her eyes intensified, and the entire group was enveloped in golden light. The dead and undead were incinerated in an instant, then the living were gently set back down on their feet, and the light faded.

Bast opened her mouth and spoke. Her words were near deafening when they echoed across the field and in the Powries' ears. "Leave this place!" she demanded. There was no need to repeat herself as she watched them all turn and run for their lives.

Bast returned to the room where King Larriforn and the others were seated around the large oval-shaped table, finalizing some arrangements. "They are gone." The red glowing flowers returned to their normal yellow color.

They continued their discussion, but the mystical barriers on the walls suddenly dropped. As soon as they did, there was a burst of black mist behind Bast's seat. When she turned to look, a woman stepped forward, gabbed Bast by the throat and hoisted her into the air.

The woman was thin, too thin. Her skin was gray, and the whites of her eyes were yellow. The woman's pupils were black, as too was her scraggly hair and clothing, which was wrappings of tattered cloth.

She slammed the Egyptian goddess onto the table with such force that it buckled from the impact. The woman leaned down, her face an inch from Bast's.

"How dare you interfere with my people?" she sneered as the darkness of her pupils expanded, and her eyes became two pools of black.

The geode portgates all activated at once, and the guards looked on in confusion, then were shocked by what came next. Goblins swarmed from the vortexes; polearms pointed forward as they charged. The guardsmen reacted quickly but were still overwhelmed by the sheer numbers as they continued to rush in from the gates.

Everyone was stunned by the spectacle before them as Bast choked from the woman's grip. Then, a burst of golden light knocked the woman away, and Bast was up in an instant. She threw a bolt at the woman, knocking her back a couple of yards. Bast closed the distance while swinging her arm, purple light trailing from her fingers. The woman put her arms up to block and winced as Bast's attack sliced her left forearm.

The woman countered with a mystical bolt of her own that looked like an orb of black mist. It hit Bast, knocking her across the room and into the wall. It was followed by a jagged shard of blackness piercing Bast's abdomen.

"Leave her alone!" the woman heard Haley shout and turned to see her and Elizabeth crackling with energy. Together, they unleashed their sustained beams at the intruder, causing her to stagger back a couple of feet, but the woman dug in her heels and stood up straight, unmoving for the remainder of their blast.

She glared at the girls, and her lips curled in disgust, "Unruly children," she spat. "This day has been your las—" The woman's words were interrupted by a potato breaking apart against her lips, but she didn't budge.

The woman's eyes narrowed as she lifted her right hand, gathering intense energy into her fingers. Elizabeth conjured her helmet and began scanning the woman. The Head-Up Display highlighted her hand and flashed the words.

WARNING: EVASIVE ACTION REQUIRED

Harry and Ryan jumped in front of the girls just when the woman went to throw her hand forward and unleash a lethal bolt, but a crack echoed in the room as a metallic cord ensnared her wrist. Sabrina electrified the whip, and the intruder began to convulse. A couple of seconds later, the woman shrugged it off and locked eyes with the Hunter. She wrapped her fingers around the electrified metal, yanked the handle from Sabrina's grasp and caught it in her left hand. Never breaking eye contact, the woman pulled her arms outward, snapping the whip in two and dropped the pieces to the floor.

Maintaining eye contact, Sabrina instantly had her bolt pistol leveled and opened fire, joined by Haley, Elizabeth, Sahmbo, King Larriforn, Neil and Maggie. The bolts hit the intruder again and again with no effect as she took deliberate steps toward the Hunter. Sahmbo launched a restraining disk at her, the tendrils wrapped around to cinch tight, but she pushed out with her arms, snapping free of the entangling metal and continued for Sabrina.

Drawing her katana, Sabrina believed her life to be forfeit, but intended to go down fighting. Then, the roar of a lioness was heard as Bast dove toward the woman. She tackled the invader and teleported, landing them on the ground of a grassy field somewhere on the continent that the First and Second Densities knew as Africa.

"Where'd they go?" Haley asked.

"And who was that?" Elizabeth added.

"That," King Larriforn said with a grave expression, "Was Hel, the Goddess of Death."

One of the Dwarves picked up the pieces of the whip. "Hmm." He turned toward Sabrina, "It was a unique weapon. Were you attached?"

"Yes," Sabrina answered.

The Dwarf then looked at the Elf who entered the room with him, a fellow craftsman with whom he often worked, "Lellan, are you thinking what I'm thinking?"

The Elf nodded with an enthusiastic grin and a gleam in his eye, "Flekkle would do nicely."

"What's Flekkle?" Haley asked.

"A type of metal," Lellan answered. "It's an excellent medium for conducting magickal energies. And electrical energy as well."

The Dwarf opened the end of the handle, and a cylinder slid out.

"That's the power cell," Sabrina told him. "It holds the charge that…"

Runden held up his hand with a chuckle and said, "I know what a battery is."

"We'll return," Lellan said. He chanted some quick words, and the two men disappeared in a flash of light, teleporting to the Dvwargarian forges in the Third Density.

The glass globes in the room illuminated with red light as horns sounded off around the structure. "The goblins have returned," said King Larriforn. He then shouted, his voice enhanced with magick, and it echoed throughout the complex, "Prepare for battle!"

The Savannah

They crashed to the ground, and Bast tumbled forward, coming right back up and spinning around. She unleashed a blast of golden light at Hel while she was getting back to her feet. The blast hit and sent Hel flying as the Egyptian goddess, while running after her, began to glow. Her body looked as if it were made of gold and purple light as she changed into the shape of a leopard bearing down on Hel as she landed.

Bast, claws out, dove at Hel but was knocked back by a concussive burst of darkness. The Goddess of Death threw dark shards at the panther, but Bast dodged and dove into the grass, seeming to vanish.

Approaching the spot where Bast disappeared, Hel was taken by surprise when the panther leaped toward her from the side. Bast slashed Hel in the arm as she went by and disappeared again into the grass.

Hel then began to glow red, flames billowing from her mouth and nostrils with every breath as the ground became covered with frost. She had taken the heat, causing the area to freeze and could now hear the frozen blades of grass cracking from Bast's movement.

A stream of flames poured forth from Hel's mouth, engulfing the hidden panther. With a shriek, Bast leaped into the air above the flames, morphing back to her true form. She flew toward Hel with her right arm pulled back, claws of purple light glowing from her fingers.

Just before impact, Hel saw Bast vanish, and she was slashed from behind. The death goddess turned around to see Bast vanish again and was slashed from her left.

She turned to the left, and Bast disappeared, but Hel spun toward her back, Grabbing the Egyptian goddess as she manifested. Hel threw her to the ground and jumped on top, digging her fingernails into Bast's face.

"Ahhh!" Bast shouted in pain while Hel ran energy into her skull. Her head felt like it was going to explode when Hel was abruptly hoisted into the air.

A 6'2 Egyptian man, wearing a tan flannel and blue jeans, had grabbed the back of Hel's neck with his right hand and was holding her up above his head. "Get off my wife!" Ptah shouted and then hurled the Goddess of Death across the field.

Hel hit the ground and kept on going, leaving a long trench leading to a large rock, which split when it was hit by the goddess's head.

There was a flash of orange light to the left of Ptah from the arrival of Baphomet, who charged straight for him.

Getting back to her feet, Hel saw Baphomet grab Ptah and take their fight to the air while Bast was still on the ground, dazed. She raised her arm, gathering energy for a devastating bolt, when an arrow pierced her right side.

Grabbing the arrow with both hands and a grunt, Hel looked up to see a Greek woman with another arrow knocked and drawn in her bow while Baphomet and Ptah crashed back to the ground.

To the side of the field, a multicolored spark appeared. It spun and formed a vortex, opening wider into a portal. A man stepped through, aging but rugged. He wore a gleaming chainmail with a shaggy blue and white striped cloak overtop and a golden helm upon his head. Long hair draped down his shoulders, mostly gray with a bit of red still remaining. His right eye was missing, and his left was a steel blue, which he used to look upon the field. In his right hand, he held a beautifully crafted spear engraved with runes, which glowed when he struck the butt-end of the weapon to the ground, quaking the earth.

"Enough!" Odin's voice reverberated.

Everyone stopped and turned their heads to the Asgardian King, who did not look pleased. Hel grimaced as she pulled the arrow from her side and dropped it to the ground. When it landed, it disappeared, returned to Artemis's quiver.

Odin's gaze settled on Hel, and he narrowed his eye. "Explain yourself."

Hel pointed to Bast, who Ptah was helping back to her feet and said, "She had no right to interfere with what my people were doing. Bastet overstepped."

"Is that so?" Odin asked.

"Yes," Hel replied.

"I had personal business at Og Palace, and it was attacked while I was there," Bast said. She was bleeding from ten deep gouges in her forehead and cheeks.

"We all agreed to let the mortals deal with mortal affairs," Hel shouted. "Just because the goblins decided to worship me doesn't give you any right to interfere in their battles. So, you came to talk to an Elf? And you now keep the company of two little mortal girls. You shouldn't be here at all!"

"Tell me," Odin said to Hel, "was it not your actions that set Bastet on her current path?"

The death goddess feigned a look of confusion.

"Did you think I would not find out?" Odin asked with a stern gaze. He pointed at Hel and said, "You and your ilk, who fell in line with Lucifer's schemes, cast that binding spell last year and had the Cetatian wizards maintain it. What was your plan exactly? Help the Cetatians and Archons conquer Midgard? It would not be long before Zeus would take note. Then what? Would you all stand together against him? Even if you could, what would your plans have been for when I got involved?"

Hel clenched her fists as she glared at Odin like an angry, pouty child. Of course, they knew Zeus, who kept watch over the first two densities, would have seen what was happening moments after the assault had begun, but that's all they would have needed to disable the

First Densities defenses. By the time Zeus would have arrived to assess what was happening, they would have already released the other gods and been gone, but the path for the Cetatians and Archons would have been cleared. "The Cetatian wizards…" Hel began.

"Do not speak falsehoods to me!" Odin bellowed. "Even with their devices to assist them, they are not powerful enough to cast such a spell. And do you also mean to tell me that you, yourself, did not instruct the Powries to attack the Alfan?"

A raven swooped down from the sky and landed on Odin's right shoulder. He looked at his raven and slowly turned his head back toward Hel. "You did what!?" He let go of his spear, which remained upright on its own and clapped his hands.

Og Palace, Tir na nOg.

The goblins were everywhere. Haley and Elizabeth were blasting away as Sabrina dropped intruder after intruder with her bolt pistol. Those who got too close to the Hunter fell upon her blade. The Elves and Dwarves were fierce as they fought back against the onslaught, and having a SEAL team on their side was a great equalizer against the overwhelming numbers. Without warning, a multicolored spark appeared in front of every Powrie. They opened into vortexes and closed around the invaders. In an instant, all the goblins were gone.

The Savannah

"You have used our society's good faith to push the boundaries repeatedly. Zeus and I have both shown great mercy and restraint, but no more." Odin said. "I've sent your people home. Now you go home as well and take your boyfriend with you. If either of you overstep again, you'll both join Surtur…" his eye narrowed, "…in Tartarus."

Hel sneered and took a step back, disappearing in a burst of black mist, and in a flash of orange light, Baphomet did the same.

With a flash of green light and another of orange, two more gods appeared. From the orange was a Greek man standing at five feet and eleven inches tall, with black hair, an olive skin tone and a neatly trimmed beard. From the green came a Celtic man who was six feet and two inches tall. He had long, wild, and wavey auburn hair with a bushy red beard."

"Awe, we missed it," Ares said in disappointment.

"But she didn't," Cernunnos replied in a heavy Irish accent while pointing at Bast. He walked over to the Egyptian goddess and waved his hand across her face, healing the deep wounds.

"Thank you."

"Do you need us to hang around for a bit?" Ares asked.

"I'd appreciate that," Bast said.

"And so would I," Ptah added as he and Bast clasped each other's hands.

The King of Asgard approached the rest of the group, and they all turned toward him. "Thank you, Odin," Bast said to him.

"You're welcome. But I'm afraid Hel brought up a good point. You have been visiting with the two young mortals quite a bit. You know where this emotional attachment will lead. Their time will have come and gone before you know it."

With a heavy sigh, Bast lowered her head and squeezed Ptah's hand tighter as she said, "I know." She lifted her head back up and looked Odin in the eye, "That's why I must appreciate their company while I can." She felt Ptah squeeze her hand back in support.

"So long as you do not interfere with the direction of mortal civilization, there are no laws against it, but you know the heartache that will come as a result," Odin reminded.

"They're worth it," Bast stated firmly.

"Very well," The Asgardian King said, "Before you all go…Ares." The God of War turned toward Odin. "Thor and Raiden are having a rematch tonight. Over the Pacific in the Fifth Density. They were hoping that you would officiate."

An enthusiastic smile spread across Ares's face as he said, "I'll be there!"

CHAPTER 12
Lost And Found

The healers were working furiously when Bast, Ptah, and Cernunnos appeared. Bast and Cernunnos used their healing abilities to tend to the wounded. Ptah began repairing the damage done to the place while Ares and Artemis were outside, keeping watch to make certain that no other nasty surprises came their way. Green light flashed next to Bast, and a woman appeared. Tuweltha, the Alfan goddess, stood at five foot five with long blonde hair and large blue crystalline eyes. She looked to Bast and asked, "What has happened here?"

Third Density. The Dvwargarian Forges

The door swung open, and light spilled into the small safe for the first time in a decade. Runden smiled as he reached in and wrapped his fingers around the chunk of Flekkle. Lellen was at his safe, sporting the same smile of eager anticipation. The ore was tough to come by, but between the two of them, they had enough to replicate

Sabrina's whip. Flekkle was a soft metal, much like lead and gold, but not nearly as heavy.

When a worked piece is quenched in mystically charged water, it would become as supple as leather and nearly unbreakable, but if heated to twice the temperature at which it was worked, the metal would melt and return to its original properties once cooled.

Fourth Density. Tir na nOg. January 7, 2000

She could not avoid it. She could not escape it. No matter where she went, it still followed her. Even here, in the magickal land of Elves, Haley had to practice. Though it was winter, the temperature was in the fifties, and the sun was shining, making for a pleasant day.

She was gifted a collapsing staff from the Elves and Elizabeth a pair of sai. They were both demonstrating their strikes again and again as Sabrina corrected their stance and refined their form. It had only been a week, and as much as she hated it, Haley couldn't deny that she was gaining noticeable improvement with the use of her staff, and Elizabeth's two sai already seemed to have become an extension of herself.

Harry and Haley were staying with Dunks in Glaid, and the Dwarf had made arrangements for the girls to use the palace training field. The two girls stood about ten feet apart as they both went through their forms. Satisfied with their demonstrations, Sabrina let them take a break and began practicing a couple forms herself.

The Elves had natural agility and were adept at dual-wielding swords of the same length. Most people of the other species weren't nimble enough to do this effectively, with a few exceptions. Sabrina was one of those exceptions, and King Larriforn had the Guardsmen's weapons master provide instruction. Haley and Elizabeth went to sit on the cool grass next to Ryan and sipped some water as they watched Sabrina work through the moves taught to her. In the adjacent fields, SEALs, Hunters, Alfan Rangers and Guardsmen were all practicing their moves and sparring with each other.

Turning toward Elizabeth, Haley asked, "Even though we haven't known her long, isn't it weird to think of her as a student?"

"Kind of," Elizabeth replied while nodding her head. "She definitely gives me more leader vibes."

"Everyone is always a student," a melodic voice said. They turned and looked up to see Flashipor, the weapons master himself, standing behind them. "Even me," he added as Ryan nodded in agreement.

Haley felt it first. That same feeling when she couldn't wait to show something to someone. Then Sabrina noticed the echoes of excitement. The two empaths turned their heads, and Elizabeth followed Haley's gaze to see Lellen and Runden approaching, followed by four more Alfan men. And one of them was King Larriforn. Runden was carrying a hinged wooden case as both he and Lellen wore smiles that could not be hidden if they had tried. Haley and Elizabeth both smiled and waved.

"How fares the training?" Lellen asked the ladies while Runden returned the wave.

"It's going well," Sabrina replied. "How are you?"

"Ecstatic!" Runden said with intensity in his eyes. "As you'll also be in a moment."

"Hunter Sabrina Carmen," Lellen stated as he stood a little straighter and motioned toward Balgar. "We present to you…" Runden opened the case, "Your new whip." It was made of Flekkle, but the bumps along the surface were much smaller, giving it a smooth look from the handle to the tapered tip. The handle was shaped into a comfortable grip and had runes etched around the top. The switch was in the exact same place, where she could turn it on and off with a convenient flip of her thumb.

Sabrina's jaw hung slack for an instant when she looked upon the weapon. Runden lifted the open case higher, indicating for Sabrina to take it. The Hunter reached into the case and slowly grasped the handle, experiencing the comfort of the grip. She lifted it up, entranced by the beautifully crafted weapon, staring in awe.

After a moment, Runden said, "Well, what are ya waitin' for? Give it a try!"

Sabrina turned toward the targets and stepped within range. She burst into motion, and the metallic whip snapped against the leather-wrapped post. And then again. And again. With speed and precision, Sabrina practically whittled the padding away from the post in short order. She finished the barrage with a loop that rolled into a wicked snap, taking a good chunk out of the wood itself.

"Whoa!" Elizabeth said while she and Haley watched with wonder.

Sabrina then toggled the switch and electrified the whip. A soft buzz was heard as little blue-white arcs snapped across its surface. She rolled it forward, striking the leather from another post, hit it again and once more, snapping the post in half.

It was Haley's turn to say, "Whoa!"

"Why is it," King Larriforn began as he turned his head toward the craftsmen, "that every time you two make something special, I have to replace the Guardsmen's training targets?"

"Because we're good at our job!" Runden answered without skipping a beat.

The Elf King nodded and said, "That you are." He flashed a quick smile, "Well done."

Sabrina turned back toward the two smiling craftsmen, feeling the pride in their good work radiating from them both.

"It has a name," Lellen said.

"What is it?"

"Skilja," answered Runden.

Out of habit, Sabrina put the handle to her right hip, this one also coiled itself and set in place. "This is incredible. How can I repay you?"

"You already did," Lellen said.

With a chuckle, Runden added, "When you shocked that nasty hag. We'll be tellin' that story for years to come!"

Haley laughed, thinking back to the confused expression on Hel's face when Sabrina tried to electrocute the Goddess of Death.

"Thank you," Sabrina said.

"You're welcome, but there is one more thing," Lellen said.

"We designed this whip to be bonded to the user," Runden said. "Remove the power cell."

Taking the whip back into her hand, she opened the grip, and the cylinder slid out. Lellen and the other two Alfan men began singing, and Sabrina felt a change in the air as mystical energy surrounded her. A moment later, their song was done.

While the power cell was still removed, Lellen said, "Now turn it on."

Sabrina toggled the switch with her thumb, and nothing happened. "Not with that," Runden said, and the Hunter looked to him with confusion.

"With your will," Lellen clarified.

Strong-willed as Sabrina was, she was not practiced in mysticism. She focused, but nothing happened.

"It's tuned to your field. It will work," Lellen said. "Keep trying."

"It's the same as focusing your chi," Elizabeth said.

Sabrina focused, and Haley could feel her frustration, like when the farmer struggled to make her eyes glow. But Sabrina was nothing if not disciplined and would not be deterred. The Hunter took a deep breath and centered herself, focusing her mind on the whip, and there was a spark. Sabrina tried to lock in her concentration, and Skilja crackled to life with blue-white and purple arcs.

Her eyes popping open wide, Sabrina said, "I did it." Then, the arcs diminished and stopped. She focused again, and the whip crackled with electrical energy.

She let the whip rest and looked to the craftsmen and Elven wizards, the appreciation written all over her usually stoic face. "Thank you," she said again.

"You're welcome," Lellan and Runden said in unison.

"But," Runden continued, "you might want to keep the power cell in there. So, if you find yerself in an anti-magick field, it'll still work. And when you use Skilja with your own energy, it will recharge the power cell."

Sabrina slid the cylinder back into the handle, and Skilja coiled itself as she set it on her hip.

West Antarctica: Second Density

It went on for miles. As far as the eye could see. Everything ahead and to their right was flat and white. Seven men trekked across the tundra, and the only thing that gave them any sense of movement was the mountain range to the southeast. The Transantarctic Mountains were the dividing line between East and West Antarctica, and the group was getting closer. All of them wore polar gear, which was white, and carried large packs on their backs. The lead man was checking a device in his hand with increased frequency as the others followed.

Two of the men were shorter than the others, under five feet tall, with thick beards and wide shoulders. One of whom turned toward the leader. "Think we're gettin' closer?"

The leader, a Cetatian man, turned toward the Dwarf and smiled. "I think we're almost there." The Dwarf grinned with anticipation and excitement. If Vedant Sahmbo thinks they were that close, then in the Dwarf's mind, the location was as good as found.

They had been on the tundra for nearly three weeks, and their supplies were getting low, especially after spending the last week riding out a nasty storm. It was summer, and the sun didn't set but instead traveled low on the horizon, rose and dipped back down. The storm had finally ended, and the sky cleared, granting them a calm and sunny trek for the last five hours, and they used it to make up for some lost time. Unfortunately, they had already missed their goal. The group was trying to find their destination at the same time as Kone seizing control of the First Density in hopes that he would be too preoccupied to notice their passage.

The mountains were just a couple miles away when Vedant glanced down at the device in his hand and held his left arm out to the side. "Hold still!" he announced.

The other men all stopped as Vedant read the data on the small screen in his palm. He stood up straight and turned to one of the men, a Human, and said, "Scan the area."

Jake unbuckled and removed his pack, setting it to the ground. He opened the top and pulled out a rectangular object. It was eleven inches wide, eight inches tall, and had a screen on one side and handles on the ends.

Holding the tablet up between himself and the area before him, the screen flashed to life, displaying the landscape. After a couple of seconds, a yellow dot flashed on the screen, indicating that technology was present. The scanner analyzed the readings and displayed the new information. "It's a motion detector," Jake told everybody. "About twenty-five feet ahead."

The scanner beeped again. "There's two more," Jake said. "Ten feet away on either side."

"Don't get any closer," Vedant told everyone. He looked toward the mountains and said, "This way."

As the group continued, they found that there were more of these motion sensors every ten feet. Noting their placement, Jake said, "These sensors are following a steady curve. If this is constant, then it's a ring large enough to surround a small city."

"Would the ring contact the mountains?" Vedant asked.

"Nah," Jake answered. "It should fall about fifteen feet short."

The group pressed on until the mountains were about five minutes away when the scanner made a different beeping sound.

"What is it?" asked Alunareth.

Jake looked up from the scanner and to the Elf, his face bearing an expression of shock and disgust. "Bodies," Jake stated as he handed the scanner to Alunareth.

Looking at the ground through the screen, Alunareth could see many bodies frozen about twenty feet beneath them. "Oh, my!"

The Elf turned and handed the scanner to Vedant. "According to this, they're almost all Human, but a few are…" After a couple of seconds, the Elf looked up to the others. "Unidentified hominoid-like species."

Vedant looked at the images being displayed and asked, "How long has this been happening?" He looked up from the screen and explained his question. "They are wearing clothes from different time periods. Kone must have found this place generations ago."

One of the men, a Cetatian Hunter, looked up from the group and pointed toward the base of the mountains, "What's he doing so far from the coast?"

The others looked to see what Samuel was pointing at. Native to the Second Density and the only land mammal to live on this continent, the snow ocelot, commonly referred to as the icelot, was about the size of a jaguar. Even though it shared the same markings as its smaller First Density cousin, the cat's fur was thicker and white in color, while the stripes and rosettes were gray. These cats fed on penguins and the occasional seal while spending time during inclement weather in caves. They were also the only known cat that could hibernate.

"He looks healthy," Alunareth commented.

The icelot was sunning on a boulder by the sensors near the base of the mountains, enjoying the direct light while it was available.

"They weather underground," Samuel said.

"So we need to know how they get there," Vedant added. "That's probably our best chance to find a way down."

"It's over a mile of ice between our feet and the ground," Jake mentioned. "What makes you think that'll be our way down?"

"Because the cat looks well-fed," Samuel answered. "And there's no food source for him up here on the ice."

Vedant looked to Samuel and nodded in approval. "Sabrina taught you well."

The young Hunter had accomplished much under Sabrina's mentorship. There was a time when they thought Samuel wouldn't be able to join their ranks even though he was a gifted fighter with a sharp mind and excelled in his woodland tracking skills. His performance seemed to be matched by only his ego as his achievements boosted his confidence, leading the brash young man to a penchant for thumping his chest and bragging to any who would listen. This, coupled with a superiority complex concerning people of other species, made him a serious concern for the Hunters.

Xenophobia was common amongst most of the Cetatian people, thanks to Kone subtly encouraging it as a cultural norm over the generations. They all were taught that Humans, long ago, used the Cetatians as slaves until Kone had fought to free them. People who grew up in the Second Density learned about how Kone thwarted the Humans' plans to subjugate their people and then worked hard over the next few generations, sending spies into the First Density to remove any records of the Cetatians until the Humans' descendants thought of them as fabricated stories. A myth. But the Hunters had a code which they all made their personal constitution. This code respected life and was incompatible with Samuel's prejudice. Not to mention his tendency to lead with his emotions.

Derek Sahmbo, at one point, had discussed other paths for which Samuel might be a better fit. "The Commandos would certainly accept you," Derek suggested.

Shaking his head, Samuel said, "No. As much as I would love the action, they're too…" He took a long pause while trying to think of the right word. "…cold," he said at last. The Commandos followed orders and sometimes, those orders would require acts that even the brash young Samuel saw as atrocious. But once a Commando, refusing an order was not an option.

"The Proctors, perhaps," Derek observed Samuel's demeanor as he considered the suggestion and could tell that this also didn't sit well with the potential Hunter.

Samuel shook his head. "It seems like lately, their ranks are being filled by people just as psychotic." Derek saw signs in Samuel's body language that were unusual for him. Signs of self-doubt. "I don't want to become like that."

Pleased with Samuel's self-awareness, Derek decided to place him under Sabrina's tutelage. Having won some hard-fought battles with her own emotions, Sabrina worked with Samuel. Teaching him meditations and mental discipline. To where he began making noticeable progress. She also helped him make dramatic improvements in his detective skills. Samuel worked hard to gain self-control. Often, he was more exhausted from holding himself back than any amount of physical effort, but as the months went by, Samuel became less volatile and more the man that he intended himself to be. Until he finally earned his place amongst the Hunters.

The group continued for the mountain, and the icelot looked in their direction. He stood up, stretched his front limbs forward and hopped down to the ice.

Vedant observed the cat turn and walk along the sensor ring near the mountain. "Turn off the scanner. Turn everything off and get behind those rocks," he said, pointing at some boulders.

The icelot moved within eight feet of a motion sensor, and a signal was sent. Out on the ice, at the center of the sensor ring, a white cylinder rose above the surface. The shutters on the top opened, and a softball-sized sphere rose ten feet into the air. A lens cover rotated open while the sphere sped in the direction of the cat. The probe was there in a couple of seconds, scanning the feline that triggered the sensors.

From the boulders, Vedant and the others observed as the cat glanced up at the surveillance device and then returned his gaze forward, moving closer to the mountain. He was familiar with this object and paid no attention to it. Although, as a cub, he would leap up and try to swat it from time to time. The probe made its scan, spun around and shot back out over the tundra. It came to a halt above the cylinder, lowered inside, and the shutter closed as the cylinder retracted beneath the ice.

The cat jumped onto a rocky ledge, walked around a jutting section of stone and disappeared. The group waited a few more minutes and then followed Vedant's lead, keeping away from the sensor ring as they approached where the cat had vanished. They rounded the jutted section of rock and found a crack on the other side that opened into a hole four feet high and three feet wide, large enough for the cat to comfortably fit.

Holding the scanner up, Jake switched it on and read the screen. "Nothing in there right now."

One of the Dwarves looked at Vedant, who nodded. Rudge reached up, pulled back his hood and donned a headband with a light attached to the front. The other Dwarf, Balgar, attached a rope to Rudge with a D-ring and tugged to verify that it was secure before attaching the other end to himself. Rudge hunched down and walked into the opening.

The light revealed to Rudge the thirty-degree downward slope of a tunnel, consistent with the size of the cave opening. After fifteen feet, Rudge could stand up straight, and the tunnel continued to widen. Another ten feet in and he saw the sides and top of the tunnel come to an end, but the floor continued. As Rudge made his way to the end of the tunnel, it flared out into a wider cave that continued to slope down.

"There's plenty of standing room in here," he said. "The ceiling's about fifteen feet up, and the slope is gentle here, though it's getting steeper."

"Acknowledged," Vedant replied on the comm. He gave a nod to Jake, who clipped a tether to Balgar and gave it a tug. Balgar donned a headlamp and walked into the tunnel.

Rudge moved deeper into the cave when Balgar arrived in the larger area. "The floor rises back up," he said when his headlamp illuminated the end of the cave. The floor abruptly rose at a steep angle, but when Rudge looked up, he saw that it fell a couple feet short of the ceiling.

Balgar came and stood alongside Rudge when Jake entered the cave. "Ready to see the other side?" he asked Rudge with a grin.

"Not yet, Balgar," Vedant said over the comm. "Wait for the rest of us."

Five minutes later, all seven were inside the cave, and Balgar peeked into the crevice near the ceiling. The light from his headlamp spilled into the space. "Looks like it drops off after four feet."

With a nod, Vedant said, "Proceed."

Balgar climbed into the crevice and slid on his belly to where he could see down the other side. "It drops back down to the floor's level, and the cave continues on."

Rudge and Jake, both being tethered to Balgar, went in next. When Balgar made his way down to the cave floor, he noticed the subtle difference. Of course, he wasn't surprised by a warmer temperature, but it was just a bit warmer than he would have predicted.

The rest of the group came through the crevice after passing their gear and began exploring the cave. It continued downward and steepened as they made their way deeper into the mountain.

"Alright," Balgar said, "this is definitely warmer than it should be."

"Agreed," Rudge said.

"What's that?" Alunareth asked, pointing down to where the cave turned.

"Interesting," Rudge said as he, Alunareth, Quinton and Balgar shut off their lights. Vedant told Samuel and Jake to follow suit. Now they could all see the blue glow coming from around the bend. With caution, the Dwarves led the rest down to the corner to find bioluminescent mushrooms growing out from the rocky walls. The average stem length was five inches long, and the girth was about the size of a thumb. Some of them had flat, unremarkable caps, but the caps of those emitting light were folded upward. The air was noticeably warmer, and there were some insects buzzing around.

"Smells like a hint of dung," Quinton remarked.

Samuel observed as a fly landed on the flat cap of a mushroom. The cap snapped shut, and veins along the underside of the cap and stem began to glow a reddish purple. "Wow!" he exclaimed with a smile.

"I've never seen carnivorous fungus before." They all watched as the glow intensified over the next couple of minutes.

Jake, who had held the scanner up to the mushroom through the process, said, "It's an unknown species."

Looking down the cavern, Vedant said, "To us." He turned back toward the group, "I wonder how many people, if any, may be down below."

With a shrug and a smile, Jake said, "Let's go find out."

Continuing, they followed the cave as it twisted and turned deeper into the mountain. The air became warmer, and the mushrooms were larger and more numerous, to the point where they could see comfortably. The slope became steeper in some areas and in another, there was an abrupt vertical drop, requiring them to jump among some rocky ledges. It wasn't long before they encountered vegetation and even a couple of rodents.

The humidity was rising when Jake checked the scanner and said, "We're below ground level now." The temperature was now sixty-seven degrees, and the vegetation had steadily increased the further down they went.

"It's getting brighter," Rudge commented right before turning a bend to see where the tunnel ended. Bright light was spilling into the exit from a massive cavern.

"It looks like sunlight," Jake commented.

Vedant nodded and said, "It sure does."

Balgar looked out the end of the tunnel and turned around to face the others with a grin. "I haven't seen a new one this big since," he shrugged his shoulders with a chuckle, "well…ever!"

Rudge looked out next, and his smile matched Balgar's. "Oh, you guys are gonna love this!"

The rest of the group stepped to the mouth of the cave to see they were standing on the conifer-covered hillside of a giant cavern. From their vantage point, they could see woods, plains, a river, a lake, some smaller ponds and a large hill that rose up from the center of the cavern, narrowed halfway up and then flared back out, merging with the cavern ceiling to form an enormous stalagmite. Along the ceiling, a thick mist billowed and glowed with brilliant yellow light, illuminating and warming the cavern. This world under the world was teaming with life as the song of birds carried through the air, and a herd of ungulates could be seen grazing on the plain.

A comfortably cool breeze swept by, carrying moisture and the smell of vegetation to mix with the aroma of pine in the immediate area.

Jake was looking at the glowing clouds and asked, "How is this possible?" He looked down at the edge of the forest to see a large animal stepping out from the trees and pointing. "Or that!" Everyone followed his finger to see a mammoth walking onto the plain.

All seven of them watched the magnificent creature they believed to be extinct with amazement. The entire cavern was surreal, and even the Dwarves, who had seen similar underground environments, were in awe at the sheer size of the place. They could see the northern wall of the cavern in the distance beyond the stalagmite, which was pale in color compared to the gray hues of the southern wall.

The eastern end was the same gray hue as the southern wall but faded to pale toward the north. The cavern stretched on to the west for miles and continued beyond their view. The Alfan could both make out lines of color on the northern wall. Alunareth turned and informed the others while Quinton opened his pack to retrieve a pair of binoculars.

"Many lines…many colors." Quinten lowered his binoculars, turned to the Dwarves and smiled. "That stone is rich with veins of crystal." He handed the binoculars to Rudge.

Taking a look for himself, Rudge exclaimed, "That's pretty…and the wall's been worked!"

"Now look down and along the treetops."

Lowering his angle of view, Rudge noticed some rooftops peeking out from between the trees. He slowly turned left, scanning westward along the northern edge to see a clearing further down with more houses and a small plume of smoke rising from the village center. "People *are* living here! What an incredible find!"

Quinton found a good spot near the bottom of the slope, and the group set up camp. After the tents were set, Jake unpacked a round metallic object one and a half feet wide, seven inches tall and it was flat on the top and bottom.

"We're going to go scout the area," Samuel said to Vedant.

Vedant looked to Samuel and Alunareth, gave a nod and said, "Don't let the locals see you." He turned back toward Jake. "That's probably the best spot."

After placing the arctic gear inside a tent, Samuel turned to Alunareth. "Ready, Al?"

With a smile, Alunareth replied, "Yes. Another adventure awaits."

Vedant looked again as the pair disappeared into the woods and smiled, thinking again of how far Samuel had come. Once ruled by his prejudice and now there he was, a Cetatian Hunter working side by side with his best friend, an Alfan Ranger. A friendship that was tested a couple of months ago when Samuel started dating Fiona, Alunareth's sister.

Jake had the device ready to go, and Vedant said, "Activate it."

CHAPTER 13
Light As a Feather

Eighth Density. Niflheim

She sat upon a throne of skulls with her chin resting in her palm, glaring at the floor.

"You look happy."

Hel lifted her eyes to see the source of the sarcastic comment. Baphomet walked up to the Goddess of Death. "Funny," she spat more than said.

"Still thinking about Tir na nOg?"

"Bast wasn't supposed to be there!" She snapped as her eyes flashed with anger. "I wanted to send Tuweltha a message. That crazy cat lady wasn't part of this."

"But the Powries have made a couple more runs at the palace this past week. That probably gets under Tuweltha's skin."

Hel shook her head. "They were easily pushed back by the palace Guardsmen. We can't risk putting them into the palace ourselves again. Odin meant it when he threatened us with Tartarus."

"So, why don't we move them in there without him knowing it was us?"

Hel looked at Baphomet like he was the biggest idiot on Earth. "Fool! As soon as the mystical bindings on the palace are removed, Odin will know it was the work of a god, and he will come right back to us." She sighed. *Why did I fall for him? Yes, he's fun, but he's an idiot!*

"Which is why we go talk to Molech," Baphomet replied with a smile. "Ask him to put that little gift you gave him to use." The Archangel's feather could be used to transport all the Powries into the palace without undoing the bindings, and no hint as to how it was accomplished.

"That would work, but he'd never go for it. He's been careful for too long to risk exposing himself right now."

"I know, and it makes him restless," Baphomet said with a smile. "So, perhaps Molech's best friend could convince him to let it be borrowed and returned as soon as the transport is done."

With a scoff, Hel said, "What makes you think he'll agree to that?"

"Because I already asked him," he replied with a smug smile and held up the feather. For the first time in days, Hel's face lit up. "So," Baphomet asked with a wicked grin, "Do you wanna have some fun? Do you wanna really hurt Tuweltha?"

Hel's grin matched Baphomet's. *Maybe he's a little smarter than I've been giving him credit for.*

Fourth Density. Og Palace Training Fields, Tir na nOg

Losing her grip on one of the wooden katanas, Sabrina brought her free hand to the other and tried to defend herself from the flurry of Flashipor's attacks, but with only the one sword against two, the experienced Weapons Master overwhelmed her in short order, tripping and sending her flat on her back with the tip of a wooden sword held to her throat. Again. But each time Flashipor defeated the Hunter, she learned and became more difficult for the Elf to best. And this time, he was actually winded.

Pulling his sword back, he tucked it under his other arm and extended a hand. "Well done. You do catch on quickly."

Accepting the hand, Sabrina stood to her feet. "Thank you. In my line of work, I must always be trying to improve."

"And honing your already impressive skills might be part of it, but if you truly want to improve, we should address your weaknesses."

"Such as?"

Looking Sabrina in the eyes, Flashipor's expression became serious, almost stern. "You lack balance."

"What?!" Elizabeth blurted. "But she can do flips and climb things just as well as you guys."

Flashipor shook his head with a chuckle. "No, not physical balance." He turned back to the Hunter. "Personal balance."

"What do you mean?"

"When did you last spend time with a friend?"

"Just last week, I spent a day with Chelsea and Sakura."

"Doing what?" he asked, raising an eyebrow.

"I helped them decide on some new weapons and gear that would suit how they operate." Before he could respond, she added, "And a couple days before that, I sparred with Zahra, and then we worked on her tracking skills."

Flashipor shook his head. "When do you ever sit down with them and socialize?"

"I sit down with them; we drink tea and talk," she replied.

"Talk about what? Besides your careers as Hunters?" Sabrina said nothing because she had no idea what to say. "You are not your job. You are a person. When the assignment is done and you're not working, what do you do?"

"Rest."

"Sabrina Carmen, what is it that *you* want?"

"To stop Kone's tyranny," she said with conviction.

"Why?"

The question seemed absurd to Sabrina. "What do you mean, why? We all want that."

"Yes," Flashipor responded. "We do. But then what? Let's say Kone is defeated and there's no hunts on your schedule. You now have time for yourself. What do you do with it?"

"That's a perfect opportunity to continue practicing…"

The Weapons Master waved his hands and shook his head, "No, no, no. That's the problem! You lack balance. He stepped closer to her; this time, his expression was deadly serious when his eyes bore into hers. "You have no life." He took a step back and crossed his arms, trying to read the Hunter's face as his words sank in. "You've probably trained nearly as much as I have. And I'm over three hundred years old."

"Well, I don't have that kind of lifespan and can't waste whatever opportunities that time allows me."

"But you do have a lifespan. And in that limited lifespan, you need to take the time to actually live it. So, putting the job aside, I ask you again, Sabrina Carmen, what do you want?"

Sabrina was at a loss for words, but Haley couldn't help but notice a twinge in the Hunter's gut. A longing that was almost painful. "That right there," the farmgirl called out. "What is that?"

"What's what?" Sabrina asked.

Placing her hands down near her stomach, Haley said. "Right here. What's making you feel this right here?"

"I…I…"

"This is something you want. What is it?" Haley asked again as a tear rolled down her right cheek at the same time as one ran down Sabrina's.

"You can tell us," Elizabeth added.

After taking a deep inhale through her nose, Sabrina held it for a moment as her eyes misted over, then finally blurted, "I want to be a mother!" After a couple of more breaths and teardrops, she said it again with a calmer and more controlled tone. "I want to be a mother." She lowered her head and closed her eyes for a moment as she tried to recenter herself when Haley's arms wrapped around her in a hug. A second set of arms from Elizabeth came next. Still feeling awkward, Sabrian extracted her arms, put them around their shoulders, and squeezed as Nomad brushed against the Hunter's legs.

Nodding his head with a smile, Flashipor said, "Now, we're getting somewhere."

A half-hour later, they had finished training for the day and were preparing to walk back to the palace. Once there, they planned to use the port depot to go back to Glaid when Flashipor removed a sheathed blade from his pack and held it out to the Hunter. "You mentioned a little problem dealing with a demon. This should help if you ever encounter one again. And with the likes of Powries attacking us periodically, it is more of an inevitability than a likelihood."

"What is it?" she asked, unsheathing and inspecting the blade, which looked like a simple dagger but appeared to be made more from stone than metal.

"It's a fordriva blade. All the Rangers and Guardsmen carry these." Flashipor explained, "Fordriva is a mineral that was discovered by the Dwarves. They manufacture these blades for us. It is disruptive to some forms of magick and can pierce a demon's hide."

"Thank you," Sabrina said and then her mind went back to the encounter with Hel. "How effective is it against gods?"

"It's not," he answered. "It might sting some of the less powerful gods, but that's the most that you could expect."

"Could it be bolstered by an enchantment or something?" Elizabeth asked. "It would be nice to have something that could work against that skinny lady."

Shaking his head, Flashipor answered, "No. Fordriva cannot be enchanted."

As they walked back to the palace, Elizabeth asked, "So why do the Cetatians want to control the First Density? Is pretty much everybody in the Second Density just okay with it?"

"For the most part, they don't care. We've all been taught that Humans used to enslave the Cetatians, so the people don't think much about Kone taking over." Sabrina explained. "Although, some of us don't believe it. Hunters have been keeping records since 300 AD, and we have nothing that hints toward this ever happening. But it's been so ingrained that most of the people don't care what happens to your race."

Flashipor looked at Sabrina with an expression of surprise and confusion. "Your race?" he asked. "So, you don't know."

"Know what?" the Hunter asked.

"Cetatians and Humans are the same species."

Sabrina's mouth opened, but no sound came out. Only stunned silence. She thought back to the syringes, now understanding why they were only saline solution. "I…and I never figured that out?!"

"Nobody's perfect," Haley said and got a big smile on her face, adding, "After all, you're only Human."

They were near the entrance to the port depot, and Flashipor recognized one of the women who was nearby. "Perfect timing. Maeve," he called out, and the Alfan woman approached. She was five-foot-five with long red hair and deep green eyes.

"Yes?"

"Everyone, this is Maeve. Maeve, would you please lift your hair and show them."

She turned her back to the others and pulled the thick, wavy hair to the side, revealing a secondary pigment on the back of her neck that matched her eyes. At her color line, the green became a filamentary pattern and faded into her white skin.

"That is so cool!" Haley exclaimed. "And you're so pretty!"

"Thank you," Maeve said with an appreciative smile as she dropped her hair back down.

"She is not Cetatian but was conceived in the Second Density." Flashipor looked back at Sabrina. "The secondary pigment is not a Cetatian trait, but an environmental one."

"Wow," Sabrina softly whispered. "I wonder if Papi knows."

"Aren't we supposed to meet him today?" Elizabeth asked.

"Yes. He said he'll meet us at the portgates." She looked at Haley, "You'll like him. He, like your father, is an engineer."

Manny stepped out of the portgate, and the vortex closed behind him. Some Elves and a couple of Dwarves were standing guard. Gwening stepped forward to greet him. "Mr. Suarez, how are you today?"

"Good," he answered with a charismatic smile. "How are you?"

"Well, thank you. What brings you to the palace?"

"I'm supposed to meet my daughter here. We've barely seen each other since we arrived."

Gwening said, "She should be done with her training by now. She'll probably be here any moment."

Right on cue, Flashipor walked in, followed by Haley, Elizabeth, Sabrina and Nomad.

"There she is," he said with a smile. "Sabrina!"

"¡Hola, Papi!" she replied, going right up to and hugging him. She turned to the others with a rare smile, "This is my papi. Papi, this is Flashipor, Haley, Elizabeth and Nomad."

"Hi, everybody." He greeted them all with a handshake, but then Flashipor, with a schedule to keep, excused himself and left through a gate.

Manny reached down and gave the friendly Nomad a scratch on the head. As Flashipor left, Neil and Maggie came down the stairs and into the depot. "Hey, girls!" Maggie called out.

"Hi, Mom," Elizabeth said. "How did it go?"

Since fully connecting with their fields, the Alfan offered to teach them how to use their newfound abilities. "Good," said Maggie. They really know their stuff here."

Introductions were made, Neil and Manny started talking about circuits and Maggie's eyes glazed over. "I'm going to head back to town," she said. "Elizabeth, are you and Haley coming?"

"Can we stay here with Neil a little bit longer?"

"Okay, but not too late."

"When do you want her home?" Neil asked.

"Two hours."

"I'll be there, Mom," Elizabeth said.

They hugged, said "Bye," and Maggie disappeared into the portgate.

Things were calm as they chatted, and the Guardsmen were patrolling up and down the length of the port depot. Pacing would be more accurate. There was no reason to patrol the quiet depot as they could see the entire room from any point, but with so little traffic coming in and out, they were becoming restless and walked along inspecting the portgates just for something to do.

Amongst the geode portgates, one had a round metallic device attached to the side at the bottom that was one and a half feet wide and seven inches tall. The object began to make a soft hum, which caught the attention of a couple Alfan.

Their eyes went wide as one asked the other, "Could it really be?"

A small blue-white spark appeared at the center of the object's flat surface. It spun and opened into a vortex that engulfed the geode and then closed, leaving an empty space next to its mate.

Second Density

The little blue-white spark at the center of the beacon's flat surface opened, moved away from the device and then closed, leaving a large geode in its place. The flat surface of the port beacon attached to the geode was pressed flush against the flat surface of the one at Jake's feet.

Jake turned to Vedant and said with a smile, "I'll bet folks are already gathering on the other end to hear what you have to say."

"We'll continue getting situated here," Balgar said.

Vedant nodded and turned to Quinton. "Keep watch while I give them a report."

"I will."

"And Rudge," Vedant said, catching the Dwarf's attention. He smiled and asked, "You're going to start working on your beef stew?"

Matching the Hunter's smile, Rudge said, "Right away!"

"I should be back shortly," Vedant drew his bolt pistol and fired a blast into the geode. The burst of energy was amplified by the crystals, and a vortex opened.

Fourth Density

The purple crystals began to crackle with blue-white energy. The arching converged in the center of the geode, and a vortex opened. The Alfan smiled and lowered their arms when Vedant stepped out from the natural portgate.

Gwening came running, "Have you found it?"

"We've definitely found something."

"Vedant!" Manny shouted with exuberance.

He heard the voice and looked to see Sabrina and Manny. "Well, this is a surprise."

Manny and Vedant clasped hands, then the former Hunter-Ralt turned to Sabrina, and they gripped each other's right shoulders in their customary greeting, which transitioned into a hug.

"It's been too long," Sabrina said. They released their embrace, and she introduced Vedant to Haley, Elizabeth, and Neil, then explained about the Hunters' evacuation from the Second Density.

Vedant listened to her story and nodded. "It was only a matter of time."

"Where have you been lately?" Manny inquired.

"I've been busy on the biggest hunt of my life." Vedant's confidant smile grew bigger when he added, "And I think I've found it."

Manny's eyes went wide. "You mean…the *big* one?"

"Yes."

Gwening's smile widened. "This is fantastic news!"

"I have not confirmed it yet," Vedant clarified. "We've found an inhabited place cut off from the rest of the world, but we have not yet made our presence known. We do not know if it is indeed Atlantis."

Haley's eyes went wide, and Elizabeth whispered, "Atlantis?" The girls looked at each other. "Cool!" they both gushed in unison.

"Meow."

Vedant looked down at the cat and smiled. "And who are you?" he asked while reaching down to pet him.

"This is Nomad," Elizabeth answered.

Vedant stood back up straight and turned to Sabrina. "You would be proud of Samuel. He's part of the team exploring the caverns right now."

"Caverns? Wouldn't Atlantis be somewhere in the ocean?" Neil asked.

"No, it's beneath the ice of Antarctica." He began to tell them about the caverns beneath the continent's surface, the ecosystem and the village they saw in the distance.

"A mammoth!" Haley's eyes were wide with excitement. "I wonder what else could be there. Maybe a sabretooth tiger!"

"Perhaps," Vedant said with a shrug. "I need to give a full report to…"

White lights flashed everywhere, interrupting Vedant's words, and the depot was filled with Powries.

Second Density. Meelyhn

"The flora is much like a South African forest," Samuel said as he and Alunareth continued along a game trail. "The fauna, on the other hand…"

"I'm still astonished by the mammoth," Alunareth commented.

"Yeah," Samuel agreed.

Heading north from camp, the pair were making their way toward the giant stalagmite that had the same dark gray hue as the cavern's southern wall, which was muddled by the green of moss.

"Do you think they like peanuts?" Samuel asked with a smirk.

"We might get to find out," Alunareth replied with a chuckle. Samuel started to chuckle, too, but they both came to an abrupt stop to stare at a point on the ground.

"Or just ask the locals," Samuel added.

It was faint, and most would have never noticed, but Hunters and Rangers have trained their eyes to see such things as an almost worn-away footprint, a reminder that they need to stay alert.

"Dang right, the whole stick! That's what makes it so savory," Rudge said as he finished cooking the rest of the bacon. Don't forget the brown mustard, either."

"How much?" Jake asked. Rudge turned and looked Jake directly in the eyes, held the gaze, but didn't say a word. Jake nodded, "All of it, of course." Rudge nodded and continued breaking up the bacon while Jake tossed the stick of butter into the cooking pot.

"So, how is all this possible? Especially the…sun-clouds?" Jake asked while looking up toward the ceiling. "I'm a geologist, and I've got no clue what can make all this work."

"Bugs," Rudge answered with a grin.

Jake chuckled, "No, really. Do you know how that is happening?"

"Yeah." The Dwarf chuckled. "It really is bugs. Give me a second." He placed the bacon in the pot, stirred it thoroughly and placed the lid on top. "And now we wait." Rudge walked around the pot and sat next to Jake. "We know of areas like this in the Third and Fourth Densities. The higher air pressure allows for a thicker mist, acting as a cloud cover. Bugs in the cavern make their sounds in a certain pitch, and when the soundwaves move through the cloud, it produces light and warmth."

Jake, looking confused, said, "That sounds like sonoluminescence."

"Exactly."

"But that would require an actual body of water. It shouldn't be able to work with a billowing mist."

"Right…in the First Density. Each density is slightly less dense than the previous. Our senses can't tell the difference, but…"

"Speak for yourself," Quinten interjected from across the camp with a smirk.

"Alright," Rudge conceded. "Anyone who isn't an Elf can't tell the difference, but there is a difference nonetheless. And it's enough of one that can allow for this," he finished, pointing at the 'sky.'

With a smile, Jake said, "So many new things to learn." He knew his field well, but since he made an unexpected trip into the Dvwargarian realm, he's been on an adventure of learning lessons about worlds within his own that he never knew existed. The first of which is how grateful he should be that he stumbled into the Third Density instead of the Second.

As soon as the invading Gnomes appeared, they charged at whoever was standing closest to them. Gwening drew his sword in an instant and took out the first goblin. The Portmaster and the Guardsmen moved quickly to meet the challenge, as did Vedant and Sabrina.

Neil, for the first time, unleashed mystical bolts that had enough potency to take down opponents. Haley conjured her potato gun and began unleashing blasts while Elizabeth flicked the lighter and started throwing orbs of fire.

Their response was quick and almost effective, but the sheer number of Powries was overwhelming and couldn't be held off.

Vedant turned and fired a bolt into the geode. "This way, he shouted as he turned his pistol back on the goblins and continued firing to cover their escape. Haley, Elizabeth, Sabrina, Neil, Manny and Nomad all hurried through the vortex as the horde closed in. Gwening moved with all the grace and agility of an Alfan, slicing down goblins with speed and precision.

The Guardsmen were doing the same, but the crowd closed in. One of the Guardsmen, a Dwarf, held up his shied and charged, screaming as he plowed through a group of the smaller opponents. He knocked them over like a bulldozer, and the other Guardsmen finished them off, just for the fallen Powries to be replaced by more Powries.

Gwening twirled and sliced in a captivating dance of death, cutting them down one after another until a mace connected with his ribs. He stumbled to the ground, and the last thing he saw was the sharp end of a polearm piercing down to his face.

Witnessing the sudden death of his friend, Vedant became enraged. He dove into the crowd, grabbing the closest goblin and with strength unexpected of one his age, picked the Gnome up and swung him, knocking three others to the ground. He fired at them, then threw his arm up, redirecting the momentum of a stabbing polearm and grabbed the assailant to bash him into more Gnomes. Vedant and the remaining Guardsmen took down many Powries, but it didn't change that they were outnumbered.

The portgates opened, and the Humans from Glaid came rushing through to join the fray as Admiral Book's SEAL team, Hunters, and the Seabees from the undersea base came rushing in from the training fields. Dunks, Harry and Ryan were also among them.

Dunks saw Gwening's body and also became enraged, throwing himself into a wall of Gnomes while swinging his war hammer. Harry and Ryan were armed with bolt pistols, and the Naval warriors did what they did best. The battle wasn't only in the port depot but the entire palace. The conflict lasted only a half hour, but before all was done, many Elves, Dwarves and a few Humans fell that day.

Derek found Vedant severely injured, Dunks was covered in Gnomish blood, and Harry and Ryan were searching frantically for their daughters.

Staggeth, who had survived the entire assault, heard Harry asking about the girls. The Dwarf pointed and said, "They escaped into that portgate before it was destroyed." Harry followed Staggeth's finger to the geode that was broken into pieces during the battle.

CHAPTER 14
The Big City Life

Second Density. Meelyhn, Atlantis

Haley and Elizabeth ran out to the other side and were standing in a camp. Rudge and Jake stood up and drew their bolt pistols but then hesitated, not wanting to point their arms at the two girls. Nomad, Sabrina and Manny were coming through behind them, followed by Neil.

"Who are you guys?" Rudge demanded. "And where's Vedant?"

Haley and Elizabeth turned around and saw the vortex close. Sabrina said, "We were attacked by the Powries. He was right behind us."

Balgar stepped out of a tent with a pistol, ready to see what the commotion was about. "Powries?"

"Yeah," Elizabeth said. "A whole bunch of them." She turned toward Haley to see her looking up. The young mystic followed her gaze and saw the radiant clouds above. "Whoa!"

"Clear the gate," Balgar huffed. The others stepped aside, and the Dwarf fired a blast into the crystals, which crackled and then nothing. "Oh, no!" He fired another shot with the same result.

"That's…not good," Jake said.

"We've got to get them outta there," Haley said and tried firing a blast at the geode herself, but it was just another crackle, followed by nothing.

"Don't bother," Rudge said with a sigh. "The other geode's probably broken, and…did you just fire a kitten?"

"We need to find a way back to help them," Sabrina said. "Papi," she pointed to the port beacons, "can you do something with those?"

Looking at the beacon that was used to bring the geode, he shook his head. "Not when both halves are already here."

"But that's not a normal beacon," Rudge said.

"I know," Manny answered. "I built it."

"So, you must be Manny Suarez," Quinten said. "And I'm guessing that you're Hunter Sabrina Carmen."

"Yes." they both answered.

"I am Quinten. Vedant has spoken highly of you both." He turned to Jake. "Call our scouts back."

Proper introductions were made while waiting for Samuel and Alunareth's return. Haley was taking in the sight of the place and asked, "How did you guys get here?"

"We followed an icelot," Quinten answered. He told them about following the cat into the mountain tunnels and that they were waiting for Vedant's return. Now, they didn't even know if he was alive.

The scouts returned, and Samuel, although happy to see his mentor, was not thrilled with the news. "We don't have the supplies to make it across the ice again."

"Then we're going to have to find them," Quinten said. "And that probably means meeting the locals."

"We were down by the village," Alunareth explained. "They're raising cattle there and despite the simple appearance of their buildings, seem to have some advanced technologies."

Quinten pointed to Samuel and Sabrina, "Perhaps you two would be the best candidates to break the ice."

"Where's the village?" Elizabeth asked.

"It's across the cavern," Alunareth answered, pointing in its direction.

Elizabeth looked where he was pointing, but they were near the bottom of the hillside and couldn't see it through the trees.

"Hmmm…" Haley thought for a moment, then smiled, turning to a tree and started to climb. Elizabeth followed her up.

"What are you doing?" Jake asked.

"Getting a closer look," Elizabeth explained.

They saw Haley climbing up the bark like a ladder, and Elizabeth grabbed a branch and pulled herself up with ease. Neil engaged the thrusters in his PJs, and small distortions in the air could be seen around different points of his body as he began to rise alongside the climbing girls.

"He can fly?!" Jake blurted.

"They have nanotech suits. More advanced than anything we've got," Sabrina explained. As she said that, Neil and the girls conjured their helmets and used the HUD to magnify the view for a closer look.

They could see the rooftops of houses through the trees and activated their scanners. Haley took out her phone and tossed it down to the ground. It landed and projected a holographic image of what was displayed in her visor for the others to see.

"That's impressive," Quinten commented.

Haley climbed a little higher and got a good angle to a clearing in the village. She could see the cattle ranch. Neil and Elizabeth both shifted for better views. "Hey, Beth!" Haley whispered, which was unnecessary because her voice was only transmitted to Elizabeth's helmet. "Check this out."

What Haley was seeing appeared in Elizabeth's HUD, and both girls smiled. He looked their age and was doing work at the ranch. Brown hair and brown eyes, he turned around, and they could see his brown secondary pigment that speckled at the color line. They watched him pick up containers and set them on a hover dolly.

"He's cute!" Elizabeth said.

They returned to the ground to see Sabrina with her arms crossed and a stern look on her face. "Are you done boy-watching?"

Haley's face dropped with shock, then her eyes opened with the realization that she had forgotten about casting her view to the holographic image from the phone on the ground, and everybody saw her zoom in.

"Umm…" She dropped her head and let out a long, slow "Yeah."

Elizabeth giggled until Sabrina's stern gaze fell upon her, too.

"Both of you," the empathic Hunter said. "This is serious. We can't afford to clown around in these circumstances. You've both listened very well over the last week. This is not the time to stop. Understood?"

"Yes," they both said.

Sabrina turned to Neil. "Come with me and Samuel. Your equipment could come in handy."

"Alright," Neil answered.

"What do you want us to do?" Elizabeth asked.

"Help them with guarding the camp. Ranger Quinten is in charge."

After leaving the camp at the bottom of the conifer-covered hillside, The three of them made their way across the cavern through the woods and past a large pond by the stalagmite. Continuing across, they went through a heavily wooded area to the other side, where the trees thinned out into a clearing that held the village along the cavern wall. Here, the wall of the cavern was pale, and they now had a clear view of the different colored veins of crystal marbled throughout the white rock.

Neil was scanning the area and looking at his phone, "Looks like the houses all have electricity and some advanced technology."

The buildings were mostly single-story houses, though a few had dormers on their roofs, suggesting an attic room or loft. Made of the same wood as the timber in the forest, some of the houses were log cabins, and others were plank-sided frames.

The PJs detected that all the houses had electronic objects that sent signals back and forth to a large data infrastructure that operated the same as the First Density's internet. "Looks like they have remote-control washing machines."

There were some people going about. A man sat in a chair on the front porch of a house, working with some kind of tablet. Neil conjured his helmet and used the sensors to listen to the man as he mumbled something about proofs and equations.

In an open shed attached to the next house, a man was tinkering with some kind of machine when a woman came running out of the house and bolted for the shed. "Look at this! If we change the gasket just a bit, it should run without slipping!"

The man took the tablet and looked at the screen.

"Run the simulation!" she insisted.

He did so, and his face went from one of interest to a widening smile. He started to laugh and exclaimed, "That's it! Thanks, Crumpet!"

"Crumpet?" Neil silently mouthed.

Two men and a woman were walking down the pathway past the houses discussing physics, and there was also the boy who had caught Haley and Elizabeth's attention, working on an all-terrain vehicle.

Neil dismissed his helmet and turned to the Hunters. "They all seem to be," he shrugged, "really smart."

"So," Samuel asked, "how shall we break the ice?"

Sabrina turned her head and looked to the village and then back to Samuel. "I'll go first, and you two stay hidden while I size them up. If it goes well, I'll give you the signal to come out. But Neil, I want you to hold back until last. If something goes wrong, you can fly back to camp and regroup with the others."

"Okay," Neil said. "Are you guys still getting my video feed?"

"Yeah," came Haley's reply over the comm. Everyone at the camp was watching on the holographic screen projected by Haley's phone, seeing the live feed from Neil's PJs. They were all having another helping of Rudge's beef stew. Haley eagerly took another bite. "Mmmm." *This is so good!*

Serge was engrossed in the information on the tablet's screen, going over his students' theories. He had been on the porch for an hour, evaluating their work, and his neck was getting stiff. He reached up with his right hand and rubbed the back of his neck, massaging along the blue secondary pigment and lifted his head to stretch the muscles just in time to notice a woman stepping out from the edge of the woods. He started to drop his eyes back down to the screen before he snapped back up, looking at the stunning woman with surprise and confusion.

"Uh…who are you?" He turned his head toward his neighbor's house. "Hey, Rodge! Are we getting a new arrival today?"

Rodge and Bernice both poked their heads out of the shed. "What are you talking about?" They saw Sabrina standing by the pathway and were just as shocked to see a stranger standing there. "Oh, hi," Rodge said. "I guess so?"

His wife walked out to greet Sabrina. "Hi, I'm Bernice. This is my husband Rodge, and that gruff but not-so-bad gentleman on the porch is Serge."

"Hello," Sabrina answered.

"Don't worry. I know this can be overwhelming, but life here is actually pretty good. Where did Kone take you from?"

"Take me?"

"Yeah. Where did you live before Kone brought you here? And what is your expertise?"

"And why weren't we told about you?" Serge grumbled. "We don't have a place set up yet and…" He paused with a sudden realization. "Did you just come out of the woods?"

"Yes."

Rodge stepped forward. "Ma'am, did Kone bring you here?"

"No. I'm not here intentionally."

"Then how did you get here?" Serge asked, now more curious than bothered.

Sabrina shook her head. "That's a long story, but right now, I need to find my way back."

"Sweetie, I'm sorry, but…what's your name?"

"Sabrina."

Well, Sabrina…pretty name, by the way. I'm afraid no one can leave here. Those who have tried," Bernice's expression turned sad, and she even winced, "it's…just don't try. Nobody deserves that kind of end."

"Where am I?" the Hunter asked.

"This is Meelyhn, a township of Atlantis," Bernice said.

"Is there someone in charge that I can talk to?"

"The governor," Rodge answered.

Serge spoke next. "He's in the city proper, above us," he said while pointing straight up. "But he can't give you permission to leave. He's not even allowed to leave. When Kone brings us here, that's it. We're here. And no one outside of Atlantis is allowed to know we exist. Trying to leave always results in the most unspeakable punishments."

"We can take you up to see him," Bernice explained, "but the best he can do is set you up with housing and try to find where you would fit best into Atlantis." Looking over Sabrina's outfit, she asked, "Are you military?"

"No, I'm a Hunter."

"We've heard about the Hunters but never met one before," Rodge said.

"I can get out," Sabrina said. "I just don't have enough supplies to make it across the tundra."

Serge shook his head. "Others have tried. All have been caught and…Is that how you got here? There's no way you made that trip in by yourself."

"You're right." the Hunter answered. "Samuel, come meet the locals."

Stepping out from the trees, Samuel made his presence known. "Hello, everybody," he said. "Yes, we came across the ice, but we got caught in a storm for days and used most of our provisions."

"How did you find your way down here?" Rodge asked.

"We followed an icelot."

"People have tried to leave that way before," Bernice said, "but this has to be the first time someone arrived this way."

"Why is no one allowed to leave?" Samuel asked. "Why does Kone want to keep Atlantis a secret?"

"The technological advantage," Serge answered. "He takes the best and brightest minds, brings us here, and we work on developing technologies and use what we make for whatever his purposes are. He controls who has access to the tech and who does not."

"Some of us were taken," Rodge added, "but at this point, most of us were born here. The city has been populated for centuries now."

"Is Kone here often?" Sabrina asked.

Serge nodded his head. "About once a month, from what we hear. I've never met him myself. And I don't want to."

"We're not exactly on speaking terms with him ourselves right now," Samuel said dryly.

"Understatement," Elizabeth whispered to Haley, who was still watching back at the camp. Neil's helmet confined his chuckle.

"What happens to those who are caught trying to leave?" Samuel asked.

The three locals looked at each other, apprehensive to speak of such things. "Perhaps," Rodge said, "those questions would be best answered by Governor Swan. We can take you to see him."

Sabrina and Samuel looked at each other for a moment, and Sabrina nodded before turning back to the others. "We have one more person with us."

"Where?" Bernice asked.

"Neil," Samuel called. "Come out and say hello."

Fourth Density. Og Palace, Tir na nOg.

Vedant sat up from the bed a couple moments after the Aflan healer finished her song. He took a moment to orient himself and looked around. "Gwening?" he asked.

She shook her head as a tear escaped her eye.

Swinging his legs to the side, Vedant placed his feet on the floor, and the Elf handed him an apple.

"You need to eat something," she reminded.

"Thank you." He took the apple and took a bite as he headed for the door. "I need to report to King Larriforn."

The door opened before Vedant reached the handle, and the king himself walked in. "You're up! Good to see you, old friend."

Vedant quickly swallowed the chunk of apple in his mouth. "I was just about to come find you. How did the people of the palace fair?"

'We defeated the Powries but suffered many losses. I'm sorry, but Gwening…"

"I've been informed," Vedant said with a hint of mist in his eyes. "He was a good man. And a good friend." He thought about the losses over the last year. From Stanek, whose sacrifice provided key information to finding Atlantis, to Gwening.

"The healers have been busy for the last hour. Many are here from Glaid, gathering our fallen friends and helping with the cleanup," the king said. "I've heard that you have quite the story to tell. A story, from what the healer said, you almost didn't get to tell."

"We have a geode in place…" He stopped speaking when Larriforn shook his head.

"The geode on this end was destroyed during the battle. The ones you helped escape are now trapped on the other side."

Second Density. Atlantis City, Atlantis

Most of the buildings were made of the white stone that was beneath the city. The walls were polished smooth, almost reflective, and the colorful crystal that was marbled through the walls gleamed under the artificial sunlight. A giant geodesic dome, with a series of full-spectrum lights, covered the city proper, separating them from the ice above.

As the day went on, many lights would dim and turn off while others lit up, mimicking the motion of a sun across the sky. The lights simulated the sun moving from the eastern end of the city toward the west and were nearing the end of the daily cycle. The temperature was near constant, right around seventy-five degrees, although it would fluctuate around five degrees up or down. The dome was large enough that there were some clouds and even occasional light rain, but there were also water lines running throughout the dome, allowing scheduled rain showers for their crops.

The city itself was round, with circular roads that looped around the city, forming rings. Moving out from the center were four main roads that intersected the circular roads on their way out toward the city's edge, to the final road circle where most of the buildings were dedicated to maintaining the dome. Lift platforms were numerous and moved on magnetic rails along the dome, giving the people access to replace any faulty lights or allowing for needed repairs.

The tallest buildings were toward the center. The inner rings, which were the smallest, were for administrative purposes, and the next were for research and manufacturing facilities. Continuing outward were some residential rings and a couple of rings for hydroponic farms. These were aided by the river, which was fed by the subglacial lake just outside the city's north.

The water was a consistent sixty degrees as the lake was warmed by the magma flowing beneath the lakebed. The river was dug and circled the entire city at the halfway point. Electric cars traveled the streets and were inductively charged from the paving itself, giving the vehicles a constant power source.

The building at the center of the city, while elevated, was not the tallest but was more akin to a South American ziggurat. A pyramid shape that proceeded in steps, and the flat surface on top was where the city hall resided. The entire city was bright and inviting and would be a wonderful place if it weren't for the iron fist of Kone controlling the populace with fear.

A vehicle came in from one of the cross streets and turned onto the inner ring, stopping in front of the stairs to the ziggurat. The doors opened, and Serge stepped out, followed by Sabrina, Samuel and Neil. Serge turned out to be a pleasant guy, once he got chatting and had a nice conversation with Neil about computer programming during the ride.

A man was standing at the bottom of the steps wearing a uniform similar to the Proctors, except the patch on his arm said Sheriff's Department. Although ruled by Kone, the people of Atlantis were able to choose their authority figures by way of elections, which determined the governor, the sheriff and a few other positions, but most were not interested in pursuing those positions because it meant dealing directly with Kone, who was not liked by the populace.

The uniformed man said, "Hi, I'm Deputy Crig. I've contacted Governor Swan, and he's on his way to meet you. I've gotta say, this is most unusual. As you're probably aware, we don't get tourists. This way," He began walking up the steps, and the others followed. While they made their way up the stairs, a portgate opened inside the city hall, where Governor Swan and Sheriff Gurden stepped into the governor's office. They were in place and waiting when the visitors arrived.

"Welcome," Swan said when they entered. He was 5'7, with dark brown hair that was turning gray, hazel eyes and an orange secondary pigment. "This is unprecedented. No one's ever come here on their own before. I'm Governor Swan, and this is Sheriff Gurden."

"Hello," the sheriff said. He looked at the knife strapped to Sabrina's left leg. "Were you a Commando? I see you have one of our blades."

"No. This blade did belong to a Commando, but I acquired it legally as spoils of the Hunt."

The sheriff nodded. "A Hunter then! I've heard of you guys, just never met one before." His eyes dropped to the coil on her hip, then back to her face. "You wouldn't happen to be Hunter Sabrina Carmen, would you?"

Even the stoic Sabrina could not hide her shock at this question. "Uh, yes."

"Kone has spoken of the Hunters often," Governor Swan explained. "Often with a mix of respect and disdain. He often tells of the amazing work of Hunter-Ralt Sahmbo and complains of how his principles curb his usefulness."

The sheriff added, "The more he complains about his principles, the more it makes me wish that Sahmbo was the Uniralt instead."

Swan let out a heavy sigh, "I've never even met the man, probably never will, but if I could replace Kone with him, I'd do it in a heartbeat." He looked at Samuel next, "So, you're a Hunter too?

"I am."

After the introductions, Swan asked, "So, how did you get here? Did you really trek across the ice?"

"Yes," Samuel answered. "And after making our way here, I've gotta ask, why doesn't anybody ever leave? It can obviously be done."

Both Swan and Gurden lowered their heads, and Sabrina detected a profound sadness, a hurt, that she had picked up from the others back in Meelyhn.

The governor lifted his head back up, a tired look in his eyes, "Kone doesn't allow it, though some have tried. All have been caught. I've been told by Kone that there are sensors on the ice that detect anyone passing the area. When they're pinged, machines come out and detain whoever it was and bring them back down here, where Kone makes a spectacle of dealing with them. He wants to make sure everybody knows what happens if we try to leave."

"And what exactly does happen?" Neil asked.

A heavy sigh of sorrow escaped from Sheriff Gurden, and he said, "Kone takes them, and any immediate family of the offender, to a temple ground in Futola. He physically tortures them at the temple entrance and broadcasts the session to the entire city. Then he takes them inside the temple and continues the torture. We don't know exactly what he does in there, but the screams are horrendous. And then, they fall silent when death finally takes them."

"What kind of temple is this?" Samuel asked.

"It's a temple to a being named Molech. The Great Owel, he's sometimes called," Swan explained. The torture is a ritual sacrifice in the god's name. Men, women and children, it doesn't matter. Kone has no problem putting even the most innocent through this vile ordeal." He leaned forward and whispered his next words with disgust. "In fact, it is said that Molech craves a child's pain most." He leaned back, distraught from the subject. "And that's what awaits anyone trying to escape."

"But," Neil began, "you have some of the most advanced technologies on Earth. Can't you use that to overpower Kone?"

"It has been tried," Gurden said.

"And it ended in the same result as those who have tried to escape," Swan spat in contempt. "Kone has magickal abilities. He held up his hand and shielded himself from a powerful particle beam as if it were nothing more than a laser pointer. He has diminishing frequencies constantly broadcast throughout Atlantis, so none of us can learn to use magick ourselves."

"Some have tried to shut them down," Gurden added, "but he must have something that alerts him because he showed up immediately after and gave the saboteur to Molech."

"Well, we made it past the sensors, and we can do it again, thanks to a cat. Kone is still just one man, and he can't control everything all the time," Samuel said. "When we get back, we can let the whole world know about this, turn the people against him. His rule can only last as long as the populace complies."

"We've learned that this would be a fool's errand. As long as we don't push against his wishes, he allows us to live a decent life, pursuing our interests and ideas. We just have to stay here, and here is not a bad place." Swan continued, "If you want to try making it back across the ice, then best of luck to you. But you could find a new life here, and Kone would probably leave you alone."

Shaking her head, Sabrina said, "No. He and I had a falling out. And he's probably still mad at me for rescuing two children last week from a fate much like what you described at the temple."

A concerned expression made its way onto Swan's face. "Then you might want to keep your head down because Kone is coming here tomorrow."

"And you just might want to let the others know," Gurden said.

"Others?" Samuel asked.

"You expect me to believe that you three made it across the ice by yourselves?" Gurden responded as he was writing something in a notepad. "You need more supplies for that, which means more people. You probably have a team camping somewhere in the forest." Neil was curious why, with all the technology at their disposal, the sheriff would be writing with a pencil and paper.

"Don't worry," Swan added. "We have no intention of turning you over to Kone. In case you haven't noticed, we don't like him. But we cannot stand against him on your behalf either. Your best bet is to stay hidden for the time being. But we're willing to help you settle in if you so choose. It's up to you."

A short time later, they were coming to the bottom of the steps, and another vehicle was waiting for them. The car brought them back to the building by which they entered the city proper. A large overhead door opened, allowing the vehicle to drive inside where there were a series of elevators, each one big enough for most vehicles, that descended to the caverns below. There was a deputy posted here at all times and a portgate next to the guard shack.

The car pulled onto one of the lifts as the portgate opened. Sheriff Gurden came out, turned to the shack and told the deputy, "Don't let them leave." The deputy hit the stop on the shaft controls, and the elevator stopped and came back to the top.

Walking up to the car, the sheriff said, "You dropped something." Samuel was next to the window, and the sheriff handed him a folded piece of paper. Before anybody could say anything else, he turned around and stepped off the lift, telling the deputy, "They can go now."

CHAPTER 15
Lockdown

Meelyhn, Atlantis

Haley and Elizabeth were sitting on a tree branch, watching the mammoth walking the grassy plane in the distance, when Neil's voice came across their comm. "We're on our way back."

"Okay," Elizabeth answered. "Everything's the same here."

"But I think it's getting a little darker," Haley mentioned.

The girls climbed down from the tree, and over the next ten minutes, the light from the clouds dimmed significantly. The others made it back, and a moment later, the clouds went dark.

"Is this because the bugs are going to sleep?" Jake asked Rudge.

"Actually, that's exactly what this is."

"What do you mean, bugs?" Haley asked.

Rudge started to explain the sonoluminescence. While he described it, the place began to brighten with reds, greens and purples. The fungus all around Meelyhn began to glow, and it turned out that there was bioluminescent vegetation as well. Even though it wasn't nearly as bright, the woods became alive with soft colored light that was gentle enough on the eyes that one could sleep undisturbed.

"Can you believe it, Beth?"

"No. This is beautiful!" she answered.

The others came and sat around the small fire under the stewpot, and Samuel handed Quinten the paper from Sheriff Gurden. "Take a look."

His eyebrows lifted as he read the words, and the possibilities gave him a bit of hope. "This could be worth a shot with the right team."

"What do ya got?" Balgar asked.

"Apparently, my comment about needing everyone's cooperation struck a chord with the sheriff," Samuel said.

"It says that there's a vault under the city hall, and Kone keeps all his information there. If we access the vault and release that information to the world, everybody will reject Kone." Quinten explained. "But there's a lock on the vault. Put in place by Molech himself. There are three crystals that work as keys. If we acquire them, we can open the vault."

After his pause, Rudge said, "Well, don't keep us waiting! Where are the keys?"

"One in the Temple of Molech."

"You've gotta be kidding me!" Rudge spat. "And the other two?"

"One in the Temple of Baphomet and the other in the Temple of Hel."

"Awe, c'mon!" Jake groaned. "Are you going to tell me that they seriously believe in these guys?"

"Me and Elizabeth are friends with Bast," Haley said.

"Who's Bast?" Jake asked.

"An Egyptian goddess. She's most well known for her association with cats," Alunareth said.

"Does she have a temple too?"

"No," Haley flatly answered.

"Sorry," Jake shook his head, "it's just that I'm finding it a little difficult to buy into the whole gods thing."

"And did you believe the Alfan to be real?" Quinten reminded.

"Good point. It…it's just a lot."

"Anyway. These three Temples have constructs in place to guard the key crystals. They will attack any living thing that goes near them that isn't Kone. Molech's temple is in a jungle called Futola, Hel's is in an icy area named Churgen, and Baphomet's is somewhere down by the magma flows of Buruum."

"Even if all these things are real, can we really trust the sheriff? Or any of them? We just met them," Jake said.

"That is a good point," Sabrina said, "but I can sense their emotions. Their disgust for Kone is genuine, and they want to be free of him. The sheriff took a big risk by giving us this info. We should be grateful that they're trusting us."

"I wonder why he thinks we can pull something like this off?" Neil said. "Or that we would even try?"

"Because we actually showed up," Balgar replied.

"So," Samuel began with a smirk as he stood up, "Who wants to ruin Kone's weekend?"

"Me!" Haley blurted at the same time as Elizabeth, saying, "I'm in!"

"No!" Neil and Sabrina said simultaneously.

Neil turned back to the rest of the group. "At first, I was wondering why the sheriff was using a pencil when he had all the high-tech gear. Now I understand."

"Why?" Jake asked.

"You can't trace these notes electronically," Neil answered. "And they have lots of electronics." He set his phone down, and it projected a holographic screen, displaying all manner of gizmos and gadgets. "Look at all this advanced tech they have. You'd be hard-pressed to send a message that couldn't be tracked. Almost all electronic activity is recorded and stored. There is no privacy."

"Well then, didn't your scans probably raise a few red flags somewhere?" Rudge asked.

"No," Neil replied. "The PJs are actually more advanced."

"More advanced than Atlantis?" Jake asked. "Where did you get them from? Space?"

"From an alternate universe," Neil replied.

"Of course, I should have known," Jake moaned with a roll of his eyes. "How foolish of me."

The sarcastic comment brought chuckles from Haley and Elizabeth as Neil continued. "The PJs can piggyback on the Atlantis infrastructure and let us use our comms across the entire city without being detected. Just like they do with the internet in the First Density."

"Were you able to pull any kind of info about Kone from the computers?" Manny asked. "Maybe we don't have to go digging in the temples."

"I'm afraid not. Looks like all data systems connect to the vault, but any info sent there can only then be accessed from a terminal inside the vault itself."

Elizabeth was looking through the info on her phone. Once Neil stepped back into range of the girls' com-systems, the PJs automatically linked the information. When his scans explored the Atlantean cyber-structure, it rendered a map of the city, and the young mystic was taking the opportunity to learn her way around. Nomad curled up in Haley's lap as she yawned, tired from the day's ordeals. The adults discussed whether to take the shot at Kone, or to make the trek across the ice. After a bit, they decided to sleep on it and make their choice in the morning.

Haley conjured her helmet, and the nanobots rippled from her sleeves, forming a game controller in her hands and she played a few rounds of Tetris on her Head-Up display to unwind before sleeping.

Atlantis City, Atlantis

The portgate in the city hall opened a vortex, and Kone stepped through. It was four in the morning, but Kone, wearing a three-piece suit, looked fresh and well-rested. He stood up straight and clasped his hands behind his back as he walked forward. "Good morning, gentlemen."

"Morning," Gurden replied.

"Uniralt," Swan said with a nod. "How are you today?"

"Doing well," Kone answered as he walked past them and sat at the governor's desk. "Tell me," Kone began as he set a tablet down and interlaced his fingers, "did they complete their designs?"

"Yes, they did." Swan held up his own tablet and transferred files of aircraft schematics. Most of them intended for use beyond the atmosphere. The engineers in Atlantis couldn't build most aircraft due to available space, but they were often commissioned to design them, and the plans would be taken to manufacturing facilities elsewhere in the Second Density for fabrication and testing.

The files appeared on the screen of Kone's tablet. He picked it up and opened one of the schematics. "Excellent." He set the tablet back down. "And the mayum knives are ready to go?"

"Yes, sir," Gurden said. "Two full crates are in the dock and ready to port."

"Good. Now what about the shell research?"

"They've set up a lab to produce the shells, but the project is just beginning. They haven't begun experimenting yet."

"Well, I expect to see more efficient shell bodies by the end of February. I want to see greater physical strength, with less food requirements."

"I'll let the biologists know," Swan answered.

Kone nodded. "I will be going through these designs for the next hour. Be in the port bay at five thirty, and we'll ship the blades when I arrive."

"Yes sir," they both said and left the office.

Fourth Density. Og Palace, Tir na nOg

"So, my daughter is in Atlantis?!" Harry asked, deeply worried. "I need a way to get there!"

"There isn't one," the Alfan man said. "I'm sorry."

"I've seen you guys teleport," Ryan said. "Can't we do that?"

"No, I have been trying," Fresell said. An aging Alfan, he looked the equivalent of a Human in their late sixties. Fresell was King Larriforn's best Wizard. "And I will keep on trying, do not doubt, but there are mystical barriers in place, the likes of which I've never encountered."

"Then we go in the way he did," Harry said while motioning toward Vedant. "If anybody has a better idea, I'd love to hear it."

Derek turned to Fresell. "How close could you teleport us to the mountains without us being detected?"

"Just like last time, only to the coast. The deeper I've focused on the energy, the more I've realized it's more than just a block against magickal transport. If I manage to penetrate the barrier, whoever put it there will instantly know."

"Can you tell who put it there?" King Larriforn asked.

"I recognize Kone's vibration as part of it, but there's something more. I fear that the spell is bolstered by the energy of a god."

Tuweltha arrived in a flash of green in time to hear King Larriforn slam his fist on the table, spitting, "Molech!" The king was always calm and collected, but in this moment, his emotions were laid bare. His intense disgust and hatred for The Great Owel was a secret to none.

"Molech?!" Tuweltha looked at Larriforn. "He has returned?" And before anyone could answer, she too became angry. "What has he done? If he is responsible for this attack…"

Bast appeared. "What happened?" The worry was written all over her face.

"That's what I'm about to find out," Tuweltha said and turned to King Larriforn.

The king told them everything that happened with the attack and the predicament in Atlantis.

"I'll take a look," Bast said. A golden glow appeared in the goddess's eyes. She stood there for a moment before her eyebrows raised in fear, and then her brow furrowed with determination while the glow faded away. "It is Molech's energy."

"Why couldn't he just stay gone," Tuweltha hissed.

"I'll be back shortly," Bast said and abruptly disappeared.

Tuweltha turned back to the king. "Who did we lose?" Her eyes welled up as King Larriforn told her the names of everyone who fell in the attack. Forty-eight Alfan, Fourteen Dvwargarians, five Humans and three Gnomes.

Bast appeared again, followed by four flashes of light from the arrival of Ptah, Artemis, Ares and Cernunnos.

"As soon as I arrive there," Bast began, "Molech will know. They will come with me in case he shows and tries anything." She turned to Tuweltha. "You should stay here. We don't know what kind of trouble Molech might have waiting for us, and we don't want to leave Tir na nOg unattended should he try something here."

Second Density. Meelyhn, Atlantis

The colors of the bioluminescent glow that bathed the caverns slowly but steadily shifted to shades of blue. It wasn't long after that when the clouds began to brighten with a yellow glow.

"…wake up," Elizabeth shook Hailey's shoulder again.

"Huh?" Haley moaned. She rolled to her side and lifted her head to face Elizabeth but did not open her eyes. "What?" she groaned.

"It's time to wake up," Elizabeth said.

The bedroll that Haley was in started to ripple as the nanobots turned back into clothing. The excess mass fell apart, turning to dust. The farmer stood up but still hadn't opened her eyes, which she now rubbed. The clouds were brightening as the bugs woke up, and the song of birds echoed from the cavern walls.

"We don't have the supplies to leave yet," Quinten was saying, "but we shouldn't try anything until after we know that Kone has left."

"Then it would be best to find supplies while we wait and see what we have to work with once he's gone," Sabrina said.

Atlantis City, Atlantis

The port bay was lined with large gates for transporting cargo. One gate had a closed metal iris that covered the archway. Kone went to one side of the gate and placed his hand on a sensor pad while a camera scanned his eye. The iris opened, followed by a vortex. Gurden pushed the hover dolly through, the vortex closed, and the iris sealed the gate.

An hour later, they met at a restaurant with Governor Swan for breakfast. They sat at a private table to discuss what tasks Kone wanted them to fulfill over the next month when the waitress entered the room, carrying a pitcher of coffee and some mugs. She sat the mugs down and began to pour when Kone noticed a slight trembling in her hand. She was nervous and the Uniralt knew it, but despite enjoying that his mere presence was intimidating, he suppressed his smile and maintained a professional and business-like demeanor.

"Thank you," he said with a polite nod. They went on to order their meals and when the waitress left, Kone began to lay out the goals he expected from the genius minds of Atlantis.

Meelyhn, Atlantis

Samuel and Alunareth had returned from a hunt, bringing with them an ungulate. They went to work cleaning and dressing the animal while Rudge was preparing to cook.

"That's a weird-looking deer," Haley commented.

"Not a deer," Alunareth said. "It's a springbok."

"Never heard of them, "Elizabeth said.

Nomad came over and started sniffing at the harvested animal but then stood up straight and looked over his shoulder. He trotted over to a rock, hopped on top and let out a "Meow." His voice echoed, and everyone could feel the energy emanating from his call.

Bast manifested, followed by four flashes of light.

Atlantis City, Atlantis

He was chewing a mouthful of his omelet when his eyes widened, and he abruptly set down his fork.

"Is something wrong?" Governor Swan asked.

"Yes. Someone has breached the magick barrier around the continent," he answered. The barrier was powerful, and a mortal wizard would be hard-pressed to make it through. In fact, any wizard powerful enough to do so would be wise enough not to try; this must be the work of gods. "I sense four breaches." With a few seconds of concentration, he noticed something more. "No, not four. Five." His eyes became two pools of swirling black and red while he pushed energy into the continental barrier, reinforcing it to new levels.

Swan and Gurden shuddered, and the hair raised from their necks, unnerved by the sight of Kone's eyes. The Uniralt then held out his left hand, closed his fingers and made a pulling motion, "Arrive."

Baphomet and Hel appeared next to the table, accompanied by two other gods, Lillith and Apophis.

Meelyhn, Atlantis

Haley and Elizabeth practically tackled Bast with hugs as soon as they saw her. "Ready to go home, girls?" the goddess asked.

"Yes!" Haley answered.

"Then let's go," Bast replied. She took their hands, and they began to fade, but immediately became solid again. "What?!"

"What's wrong?" Elizabeth asked.

"Give me a moment," Bast said and disappeared. She came right back. "The barrier has been reinforced. I've never encountered a field quite like this."

"Let me check something," Cernunnos said and then sank into the ground. A few seconds later, he came back up, "It's a complete sphere," he said. "Even underground. The continent is completely surrounded by it. How did it get so strong?"

"Molech has never been this powerful," Artemis stated. "How can he be doing this?"

"Bast, there is no barrier you have not been able to breach," Ptah said. "Can you get through this?"

"I believe so, but it's going to take me some time and concentration." She sighed. "But it's now more than it was. Before, the barrier would only stop magickal transport and shield the place from scrying. Now, it prevents physical passage as well." Bast closed her eyes, started to fade as she attempted to shift to another density, but this, too, was ineffective, and she immediately became solid. "I've never seen a spell like this."

"How did my father not notice this?" Ares wondered. "You would think that a continent-sized barrier would catch his attention."

"It is both subtle yet strong," Bast explained. "If Zeus doesn't have a reason to actively look at Antarctica, then there's no reason that he would have noticed the barrier."

"And, unlike the First Density, there's almost no activity on the surface of the ice," Cernunnos added. "Easy to overlook when you're keeping watch over two densities."

"I'm going to need some time out at the barrier," said Bast. "If I can focus undisturbed for a while, I should eventually be able to phase through…"

In a puff of black mist, Hel manifested right behind Bast and grabbed her by the collar. "You just can't mind your own business, can you?" She said as she threw the Egyptian goddess into the trees, knocking many of them over. Bast landed in a heap five hundred feet down the cavern; the cracking of wood was heard by the village on the other side of Meelyhn.

Artemis pulled her knife and slashed at Hel but only managed to cut through black mist as she vanished.

Ptah was already running after his wife when Lillith, Baphomet and Apophis manifested and attacked the other gods.

Hel reappeared, her hand began to pulsate with black energy, and the ground started to ripple. She disappeared again before Artemis could land a blow. Lillith dove at Artemis, tackling her to the ground.

"Whoa, this just got real!" Elizabeth blurted.

Sabrina didn't say a word. She just grabbed Haley and Elizabeth by their hands and began running. The other mortals followed as the bodies of dead animals reconstituted while clawing out from the dirt.

Ares cracked Apophis in the jaw, knocking him on his backside when Baphomet grabbed him from behind. Ares's elbow came quick, though, and Baphomet stumbled back while Apophis jumped up and

Cernunnos went after Baphomet. They all vanished, taking their fights to different locations around the frozen continent, away from the mortals.

Fourth Density. Og Palace, Tir na nOg

"They should be back by now," Tuweltha said. A green glow emitted from her eyes as she began to peer into the Second Density's Antarctica. "What?!"

"What did you see?" Larriforn asked.

"The barrier. It's even stronger. Even I couldn't penetrate it now."

"So, we'll have to go in the old-fashioned way," Vedant said.

Shaking her head, Tuweltha said, "No. We can no longer physically pass."

"But you're a god," Fresell said. "How can you be blocked?"

"By a more powerful god," Tuweltha answered. "I don't know how, but if it is Molech, his power has grown to new heights that I never would have thought possible for him."

"Do you know of anyone strong enough to overcome this field?" Larriforn asked.

"Perhaps Zeus. Since he keeps watch over the immortal activity of the first two densities…" She thought for a moment, then looked back to the others. "I will go to Olympus and see if I can gain an audience with him. Maybe he will be willing to break these barriers if I can show him that Molech is directly interfering with mortal lives." She disappeared in a burst of green light.

CHAPTER 16
When The Past Comes Back to Bite You

Running, Alunareth jumped and spun in the air while he unleashed a couple of mystical bolts. His feet touched the ground, and the Elf continued without breaking momentum. The rotted hyena took both shots but didn't go down. Samuel cranked his bolt pistol to full power, turned and fired, which finished off the abomination, and Alunareth threw a few more bolts at the other hyena.

A skeletal raptor found the Dwarves right before it found their hammers. "Ha ha!" Balgar roared as he took a mighty swing, bashing it to pieces while a large primate charged the bearded folk from behind, but an arrow tore through the reanimated gorilla, and it turned its attention from the Dwarves to the Elf.

Jake fired his bolt pistol at some kind of reanimated feline while Neil put his abilities to use. Powerful blasts of yellow energy shot forth from his hands, taking down a couple of the creatures. A large bird dove at him from above, but Neil waved his hand, connecting with the energy of air. The sudden gust knocked the bird into a tree trunk with a crack, where it tumbled to the ground and flopped in circles.

"I don't have a gun," Manny announced, hoping someone could toss him one, which Jake did.

A few more large birds dove from the air toward Haley, Elizabeth and Sabrina. Haley and Sabrina began blasting while Elizabeth threw a few of them off with her aerokinesis.

They were forced to split into groups as they ran. Samuel and Alunareth went toward the eastern end of Meelyhn, while Neil, Manny and Jake made way for the northern side. Quinten, Rudge and Balgar headed west, deeper into the large cavern. Haley, Elizabeth and Sabrina ran northwest toward the village.

They could hear the impact of large feet accompanied by slight tremors in the ground. Trees cracked as they were broken out of the way of a decomposed mammoth charging straight for them.

"This way!" Sabrina shouted. They shifted north and kept going, but the mammoth only followed, getting closer and closer. "You two keep going; I'll draw him off," Sabrina said and stopped, turning around to face the mammoth. The girls continued to run, and Sabrina launched an anchor at a tree limb fifty feet away. The mammoth bared down, but the Hunter activated her harness, zipping sideways and up to the branch. The mammoth turned to pursue as Sabrina dropped down to the ground and ran to the side.

Continuing for the town, Haley and Elizabeth heard the leaves shaking above. They looked up and dove to the side as a sabretooth tiger dropped down from above. Had this been a living feline, Haley would have nothing to fear, but this was an animated carcass with no spirit within.

Haley charged and unleashed a bobcat-shaped blast at the creature. It hit with a concussive burst, and the tiger staggered back from the blow but did not relent. Elizabeth threw a couple of bolts and jumped up with a gust of air, boosting her leap to grab a branch. It watched her go up but decided to continue going after Haley. Elizabeth let go and pulled a sai, holding it with both hands, pointed down as she dropped from the branch. She didn't even think about it, but she gathered her energy into the sai and released it as she plunged it between the tiger's shoulders. A hole blew out its rotted stomach, and the abomination began to thrash.

"Let go, Beth!" Haley shouted.

Elizabeth released her grip as the tiger flung her to the right, where she tumbled and came back to her feet but caught her head on a low branch coming up. "Ow!"

The tiger turned to Elizabeth, not noticing Haley, who was now crackling with blue and purple light. She released the wide stream of blue, encompassing purple ethereal figures of many different cats, and it plowed into the desecrated feline corps. The beam continued, and the tiger tumbled toward Elizabeth, who jumped up onto a limb, watched it go by and slam into another tree, where it crumpled and dropped to the ground.

Elizabeth dropped back down, and Haley ran over to her, "Beth, are you okay?"

Elizabeth looked at Haley, a big grin spreading on her face. "That was awesome!"

"You shot through your sai!" Haley said.

"What are you talk…" Her eyes went wide with realization. She didn't even know it at that moment, but Elizabeth did channel energy through her weapon. "I did? I did!"

They high-fived and hugged, but the hug was interrupted by a rustling sound. The girls looked and saw the broken and deformed tiger doing its best to charge them. Both girls began to gather their energy until they heard a growl. An Icelot leaped onto the sabretooth's back and bit into its neck. With a sickening snap, the beast collapsed to the ground while the icelot slashed furiously with her claws. The cat released her jaws and clamped down on the head. With a powerful bite, the skull broke apart like an eggshell. The tiger's body turned back to dust, and then the icelot locked eyes with Haley and Elizabeth.

"Uh…can we trust it?" Elizabeth asked.

"Yeah," Haley answered. "But where's Nomad?"

"Meow," Nomad answered from a branch. A small bird in his mouth was turning to dust.

"Yuck!" they both said.

The icelot chuffed, catching their attention. Haley slowly walked up to the large cat and looked into her blue eyes. With a sharp inhale, Haley felt the snow ocelot's adrenaline. The rush from a victorious pounce. The purple, ethereal claws extended from Haley's fingernails, and then the icelot extended her claws. As she did, Haley's claws began to glow. The icelot let out a loud yowl and swiped at a tree trunk, leaving deep gashes in the bark. Haley moved in time with the cat and slashed with her claws, trails of purple light flowing behind them as she slashed into a tree, also leaving gashes in the bark. She held up her hand, stared at her nails and whispered, "Whoa!"

Haley felt a bump to her shoulder and looked to see the icelot nuzzling her. She smiled and scratched the cat's head. "Thanks, Big Kitty." The Icelot turned and pranced into the woods. The farmer turned to Elizabeth and Nomad, then the realization hit them all at once. "Where's Sabrina?"

"Is that the lady who came to town yesterday?" a voice asked. They turned to see the boy from the ranch.

That's when their coms came to life with Neil's voice, "Girls, are you okay?"

Not taking her eyes off the boy, Elizabeth responded, "Yeah. But we don't know where Sabrina is. She was chased by a mammoth."

Sabrina's winded voice came on the com. "I'm here." Picking up the Hunter's signal from different places, the PJs were able to pinpoint her location.

"Got you," Neil said. "Stay put, we're coming."

"Do you want us to go there too," Haley asked, "or wait here?"

"If there's no danger where you are, then stay there," Sabrina said.

"Okay!" Haley replied with a smile.

Elizabeth asked the local, "What's your name?"

"Dalton," he answered. "What are your names?"

"That's weird," Neil commented and looked to Manny and Jake. "Usually, they'd want to go rather than wait."

Sabrina picked up her katana from the dust pile and flipped it over her shoulder. The scabbard opened, the magnetics guided the blade in, and the scabbard shut. Engaging her grapple harness, she zipped back into the tree, retrieved the anchor and got a good look at the area. Looking toward the east, she could see Neil, Manny and Jake approaching. Jake's voice came on the radio, "Quinten? Samuel? Rudge? Guys? Are you okay?"

Alunareth's voice answered the call. "I'm here with Samuel. Balger? Quinten?"

Balgar's voice was the next to be heard. "I'm here with Rudge, but…" He let out a deep sigh. "We've lost Quinten. These…stupid ape-things."

"Oh-no!" "What?!" the girls said at the same time, drawing their attention from the boy and back to the comms.

The PJs calculated their positions, and Neil called out, "We're east of you and almost to Sabrina."

"We need to regroup," Samuel said. "Stay with her when you get there. Haley and Elizabeth, can you see her position too?"

"Yes, we can," Elizabeth answered. "On the screen, but not with our eyes."

"Okay, stay where you are, like Sabrina said, but have a route to her prepared in case something comes up."

"Alright," Haley said, and the map on her phone calculated the best probable route through the woods to the Hunter's location.

"Sorry to hear about your friend," Dalton said.

"He seemed so cool," Haley sighed. "And we barely got to know him."

"Yeah," Elizabeth agreed. She looked up at Dalton and asked, "How come you're here?"

"I live here," he said flatly.

"I mean, out here in the woods?"

"I was out for a walk when I heard some commotion. So, I came to see what it was. Were you really petting an icelot?"

"Yeah," Haley said. "I'm really good with cats."

"I guess so," Dalton said. "They usually don't bother anybody, but they don't let us get that close either. But they do sometimes take a shot at our livestock."

"How often does that happen?" Haley asked.

Dalton shrugged, "Not in a couple of years now. The new force-field fences keep them out pretty well. But what was all the noise? It sounded like trees were breaking and shots were blasting."

"Well, that's because…they were," Elizabeth said. "We were attacked by…this is gonna sound weird…dead animals. But the cat helped us."

Dalton smiled but suppressed his chuckle. "Good one. But what really happened?"

Haley looked at her phone and said, "They're almost here."

"We gotta go," Elizabeth said. "Nice to meet you, Dalton," she added with a smile.

"Yeah," Haley said with the same kind of smile, "Always nice to meet a fellow farmer."

"You're a farmer?"

"Yep. Gotta go."

Dalton stood there and watched the girls turn and head for the others who were just over the small hill.

They started making their way up the hill and saw Samuel and Sabrina crest from the other side first. The others were coming up behind them. The Fjallgaard brothers were carrying Quinten's body on a makeshift stretcher.

Haley and Elizabeth started to run up the hill to meet them when, in a burst of yellow light, Apophis appeared. With a wicked grin, he threw out his hand toward Sabrina and the others. The ground started to ripple like swells of waves on the ocean, and snow fell from the clouds. Neil fired his thrusters to lift himself from the moving ground.

"Knock it off!" Cernunnos shouted as a small bolt of lightning hit Apophis. With the strike, the ground stabilized, and the snow stopped.

Lillith arrived in a burst of red, right behind Haley and Elizabeth, grabbing them by their shirt collars. "Aren't you two just so precious!" she squealed with a wicked grin and hoisted them into the air. "The boss would *love* to meet you." The vile goddess was already starting to teleport when the hands of another grabbed her shoulders, and Bast was pulled into the transport. They disappeared, but Bast pulled back with a teleportation of her own, and the magickal tug of war landed them in the western end of the cavernous Meelyhn, where the cave systems bent to the north.

Letting go of the girls, Lillith unleashed a wave of painful red energy into the Egyptian goddess, and she flew back into the cavern wall, shuddering the area around them. Red sparks flew out from Lillith's fingertips, trails of neon light behind them as they shot forward. Bast moved and was nicked by only one of them as she returned the sentiment with a bolt of golden light while shouting, "Run!"

Elizabeth was already charged up, crackling with energy and unleashed a stream of energy at Lillith's back when they were told to run. The young mystic's beam knocked the woman forward and into Bast's incoming bolt.

"Uhg!" she grunted with the impact. "I will slowly choke you both," Lillith's shrill scream echoed while they ran into the northbound caverns. There was another shuddering of the world around them, spurring Haley and Elizabeth to move faster.

Everything seemed too quiet when Cernunnos ported Apophis away to continue their fight. The girls were gone to who knows where, and a short distance from where Haley and Elizabeth stood only seconds ago was a slack-jawed Dalton, trying to process everything he had just seen.

"What is going on?!" the exasperated boy finally asked.

"What are you doing out here?" Sabrina asked right back. "It's too dangerous. Go back to the village."

"I live here," Dalton shot back. "Meelyhn is my home, so tell me what is going on. What knocked over those trees? How are people teleporting without gates? How did that guy…" he pointed at the hill on which they stood, "…warp the ground?!"

Sabrina heard the true emotional state echoing from inside the young man and realized that he was the type who, when nervous, would plant his feet and become defiant. Making a stern demand would not result in his compliance. "Very well. We'll explain, but we need to head back to the village. Neil, scan for the girls."

"Already trying," he said.

"I'm trying," Haley said. "We must be out of range." They were so far from the group and had walls of rock all around. Not to mention, there were no electronic systems to carry the signal.

Remembering back to when she snuck into Camp Yeoman with the Marshals, Haley held up her phone, a thin slot opened along the bottom, and a thin piece of transparent material the size of a credit card slid out. She took the inconspicuous repeater, stuck it to a tree, shrugged and said, "Might as well start putting them up in case they get close."

The cavern here, though not nearly as large as Meelyhn, was big enough that there were still glowing clouds above. Birds flew by, and critters rustled the brush as they walked, heading north. The eastern wall was the same pale rock marbled with crystal as the wall by the village, and the western side was made of grayish-blue stone. The cave system was bending back toward the east as they continued, and the air was getting warmer.

"So, I was thinking," Elizabeth said as they walked, "if we can't find the others, maybe we can find those key things." She slapped a repeater on the trunk of another tree and noticed the different bark. Looking up, Elizabeth saw that it was a type of palm tree. Then she saw coconuts. The tangled foliage was thickening the further they went, and the temperature was nearing eighty degrees.

Haley shrugged, "That would be cool, but do you think we can find the temples?"

A blur of gray whooshed past them, startling the girls from their conversation. "What was that?!" Elizabeth asked while they turned their heads to follow whatever buzzed past them. It swooped upward and landed on a tree limb about ten feet up from the ground.

Conjuring their helmets, the girls zoomed in on the creature. It was almost as big as a Nomad, with gray fur and a head similar in shape to a possum. A lanky body and a flat, fuzzy tail, this animal had flaps of skin between its front and back limbs, which allowed it to glide like a flying squirrel. The animal's fur did not cover the patagia, and the bare membrane looked similar to bat wings. The com-system finished its scan, and the words in the HUD read:

SPECIES: UNKNOWN

THREAT ASSESSMENT: NONE

**POTENTIAL RELATIVE OF THE
SUGAR GLIDER (PETAURUS BREVICEPS)**

"He's neat looking," Haley commented.

The animal observed them for a couple more seconds, then jumped off the limb and swooped away.

Turning back to Elizabeth, Haley said, "One of the temples is supposed to be in a jungle. Maybe we're in the right area."

Haley shrugged. "Maybe. It would help if we could find somebody who knew the area," she said with a smirk.

Sharing the smirk, Elizabeth said, "Like Dalton."

A long, slow "Yeah" flowed from Haley's mouth, accompanied by a grin and a faraway look in her eye.

As the girls ventured on, they noticed that the foliage was changing and becoming thicker. Haley pointed to the more colorful birds flying through the caverns. "That one's pretty!" The gliding animals became common as the cavern swung around to the east and continued, where another village was established along the southern wall. "Do you think we should go ask the people there for help?"

"Probably not," Elizabeth replied. "We don't know who we can trust." After the village, the cavern abruptly turned left, heading north again, deeper into the tropical climate.

Sabrina and the others were halfway back to the village of Meelyhn when they met a group of locals coming their way.

"Dalton," Rodge called. "Are you alright? What was all that commotion out there?"

"I'm alright," he answered.

"What were you people doing out there?" a deputy asked Sabrina and the others.

"Running for our lives," she said. "We found him just a few moments ago."

"So," Rodge asked, "what was all that noise? It sounded like a bunch of trees snapped in half."

"Indeed," Neil answered as he stepped forward. He held up his phone and projected a holo-screen displaying footage of Hel flinging Bast through the woods and them being chased by undead animals.

"What is…how are they doing this?" Rodge asked.

"They're gods," Alunareth replied. Just then, when everybody was looking at him, did they notice his larger eyes and pointed ears. Then, they noted the shorter stature of Rudge and Balgar, with their slightly larger noses and thick beards and saw Nomad following along. And they saw the body of Quinten on the stretcher. The townsfolk's stunned expressions said it all, but it took a moment for reality to sink in.

"Apologies," Bernice finally said when she realized she was staring. "We've known that your people exist but never expected to meet any of you."

"Many could say the same about Atlantis," came Rudge's reply.

"Come," the deputy huffed with a wave of his hand. "It's obviously not safe to be out here right now."

CHAPTER 17
No Bull

Atlantis City, Atlantis

The cruiser was in auto as it hovered along the unending curve of Atlantis's third ring. He was moving at fifty miles an hour and observed the other vehicles passing him in the opposing lanes. Many still had wheels even though they could hover, which was the method most commonly used and all of them could use autosteer, so long as they were on a road. The system could track where all the vehicles were via the induction charging, but not once they left the surface of the street's panels. Manual steering was the only option.

The sheriff was out on patrol just to stay out of town hall, a common practice when Kone was around and was contemplating the depth of the current situation. Gurden knew of the gods but had never met them before. And after this morning, he never wanted to meet them again. But a breech in the barrier while the newcomers were here…*Can't be a coincidence.*

Both he and the Governer were taking a huge risk in not reporting them to Kone, and with the breech in the field, Gurden knew he better go ask some questions, so he was already on his way when his comm sounded.

"Go 'head."

"It's Deputy Karn. Burnice down here in Meelyhn was hoping she could speak with you in person." The entire Sheriff's Department was on the same page with communication. When Kone's around, be as discrete as possible on all comms.

"On my way."

"And, Sheriff, someone's a little down."

"I'll bring ice cream," Gurden answered with a sigh. He stopped at a satellite station and had another deputy follow him to Meelyhn in a coroner's wagon.

Meelyhn, Atlantis

Ten minutes later, the two Deputies were loading Quinten's body into the back of the wagon while Gurden spoke with the others.

"How long ago?" he asked, looking at the pictures of Haley and Elizabeth.

"An hour," Neil answered. "They're only eleven."

"Of course, we'll try to find them, but vanishing with a god doesn't give us much of a trail." Gurden rubbed his face. "And to make matters worse, the god you showed me there was called here by Kone himself. Her name is Lillith, and Kone is her boss."

"No, no," Neil started. "We can't let Kone get his hands…" He stopped talking when Bast came into view.

"Have you heard from the girls?" she asked.

"No," Sabrina said.

"We were hoping you had them," Neil added.

"They got away from Lillith, but I don't know where we were when they escaped."

The sheriff asked, "Was it a city or cavern?"

"Cavern, it was…" Baphomet came out of nowhere, attacking Bast, who teleported their fight away before someone could get hurt.

"Sheriff, how many caverns are there here?" Sabrina asked.

"Five. Below us is Churgen, going north from there is Freq and past that is Buruum. And above Buruum is Futola. Churgen is cold, with lots of ice and frost. Freq is all crystal underneath the quarry, Buruum is where the magma flows are, and Futola is tropical." He turned to one of the Deputies, "Don't put this out on the comms." He looked back to the group and continued, "You can probably rule out Buruum because it's so hot that you need a thermal suit and a breathing apparatus."

"They have that equipment built into their clothing," Neil said.

A look of surprise was upon the sheriff's face. "Really?! That's some advanced tech, even for us. Do all of you have that?"

"No," Neil replied. "Just them and me." He projected a map system from his phone and started rendering the caverns below Atlantis City.

"We need to split into teams and find them," Sabrina said. "Neil, you can travel the fastest, so you go to Futola. Samuel and Aluneareth, you go to Buruum. Rudge and Balgar can investigate Freq. Jake and I will check out Churgen. Papi, stay here in case they come back.

"Hang on," the sheriff said as he pulled out a notepad and pencil. "When you two get to Buruum, you're going to need protective gear. So, stop at Freq village and give this note to Deputy Winthrope," he was writing as he spoke, "He'll make sure you have the right gear. Karn, get these two some proper coats, gloves and gear."

Ten minutes later, with their courses of action laid out, Neil activated his thrusters, flying west for the other end of Meelyhn. He would follow the bend around to the north, continuing the curve to the east, then a hard turn north again into the jungles of Futola.

After the deputy provided some coats, Dalton guided the others to the corridor that went down to Churgen. From there, Samuel, Alunareth, Rudge and Balgar went north, while Sabrina and Jake went south and down deeper into the icy cavern.

Atlantis City, Atlantis

He had been going through the proposed design schematics for the last hour, impressed as usual by the engineering talent of the Atlanteans. Some of these proposals would suit his needs nicely, and the Uniralt's only concern was which ones needed to be prioritized first. With a sudden flash of light, Apophis was standing before him.

"Has it been handled?" Kone asked without looking up from the papers.

"Not yet," he answered. Apophis continued with a chuckle, "But it will be. And yes, it's the usual suspects. Ares and his sister. Cernunnos. Bast and Ptah."

Kone nodded, still looking at the designs for a few more seconds before setting them down to look the god in the eye directly. "We need to end them this time. Nobody can scry through the barrier, so make sure they disappear."

"By the way, you know those two girls you mentioned last week?" Apophis asked with a snicker.

"Yes," Kone replied, wondering why the god would choose now to discuss them, but Apophis is nothing if not chaotic.

"They're here."

Kone was always calm and controlled, so it entertained Apophis to actually see a stunned expression on the Uniralt's face. "How did they get here?"

Unlike Kone, Apophis did not bother to hide his feelings. With a shrug and a chuckle, Apophis said, "Who knows? But they won't be leaving. Lillith is looking forward to getting her hands on their throats."

"No," a different voice said from Kone's mouth. "Their agony will be my celebration feast once Ares and his friends are disposed of." Molech reached out with Kone's hand and made a pulling motion and six reptilians phased into the room, confused as to how they arrived. "Where were they last seen?" Molech asked.

"In the caverns."

"Then make sure the caverns are treacherous outside of the villages."

"With pleasure," Apophis replied. "Oh, one other thing. That whip chick is here too."

"Hunter Carmen?" Kone asked.

"Yep!"

"I see. Thank you." Turning to the Archons, Molech said, "I have a job for you. Haley and Elizabeth are here. I want you to find them but keep them alive, and I'll reward you by letting you join in the harvest of agony."

Ahnk-Hume smiled. "Oh, yes. We will find them."

"Atlantis is a big place. A few extra eyes are in order." Molech moved his hands again, summoning three large men. Over seven feet tall, they had long hair and bushy beards, knotted skin that covered their large muscles and body hair so thick, their forearms almost appeared to have fur. The three newcomers looked around in surprise, then their eyes settled on the Archons. "What are you?" Curgel asked.

"They're Archons," Kone said. "And that one," he continued while pointing at Ahnk-Hume, "Is your boss for today."

"What?" Shnaps blurted. "You pulled us out of the box to be pushed around by some oversized snake guy.

"The job is to capture two little girls and return them to me," Kone said. "If you can do that, I will pardon you for your failures, and you'll be free to go."

"So, why do we have ta listen ta…that?" Funts asked, pointing at Ahnk-Hume.

Kone nodded to Ahnk-Hume, and the Drakel smiled as he walked right up to Funts. "Would you like to find out why?"

With a sudden burst of movement, Funts took a swing at Ahnk-Hume with his right fist, which was caught by Ahnk-Hume's lower left palm. Funts swung with his left, but Ahnk-Hume caught this, too, by the wrist in his upper right hand. With his lower right, Ahnk-Hume grabbed the waist of Funts's trousers, and his final hand clamped around the neck, hoisting him into the air. These three men were known for their incredible stregnth, but Ahnk-Humes physiology, bolstered by his mystical abilities, allowed him to match the challenger's strength without too much trouble. Funts struggled but could not break free from the Drakel's grasp. Ahnk-Hume began to squeeze Funts's neck as he hissed with glee, "This is why. Do we understand each other?"

"Yes," came the strained reply without hesitation.

"Good," Ahnk-Hume said as he placed Funts back down, let him go and straightened his shirt right before brushing off his shoulder with his usual wicked grin. "Then we should get along just fine."

"But," Kone began, "you are to leave the citizens here alone. Do not disturb them. Understood?"

"Yes," they all said.

"Good." With a wave of the hand, Kone transported them to the caverns below as his mind turned to the Hunter. He summoned one more man and said, "I have a special assignment for you, and her name is Hunter Sabrina Carmen."

Futola, Atlantis

"Wait! Don't climb up yet," Elizabeth said. "I want to try something." The young mystic drew one of her sai and visually measured the distance. A flick of the wrist, the sai flipped and she caught it by the shaft, lifting it over her shoulder for a throw.

Her arm swung forward, and she released her grip, letting the sai fly up toward the tree. The sai slid between the coconut and limb where the tine hooked, leaving the sai to dangle in the tree. "Son of a b…"

"Hey!" Haley snapped.

Elizabeth gave a stern look in return. "…branch."

Haley attempted to match her friend's expression, but after a couple of seconds, she began to giggle.

After a shrug, Elizabeth started to ask, "Could you, uh…?"

"Yeah," Haley smirked as the ethereal purple claws extended from her nails, "I got it." She leaped up, clung to the trunk and climbed to the top, where she retrieved Elizabeth's sai and dislodged a couple of coconuts. After tossing them down, Haley released her cling and dropped to the ground. Her feet touched down and she bent her knees to absorb the impact, bringing her down to a squatting position, and she picked up one of the coconuts before standing back up.

Holding the coconut in her left arm, Haley pointed at it with her right index finger and the ethereal claw extended again. It started to glow, and she used it to cut a couple of holes into the coconut before handing it to Elizabeth. "That worked better than I thought it would," she commented while reaching for another.

They drank. The water from inside washed down their throats, quenching their thirst and refreshing them.

"Mm, I wish I had some pineapple to go with this, "Haley commented with a smile.

"I wonder how long it'll take us to find it," Elizabeth said.

"The pineapple?" Haley smirked, knowing that Elizabeth was referring to the temple. When they had passed the village in the area, the girls were tempted to go and meet the people there in hopes that they would know where the temple was, but they decided against it since they didn't know who they could trust, and the last thing they needed was word of their location reaching the wrong ears.

It's been about a half hour since, and they had been moving toward the north. Finishing their drink, the path brought them close to the eastern wall of the cavern. The humidity increased along with the temperature, and the pathway led them to the source of that increased heat, a chasm that ran along with but separated them from the eastern wall. The chasm was deep, with heat wafting up from the faint red glow of magma flowing in the caverns below them.

The vegetation thinned along the chasm, and they found an old bridge, or what was left of an old bridge, that ran to the other side where a small building sat against the rocky cavern wall. The edges of the bridge were still present, but the center had collapsed, and even with their enhanced abilities, thirty feet was too far of a leap for them to make.

For a moment, Haley considered trying anyway. She couldn't make the other end of the bridge, but an outward leap would get her to the other side of the chasm wall part way down, where she could cling to the cliff side and climb back up. Unfortunately, the thorn-covered vines were thick around the edge and even under the remains of the old bridge, blocking her way.

They scanned the small building on the other side. "An elevator!" Haley said. "Too bad our thrusters don't work yet."

Elizabeth sighed. "C'mon, eighteen."

With nothing left that could be done here, they continued along the path, which bent back away from the chasm. They continued, looking for any sign of the jungle temple. It didn't take long.

It was in the air, a nasty feeling. A vibe much like that of an Archon. As they continued, it steadily increased and made them both uneasy. The foliage around the path started to thin out, except for the briars, as they proceeded into an area of hills. And the path, with an abrupt turn, ran right up and over one of those small hills.

"Those feelings are almost pouring down from over that hill," Elizabeth said.

Haley was staring at the path. "That's weird."

"What?"

"The clear path. I…I guess I just thought that it would be difficult to get to."

"It's a temple," Elizabeth reminded. "Don't people need to be able to go there for services?"

"I don't think it's *that* kind of temple."

It took them a moment to start up the path, with the vibe radiating from the trail making them want to run the other way, but the girls needed that key crystal. And they intended to get it. Thinking back to the SEALs and how they continued despite their fear, Haley drew inspiration from that memory and pressed on. Although she couldn't help but ask, "Are we daring…"

"…or stupid?" Elizabeth finished.

It was like having cement shoes when they took that first step, forcing their legs to go in the opposite direction that every instinct told them to go. No creatures scurried in the brush here. No birds sang or leaves rustled, only the occasional buzz of an insect. The color of the foliage itself was less vibrant, and it thinned the further they went. They crested the hill and started down the other side, where soon, it was all briars and vines leading to a building. Cave was more like it. The structure itself was a large gray cube carved from a rocky outcropping with no distinguishing features other than an archway for entry.

"Shouldn't there be a door?" Haley wondered.

Elizabeth shrugged. "How many people actually want to go in there?"

"Good point." She took a deep breath and blew it out. And they stepped forward, through the archway, down some steps and entered the long hall carved into the earth. The walls were polished smooth, and light reflected off them from the glowing eyes of the small statues that lined both sides of the arched corridor. The statues were owls, three feet tall and staring straight ahead at their counterparts on the other side of the entry hall. Elizabeth scanned the area down to the door at the other end, but nothing registered other than the low energy emissions of the statues' eyes.

"This is creepy," Haley muttered and was startled by the echo.

They made it six steps forward before all the owls shifted their heads, looking directly at the girls.

"Whoa!" they both whispered; even that echoed. The girls held still for a moment, but nothing happened. So, they dared to continue, and the owls' heads slowly turned, following their movements. Sending shivers down their spines. Halfway down the hall, the large wooden double doors at the other end slowly swung open. The feelings of horror, dread and terror assaulted Haley's senses. The agony of so many unspeakable deaths lingered in the air itself, and it turned the empath's stomach as if it were the stench of rancid eggs.

Suddenly, the silence broke. An ear-piercing screech echoed through the hall while the soft yellow glow of the owls' eyes turned an angry red. The girls pivoted to run but saw a set of doors at the top of the stairs that weren't there a moment ago slamming shut. The owl statues glowed with yellow and green light. Then, the glowing lights stepped away from the statues while retaining their form. Ten ghostly owls with glowing red eyes staring at Haley and Elizabeth. The owls opened their beaks and screeched. The horrific sounds echoed and reverberated to such a degree that Haley and Elizabeth conjured their helmets to block out the sounds.

The three closest to them jumped up near the ceiling while spreading their wings and swooped down at the girls. The first one took an amber orb to the face, followed by another to the chest, and it swerved away. The second was slammed four times in rapid succession by blue and purple kitten-shaped orbs, bursting upon impact. The concussive blows were too much, and the owl faded to nothing.

A charged blast from Elizabeth knocked the third owl off course before she turned back to the first and finished it off. Haley's next blast took down the third, and Elizabeth threw more bolts down the hall at the others before they started to move.

All of them scattered, and a couple dove in. Haley threw her shield up just in time for a talon to grind against her barrier. She dropped it and blasted the one near Elizabeth, who then covered Haley as she started charging for a larger blast.

She launched the bobcat, and it burst on impact, knocking down two of them. Haley finished them off as Elizabeth defeated the last one.

They looked at each other and then at the open doors to the main chamber. "Now, where's that crystal?" Haley asked, feeling pretty good about herself.

"Yeah," Elizabeth added with a cocky grin. "We earned that one!"

They entered the room and took a good look around. It was large with a much higher ceiling, and straight ahead was the centerpiece: a large, hollow metal statue of a bull, Molech's original symbol before the owl. It was fifteen feet tall with a humanoid body, sitting upright on a giant throne. There was a hatch on the belly big enough for a person to fit in, and there was some kind of hearth under the throne to light a fire that would heat up the statue for the slow cooking of a living sacrifice. An eye was engraved into its chest above the hatch, and its pupil a green gemstone.

"That's probably it!" Haley said softly, pointing at the engraved eye.

They took a step forward, and the room brightened. Yellow and green orbs of light flew past them and toward the bull, converging to form another owl. More orbs were flowing into the ethereal construct, increasing its size and changing its shape as it grew. Wings became arms, the feathers were no more, and large, long horns extended out from the head, transforming it into a twelve-foot-tall minotaur. The construct became solid as the glow faded, but the red glow in the eyes intensified.

Having already gathered her energy, Elizabeth was crackling with amber and indigo light. She held her hands up and released her stream of energy right away, hitting the unholy construct and forcing it back a step.

The red eyes flared, and the minotaur's mouth opened, unleashing a beam of yellow and green energy. The girls dove to the side, and Haley came up with a charged shot in the barrel of her arm cannon. She released the bobcat-like orb, and it burst into the minotaur's face.

Smoke billowed from the thing's nostrils right before two bolts of red shot from its eyes, one at each girl. Haley blocked it with her protective field while Elizabeth sidestepped the blast and pulled her sai. Then, the minotaur charged.

"Whoa!" Elizabeth blurted while diving between the minotaur's legs. The bull kicked, and Haley threw her field out again before the impact. Her sphere absorbed the impact, but she was still launched across the chamber and into the wall as Elizabeth came back up to her feet. The young mystic held up her sai and channeled her energy through the weapon and out the tip, launching bolts of mystical energy at the back of the monster. When the orbs hit, the minotaur turned its focus upon her.

She turned and ran to the other end of the chamber while the minotaur gave chase. A powerful gust of air assisted her leap as Elizabeth bounded up and kicked off from the wall with another gush of air, right for the head. She kicked her heel into the minotaur's snout, releasing a burst of energy through her foot. While it didn't do much damage, it was enough to make the thing lean back just a bit, and Haley was right behind it, holding her staff horizontally and pushing it into the back of its knees. Haley collapsed the staff and darted forward between the legs, letting the minotaur topple backward to the floor on its back.

Elizabeth ran for the head, her sai both glowing with energy while Haley climbed the statue. The farmer poked a clinging claw into the key crystal and pulled, dislodging it from the engraved eye and instantly felt something, but didn't know what.

Plunging both sai into the minotaur's face, Elizabeth growled as she released her energy through her weapons until it swatted her away with its arm and sat up, her two sai still stuck in its cheeks.

"Up here, you stupid cow!" Haley shouted as the construct pulled the sai from its face and looked above. She leaped from the statue and pounced.

Propelled down by her energy, Haley's feet connected with the top of the minotaur's head, and the released energy shuddered the construct while rebounding Haley back up, who coalesced her energy for another pounce. She rebounded again, shot downward for a third, and began to crackle with blue and purple light on her way back up.

Elizabeth, too, was focusing a mass of energy and began to crackle with light. Haley clung to the statue and conjured her potato gun, aiming for Molech's guardian. Both girls released streams of energy upon the minotaur, knocking it back flat to the floor, the combined beams finally bringing the threat to an end. It lay still for a couple of seconds before it started to lose its form and dispersed like a glowing mist of yellow and green.

Haley hopped back to the floor next to Elizabeth and held up the green crystal between her finger and thumb, "Check it out." She handed it to her friend, and Elizabeth noticed right away that it had some subtle interaction with her energy.

"Weird…" she said softly while focusing on the feeling.

"Any idea what it might be doing?"

Elizabeth answered with a shrug. And looked out to the hallway entrance. "Hey, the doors are gone again. Let's get out of here!"

They began moving when Haley said, "And we have to do this two more times…" They jogged to the entryway, up the stairs and out the door to the path that brought them in, happy to be leaving.

He sat cross-legged. Sat might not be the appropriate word, considering he was hovering six feet in the air. Apophis's eyes snapped open, and his crazed grin widened, making the already insane expression even more unnerving. "Make the wilderness…" he started to chuckle and stopped himself, "…truly wild!" he shouted, throwing his arms out wide.

The chaos god laughed hysterically as his energy washed across the caverns of Atlantis, affecting all but the populated villages as Kone had instructed. Though most Atlanteans were as energy blind as those of the First Density, everybody felt the odd wave pass through the area like they were near a transformer shorting out. Everything shimmered, looking like reality was underwater for a few seconds and then settled.

But inside the caverns, through the woods of Meelyhn to the jungles of Futola and everywhere in between, random bits of whatever was around pulled together, forming strange and dangerous creatures. Some were twisted versions of already existing animals; some were compilations of foliage, rock or ice. Most made no sense, and all were dangerous. And all had one goal: to seek out Haley and Elizabeth.

CHAPTER 18

1up

The descent into the depths of Churgun was slow. The ice-covered slope required the placement of anchors and ropes, which Jake set as they went. "This temperature drop makes no sense," he commented. Once they made it down to level ground, they found a forest encased in ice that emitted a dim purple and blue light. There was a chasm that followed the eastern wall of the cavern. A path that continued straight ahead to their south, and to the west was all frozen forest. A few small animals were around, but they scurried away from the sounds of Jake's footsteps.

"I wonder what they eat," Sabrina said as they trekked forward.

The walk down the path was uneventful, and a short time later, they found a pair of statues standing like sentinels on either side of the path. There was no mistaking the likeness when Sabrina laid her eyes on the visage of Hel, except half the face on the statue looked old and withered while the other half looked young and vital.

"I hope we never have to meet her again," Jake said.

"Agreed."

They took another step forward and felt a wave of energy flow through the area. Looking at each other, they both asked, "What was that?"

With a shake of the head, Sabrina said, "I don't know, but we've come far enough in, and I still can't sense anybody. This is probably a good time to leave."

Heading back to the slope, they quickly noticed a lot of bare patches on the ground, free of ice. "I don't think that those were there before," Sabrina said, pointing to the missing ice.

"No, they weren't," Jake confirmed.

"Let's keep moving," Sabrina said.

A moment later, they could hear the slapping of feet against the ground coming from the west. "Those are footfalls, but different than any I've heard before," Sabrina said as they picked up their pace while being mindful of slick spots on the ground. The sounds got closer, and one of the creatures broke away from the rest, coming near the path and into sight. A large white lizard with leathery skin, as tall as a wolf, three times as long. Its yellow-slitted eyes locked onto Sabrina and Jake.

Futola, Atlantis

"What was that?" They asked aloud at the same time. Haley and Elizabeth were unnerved by the pulse of energy, and everything seemed just a bit dimmer after the wave had passed. Then, a notification sounded from their com-systems, followed by a voice from their speakers.

"Elizabeth? Haley? Can you hear me?" Neil's PJs located the first repeater as soon as he was in range, which relayed through all the repeaters that Haley and Elizabeth had placed, giving him a nice trail to follow. He had tried to contact them as soon as he connected but received no response. Now that the girls had stepped out from the temple, they reconnected to the network and instantly linked. They could see each other's positions in their displays.

"Neil!" Elizabeth exclaimed. "We're okay!"

Having just passed by the village, Neil increased his speed, flying to the girls. "Stay there. I'll be there in a couple minutes."

"Okay," Haley said and then asked, "Did you feel that weird energy a minute ago?"

"Yes," Neil replied. "I don't know what that was, but I don't like it. Just hold tight, and I'll be right there."

"Acknowledged," Haley said in a serious tone. She noticed Elizabeth was looking at her as if she had three heads. "What?"

"Acknowledged? Where did that come from?" Elizabeth asked.

With a shrug, Haley said, "They say it in *Star Trek*."

Elizabeth blew out a long sigh. "You're such a nerd."

A rustling sound from behind grabbed their attention, and they partially turned to look over their shoulders. A strange creature, bipedal and four feet tall, stepped out from the brush. Old leaves, twigs, stone and dirt were all clumped together in a humanoid shape, making this strange little man-shaped thing. There were no ears or a nose, but two rocks made its eyes, and its large round head gave room for a wide mouth lined with thorns for teeth.

The girls turned to face it directly and conjured their helmets, scanning the weird thing. Their HUD's displayed:

IDENTIFIED: MYSTICAL CONSTRUCT

LOW LEVELS OF ENERGY DETECTED

THREAT ASSESSMENT: MINIMAL

"It looks like an angry salad," Haley chuckled, but a loud and raspy shriek knocked her out of her mirth. Indeed, it did look like an angry salad, to the point where it appeared cartoonish. But when the creature opened its mouth and let out that squeal, the farmer took it seriously, throwing up her protective field and waiting to see what it would do. Unexpectantly, it did nothing. Until eight more ran out of the brush behind it.

"Run!" Elizabeth shouted while channeling energy into her hands.

Haley dropped the field, and they booked it. Elizabeth released a charged blast at the first in the group as they ran. The mystical bolt knocked it down, and a couple others tripped over it. Haley looked over her shoulder and reached behind with her right arm, launching blasts from her potato gun. The concussive bursts from her orbs' impacts came in handy as it knocked many of them over and managed to obliterate a couple of the weird creatures.

The path took them to an area thick with trees before it would continue back toward the chasm. Elizabeth threw another charged blast and then began focusing deeper, coalescing much of her available energy as her eyes glowed amber and light began arching from her body.

She stopped with a pivot and unleashed her beam, taking out many of the swarming creatures. It thinned them out enough that the girls chose to stop running and take them on directly. Haley charged her orb, and a bobcat burst, taking out seven of them, while Elizabeth let loose another charged blast.

More of them came dropping from the trees, and Haley started picking them off with well-placed shots. She looked and aimed up, where a couple more were dropping from overhead. She hit one and was about to blast the smaller one when a gray blur whooshed by and latched onto the weird little foliage man. "Reeeeow!" The gray ball of fur sounded like an angry cat when it shredded the thing's neck, jumped off and glided away.

"Was that one of those gliding things?" Elizabeth asked while blasting a few more of the creatures.

"I think so," Haley answered while letting out another bobcat.

Elizabeth pulled out her sai and pointed it at another group of the strange creatures. She ran her energy through the sai in her right hand, launched orbs out the tip at the oncoming constructs, and used the shafts to skewer any that got too close.

Mystical bolts of yellow light came zipping from the south to hit more of the creatures. Neil rocketed in and let loose a few more blasts. "You girls just can't have a normal day, can you?"

"Nope!" Haley said with a smirk and released another charged blast.

Among the three of them, they were able to clear out the creatures without much more trouble. They all fell apart into piles of leaves, rocks, and dirt under the barrage of blasts.

"Woo-hoo!" Haley shouted with her arms in the air. "We beat the evil jungle monsters!" She turned to Neil, "How many points do we get?"

"Unfortunately," Neil began with a chuckle, "this isn't the arcade. But I think that should earn you both an extra life."

"Awe, c'mon!" Elizabeth grumbled, "Do you two have to nerd out with everything?"

"Yeah," Haley and Neil both said while nodding.

"Well, you're gonna have to…" Her words started to slur, and the young mystic stumbled.

Haley caught her and lowered her to the ground. "Hang on," she said and handed her a B12. Next, she climbed up one of the trees for a coconut, then came back down, cut a couple of holes into the shell and handed it to Elizabeth. "You used too much energy at once. That hasn't happened in a while."

Steadying herself, Elizabeth tipped the coconut back and began to drink the slightly sweet water. It felt refreshing as it washed into her stomach, and she sat still, letting herself recoup. "I did throw a lot of energy around."

"Where were you getting it all from?" Haley asked. As time went on, their continued practice allowed them to use more and more energy without burning themselves out, but this time, Elizabeth continued throwing high-intensity blasts. When energy is used, it replenishes on its own, but Elizabeth seemed to be tapping into a bigger pool of it than normal.

Elizabeth gave a tired smile, pulled out the green gem, and tossed it to Haley, who caught it.

"Is that what I think it is?" Neil asked.

"Yep," Haley replied. "The key crystal from Molech's place."

"We didn't know what else to do," Elizabeth added. "So, we crashed a temple. Hey, Haley. How do you feel holding that."

The farmer did notice something a little different with her energy while holding it back at the temple, and she felt it again here. "Something, but I don't know what." She handed it to Neil, "What do you think?"

Neil took the crystal and closed his eyes, focusing on the subtle sensations. "Hmmm…" He opened his eyes and gathered some energy for an intense blast. Throwing his arm forward, Neil released a charged bolt at a large moss-covered rock, focused more energy and did it again. He closed his eyes and waited a couple of seconds, focusing again on the sensations before he opened his eyes and said, "My energy is coming back quicker than usual. About twice as fast!"

"That's what I thought was happening," Elizabeth said. "But I wasn't used to running so much of it."

Neil handed her the gemstone back. "Well, finish recouping. Then we're going back to Meelyhn to regroup with the others."

There was a rustling on a tree limb above, and they looked up to see a gray, furry body glide from one branch to another. The fur gave way to a bat wing-like membrane between the front and rear limbs and a somewhat flat tail.

"It's another one of those big sugar gliders," Elizabeth said.

But then they heard "Meow."

"That's not a glider," Haley said. She jumped onto the tree and climbed. She came up to the limb and looked upon a short-haired cat. Gray fur with spots of white down her back, in a pattern much like that of a white-tail fawn. With deep blue-green eyes and white around the snout, she was absolutely gorgeous. But there was more! This cat had patagia between her front and rear limbs. The fur did not cover them, and they were reminiscent of a bat wing. The gray tail was also unusually flat in shape. "Whoa," Haley said. She conjured her helmet and scanned the cat.

SPECIES: CAT (FELIS CATUS)

GENETIC MANIPULATION DETECTED

THREAT LEVEL: MINIMUM

"Who did this to you?" Haley asked. Looking deep into those beautiful blue-green eyes, she empathically bonded and took a sharp inhale. Iris felt free in her leaps when she could feel the rush of air and glide from tree to tree. Iris turned and looked to a limb, and Haley followed her gaze.

A leap too far for Haley to make, the empath could feel Iris preparing to jump and started drawing upon her energy as she readied to do the same. Together, they bounded from the branch. Iris spread her limbs and began to glide while Haley released her energy. She kicked forward in a mid-air dash and made it to the limb with time to turn and greet Iris on the way in. Iris landed next to Haley and gave a soft chuff before rubbing against her shins. The empath reached down and gave Iris a pat on the head, then Iris turned, leaped and glided away.

"Wow!" Haley breathed as she thought about what she had just done. Energetically, it was no more strenuous than a pounce.

"Did you just fly?" Elizabeth shouted. "No fair! You got to fly last time."

"No," Haley responded. "Not exactly. I was…Um, darting forward?" She clung to the tree limb with her hands and let herself dangle before letting go for the drop. "The cat was given flaps like the glider things."

"That's…weird," Elizabeth said, her expression confused.

"We need to get back with the others," Neil said and led them along the path heading south. They were coming along the chasm when the hair on the back of their necks stood up.

"Archons," Elizabeth said through gritted teeth.

They all could feel it from ahead and coming in from the brush behind them.

"Uh-oh," Haley blurted while looking over her shoulder. She spun around and charged her potato gun.

Elizabeth held a sai in each hand, and Neil held an orb of yellow light in his hand. They could hear the rustling of foliage before the two archons stepped into view.

"Hello again." the Archon ahead of them said.

The one that was behind them stepped from the brush; scars were on his forearms, and a burn mark was on his neck, reminders of his fight with Sabrina. "Doesn't matter how far you go…"

Then both spoke as one, "…we will always find you."

Because of the continental barrier, they could not summon any demons, but they had plenty of magick at their disposal and looked forward to using it.

Neil flung his orb and immediately raised a protective field in anticipation of the incoming shards. They hit his field and dissipated but drained a bit of his energy.

Haley and Elizabeth released their blasts at the other Archon, who blocked them, dropped his field and released a couple blasts of his own, then quickly chanted. The girls blocked the incoming blasts and dropped their fields to return fire. When Haley dropped her field, the Archon spoke a final word, and she felt mystical energies converge upon her. She tried pushing her protective field back out, but it was too late.

Elizabeth let a few orbs fly; the first one hit, but the second one was blocked before he flung a few shards of red light in return.

Neil engaged his thrusters and lifted from the ground while throwing orbs at his opponent, who held up a field and began chanting while Neil shielded himself from the expected counterattack.

She started to shiver, feeling like her blood was turning to ice within her own veins. Haley kept her shield up and focused on her regenerative ability, hoping it would counteract whatever dark magick the Archon had cast upon her. Thankfully, it worked, and a second later, she felt like she was back to normal, so she dropped her field and blasted.

Elizabeth dodged the red shards and launched a charged orb, but the Archon already had his field back up and was chanting again. As soon as the mystic's blast hit his shielding, he dropped the barrier and went to speak the final word, but a hail of ethereal kittens hit him. The concussive bursts knocked him to the ground, with his ears ringing.

Disoriented, the Archon threw up his protective field, trying to focus and regain his bearings.

Neil shielded the expected blast from the Archon and dropped his field to throw another orb. That's when the Archon uttered the final word. Neil felt the enchantment right away but didn't know what it would do. He threw the orb to make him raise his field in hopes of having a couple seconds to figure out the predicament, but the orb went wide to the right.

The Archon followed the spell with a couple of blasts, and Neil fired the thrusters, going straight up and out of the way. A few more blasts came Neil's way, and he cut the thrusters to drop back down below the bolts that zipped by. The Archon launched another mystical bolt, and Neil tried to dodge to the right but went left instead. Directly into it! The blast knocked him off his feet and to the ground. Between his own energy and the PJs, Neil was able to take the hit, but it was still far from pleasant.

A volley of blasts was unleashed by Haley and Elizabeth at the dazed Archon, who kept his field up, surprised by how much punch the girls had in their attacks. He could feel his energy draining with each blast that hit his field, so he dropped it and darted off the path and into the jungle for cover and a chance to recoup. Haley took a step to give chase and stopped as she felt the icy cold again gripping the blood in her veins. Elizabeth stopped at the edge of the path, not stupid enough to chase him into the thicket alone.

"What's wrong?" Elizabeth asked, now noticing the energy clinging to Haley.

"It's making me freeze…I gotta heal," Haley chattered while focusing her energy on regeneration once again. The internal sting vanished, and her blood felt normal again as she took a breath. "I'm okay."

"No, you're not," Elizabeth said. "I can still feel his spell attached to you, and we…" She was knocked down by a charged orb from the Archon, who came rushing from the brush. She threw out her field just in time. The Archon lunged at the mystic, but his hands stopped, pressed against her barrier right before a bobcat burst against his torso, knocking him away from Elizabeth.

Neil hit the ground and scrambled back to his feet. Another blast was incoming for his right shoulder, so he tried to lean left and out of the way but instead leaned right and took it in the center of the chest. He fell to the ground, a little sore, but physically okay for the most part. And now he understood what the enchantment was doing. It was some kind of confusion spell that switched his comprehension of left and right.

He threw a blast toward the Archon, which again went wide, then held out his field and tried to concentrate on the enchantment's vibration. A couple of blasts hit the field while he set an intention of cleansing. He focused that cleansing energy and overlapped it with the enchanted field that clung to him, undoing the spell.

Dropping the field, he threw an orb at the oncoming Archon and smacked him square in the chest. The reptilian stumbled back, surprised at the return of Neil's coordination.

"You want to use spells like that?" He sneered. "Congratulations!" he continued with a raising voice. "You just unlocked hard mode!" A yellow glow appeared in his eyes.

Energy was gathered, intentions were set, and Neil waved a hand. Vines snaked out from the jungle around the path, reached for the Archon's limbs and ensnared the reptilian. The vines lifted him ten feet into the air, and the glow in Neil's eyes intensified.

With a shout, Neil swung his arm and moving in time with Neil's arm was a nearby tree limb. It swung out and down, the vines released their grip, and the limb smacked the Archon, sending him flying to the east. He hit and skipped off the ground, tumbled through a thick bush of briars and over the edge of the chasm. Neil collapsed from the intense energy use and nearly passed out.

Haley and Elizabeth both had energy charged and ready to go, scanning the brush for the hiding Archon. They heard Neil shout at his opponent, followed by a weird wood creaking sound echoing through the cavern from a swinging tree limb. They turned their heads to see the other Archon launch toward the chasm, and Neil collapsed to the ground.

"Neil!" Elizabeth shouted, and the girls turned to rush to his aid. That's when the Archon jumped from the bush and, with a word, threw out his arms. A bolt of lightning discharged from both his hands, jolting into the girls, knocking them to the ground in convulsions. Even disoriented, Haley could feel the rage flowing out of the Archon over the loss of his companion. He uttered the word again, and two more bolts of lightning struck the girls before they could shield themselves.

"You will *writhe* for this," the Archon growled and pulled his right arm to his chest, his hand clenched tight into a fist, and the red light started to shine out from between his fingers.

Neil pulled it together and pushed himself up. He raised his head to see the girls get struck by lightning and then again. He tuned in on the energy of the foliage around them, set an intention and focused his remaining energy. He noticed the Archon pull his arm in and make a fist as red light began to glow from between the fingers, so Neil engaged the thrusters and shot himself forward.

The Archon swung his arm out, releasing a couple shards of red light at the girls. The missiles sped toward their targets but slammed into something else instead. That something else dropped to the ground, and there Neil lay with two shards of red light in his chest. He lifted his head and looked the Archon in the eyes while a yellow glow appeared in his, and a tree limb swept down, launching the reptilian into the chasm. Neil dropped his head back to the ground as the shards dissipated, but now there were two open wounds in his chest. The PJs immediately applied pressure to his injuries to stop the bleeding, but one had nicked his heart and the other punctured a lung.

The girls were regaining their senses and started to register everything that had just happened. "Neil?! Neil!" They scrambled to him.

"What can we do?" Elizabeth asked.

"Stop, Kone," Neil rasped. "And tell Sandra and Junior that I love them." Those strained words were carried on Neil's last breath.

And then he was gone.

"No! No! No! No! No!" Haley cried while Elizabeth knelt on the ground beside him, tears streaming down her cheeks and her silent frown contorted, twisting with sorrow and rage. Neil's sleeve started to ripple and formed a metallic bracelet around his wrist. Haley wiped her face with her forearm, reached out and took hold of the bracelet. The clasp unhooked, and it opened. She clicked it onto her forearm, where it broke apart and rippled into her sleeve. Neil's com-system went dormant, stored inside of Haley's.

CHAPTER 19
Arachnophobia

Churgen, Atlantis

With the faint sound of whooshing air, Sabrina's katana swung and sliced into the attacking lizard. A follow-up stab with the other sword finished it off, and it collapsed into a pile of broken ice. They were at the bottom of Churgen's slope and had dealt with a couple of lounges on their way back. This latest one attacked just as they were about to start their climb.

A bolt pistol in each hand, Jake fired furiously, turning a lizard into ice chunks as another leaped toward him. He dropped his pistols and pulled out his climbing pick, swinging it with both hands and burying it in the lizard's head. It collapsed as he looked over his shoulder to see the last three lizards charging Sabrina. He rushed toward her to help as she put her katanas to work, but he slipped just as he got to her, and his foot wedged between a couple of rocks.

She plunged both katanas forward, skewering two lizards and they crumbled to ice as the third one bounded at the Hunter. It was too late when she tried to counter, and she collapsed beneath the lizard, but right as it tried to bite, Jake's pick embedded in its skull, turning it into a pile of ice. Sabria sat up and brushed the little ice chunks off her to see Jake lying on the ground, moaning in pain. His foot was still stuck between the rocks. He had snapped his ankle to reach the lizard.

"Jake!" She hurried to her feet and went to assist. It was definitely broken, and she was cautious not to make it worse when they extracted his foot. After applying a splint from a small med kit, they looked up the slope. "Can you still make this?" Sabrina asked.

"Yeah," Jake answered with a grunt. "I've had to climb with an injury like this once before. Thankfully, I'm not alone this time." He groaned as Sabrina helped him up, and he stood on his good foot. "It still isn't going to be a lot of fun, though."

"Once we get to the top, we might have someone in comm range and…" She gasped, and tears began to flow from her eyes.

"What happened?" Jake grabbed her arm to help her steady herself and almost fell for the effort.

"I…I…" She took another couple of breaths. "I know where Haley is. Or…which way she is."

"What happened?" Jake asked again.

"I just felt her emotions and…" Sabrina looked into Jake's eyes with tears in her own, "…I think someone just died."

Atlantis City, Atlantis

All three men were focused. Keith was hunched over, peering into a microscope. Nigel was adjusting the temperature on a vial of chemicals and Dimitri was going through documents on a holographic screen, deep in research.

"Still nothing," Keith said and stood up from the microscope. He grabbed a pencil, wrote a few notes on the bottom of a sheet of paper, and brought it over to Dimitri.

"I'll input the data once I finish this article," Dimitri said without looking away from the screen.

Nigel closed the burner's valve and held up a scanning device, monitoring the chemical concoction as it cooled. "These readings are giving me déjà vu." He rolled his eyes with a sigh, set the scanner down and turned toward Dimitri. "I sent the readings to your terminal if you want to see them…again."

"Thanks," Dimitri half-heartedly replied. He closed the article on his screen and stood up to stretch his back. "Ahhhh," he sighed, rolling his shoulders back as far as they would go, then he scooped the paper up from the desk to give Keith's notes a read.

"Ahem," they heard from the corner of the room, and the three scientists looked over to see a man. He was tall, around six feet, with a slender frame. His long black hair, contrasting his pale skin, was slicked back in a tidy fashion and matched the suit that he wore. The black trousers were of high quality, as was his dark purple silk shirt, which was buttoned up with a black tie and covered with a fine blazer. His shoes, also black, were polished to a shine. He took a couple of steps toward the scientists as he threw his arms out wide and with a big smile and said, "Greetings, curious people."

The three men looked to the newcomer, jaws dangling in shock. This was the first new face that any of them had seen in years.

The man in the black suit stopped about twelve feet away and said, "I'm looking for this woman." He swept his arm out wide to his right, and a woman appeared next to him. Thin with gray skin and black hair. Her clothing seemed to be made of black bandages.

None of the scientists recognized Hel, but Dimitri cocked his head and asked, "Is that a hologram?"

The man in the black suit smiled and, with a brief chuckle, looked to Dimitri as if he were a kindergarten teacher speaking to a slow student. "My dear simpleton," he waved his arms out and around, "Everything is a hologram." He gestured like he was giving a presentation to a large auditorium as he spoke. He thrust his finger into the air, "But," he held his hand out toward Dimitri, palm up. "In the way you meant it," he spun around, waving his hand by the illusion of Hel as it disappeared. He turned back and held his hands out in a ta-da gesture, "No."

Keith said, "I don't mean to derail this fascinating conversation, but…" he held his hands out in front of him, palms up, "…who are you and how did you get in here?"

The man flashed an amused smile as he placed his left hand in his pants pocket and held up his right, extending his index and middle fingers, "I…" He paused until all three of them were looking at his right hand to see the business card between his fingers. "…am just passing through." He walked up to Demitri, who was closest to him, reached out and set the card on the desk next to the scientist. "And I came here the same way I'll be leaving." He turned and walked back to the center of the room and smiled. "By magick."

"That's impossible here," Nigel said.

With a beaming smile, the man said, "Impossible is what I do! Now if you see her," he pointed at the card on the table and smiled, "Let me know."

The three scientists all looked at the card on the desk as he pointed, but when they lifted their eyes back up, he was gone.

Nigel regained control of his slack jaw and asked, "What in the Uniralt's name was that?"

"And how did he teleport here with all the bindings on the complex?" Dimitri added as he picked up the card. One side had a yellow and blue pattern that looked like it belonged on the back of a playing card. Dimitri flipped it over to see that it was a playing card with the dimensions of a business card. And this one was the joker with the words 'impossible is what I do' printed beneath the face.

"What kind of nonsense is this?"

The image of the joker morphed into Hel and then back into a joker. Dimitri swung his arm, intending to toss the card back onto the desk, but it stuck to him. "Huh?" He shook his hand, but the card would not separate from his fingers. Demitri limped his wrist and flailed his hand back and forth, but the card remained. "What the…?"

Nigel and Keith came to Dimitri's side to see if they could help. Dimitri dared to grab the card with his left hand and found he was able to let go with his right. Only to have the same problem again on his left.

"Here, let me," Keith said as he reached up to take the card from Dimitri's hand, but when he tried to take it, he discovered that it was two cards stuck together. One slipped off into Keith's hand while the other stayed in Dimitri's.

Nigel went to his bench and came right back with a pair of pliers. "Allow me."

"Certainly," replied Demetri as he held the card out.

Clamping down on one end of the card, Nigel pulled, but the card wouldn't separate.

"Go ahead," Dimitri said. "Really pull."

"Hey, guys!" Keith called out.

"One second," said Dimitri.

Nigel gave a strong yank, and Dimitri almost toppled forward. But the card remained.

"No, *really* pull."

"Guys!" Keith called.

Dimitri steadied himself as Nigel gripped hard and said, "One moment, please."

Nigel pulled with all his weight and fell backward as the pliers slid right off the card. "Ow." he blurted when he hit the floor.

But the card remained.

"Are you okay?" Keith asked while reaching out to help Nigel get back on his feet.

"Yes," he replied while straightening his shirt. "I'm just…" Nigel took note of Keith's hands as he reached. "Where's your card?"

"That's what I've been trying to tell you." Keith reached into his pocket, pulled out the card and showed it to them. Smiling, he slid it back into his pocket and then held up an empty hand.

"Oh," Dimitri said in a soft voice and slid his hand into his pocket.

And the card released.

The Tundra, West Antarctica

Her hands opened and released a burst of energy in Hel's face, but then Bast noticed the emotions. The sorrow, the anger and the despair.

They were strong and she instantly knew who they came from. She needed to disengage from the fight without Hel following, so, Bast vanished from the tundra just as Hel's next attack came in. Hel spun around, expecting another sneak attack, but was confused when nothing came.

Futola, Antarctica

Haley removed Neil's glasses from his face and closed his eyes. She burst into another round of sobs, stood up and hugged Elizabeth, who was also falling apart.

Bast appeared. "Girls, what hap…" She gasped. "Neil!"

In an instant, she was kneeling on the ground beside him, her eyes glowing with golden light, and held her hands above his body. She stood up and swept her hands back and forth, searching the area for Neil's spirit.

Nothing.

She would usually proceed to the astral plane to search there, where she could bring a spirit back if one had not yet moved on, but with the continental barrier in place, she could not even try that. There was nothing she could do. "Neil," she cried softly.

The golden glow faded from the Egyptian goddess's eyes, replaced by tears as she turned slowly to Haley and Elizabeth. "I'm sorry. He's beyond my reach." The girls leaned into Bast. She wrapped her arms around them, and the tears continued to flow. After a moment of grieving, Bast said, "I need to bring you back to the village." She barely finished the sentence when an orb of black mist slammed into her side, knocking her to the ground.

"Oh, you two again," Hel smirked, pulling her hand back to throw a blast when Bast shouted, "No!" The Egyptian goddess vanished from her spot and was instantly in front of Hel, grabbing her by the wrists. She teleported away, pulling Hel with her.

Haley sniffled, looked to Elizabeth and asked, "What do we do now?"

Wiping her eyes, Elizabeth furrowed her brow, sniffled again and said, "We stop Kone." She turned to face Haley and tried to keep herself from crying. "We have one of the keys already. We get the other two and finish it. One of 'em is in a lava area. Can you make it across the chasm?"

Her lips still quivering, Haley answered, "I think so." She looked at Neil's body. "But we can't just leave him here."

After a few seconds of thought, Elizabeth said, "We'll come back for him." She turned to Haley before the farmer could respond. "I don't like it either, but there's nothing we can actually do about it right now."

Haley started to nod. She hated it, but Elizabeth was right, and to stay here was to invite another attack. The girls had to move, and the bridge was a stone's throw away. They each took one of his hands and said goodbye. Then Haley added, "We're gonna beat him. I promise." Finally, they stood up and pressed forward.

Within a minute, the girls were by the chasm, standing on the edge of the broken bridge and looking down. "You sure you can do this?" Elizabeth asked.

"Um, yeah?" came Haley's response.

"Too bad the rope is on the other side. Would have been nice if you only had to do this once," Elizabeth commented.

"After all this, the elevator better work."

"Right? But the PJs *did* say that it'll work."

"Okay," Haley let out a long sigh. "I need a running start."

Haley jogged back ten feet, turned and sprinted. She reached the edge of the bridge, kicking into the air with a great leap. She focused her energy and, at the apex, kicked forward. The air dash took her most of the way. "Uh-oh," Haley said while gathering more energy. "Please work!" she shouted as she kicked forward again, over the edge of the chasm and above solid ground, where she dropped to a stop. "Yes!" she shouted with clenched fists.

Grabbing the rope, she uncoiled it to see that it would be long enough. After securing one end with a few good knots, Haley held the loose end and ran out, jumping from the edge. She kicked forward once and then again, landing near Elizabeth.

"Alright!" Elizabeth said.

Haley went to work, tying the knots after pulling the rope tight when more of those strange vegetation creatures arrived. "Climb across now! I'll keep 'em away!" she shouted.

Elizabeth reached into her pocket, pulled out the green gem and placed it in Haley's hand. Haley started gathering her energy as Elizabeth knelt, grabbed and climbed out onto the rope. The nimble girl had no problem shimmying across as Haley crackled with blue and purple light. She unleashed her sustained beam and swept it across the oncoming group of weird little creatures. Her energy came back quick enough to focus some for a charged shot, and a bobcat-shaped orb hit the next closest group, scattering them across the ground while Elizabeth neared the other side. The young mystic reached the edge and said, "I'm across. Go!"

Haley released one more charged blast, turned, ran, and jumped. She kicked forward once and then again to tumble onto the ground near Elizabeth, dizzy. She tried to stand but stumbled back onto her butt. "Looks like it's my turn," she groaned before reaching into one of her pockets to pull out some B12 supplements. She took one and looked up to see the remaining leaf men charging at them right off the edge of the broken bridge.

"They literally have no brains," Elizabeth commented.

Haley stood up and said, "I'm feeling better." She handed the gem back to Elizabeth, and they went to the building. Inside was a lift platform big enough for a vehicle and a control booth that had power but was switched off. After another scan, Haley found the power switch, and the control console's screen lit up. The PJs synced in, and control of the elevator was theirs.

"Ready?" Elizabeth asked.

"Not really," Haley answered.

"Well, we're going," And the lift platform began its descent.

Buruum, Atlantis

The air was getting stuffy and difficult to breathe. Haley's bandana slid up and over her face. The simple-looking cloth would do more than filter the air. It could even function as a rebreather if needed. Elizabeth also conjured a bandana from her PJs right before the lift stopped at the bottom. The large doors separated in the center and moved to the sides, sliding into pockets carved in the stone.

The girls stepped out through the spacious doorway to see that the elevator shaft was inside a large stalagmite in the middle of a cavern flowing with magma streams. The heat was too much for Haley's exposed skin, so she conjured her helmet and some gloves. The nanobots of her clothes opened along her back, pulled the pigtails under the layer of clothing, and sealed itself shut. She was completely covered from head to toe. Elizabeth was surprised that she could still feel the heat yet was not overwhelmed by it; apparently, a result of her pyrokinesis.

The cavern stone was black, and the glow of the magma streams gave everything an eerie appearance. There was once a bridge that went to the western wall, but it, too, collapsed like the one above. Along the eastern wall was a large area that had a two-story building with vents along the upper wall. Elizabeth scanned the structure, learning that the vents were carbon collectors and within the collection station was a portgate. "Guess we know why they're not worried about the bridge anymore."

Looking along the cavern floor, they picked a path to the collection station, which required jumping to a couple of small rocky islands. "How hot is this stuff?" Haley asked. The inside of her visor read:

2700 FAHRENHEIT

"How much heat can the PJs take?!"

**THERMAL THRESHOLD:
4500 FAHRENHEIT**

"Oh, good," Haley sighed.

They jumped from island to island, making it to the western pathway with no trouble. Elizabeth scanned the portgate and synced the com-system with it but did not override the controls because that might show up on Atlantis City's system. They were not interested in drawing that kind of attention.

"So, which way do you think it is?" Haley asked. "I think it would be that way," she continued, pointing to the north. Away from the city.

Elizabeth shrugged. "Who knows. We might as well check that way first." She started walking up the northern path, and Haley walked beside her.

"So, does it feel hot to you?"

"Yeah," Elizabeth said. "It's weird. Even though I can feel that it's hot, I'm not uncomfortable. I'm not even sweating. But it's still too stuffy to breathe without the bandana."

"Can you make the air easier to breathe?"

"I...I don't think so," Haley felt Elizabeth's energy increase, she was trying to do it, but after a moment, "Nope."

They passed another collection station and synced their PJs with the portgate before continuing, and it wasn't long before they reached the end of the path. The only way forward was a series of rocks jutting out like platforms from the cavern's western wall, leading to the northern end, where there was a wide ledge with a couple of tunnels that continued north. In between those two tunnels was a statue carved into the stone. A Human body with the head of a goat, two horns protruding out from the head and curved back behind the ears. The wall behind it was carved into a pair of feathery wings, and the six-foot-tall figure sat cross-legged with its right hand pointing up, two fingers extended. The left hand also had two fingers extended, pointing down. An uneasy vibe, like that of Molech's temple, washed over the girls from those tunnels.

"Are you kidding me?" Haley whined.

"Wasn't 'hard to get to' part of what you expected?" Elizabeth asked in return.

"Yeah, but…Kone has to get there if he wants the gem. How does he do it?"

"Maybe he can just teleport there," Elizabeth speculated.

Haley sighed and then leaped to the first rock. Once she jumped to the next, Elizabeth jumped to the vacated platform. As they hopped from landing to landing, the magma below began to bubble right before it rose from the stream with a humanoid shape, followed by a second. And then a third.

"Haley…look down."

Heeding Elizabeth, Haley saw the lava people who were growing in number. "Oh, great," she huffed.

"Let's go!" Elizabeth shouted, and they picked up their pace.

One of the lava men splashed against the wall and turned into a puddle, which flowed up the wall toward the girls, followed by another.

Elizabeth reached out with her mystical senses and felt what they were: a combination of earth and fire mixed with fluid form. She focused and took hold of that heat, could feel the vibration of stone and peeled the molten puddle from the wall, dropping it back down to the magma flow. Haley shot a blast at the other, flowing along the wall, and the concussive burst knocked it back down to the stream.

Another slid along the wall, dropped onto a platform and regained a humanoid shape. The lava man drew its arm back and threw a blob of magma. Even with the limited footroom, she could easily dodge. But when that one was joined by many, those blobs quickly became a problem. Elizabeth shielded herself from a couple of blobs and then used her kinetic abilities to rip a few of them from the landings.

Haley fired a few blasts, hitting her targets, but then a blob landed on her. Though hot, the PJs were able to protect her from any burns, but the blobs were mystically charged and still hurt. Her potato gun became covered with whisps of blue and purple light. She raised her arm toward four of them in one spot and released a bobcat, bursting the lot of them apart.

They made it to the ledge and ran for the tunnels. "At least they're slow," Haley said with a smirk.

"I'm okay with that," Elizabeth chuckled back.

They heard a strange sound from above, like a bristled metal brush dragging against stainless steel. The girls looked up and then dove to the sides when a giant spider creature dropped down between them. It was as big as her dad's truck and formed of many small but sharp chunks of obsidian. "I hate spiders!" Haley shouted and hit it with a blast as soon as she came back up.

The kitten hit the arachnid and gave it a shudder, but it seemed unharmed. The spider squealed and launched pieces of obsidian at Haley, who shielded herself from the volley.

A few shards fell off from the spider, turned into smaller spiders and scurried toward the farmgirl while Elizabeth was focusing. The young mystic, crackling with amber and indigo light, ran around the spider, placing it between her and the edge, dug in her heels and unleashed her beam. The spider staggered back toward the edge but did not go over until a bobcat burst against it.

The other spiders got too close to Haley, and she had to fall back into the eastern tunnel while lava men swarmed Elizabeth, forcing her into the western.

Without the glow of the magma, the tunnels became dark. Haley's visor switched to night vision so she could see the spiders chasing her. Blue and purple light wisped on her arm cannon, and she fired a charged blast at the closest spider, and it staggard back from the hit. Another was crawling along the wall, and she fired a few shots at the legs, dropping it to the floor. She jumped up and clung to the ceiling with her left hand while firing a few more blasts. She charged and let loose with another bobcat at the first spider, and it fell apart into a pile of shards.

Releasing her cling from the ceiling, Haley kicked forward through the air, and when she came directly above the next spider, she pounced. Haley's feet slammed on top of the second spider's back, releasing a pulse of blue energy that rippled out as she rebounded back up to the ceiling. A blue glow reflected on the inside of her visor from her eyes as she looked upon the final creature and hissed, "I hate spiders!" She released her cling and pounced, plunging feet first into the spider's back, but this time, she did not rebound on the pulse of energy. Haley drove her feet to the ground and the energy pulse rippled out, spreading the obsidian shards that used to be a spider everywhere.

"Beth!" she shouted and started to run back when she could hear the screech of many more spiders coming through the tunnel.

"I'm still here," she heard Elizabeth's voice barely scratch through in her speakers, but then, with too much rock between them, the signal was lost.

Haley turned and ran deeper into the tunnel.

CHAPTER 20
True Faith

Meelyhn, Atlantis

His eyes fell to the workbench and the small round object set on its surface. "That looks a lot like a restraining disk."

Serge sighed. "That's about all it's good for," he told Manny. "We've been trying to make a portable disruption emitter, but the wattage required is too high for what the power cell can produce." A restraining disk could disrupt one's conscious connection to their mystical field when in direct contact with a person but could not push the signal out any further.

"I have a design that might do the trick, but no way to test it without the right material. I need something even more conductive than a graphene-silver mesh."

Manny tilted his head, "There's only one thing that I know of that's more conductive."

Serge lowered his head with another sigh. "Flekkle."

"You have access to the greatest technologies on Earth, and you can't get Flekkle?"

Serge started to explain, "About a hundred years ago, Kone traded almost all the Flekkle we had in the Second Density to the Sabidars for a mass shipment of mayum and some scientists who understood how to work with it." He shrugged and continued, "I guess he plans to eventually have access to the Third Density's supply, but the mayum was far more valuable to his purposes at the time. Mayum isn't found on Earth and is kind of rare throughout the galaxy. Word is that some of the wealthier civilizations use it to plate the hulls of their ships, allowing them to withstand the heat of a star. But Flekkle is far rarer as was the only way to acquire the amount of mayum being offered."

"How much Flekkle would you need to test your theory?"

"All we have is an ounce. I need two ounces just to make one. And I don't even know if it will work."

"No, not one," Manny replied. "Two." He was gripping the pouch that hung from his neck.

Serge was confused by Manny's statement. "What?"

"You'll make two. And *when* they work, give one of them to Sabrina," Manny said. He released his grip and let the pouch hang as he used his index fingers to pull the top open. "Along with enough mayum to forge her two new katanas. In exchange," he reached into the pouch with the fingers of his right hand a removed two metallic ingots, "I'll give you enough Flekkle to test your theory."

Serge's face was one of shock. "I, I uh…I," he shook his head, "I have to talk to Laris, but I don't think he'd object. But we're still one ounce short to make two, and how are you so certain that it will work?"

With a grin, Manny replied, "Because I've already done it. I combined Flekkle and graphene to make the power cells for the port-outs. That's why there are so few."

"What's a port-out?"

"A hand-held device I made that can be linked with a gate or beacon. It makes for a nice getaway. And three will be enough." He held out the two ingots.

Serge still had a stunned look on his face, staring at the two one-ounce ingots in Manny's hand. He probably would have stood there a while longer if Manny hadn't snapped him back by asking, "Don't you have a call to make?"

Atlantis City, Atlantis

"Katanas? You know that we can't use the mayum for personal projects." Born in Atlantis, Laris was a Sabidar man, a descendant of the scientist slaves Kone purchased generations before. A deep yellow skin, Sabidars had no hair but, instead, what looked like flexible scales covering the tops of their heads. Their anatomical proportions, however, were much the same as most other humanoid species.

Having been born in Earth's Second Density, he too had a secondary pigment, which was orange and speckled at the color line. Laris was in charge of fabrication and had to keep track of their mayum inventory. The only authorized use at the current time was to produce more combat knives for the Commandos. And even that was done sparingly.

"Laris, turn on your screen."

He sighed and reached out, tapping the panel, and his monitor came to life. "Who's that?"

"This," Serge said with a smile, "is Manny. And he is the one commissioning the Katanas in exchange for this." He held up the two ingots, and Laris's jaw dropped.

"Is that…?"

"Yes. Flekkle. He gave us two ounces."

Laris rubbed his face, then his eyes and looked back at the screen. A couple of taps on the control panel and the scanner confirmed the news. "And it's enough to make that power cell!" A smile spread across his still-shocked face, and he exclaimed, "For that, I can justify making a doorstop!"

"Great!" Serge began tapping his own control panel and said, "I'm sending you the specifications."

Manny added, "Also, keep in mind the handle. It's designed to alter its shape in particular circumstances."

Looking over the data, Laris saw that the handle could expand or contract to the user's grip, allowing Sabrina to use it in one hand without slipping. "Yeah, we can do that. They should be ready within the hour."

"What?! Only an hour?!" Manny figured that it would take a considerable amount of time to make the swords.

"Yeah. I just put the info into the settings, and the sonic forge will do the rest." Now that the excitement of the Flekkled promise had fully sunk in, he remembered the reality of the situation and asked, "Wait? Manny? How come I've never heard of you before? Where'd you come from?"

"New York originally."

"Never mind," Laris said. "The less I know, the less trouble I'll get in." He turned his head a bit, looking at Serge on his monitor. "Bring him here in a little bit. The katanas will be ready."

"Thanks," Serge said. "Now, remembering our theory, I want you to take a look at this." He made a few taps on the panel, sending Manny's power cell design to Laris. "This is a functional power cell that he uses for personal port devices. And this…" he sent another design, "…is his modification for the portable disruption emitter."

Upon inspecting the diagram, Laris saw that it was very similar to the version that he and Serge had made but could already tell that it would be more efficient. "Wow!"

With a smile and a shrug, Manny said, "I've had the opportunity to tinker with it a little over the years."

"While you fabricate the swords, I'll get to work on that power cell." Having everything he needed and most of it already set up, he figured he could have the new batteries ready in that same amount of time.

Buruum, Atlantis

She focused her energy, set an intention and pushed it out to the environment around her. A little something Elizabeth learned over the last week in Tir na nOg: tiny specs of soft yellow light spread through the tunnel, illuminating the area.

A group of lava men and a couple of obsidian spiders were closing on Elizabeth. There was even another kind of creature coming from the other direction. A fleshy three-foot ball with two eyes, a large toothy mouth and a pair of long, skinny legs were rushing toward her on its big, flappy feet. It didn't even look like it belonged here or anywhere, but that was par for the course when Apophis would cast a spell.

Having just lost contact with Haley, she looked around and realized that there was only one option. Ripping a page from Haley's book, Elizabeth sent a mental command to her com, readying a song. She flicked the lighter with her left hand, and a lick of flame ran up her arm, across her shoulders and down to her right fist. She focused and built up the energy in that fist, and the fire surrounding it flared. The lava men on one side and weird fleshy-head creatures on the other, they came closing in at the same time.

Elizabeth waited until the last second and slammed her fist to the ground. A wave of flame rushed out in all directions, knocking the creatures back as a hard-hitting electric guitar riff blasted from her PJs speakers, playing Motley Crue's Looks That Kill. She stood up, an amber glow in her eyes and holding a sparkling amber and indigo orb in each hand.

She threw them at the closest lava men, taking down two, then drew her sai as she pivoted to deal with the…whatever they were. She pierced the tip into the closest one and ran a blast of energy through the shaft, blowing it backward and knocking over two others.

She spun around again, charging up and crackling with light. She unleashed her beam through her sai and cleared out most of the lava men along with one of the spiders. She pivoted again, lifted her right leg and launched a forward kick into the jaw of another head-creature.

It tumbled back, and she launched a volley of blasts, destroying it and one other. Her energy came back quick due to the gemstone, but she wanted to give her mystical attacks a rest before she wore herself down, so she went into a series of melee attacks with a few casual blasts mixed in.

Since she would need her energy to take down that other spider and the last few lava men, Elizabeth continued to physically beat back the head-creatures while she recouped.

Between her augmented strength and the last year of training, this was almost a fun challenge for the young mystic as she fought her way further into the tunnel. There were a few of the head-creatures left when the lava men and spider caught up, but Elizabeth was ready. She reached out and felt the fire-based energy of the lava men.

Pulling on that element, she merged it with her own energy, and her eyes glowed with amber light. Flares erupted from the lava men as they burst apart and expanded into rolling flames, filling and spiraling down the tunnel to wipe out the rest of the head-creatures. She turned with a charge blast readied and launched it at the spider. It hit, and she followed it up with a volley of regular blasts. One more charged blast and the spider fell into a pile of shards.

"Haley?"

With no answer on the comm, Elizabeth sprinted back to the tunnel entrance.

The air was getting cooler as Haley continued running down the widening tunnel, launching a charged blast behind her as she went. She ran a bit more and started to crackle with light before she spun around and unleashed her sustained blast, demolishing the spiders. "Phew!" she exclaimed and took a few seconds to catch her breath. Looking around, Haley saw that the tunnel opened into a large, worked room with a thirty-foot goat-man statue standing at the far end of the chamber; a red gemstone in the middle of its chest. She heard a similar sound to the screech of the spiders, but at a lower pitch and it was coming from behind the statue.

"Beth?" she tried on the comm. Nothing.

A doorway manifested and closed, blocking Haley's exit. The screeching sound got louder and louder and so Haley readied a charged blast as she heard the tapping of multiple obsidian limbs clacking on the temple floor. The construct scurried around from the back of the statue, Haley did not like what she saw and scanned the new threat.

This creature, like the spiders, was comprised of many obsidian shards, but was bigger, with pinchers and a tail. A giant scorpion, twice the size of the big spider was charging for her. "Ah, spuds!"

An advisory popped up in her HUD:

CONCENTRATION OF FIRE ON
JOINTS RECOMMENDED

The visor highlighted the vulnerable joints in yellow when the creature came into view. Haley took aim and fired a bobcat at its left front limb. The blast hit, and the creature wobbled but quickly regained its bearings. A volley of four blasts followed, and three of them hit the target, but the scorpion kept on coming. It closed the distance, and Haley threw up her field as the tail shot forward, overtop the scorpion's body and down onto Haley. The tail's pointed tip skipped off Haley's protective field, but the hard impact drained a good chunk of her energy. She dropped her field and fired a few more blasts, breaking the left claw limb from its body.

Staggering, the scorpion shrieked and gave a snapping swipe with the right claw. Haley leaped back and out of the way before firing another volley of four blasts. She continued using only her regular blasts while dodging to let her energy replenish. She took out two more legs when the tail snapped up, and the tip started pulsing with red light.

"Uh-oh!" She pushed out her protective sphere just before a red beam fired at her. She held it off, but it used almost as much energy as the stab from the tail. With a few limbs out of the way, Haley made that tail her new priority. She dropped her field while running around the side and launched a bobcat at the base of its tail. The scorpion turned to face her and swiped with its claw, which Haley again dodged right before making another run to its side. It turned with her, not allowing Haley to get a clear shot while another red glow pulsed from the tail's tip.

I hope this works! She watched the number of pulses and then dove forward, underneath the scorpion as the beam unleashed to hit the rocky ground. Haley came out from behind and launched another charged shot at the base of the tail, the concussive burst dealing visible damage.

She climbed the wall as the scorpion spun to face her. Haley launched herself with a mid-air dash to land on the scorpion's back and ran to the base of the tail. The ethereal claws extended from her nails, and she clawed at the tail's base. Swipe after swipe, Haley slashed with reckless abandon, gouging out chunks of rock as the creature spun around, unable to reach her with a physical attack. The tail's tip started to pulse again, but Haley fired a charged blast into the gouges, and the tail finally broke free from the body as the red pulsing light flickered to a stop.

The scorpion thrashed about like a bucking bronco, but Haley clung to it with her claws, refusing to be thrown. It backed into the cave's wall in another attempt to dislodge her, but she jumped toward the head just before impact, and when she was directly above, Haley pounced.

Her feet hit the top and drove it to the ground. The rippling wave of energy released blew the head apart, and the rest of the body fell to pieces. She stumbled to the wall and slumped down onto her butt, winded. "Beth?"

Nothing.

After catching her breath, Haley stood and jogged to the statue. She looked up at the demonic-looking figure that towered over her, inhaled deeply and blew out a sigh. "This thing is creepy." She popped her claws and scaled the front of the statue, claimed the gemstone and hopped down. "Yes!"

Her quiet little celebration was interrupted by a feeling…a sense of dread…Elizabeth was terrified!

"Beth!" Haley shouted and bolted back down the tunnel.

Sprinting, Elizabeth returned to the tunnel entrance, intending to go into the other tunnel in search of Haley, but was startled by an

unexpected sight. Down on the cavern floor stood a man. He had short brown hair and a clean-shaven chin, brown eyes and tan skin. Clothed in blue jeans, sneakers and an orange sweatshirt, the man was five feet and seven inches tall and had his hands in his pockets with a casual stance. No protective gear whatsoever. He looked up at Elizabeth with confusion, then in a flash of orange light, he was standing on the ledge, ten feet in front of her.

The hairs on the back of her neck stood up, and Elizabeth found his bulky and muscular frame to be intimidating as the man stared at her with a sinister smirk. "Who are you?" the young mystic asked.

"So, you're one of the girls causing them so much trouble," he said, ignoring the question. "What are you doing down here?"

"Trying to find a way out."

He started to laugh and pointed at his symbol, the statue to Elizabeth's left, "Oh boy, kid, did you go the wrong way!" He continued to laugh but then gave a quick sneer when his eyes settled on the cross hanging around her neck.

"What?" she demanded.

With a scoff, Baphomet pointed at the cross and said, "One of *His* kids, I see."

"Aren't we all," she stated.

A smile spread across Baphomet's face, and he held up his hand, conjuring an orb of hellfire as he replied. "Let's find out."

The malicious god flung the orb at Elizabeth, and she dove to the side, throwing her own in response. Baphomet swung his left arm up in front and backhanded Elizabeth's bolt away as he threw another and another, making the young mystic dance.

"You're fast. Good," he smirked and added. "This might actually be fun."

He unleashed a barrage of orbs and shards. Elizabeth twisted, ducked and darted side to side, avoiding the attacks, but Baphomet smiled and held his hand out, fingers forward and unleashed a bolt of lightning.

The bolt contacted Elizabeth mid torso, sending her into convulsions while she flew backward. Amber and indigo light splashed out from Elizabeth, impacting the wall, then she dropped butt-first to the floor with an "Ooph!"

Elizabeth grunted while scrambling back to her feet as Baphomet folded his arms across his chest, smiling. Gathering her energy, Elizabeth conjured another orb in each hand.

Pulling his right hand out from under his left arm, Baphomet held out his hand with his palm up and shrugged. "Well?" He slipped his hand back and stood there with his arms crossed.

The young mystic let loose, throwing a volley of bolts at the malicious god, but he just stood there, arms folded, as every shot slammed into him with no effect.

With a smile, Baphomet unfolded his arms and threw an orb of hellfire. Elizabeth side-stepped the blast while tugging at it with her pyrokinesis as it zipped by. She pulled a lick of flame, and it wrapped around her hand, funneling her own energy into it and with a burst, it expanded into streams of flame swirling around her torso and arms.

"Interesting," Baphomet muttered.

Elizabeth began hurling balls of hellfire right back at the man, but this, too, was ineffective.

Baphomet slipped his right hand into his pocket while shaking his head with a chuckle. "You don't get it, do you?" He held his hand out, palm up and pointed with his index finger. As he curled his finger, Elizabeth rose from the floor. She couldn't move her arms and felt her stomach sink into an anxious nausea as Baphomet approached. "You can't do anything to me." He walked right up to the suspended mystic and leaned in close to where she could feel the heat of his breath on her face as he spoke. "You are just a mortal child." The sinister smile on his face grew larger. "I am a god."

He reached up and gently tapped his finger on her sternum, and she sped through the air, back into the wall. "Uh," she blurted as she crumpled to the floor for a second time. Elizabeth grunted, propping herself back up with her elbows and looked at Baphomet. "You…" she grunted some more as she stood back to her feet, "…are *not* God."

"Yet here I stand, ruling over you," Baphomet replied. "Tell ya what, kid. Those little Nerf balls you toss around ain't nothing, but if you do just three little things," another grin made its way onto Baphomet's face, "I'll let you live."

Elizabeth looked at him with contempt.

"Relax," Baphomet said, "It's nothing crazy. I'll boost your powers and get both you and your friend out of here."

"I don't believe you, and I don't trust you," Elizabeth flatly stated. "Why would you even do that?"

"Because you've got talent, kid. And I'm curious to see what you could really do with the right opportunity. And kid, I am that opportunity." He held his hands out to the sides with the palms up. "All you gotta do is stay out of Kone's way, perform a minor task or two for me and…" Baphomet pointed at the cross around her neck, "…and take that thing off. I don't wanna see it."

Elizabeth shot him an incredulous look as she wrapped her fingers around the small wooden cross with a tight grip. "No way," she said with resolve.

"Let me put it this way," Baphomet said. "take my offer, or you'll suffer a slow and painful death…starting now." Her stomach was churning like a washing machine on a spin cycle. Baphomet was in total control, and a horrific end awaited Elizabeth if she did not comply. "C'mon," Baphomet pushed. "All ya gotta do is say okay, and everything will be fine. You and your friend will be safe. You don't want to die, do you?"

Elizabeth lowered her head and blew out a sigh. A couple of seconds later, she began raising back up to make eye contact with Baphomet as she said, "If it's His will…" she narrowed her eyes as an amber glow flared from within, "…then fine!" Her defiant streak coming back in full, Elizabeth pulled together all the energy she could muster and unleashed a sustained beam at the god.

Baphomet stood there and took the blast as if nothing were even happening. It lasted for a couple of seconds, then Elizabeth lowered her arms. That was her most potent blast, and it still did nothing.

"Then fine it is. So long, kid," Baphomet said with a shrug and threw his hand out, unleashing a stream of hellfire.

Holding her own hands up, Elizabeth used the energy she had left to erect a protective field to block the stream of flame. She could feel herself drain as the hellfire licked at her field, and she was becoming lightheaded. Her eyes glowed as she strained to maintain the shielding, but she knew that there was nothing left. "Father," Elizabeth softly grunted. "Looks like I'm coming home."

She rocked back and forth as her balance shifted into a wave of vertigo while the amber glow in her eyes dimmed and flickered. She closed her eyes and felt her consciousness slipping from the world as it spun around her, but the spinning sensation stopped, and she opened her eyes to find that she was still there. The flickering in her eyes became a steady glow and intensified, shifting in color from amber to a brilliant white. She then realized that her protective sphere was still holding, but the amber and indigo ripples now matched the intense white glow from her eyes.

The stream of hellfire continued, yet Elizabeth stood firm, holding it back. Baphomet finally relented and couldn't believe his eyes. There stood Elizabeth, her eyes still flaring with white light. She conjured an orb, and it, too, was white. The young mystic took a step forward, throwing her blast into Baphomet.

And he winced.

Baphomet reflexively placed his hand over the side of his stomach, surprised by the sting. He lifted his head and looked into Elizabeth's defiant eyes with a glare of his own as he hissed, "So be it…Paladin." He stood back up, straightened, and a red glow appeared in his eyes, accompanied by two ethereal goat horns of red light protruding from his head. "But your new career will be short-lived!" he roared and hurled a bolt of lightning.

The young mystic summoned her field in time to block the attack, then charged forward, throwing more bolts of white light. Baphomet returned fire as the nimble Elizabeth twisted and dodged, closing the gap between them. She sidestepped a blast just a few feet away and leaped forward, channeling energy into her fist as she swung it forward.

The attack connected with his jaw, and he twisted to his right, rolling with the punch. Baphomet turned and stood straight back up with a bruise on his chin and a smile. "You are too cute…but I'm still gonna kill ya."

She threw another punch, but Baphomet caught it in his left palm. Elizabeth spent the last year training, but Baphomet loved a good brawl, and he had been at it for thousands of years. The new paladin had nothing he hadn't seen before. He squeezed down on her hand, and she shouted in pain. "Ahhhh!"

Her hand was about to break, so she held up her left and released a bolt of energy. Not letting go, Baphomet winced again, so Elizabeth unleashed a couple more, balled her hand into a fist and threw a punch. Baphomet caught it in his right and squeezed down on this hand, too.

"Ahhhh!" she shouted again. Both her hands were trapped in his, and he kept the pressure steady—right before the breaking point—to prolong the pain.

Trying her best to push through, Elizabeth found one clear thought and went with it. She jumped and kicked both her feet forward, funneling as much energy into her limbs as she could, and connected with Baphomet's solar plexus. The surprise move made Baphomet let go as he stumbled backward, and Elizabeth landed on her back. She rolled onto her stomach and started to push herself up, but a hand clamped down on the back of her collar, and she was lifted into the air.

Baphomet pulled her up about four feet off the ground, letting go as he kicked, and a splash of white, amber and indigo light burst out when his foot slammed into her stomach. Elizabeth was launched across the ledge, and Baphomet leaped into the air, following her trajectory.

Crashing to the floor, Baphomet landed feet first on her back, making her flail as the wind was knocked out of her. Gasping for breath, Elizabeth was hoisted up again by the back of her collar. He held her there for a moment while her wind came back. "Got some air now?" he asked in a condescending tone. "Feel better, Little Girl?" Baphomet let her go, and she dropped down. As soon as her feet touched the floor, a kick slammed into her back, between the shoulder blades, launching her forward ten feet before landing face-first near the edge.

"Uh…" Elizabeth groaned. Blood trickled from her nose and the corner of her mouth, and she felt Baphomet's grip on the back of her collar once more. She couldn't catch her breath, nor could she even think straight, gripped by pure terror.

"Now that we've gotten the warmup out of the way, the real fun can begin. How about we…"

She could still feel his grip on her collar, but Elizabeth grunted as she dared to lift her head and see why he had stopped talking. Another man stood on the cavern floor. He was six feet and two inches tall with pale skin and long auburn hair that was thick and wavey. His beard, a lighter red color, was just as thick, and his eyes were green like emeralds. He wore a blue and white plaid flannel shirt, blue jeans and hiking boots.

"Of course," Baphomet muttered as the man's eye illuminated with green light. At the same time, a green and purple rack of ethereal antlers became visible, intensified, and then faded along with the glow in his eyes.

Baphomet let go of the young mystic's collar when Cernunnos took a step forward, and Elizabeth rolled over just in time to see her assailant disappear in a flash of orange light.

After a wave of Cernunnos's hand, all of Elizabeth's pain disappeared, along with all her bruises and her broken rib fused back together. "Thank you." the young mystic sighed when she felt the relief.

"Beth!?" Haley's voice called on the comm.

"I'm okay," she replied.

Haley was sprinting down the tunnel. "I'm in the tunnel. I'm on my way." A moment later, she darted out to the ledge and saw Cernunnos standing beside Elizabeth. She hugged her friend, looked at Cernunnos and said, "Hi. I'm sorry, what was your name again?"

"I'm Cernunnos, but enough is enough," he said. "I'm getting the both of you back to…" Baphomet came out of nowhere, tackling the Greenman, and they both disappeared.

With a sigh, Haley said, "They're gonna keep doing this all day, aren't they?"

Elizabeth shrugged. "Probably. I hope he'll be alright, but we should get those other two keystones while he's keeping that jerk and his scrawny girlfriend busy." Looking into Haley's visor, Elizabeth could see a giant grin on the farmgirl's face as she held up a red gemstone.

"Other *one,*" Haley corrected.

CHAPTER 21
Quit Bugging Me

Haley held the gem out to Elizabeth, "Beth, I think you should feel this."

Elizabeth took the gemstone and wrapped her fingers around it, closing her eyes and focusing on the vibrations. It was a similar feeling to the green stone, how its energy interacted with her own.

"Hmm…" She opened her other hand and conjured an orb. "It feels like…more." She threw the orb at the rock wall and took out a small stalagmite in its path. "It's like, two times as strong…I wonder…" Elizabeth focused on the vibration of the rock all around her.

She loved the way she could sense rock and crystal but had been frustrated with how she couldn't manipulate it like she did with air, fire and water. But with the potency of her energy doubled…*Maybe I can finally do it,* she thought.

She reached out to the smaller pieces of broken rock with her empty hand. The stones on the floor shifted and slid toward the young mystic. Elizabeth closed her hand, and three golf ball-sized stones moved through the air and circled Elizabeth's closed fist like moons orbiting a planet. "The gem doubles our power!" She opened her hand with a flick, and the rocks shot forward against Baphomet's statue, leaving cracks where they hit.

"One more to go," Haley reminded. "I wonder what that one does."

"Yeah, let's go find out!"

They made their way from the ledge to the rock platforms jutting from the western wall. Hopping from one platform to the next was far simpler going down than going up with lava creatures chasing them. When Haley got close enough to the cavern floor, she used her mid-air dash to kick forward and drop to her feet. Once down to the floor, they began making their way back through the cavern to the south.

"So," Haley said with a grin, "I fought a giant scorpion."

"Really?"

"Yeah!" Haley held out her phone and projected a holoscreen, "Check it out."

"Whoa!" Watching the footage of Haley picking apart the scorpion, a wide grin spread across Elizabeth's face beneath her bandana. Then she saw the finishing pounce. "By yourself!" She high-fived the empath and followed it up with a hug. "I gotta show you my fight! You'll like it. I even played music."

"Really?!"

"Yeah. But don't expect me to make it a habit."

"It helped, didn't it?" Haley asked with a smirk.

With a shrug, Elizabeth said, "Well, kinda. But…" she looked Haley in the eye with a gleam of her own, "I fought Baphomet."

"Wha…no!" Haley blurted. "How did you beat him?"

"I, uh…didn't." She projected a holoscreen and showed Haley her battle in the tunnel and then her confrontation with Baphomet.

"White light?!" Haley continued to watch the recording. "What's a Paladin?"

"I don't know." The information in their com-systems contained the answer:

A MYSTICAL WARRIOR OF FAITH

Before Haley could comment, she winced and groaned, seeing Elizabeth get ruthlessly pummeled by Baphomet in the recording. Haley became furious at the sight of what he did to her best friend, and also terrified; knowing there's nothing that she could have done if she were there.

They approached one of the collection stations when Haley asked, "Do you think we can use the portgate without anybody noticing?"

The answer to her question was displayed inside the visor:

SYNCED PORTGATES ARE SAFE
PORTING TO AN UNSYNCED GATE
WILL RESULT IN DETECTION

Simultaneously, a notification toned from Elizabeth's phone. She opened it to find the same information displayed on her screen. "Cool! We can go to the other station."

"We should be able to get to…" the info popped up in her visor, "…Freq if we keep going south. And go right through to Churgen."

They used the gate and ported to the other station near the elevator. Upon stepping into the room, Haley could sense emotions that were not theirs, and she held her arm out in front of Elizabeth. "Hold on." The air was kept cool and breathable inside the station's building, so she dismissed her helmet and turned her senses outward to detect the presence of two people nearby. "We're not alone."

Focusing her own senses outward, Elizabeth could feel the energetic fields all around them. And she felt it. Feint at first. It was a concentrated spot of extra energy, but once she focused on the anomaly, it became obvious that what she felt was a person who also harnessed their mystical abilities. Looking to Haley, she said, "I'm gonna try something," and activated her comm. "Anybody there?"

"Elizabeth?" a man's voice answered.

"Yeah."

"This is Samuel. Where are you?"

Haley clenched her fists and quietly exclaimed, "Yes!"

"We're at the collection station."

"Okay, wait there. We're coming."

Haley felt the excitement spike from outside as Samuel and Alunareth broke into a sprint to the station.

It took them a minute to reach the building and it would have taken less time if they didn't have to wear the bulky thermal suits. Samuel pressed the button, and the heavy, insulated door swung outward with a whoosh as hot, high-pressure air rushed into the airlock. They stepped inside, the door closed, and the vents activated, clearing the air before the inner door slid open to the side. There before them stood Haley and Elizabeth.

Reaching up and removing his helmet, Alunareth asked, "Are you two okay?"

"We are," Elizabeth began to answer, "but, but..." Her eyes watered as her bottom lip quivered.

Haley's tears were already streaming, "We lost Neil." she croaked before covering her face with her palms.

"I'm sorry," Samuel said softly.

Understanding that they were in a hostile environment, the girls were already pulling themselves back together. Haley was trying to dry her eyes, and Elizabeth's brow was furrowed, her jaw clenched.

Alunareth noticed their claiming control and nodded. "Where is he?"

"Back in the jungle," Elizabeth answered, trying to keep a growl out of her voice.

"We're going to bring you to Freq village," Alunareth said. "Balgar and Rudge are there as well. We'll contact the sheriff and go retrieve his body."

The girls both nodded. "Where's Sabrina?" Elizabeth asked.

"She and Jake went to Churgen," Samuel answered.

"That's where we're going!" Haley blurted.

"Why do you want to go to Churgen?" Alunareth asked.

"We can get one of the key crystals there," said Haley.

"I don't know about that," Samuel said, "but we do need to go. Do you have thermo-suits?" he asked.

"Our PJs," Elizabeth said.

Haley conjured her helmet, and Elizabeth's bandana slid up over her mouth and nose. "We're ready."

Samuel motioned to Elizabeth. "Your helmet?"

"I don't need it," she replied with a smirk. "Turns out that I do well in the heat."

"I don't think you realize how hot it is out there," he said back.

"I've been out there. The heat doesn't bother me, but I can't breathe without this," she replied while pointing at her bandana.

"It's true," Haley said. "Probably because of her pyrokinesis."

"Are you sure?" Alunareth asked.

"I'm sure," Elizabeth said as the door slid shut.

Samuel pushed the button and the thermal door opened as another whoosh of hot air flowed into the airlock.

"We've already spent more time out here than we want to," Elizabeth said. "Fighting lava monsters and angry salad men."

"Angry salad, what?" Alunareth asked.

"It all started when a wave of weird energy went by," Haley started to explain. "After that, weird creatures have been popping up everywhere and attacking us."

"I felt that spell roll through the caverns," Alunareth said. "We've been fighting strange creatures since then, as well."

The girls told their story as they made their way for Freq, telling them about Molech's temple and the Archons.

"You already have one of the keys?" Alunareth asked.

They could practically see the smile through Elizabeth's bandana when she held up a couple of fingers and said, "Two."

"Wow!" Samuel said after a whistle. "You've been busy."

The girls continued telling them about the second temple, the scorpion and Elizabeth's encounter with Baphomet.

"A Paladin?! Are you really a Paladin?!" Alunareth exclaimed.

"Uh…I guess."

"The belief one must have in the face of certain death…" His stunned expression was clearly visible through his helmet's face shield, "How is it you possess such faith?"

Elizabeth shrugged and nonchalantly said, "I'm a Baptist." She projected a holoscreen from her phone. They continued walking and Samuel searched for threats while Alunareth watched the PJs recording of Elizabeth's encounter with Baphomet.

"Samuel, check this out," Alunareth said and then took watch while the Hunter looked to the holoscreen.

"Wow! I've never even heard of this and…" He saw the part where Baphomet thrashed Elizabeth. "This guy's a real piece of work…Oh, he showed up earlier. What was his name again?"

"Cernunnos," Haley answered.

Elizabeth shut off the screen and put the phone in her pocket.

"There has not been a Paladin that I know of in nearly two hundred years," Alunareth said.

"Does that mean something in particular?" Samuel asked. "Like a prophecy or something?"

Shaking his head, "Alunareth said, "Prophecies are a vision of a potential future based on the current path. They are not absolute. If Ragnarök went as predicted, none of us would be here. But Paladins are rare, especially of late." He let out a sigh. "Grandfather Aodhan spoke of a time when he knew three Paladins, but that was long before I was born."

"But what is it that made me, or anybody, become a Paladin?"

"True faith is obvious, but beyond that," he shrugged, "nobody can know for certain. There are those who have strong faith but never become one." Alunareth gestured to Elizabeth. "You became one when you held to your faith against all odds. David McCarthy told Grandfather Aodhan that he was training with his sword when it happened to him. 'I was flowing,' he told Grandfather, 'Moving as one with the sword and in a place of mental calm. When my movement ended, and I held my sword at the ready, it began to glow with white light.' He was in a far different circumstance, yet the potential to be a warrior for the Creator unlocked. There have been many people of faith who have trained in hopes of becoming a Paladin but could not achieve it. The best we can discern is that the Creator chooses who can be a Paladin, and it is up to the individual to become one."

Haley's eyes popped open wide, "We're being watched!" She had felt a curiosity and interest that was not coming from any of them. She almost had not noticed due to everyone else here having the same interest in Alunareth's words. The empath turned around and turned her senses outward while scanning the area with her visor, but nothing registered. She pointed to a large rock fifty feet behind them. "There." She could feel the curiosity radiating from that spot, but then it suddenly faded and disappeared. "Huh, now it's gone."

Alunareth approached the boulder. Haley and Elizabeth hung back behind him, focusing their senses on the boulder while Samuel kept his attention outward.

"I can't sense anything," Alunareth said as he circled the boulder.

"Me neither," Elizabeth said.

"There definitely was something there, but it's gone now," Haley said.

"Then we should go before it comes back," Samuel said, and they continued toward Freq.

He inhaled and exhaled with slow and deliberate breaths, keeping his mind as blank as possible, projecting nothing for the empath to detect until the four adventurers were far from his spot. Having made himself completely invisible and undetectable, the man in the black suit was enjoying the story he had heard until Haley felt his emotions. As a smile spread across his face, he thought, *A Paladin. Neat! I must admit, that was sloppy of me to forget the empath. I guess I'm a little rusty.*

The further away they got from the magma flows, the cooler it became, and it wasn't long before Haley was able to dismiss her helmet and shake out her pigtails as the two men took off their helmets. They stopped at a certain point, and Alunareth retrieved two duffle bags from behind a boulder near the cavern wall. He and Samuel removed their thermal gear and packed it into the bags, making it easier for them to move.

"That feels much better," Alunareth said.

They continued south, and the stone became lighter in color as they began to see spots of crystal here and there. It wasn't long before the walls were pale with different color veins of crystal. It was getting brighter, and not just because of the walls. The cavern widened as they went, and they entered an area with a much higher ceiling and billowing, glowing mists. It was daylight in the Caverns of Freq, and the groups of trees and foliage littered the cavern; the smell of moisture in the air was welcoming and refreshing after the burning tunnels of Buruum. There was a large pond to their left, which was fed from a stream along the eastern wall. The greenery was thick around the water and birds were singing in the trees.

"This place is beautiful," Haley said as she turned her head, taking in the sights. Pillars remained from times when the stone was carved away, but now these multi-colored pillars had been worked into beautiful public garden sets. One was carved into a spiral with a trough all the way down, which was filled with soil and a lovingly selected variety of vines growing and draping over the sides. Another, which was plumbed, had water flowing from the top, cascading down through pools until it reached the bottom by the pond. Different birds were perched along the pools, and some were in the water, flapping their wings and enjoying the bath.

"Yes," Alunareth agreed. "The deputy here told me that this was the old quarry, and they used the stone to restore the buildings in the city. After that, the Atlanteans spent years working the area, piping in water, bringing in volcanic soil and composting their waste to turn Freq into a livable area. And now, the cavern is teaming with life."

"It's incredible," Elizabeth whispered with awe.

"Can anybody read me?" Samuel asked on his comm.

"This is Balgar. Any news?"

"Yes, we have Haley and Elizabeth," Samuel replied.

"Fantastic!" they heard Rudge's voice say. "Are they okay?"

"We are," Elizabeth said.

"Great! Rudge and I are heading to the western wall of Freq with the deputy. Gotta rescue mission."

"What's the situation?" Samuel asked.

"There's an old quarry building on one of the upper ledges of the western wall. Someone's trapped inside by strange creatures."

The PJs approximated the position of the Dwarves, and Elizabeth displayed it on her holoscreen. "We can catch up with them."

"We're heading your way," Samuel said.

"Watch out for big crystal bugs and leaf-people," Balgar said.

"We will," Alunareth said. "Might be a nice change of pace from the lava-people we ran into."

"Or rock spiders," Haley added with a shudder.

The deputy's phone bleeped, and he answered it. "What's going on?" After a few seconds, he said, "Alright. We're on our way now," and ended the call. "More bugs, and now some plant-people are at the lookout."

They encountered some leaf-men along the way, which they dispatched with little effort. Elizabeth's gemstone-amped blasts could take them out with a single shot! They continued at a brisk pace, taking only fifteen minutes from when they established contact to meet near the bottom of the cavern wall, where they saw a giant crystal beetle, ironically the size of a Volkswagen, and Balgar bashing its head with his hammer; a climbing pick at the ready in his other hand. The head broke into chucks, a few were sent flying, and the rest crumbled to the ground as the body dropped where it stood.

"Hey!" Samuel called.

Balgar, Rudge and the deputy looked from the crystal bug and over to the approaching allies. The Dwarves smiled. "Just in time," Rudge said. "Ready to climb?" He pointed up the steep ledges toward the observation deck on the top ledge.

The deputy sighed. "Rescue-med has been on us for a while to put a portgate up there. Now I wish we hadn't dragged our feet on that."

The crystal beetles could be seen sporadically across the cavern walls, but a group was forming at the lookout high above. The deputy slung the shockwave cannon over his shoulder and started up one of the ladders. Alunareth and Samuel went to another while Rudge and Balgar followed the deputy.

Haley looked over her shoulder at Elizabeth. "Piggyback," she said while patting her own shoulder. Elizabeth put her hands on Haley's shoulders and hopped up, wrapping her legs around Haley's waist, then her arms around Haley's neck. Haley popped her claws and began scaling the cavern wall.

Atlantis City, Atlantis

The large room of reinforced cement, designed to handle intense heat, contained a large block of gleaming mayum. Laris and Demitri stood outside the room, looking through the thick glass while Laris entered the data into the system. The sonic beams aimed at the alien metal activated, and the pulses vibrated through the substance, allowing the heat to set in. A large robotic arm lowered from the ceiling and aimed its end at the mayum, unleashing a continuous blast of heat while lasers began carving out two pieces from the cube.

Keeping the sonic pulses aimed at the two pieces, more arms lowered from the ceiling and pointed their high-intensity lasers at the work, carving at the metal until two glowing swords of Manny's specifications remained. The process itself only took fifteen minutes, whereas the handles, made of a substance much like polyurethane, took over a half hour.

As soon as the sonic pulses stopped, the metal cooled, but he still had to use robotic arms to pick them up and set them in a cubby because the room itself was too hot to enter. Laris went around to the side and opened the cubby from the outside to retrieve the katanas. They were already cool to the touch, and with all the components made, Laris attached the handles and secured them. They were ready, and Sabrina would now have two indestructible katanas that, provided she had the strength, could slice through anything that wasn't worked Flekkle.

Serge entered the fabrication control room with Manny following behind, and Laris turned and extended a hand to greet them. "Hello, pleased to meet you."

"And you," Manny replied.

Laris turned and started walking toward the Katanas as he said, "We don't often get the opportunity to meet new people."

"So, I've heard."

He led them to a table where two gleaming swords with identical handles to Sabrina's current katanas, except for the diamond shapes down the sides of the handle wraps were two different colors, at Manny's request. One was bluish-white diamonds, and the other, purple. They were laid out parallel on the surface of the table, awaiting inspection. Laris looked at Manny and motioned with his hands toward the new blades. "Pending your approval."

He set his eyes on the gleaming metal. The two swords looked identical to Sabrina's current katanas. Reaching down with his right hand, Manny wrapped his fingers around the handle of one and lifted it from the table. He immediately felt a different weight, much lighter than a regular katana, and he picked up the other with his left, smiling from ear to ear.

Serge turned to Laris, held up two of the disruption emitters that they had been working on and said, "Here they are."

Hel appeared in a sudden burst of black mist, looking for a place to rest from a battle she was having with Artemis. She figured the Goddess of the Hunt wouldn't come looking to clash around mortals. "Leave if you know what's good for you," she barked.

Dimitri's jaw hung open as he stared at the Goddess of Death.

"What?" Hel asked, annoyed by his dumbfounded expression. Reaching into his pocket, Dimitri pulled out the card. Hel now bore the expression of shock. "Where'd you get that?"

"From me," said the man in the black suit. Hel spun around to see his smiling face as Dimitri began tapping on a keyboard. "Mind if we talk for a moment?" Hel disappeared in a puff of black mist.

Dimitri was scanning the woman while she was there. Now he was looking at a monitor, confused. "I don't understand," he said. "How can someone who has that kind of energy signature disappear from our sensors?"

The man in the black suit placed his hands in his pockets and dropped his head with a sigh. "I taught her that." And he vanished.

Freq, Atlantis

She was huddled in the corner furthest from a window, peeking out from behind a medic's privacy screen and watching the beetle-like creature scurry by. It was made of crystal, and Shanda would have thought it to be quite beautiful if it hadn't charged at her, chasing her into the building. Not knowing what kind of damage this large crystal bug could do, she ran inside the observation station, slammed the door shut and locked it. Thankfully, the bug didn't try to break through the door, though Shanda had no doubt that it could, but this left her trapped.

Being so far away from the village proper, the station was equipped with emergency medical supplies, rations and a com-unit, which she used to contact the deputy's phone. More bugs have come to the area since making the call, along with some strange two-foot-tall men made of vegetation and dirt.

She made another call to the deputy, "There're more bugs here now. And weird little plant people. Lots of them," she whispered, and he told her that he was on his way with a team. That was twenty minutes ago.

Riley was still somewhere outside, and Shanda hoped he was okay. *Most likely under the decking. I hope.* She stepped out from behind the screen and checked around, searching for something she could use to defend herself when she knocked a med scanner off the table. It hit the floor with a metallic slap, and the sudden break in silence seemed as loud as a gunshot to the frightened Shanda.

Her gaze shot to the window, and she was not happy to find that a couple of bugs and a leaf man were looking right back at her. "Oh, no."

The bug charged at the wall, and snapping sounds reverberated in the building when the crystal pinchers broke through the wood beneath the window. The bug thrashed back and forth, then pulled back, extracting its pinchers from the wood and readying for another charge. The leaf-man stepped to and pressed against the window and started pounding until it became skewered on a pincher as the bug drove itself into the wall again.

The pincers pierced two more holes into the wood and snapped one of the planks while crushing the leaf-man and cracks formed a spiderweb up the glass of the window. The muffled sounds of banging and shouting were heard outside the walls, and the other bug turned to scurry toward the disturbance.

Looking frantically for something she could use, Shanda was nearing panic. Finding nothing that would fend off a giant bug of solid crystal. Another crash with the tinkling of shattered glass, and Shanda spun on her heel just in time to face the bug as it pushed through the broken wall. Cold shot down her spine, her eyes widened, and she screamed, knowing there was nothing she could do to stop the incoming pinchers, but the bug jerked to a stop; the sharp crystal of the two prongs was an inch from her stomach. She stood there shocked, with her jaw hanging and her eyes locked on the tips of those wicked pinchers.

In a strained voice, Haley shouted, "I can't hold him forever. Run!" Her fingers were clinging to the back of the beetle's shell, and her toes clung to the floor, pulling back on the bug. Her enhanced strength augmented further by the PJs, she yanked with everything she had, and the beetle dug in its feet, pushing itself forward in a tug-of-war that Haley could not win.

Shanda ducked left toward the door, and once she was clear, Haley let go, and Elizabeth hit the bug with a couple of blasts, starting a crack in its shell. It spun around to catch another amber blast in the face, followed by a bobcat that burst on impact, staggering it back to the wall. Cracks could be seen throughout the crystal of the translucent bug. Haley charged up and launched another bobcat. It hit with a burst, and the beetle broke apart, falling into a heap of crystal chunks.

Standing by the door, Shanda was still inside, not knowing what to do, considering that more creatures were out on the ledge, but so was everybody else. The deputy set the range on his shockwave generator to ten feet and aimed for some beetles. He squeezed the trigger, and a beam of pulsating rings streamed forward from the dish. The beetle began to shudder and scampered back as the deputy stepped forward, keeping the focal point on the bug. It shuddered again and fell into a heap of chunks and dust.

Samuel tore through the veggie-men, and Alunareth lured some of the beetles into a trap where Rudge and Balgar dropped down on top of them with their hammers and picks.

Looking at Shanda, Haley said, "Maybe you should stay in here until we're done." The girls hopped out the broken window and began blasting beetles.

Elizabeth was enjoying the extra oomph in her casual blasts. They packed almost as much punch as her charged orbs, which could crack open a bug with one shot. But she watched Haley launch one of her charged orbs. Blue and purple light in the shape of a bobcat's head sped forward into a beetle, and the concussive burst on impact shuddered the bug.

The burst! Elizabeth thought with a wicked grin. "Haley!"

She turned and saw Elizabeth smiling while holding out the red gemstone. "You wanna really rattle 'em?"

With a smirk as mischievous as Elizabeth's grin, Haley wrapped her fingers around the gem, gripping it in her left hand. She charged up and launched an orb that she expected to be a bobcat but instead resembled the head of a lion. It hit the nearest beetle square in the face, and the concussive burst drove cracks through its body while blowing off a pincher.

"Whoa!"

Haley charged again and launched a second. The burst finished off the bug while staggering the one closest to it.

"Yeah!" Elizabeth exclaimed.

Haley followed up with a volley of kittens, dropping beetles with impish chuckles.

Shanda watched in astonishment from inside the building while Haley and Elizabeth dropped all the bugs that she could see. Samuel, Alunareth, Balgar, Rudge and the deputy coordinated well together, taking out many more of the dangerous creatures. She couldn't see any more bugs, so Shanda opened the door on the side of the building to look and call for Riley, but when she did, one of the two bugs fighting with Rudge turned toward her and charged. She screamed and jumped backward, intending to duck back into the building, but stumbled instead. Falling to the decking, Shanda landed on her right side and tried to scramble to her feet.

Haley came around the corner and started running for Shanda while blasting a volley of shots. The beetle cracked with each blast as it bared down on Shanda. It rammed into her just as Haley's last shot landed, and she collapsed back to the ground when the bug crumbled to pieces, but not before Shanda was skewered by one of the pinchers. She lay there on the decking just outside the building door, staring wide-eyed at the sharp length of crystal protruding from her side while quivering in shock.

"Oh, no!" Haley cried as she ran to Shanda and knelt beside the wounded woman, Elizabeth coming up right behind her. Haley felt her shock and sensed her pain.

"Don't pull it out!" Alunareth shouted as he hurried for them. The girls stepped aside when he approached, and he dropped to a knee beside Shanda, who was now hyperventilating. "Try to stay calm," Alunareth said in a gentle tone. "I can help."

The others arrived as the Elf placed the palms of his hands on either side of the wound, and he began to hum. He held the hum for a moment and then transitioned to an ah, using the harmonics of his voice to raise and direct his energy into healing the woman. Though he was mystically inclined, Alunareth did not use his energetic abilities often other than his more passive senses and the occasional blasts.

All Alfan are taught the tones of healing, but he was out of practice, and the wound severe. "Elizabeth!" he called.

"Yeah?"

"I need your help. Come, kneel next to me and place your hands here." He pointed to where his right hand was. She placed her palms on the woman's side to the right of the crystal shard, and Alunareth placed his hands to the left. "Do what I do and try to match my pitch. While you do, set your healing intentions and let your voice carry the energy."

He began humming, and Elizabeth did the same while raising her energy. She pictured the woman as if she were already healed, healthy and vital. Alunareth transitioned to an ah, and Elizabeth followed his lead. He looked the young mystic in the eye and tilted his head back a couple of times, indicating Elizabeth to raise her pitch a bit. She understood, did so and Alunareth gave a quick nod to let her know that her voice was where it needed to be. She pushed her energy out and felt it as it flowed with her voice and into the wound. They stopped, inhaled and began again, pushing the healing energy into Shanda, whose breathing began to steady.

When they stopped for their next breath, Haley handed the red gemstone to Alunareth. "This should help."

"Yes! Thank you." He turned to Samuel, "When I nod, pull the shard out."

"Alright," Samuel said and stepped into position.

Alunareth and Elizabeth began their song again with another hum. As they transitioned to the ah, Alunareth nodded, Samuel yanked, and Shanda screeched and passed out. They held their voices steady, and the injury began to close. A few seconds later, the wound sealed shut.

CHAPTER 22
Need For Speed

Shanda woke up with a gasp and looked down at the tear in her shirt where the wound was. She placed her hand over the newly regenerated skin while her breathing steadied and she calmed. "Thank you so much. I've never seen anything like tha…" Her eyes popped open wide. "Riley!" She jumped to her feet and looked to a spot where he often slipped under the decking, worried. "Riley?"

Everybody followed her eyes and turned their heads to the same spot where the white and gray head of a cat emerged. Riley climbed onto the decking while sizing up the group. Keeping low as he walked, the cat circled around everybody and made his way to Shanda.

"Riley!" Shanda smiled as Riley nuzzled her leg, and she bent down to pet him.

As Shanda stood back up, Haley said, "Hi, Kitty!" and Riley turned to the farmgirl.

"Meow."

"He must like you. Riley doesn't talk to many people." She reached into her left vest pocket, pulled out a small container, and opened it, revealing the ground and dried leaves within. Riley spun around with wide eyes when he smelled the catnip, and Shanda put a pinch on the decking in front of him.

Riley put his nose to the small heap, then he rubbed his face across the deck board. He dropped to his stomach and placed his chin over the cat nip, rubbing it back and forth before he rolled to his back and stretched. He flipped over to his feet and looked like he was ready to run a marathon, his blue eyes wide as nickels. "Meow!" He darted down the deck-covered path, turned and ran back, screeching to a stop between Shanda and Haley, where he hopped in circles a couple of times while everybody laughed.

"You're funny," Haley said with a smile and reached down to pet him. Riley looked up, their eyes met, and the empath took a sharp inhale. She felt beyond energized and like she could run forever! Then she realized that Riley was not moving, and all sound fell to a deeper pitch, then stopped. She stood up straight and looked around to see everybody was perfectly still as if the world were on pause. Out in the cavern, birds were suspended in the air. The water that was running down the wall was still and looked like glass. Haley walked over to the waterfall and stared for a second with her mouth hanging open. She tapped her fingertip against the water, and it splashed out in slow motion. She watched as the water arched up higher than it should have yet was moving so slowly, and as the droplets reached their apex, she heard that deep pitch sound again as it rose and sped up. The sound had returned to the world as the water visibly flowed.

"Whoa!" Elizabeth shouted.

"Where'd she go?" Alunareth asked.

"What happened to her?" Rudges blurted.

"I'm over here," Haley said, and they all spun to see her by the water.

"Did…did you just teleport?" Samuel asked.

"Uh, no…I don't think so."

"You just vanished from in front of us," Elizabeth said.

Haley shrugged. "Everything stopped for, like, fifteen seconds. Except me."

"You paused time?!" Elizabeth asked.

"I…I don't know."

Riley took off like a shot, chasing after a rodent.

"We'll figure it out later," Samuel said. "Let's get back to the village before more of these things show up."

The scampering of Riley's feet could be heard as he charged back down the decking. He skidded to a stop and bonked his head against Haley's shin before trotting back to Shanda to brush against her leg.

As they made their way down the vertical gardens, Elizabeth asked Haley, "What was stopping time like?"

"I don't think I did." Haley went on to describe the experience of the sound distortions into silence and touching the water. "If I did, would I have been able to splash the water?"

"I don't know."

"But my energy was drained after. It's coming back, but it seems like it's taking longer."

They made it back to the cavern floor before encountering more leaf-men, which they easily dispatched. Heading back to the village, they encountered a few more beetles. Alunareth handed the red gemstone back to Haley, who made short work of them, and finally, they arrived at the village.

"We need to go to Churgen soon," Haley said to Samuel.

"No. We need to stay somewhere safe and keep our heads down," Samuel replied.

"But we need to get the last key before anyone realizes the other two are missing," Elizabeth added. "Otherwise, we might miss our only chance."

Samuel's eyes popped wide as the realization hit him like a ton of bricks. Such a simple and obvious thing that he hadn't considered. If Kone finds that two stones are missing, he'll secure the third, and they'll never get access to the vault. Ending any plans of revealing his secrets to the world. They couldn't afford to stop. "You've got a good point."

Upon arriving at the village, the girls were surprised and not at all unhappy to see that Dalton was there.

Meelyhn, Atlantis

It was only five minutes since she made the call, and now Sabrina and Jake saw a vehicle hovering in the pathway. She felt relieved, then giddy. Too giddy! She recognized the source of the emotion and realized, "Haley's in Freq!"

"How do you know that?" Jake asked with a grunt.

"Because I recognize that feeling. She sees Dalton."

"Must be strange to feel other people's emotions." He squinted his eyes as he dealt with another wave of pain. "And I hope you're not stuck feeling this ankle."

"No, I'm not," Sabrina answered. She could sense but not physically feel his pain unless she focused on it. Then, her ankle would start to hurt as well. "I'm still surprised that I can sense her so far away. I wish I knew this before we began our searches."

"Believe me," Jake replied with a grin through his grunt, "so do I."

The vehicle that looked like a monorail car but without a rail or wheels, slowed to a halt on the trail and hovered next to them, followed by a two-seater ATV. Two medics got out of the rover and ran over to Jake, one of them scanning his leg with some kind of device. "It's broken."

The other held a different device to his ankle and switched it on. It began to hum and warble while Jake let out a sigh of relief as the pain vanished. "Don't move," the medic said. "I may not hurt now, but it's still broken, and you don't want to cause more damage."

Sabrina could feel an odd mix of emotions coming from the ATV. She looked over as the medics applied a new splint to Jake's ankle to see Manny and Deputy Karn stepping from the vehicle. "Papi?!" There was a look on Manny's face that she knew well. He was not coming with good news.

"Mija, I'm sorry." He blew out a sigh. "Neil's been killed."

After a hard swallow, Sabrina gave a slow, solemn nod. *And now I know what had Haley so upset. I wonder how Elizabeth is taking it.* "He seemed like a good man. I felt Haley's emotions earlier, probably when it happened. I believe she's now in Freq."

"Why do you think she's in Freq?" the deputy asked.

"When I sensed her emotions, I could also tell which way they came from."

"So, you're heading back down?" Manny asked.

"I am."

"Well, before you go," Manny said, and a grin spread onto his face as Sabrian felt his heart changing to a different tune, "you might want to take this." He reached into his pocket and held up an object.

"A restraining disk?" she asked, taking the device.

"No." The grin on his face widened further. "It's a disruption emitter. It'll affect a seventy-foot radius and work for ten to fifteen minutes on a charge. Thought it would come in handy."

"Thank you, Papi." She attached it to the harness of her jumpsuit.

"However," Manny said and waited for Sabrina to look in his eyes. "These other items aren't magnetic." He waved for her to follow, trotted back to the ATV and his heart reached a crescendo as he pulled two swords from the back. "You know those katanas I always said I wanted to make for you?" He laid them on the ATV's hood.

"Mayum?"

"Yes." They were laid out parallel on the surface of the hood and Sabrina set her eyes on the gleaming metal. Pointing to the handles, he said, "Just like the colors of the whip.

Reaching down with her right hand, the Hunter wrapped her fingers around the handle of one and lifted it from the hood. She immediately felt the difference, much lighter than a regular katana and picked up the other with her left. Though light, the balance was spot on, so she moved twenty feet away from the others and began with a double flourish. The blades moved in a blur while the others watched, and she went from a flourish into one of the routines taught to her by Flashipor.

Manny, smiling from ear to ear, beamed with pride while they watched her performance.

"Remind me not to make her mad," one of the medics remarked.

Concluding her trial of the new swords, she came back to the ATV. She placed the katanas back on the hood and removed the two from her scabbards, setting them down as well. She picked up the new ones and placed them in her scabbards. The magnetics that guided her old katanas would not work with the new mayum blades, but she had been through the motions many times and set them perfectly into place without a thought. Turning back to Manny with an appreciative smile, she said, "Thank you, Papi," and hugged him.

Freq, Atlantis

"Hey," Haley said with a bit of a goofy grin.

"What's up?" Elizabeth asked with a confident smile.

Dalton returned their smiles. "Hi. Everyone's been trying to find you."

"Well, here we are," Elizabeth said with her arms out in a ta-da stance.

"See," Haley said. "You've found us."

"So, where have you been?"

The girls started to tell him of their adventures from when Lillith had abducted them when Alunareth's sharp ears picked up on the conversation and he immediately approached them. "Sorry to interrupt," he said politely and turned to the girls, "but there's something we need to discuss."

"Okay," Elizabeth said and turned back to Dalton with a smile, "Talk to you later."

Haley, with her own smile said, "See you later."

Alunareth headed back toward the others, and the girls followed. Once they were out of earshot of any locals, he turned to them and said, "I don't know what you were about to tell him, but I had to make sure you didn't speak of the keys. We can't risk any word slipping, or our opportunity may be lost."

"Okay," Haley said. "We won't say anything."

Elizabeth nodded. "And we should get going again."

"Yes. The sheriff is on his way and should be here shortly. We'll see what else we can learn from him, and then we'll go." As Alunareth spoke the words, the elevator bay doors in the cavern's eastern wall opened, and the sheriff's vehicle pulled out and onto the village road. The cruiser came to a halt next to them in front of the deputy's office. Sheriff Gurden stepped out of the car and exchanged a few discreet words with the deputy. The expression on the deputy's face did not reflect good news.

The sheriff turned to the others. "Glad to see you found the girls. Hello Haley and Elizabeth. I'm Sheriff Gurden." The girls waved as he continued. "I'm afraid I've got some bad news about your friend Neil."

Samuel let out a sigh and said, "We know." He motioned to Haley and Elizabeth. "They were with him when it happened."

"You both witnessed it?"

"Yes," Elizabeth said while Haley nodded her head.

"Everyone," the sheriff said while motioning to the building, "please come inside. We don't need to keep discussing this out here, and I need statements from both of you," he finished as he motioned to the girls. They followed Gurden into the deputy's office, where he took a seat at a desk. There was one chair in front of the sheriff's desk, so the deputy grabbed another chair from in front of his own and moved it over, giving both Haley and Elizabeth a seat while Samuel stood alongside.

A tablet-like device was on top of the desk, and the sheriff switched it off. Reaching into the drawer, he retrieved another that did not have wireless transmission capability and switched it on. "Rough day?"

Haley let out a long, sad, "Yeah," as her eyes began to mist while thinking about Neil and the story they must tell. Starting with their abduction by Lillith, the girls told the sheriff of their trek into Futola, of acquiring the key crystal in Molech's temple and then of the strange creatures that began to appear.

"Those creatures have been spotted in all the caverns," Gurden said, "but so far, they've been staying out of the villages."

They got to the part where Neil had arrived and even told him about the gliding cat.

Gurden said, "I'll let Ralph know that Iris has been spotted. He's been worried sick. Been looking for her for days."

And now was the difficult part. Both girls began to sob heavily while they told the sheriff of the Archons, their battle and Neil's sacrifice. Haley flipped open her phone and projected a holoscreen showing the PJs recording of the events. The sheriff had seen plenty of holotech like this before but was surprised to see it in possession of two girls from the First Density. After finishing their story about Neil, Gurden recognized their emotional exhaustion and gave them a few minutes break.

The girls regained their composure, and Gurden said, "I am going to need a copy of those video files."

Haley held up her phone, scanned Gurden's tablet and found that it could not receive data through a wireless transmission, but the scan detected a port on the side and the nanobots in her phone began shifting and reconfiguring to form a wire with a matching plug on the end. It snaked from her phone to the port on the side of the tablet and Haley transmitted a copy of all her video records from when she arrived in Meelyhn to when they entered the deputy's office. The cable retracted into the phone.

"Is that nanotech?"

"Yeah," Elizabeth answered.

"Self-replicating?"

"Uh-huh," Haley replied and then felt a sinking feeling in Gurden's stomach as he swallowed hard.

"We, uh…we'll discuss that later."

Haley's eyes widened when she gasped and blurted, "Oh, no! You had a gray goo!"

Another hard swallow and Gurden nodded; the pain of those memories was reflected on his face as he remembered the loss of a good friend and the event that resulted in Atlantis banning nanotech. It was the only time that they ever had to call on Kone for help.

"Discussion for another time," he said as he pulled himself back together. "Please, continue."

Continue they did and seemed to become invigorated while telling of their battle in Buruum and the acquisition of the second key crystal. The sheriff couldn't hide the surprise on his face as he heard about the challenges with which these two eleven-year-old girls had to contend. They even managed to secure two of the three crystals.

As they were finishing their story, the deputy came back in carrying a couple of bags. He set them down and asked, "Who's hungry?" and pulled a variety of sandwiches from the bag, placing them on the desk.

Haley found a turkey sandwich and tore into it with enthusiasm. After devouring half the sandwich, she turned to Sheriff Gurden. "These are really good, but where did the turkey come from?"

"Most of the livestock is in Meelyhn, but the turkeys in Atlantis are raised on the agricultural ring of the city."

The sheriff looked through the video footage on the tablet while the others ate. There were potent diminishing signals always broadcast in Atlantis to ensure no one would consciously connect with their energy fields. The caliber of intelligence was high in Atlantis and Kone knew not to ever underestimate the population, but those already connected with their fields would have no problem maintaining their connection once established. Sheriff Gurden had only seen mystical abilities displayed by Kone, but to see the girls in action truly surprised him. He watched their battle in Molech's Temple and then Neil's final moments. He was astounded by Haley taking down the giant scorpion and Elizabeth standing up to Baphomet. So engrossed in the records was he that Samuel's voice startled him.

"Sheriff."

Gurden snapped his head up in a startle and quickly regained his composure. "Yes?"

"We're going for Churgun. We need to finish this before we lose our opportunity."

"I can have Lilly Wells watch the girls for you. She lives here in Freq and she's trustworthy. I would know, she babysits my kids."

"Haley and Elizabeth are coming with us," Samuel said flatly.

Gurden's jaw dropped with surprise. "After everything you went through to find them, you're going to bring them right back out there?"

"Yes," Samuel said with a nod. "You might have noticed that they have special skill sets that will be necessary in places like Hel's Temple." Haley walked up and stood next to Samuel as he spoke.

The sheriff looked to her and asked, "What are you again…twelve?"

"Umm…eventually?" Haley replied with a sheepish grin.

"You're not even twelve!"

"I'm eleven."

Gurden looked back at Samuel. "You're seriously going to bring an eleven-year-old into potential battle?!"

"This isn't her first time. She defeated us last year," he added with a smirk.

"Defeated you…at what?"

"We tried to take over her town in the First Density. Haley and Elizabeth stopped us, long story." Samuel finished his sentence with a quick shrug.

Alunareth approached the desk while pointing to Elizabeth saying, "Plus, she's a Paladin."

"I don't know what that means," the sheriff responded.

"It means that she's dangerous to demonic forces," Samuel answered.

"And it's better for us that we go," Haley said.

"Why do you think that?" Gurden asked.

"Because if we stay, we…well, Kone's still there and…"

"Because if we don't stop him now, Kone will eventually come for us," Elizabeth jumped in. Haley was both thankful, yet annoyed that Elizabeth had talked over her. "We have our shot now and if we miss it, then it's just a matter of time before he gets us. Instead of sitting and waiting for him to come, we can finish this job," Elizabeth's eyes shined with amber light, and she smirked as she held up an orb in her right hand, "and me and Haley have got what it takes to do it."

The idea of letting two eleven-year-old girls go back out into danger sickened the sheriff, but he couldn't deny that these two girls and their quirky abilities might be the one and only chance to stop Kone. Gurden dropped his head and let out a sigh. "Well, at least get some more food before you go."

They left the deputy's office with full stomachs and determination, but Haley still wrestled with the butterflies in her stomach as she thought about everything that still needed to be done. Regardless of the success they'd had so far, she started to play out every step in her mind at once and began to see the task before her as a towering mountain of overwhelming odds that cast a shadow of hopelessness. She could feel quite the opposite from Elizabeth. The young mystic was focused, enthusiastic even, and eager to continue, so Haley focused on that feeling and used it to bolster her own confidence.

Dalton saw them come out of the office and start along the road toward the edge of the village, so he jogged over alongside them. "Are we going back to Meelyhn?"

"You're not going with them," the sheriff said. "I've got a couple things to tend to here and then I'll give you a ride home."

The disappointment was obvious as Dalton let out a sigh. "Alright." He accompanied them to the edge of the village but that's where he had to remain as they continued.

CHAPTER 23
Speak Your Piece

As they trekked south through the cavern, the foliage became wild in contrast to the neatly kept gardens of Freq. A few crystal beetles came charging from the brush, but they were able to make quick work of them. Haley, holding the red gemstone, obliterated most of them with lion blasts. The smacking of floppy feet against the cavern floor was heard and Alunareth turned to see a horde of head-creatures running straight for them.

"What are those?!" The Elf threw a mystical bolt and staggered the one at the head of the pack.

Turning toward the incoming creatures, Elizabeth answered, "They're easy! Just avoid the teeth." She drew her sai and charged.

Haley was charging up a blast herself when one of the head creatures leaped at her with its large mouth open. Haley shoved the barrel of her potato gun into its mouth, releasing the blast, and the creature burst apart into chunks.

"Ewe!"

Another came running up behind her and Haley pivoted as she popped her claws from her left hand, streaks of purple light flashed across the creature. It dropped to the ground, squirmed and broke apart into clumps of dirt. It was over in just a couple of minutes, and so they continued their journey and the temperature started to rise.

"I thought it would be getting colder," Haley commented.

Elizabeth nodded. "Yeah, me too."

"It will," Samuel explained, "after we cross the chasm. There's a bridge up ahead."

"More lava?" Haley asked.

"Yep. But it's down at the bottom, and the chasm is deep. We won't need any gear like Buruum."

"I wonder how Sabrina is do…uh-oh." Haley spun around to the north but didn't see anything.

"What's wrong?" Samuel asked.

"Somebody's back there. Scared and excited at the same time…it's a fight!"

Turning his ear to the north, Alunareth closed his eyes and listened while Haley and Elizabeth both conjured earbuds from their PJs. And then they heard the muffled commotion of scuffing feet and energy discharges.

Haley pulled out her phone and flipped it open. "Can you identify that sound?" Drawing on the information from Neil's scans when he was in the city, the screen of her phone displayed the words 'pulse rifle' and a photo appeared. It was a common rifle used amongst the Atlanteans who lived in the caverns for defense against the occasionally aggressive wildlife. It fired pulses of intense electrical energy that was intended to temporarily incapacitate without killing. She looked at Elizabeth, they both nodded and then took off in a sprint right alongside Alunareth. Samuel, Balgar and Rudge immediately followed.

Rounding the slight bend, they found Dalton scuffling with some head-creatures and a couple of beetles. Dalton fired his pulse rifle, a burst of electrical energy shot forward and hit one of the head-creatures. It fell to the ground and shuddered as another one was hopping back to its feet. A beetle charged and he dove to the side, firing another shot at a head-creature. The beetle scurried past and began turning around as the other beetle charged at Dalton.

Haley was running as fast as she could when she saw Dalton fire a pulse at the beetle, but it did nothing to the crystalline creature. Elizabeth, a little quicker than Haley was a few feet in front of her, but even she wouldn't reach Dalton in time. All sound took on a deeper tone as it distorted, then faded away. Haley ran in silence, past Elizabeth, who now looked like a statue to Haley, and straight for the beetle. She reached her arms out with her palms up and slid her fingers under the edge of its shell.

Haley flipped the bug over onto its back, gave it a shove and it started to slide away. Dropping back to her normal speed, sound returned to her ears as the speed of the sliding beetle appeared to increase. The next thing she saw was the beetle taking off like a shot and shattering against the cavern's western wall.

"Whoa…!"

She snapped back to the situation at hand and saw the other bug about to charge at a stunned Dalton as Elizabeth came running up. Haley pointed at Dalton, said, "Shield him!" and ran past the two of them for the bug. She leaped into the air above the charging beetle and pounced. Her feet drove down on the shell and straight through to the ground, shattering the creature as chunks of the beetle skipped off Elizabeth's protective field.

Dalton's jaw hung slack as he watched the ripples of amber and indigo light flow out from the points of impact. "You have a portable deflector?"

The others had already eliminated the head-creatures and were coming over to Dalton. "What are you doing out here?" Samuel asked.

"I was trying to catch up to you guys."

"But the sheriff said…"

"So what? Sheriff Gurden probably doesn't even know I'm gone yet. He was going to be at least another hour. What's he going to do, arrest me? We're all prisoners here already and if you guys are trying to stop Kone, I want in."

"Who says that we're trying to stop Kone?" Samuel shook his head. "That would be ridiculous."

"Umm…" Dalton, with a sheepish grin, unconsciously rubbed the back of his head. "I…heard you guys talking about it…in the deputy's office."

"Eavesdropping?" Alunareth asked with a stern look upon his face.

Dalton let out a sigh. "Yes."

Alunareth took a deep breath. He had pulled a few reckless stunts like this during his adolescence and didn't blame Dalton at all for wanting to be free from Kone. If he were in Dalton's shoes, Alunareth may have done much the same thing. The Elf let out a sigh of his own. "We need to finish our job quickly and with discretion. I know you are a brilliant and capable young man who wants to help, but it's too dangerous to be out here right now. Balgar, Rudge, please escort him back to Freq."

"But…"

"But nothin'! You saw what your rifle did to that bug?" Balgar asked and without giving Dalton a chance to answer, he continued. "Nothing, that's what! Your gear is fine for the normal critters, but there's a bad energy right now and you need to stay in the village where it's safe."

"C'mon," Rudge said to him with a grin. "Maybe we'll get the opportunity to show you a couple o' tricks for taking the bugs down on our way back."

He was about to leave, and Haley was trying to think of something, anything to say before he was gone again. She pushed through her fear and asked, "Are you going to be in Meelyhn later?"

"I should be."

"Great," Elizabeth said as she strode up alongside them with a playful smirk. "We'll come visit when we're done. I'll see you then."

"Okay," Dalton said with a grin.

There was an uncomfortable shift in Haley's stomach when Elizabeth stepped into the conversation. The farmgirl had pushed past her nervousness to speak up; her best friend capitalized on the effort, and now another feeling began to burn like acid in her stomach. Despite the inner turmoil, Haley smiled and waved as the Dwarves walked with him back toward Freq.

Haley glanced at Elizabeth as they walked, knowing that she was off in dreamland before even seeing the look on her face. But the empath could not share in her friend's good feelings at that moment while dealing with the turmoil deep within her stomach. *I don't think she meant anything by it, but it was really hard for me to say something, and she took it over!*

Despite Elizabeth's confidence in this moment, the empath had no idea just how nervous Elizabeth was because it was masked by Haley feeling the same thing. She was about to ask Elizabeth if she even realized what she did but then thought, *Maybe now isn't the best time. This is a dangerous place, and we can't argue. I need to think now and be mad later.*

"I really like his eyes," Elizabeth said.

Haley looked at her and saw she that she was looking straight ahead as she walked with a hint of a dopey grin. Returning her gaze forward with a subtle sigh, she said, "Okay." *I do too.* Perhaps her 'think now, be mad later' mindset would not be so simple this time.

The foliage was still thick as they traversed the Freq cavern, but the main path was well worn, almost wide enough to be considered a road, from the many hikers and ATV's over the years. Numerous game trails intersected with their path and wildlife was abundant, though agitated from the many strange creatures of Apophis. The pale color of the eastern wall became darker as they went and eventually was the same gray as the upper caverns. The western wall presented with the same transition soon after.

Replaying the incident with Dalton in her head, Haley was ripped from her thoughts when she felt emotions emanating from up ahead. Focus, anticipation and eagerness. It felt like someone was hunting, and it felt sinister. "There are people ahead. And they don't feel nice."

She conjured her helmet, as did Elizabeth, and they began scanning the area with the PJ sensors. Whoever they were, they weren't making any noise that could be picked up, and they were still too far away for the visual scans.

Without making a sound, Alunareth hurried ahead and disappeared into the foliage while the others continued forward with caution. He didn't get too far when the fine hairs on the back of his neck stood up. He had felt similar energy before from demonic entities, but this was a little different.

Getting close to the chasm, he moved forward in complete silence and heard footsteps from near the bridge. The Elf chose his steps carefully and moved into a position where he could see the bridge and the source of the footsteps. A near eight-foot-tall reptilian man with six fingers on each hand. *So, these are Archons.* With the same stealth that brought him here, Alunareth returned to the group before they got too close.

"What did you find?" Samuel asked when the Ranger emerged from the foliage.

"I think they're Archons. Three of them."

Haley opened her phone and displayed a picture of an Archon on her screen. "Did they look like this?"

"Yes."

"Do you think they have any idea that we're here?" Samuel asked. "I wonder why they seem to be just…hanging around."

"Hoping for us to show up," Elizabeth said. "They're a hive mind and know that we're down here somewhere. They felt it when the other two died."

Samuel nodded. "So, they're probably hoping that the bridge is a good bottleneck that you'll eventually need to cross. And unfortunately, they're right."

"I don't think that they know we're here, so at least we have the element of surprise," Haley stated.

"What do you want us to do?" Elizabeth asked Samuel.

"I want you two to stay out of it, if you can." His expression was stern, yet sympathetic. "I know you're both capable, but it would be best if Al and I handle this alone. You know better than most how dangerous they are."

With a mist in her eyes, Haley nodded while remembering Neil's last moments.

"Okay," Elizabeth said, also saddened by thoughts of Neil.

"Follow me." Alunareth turned and stepped into the foliage and the others followed to a spot that was used frequently by campers. A tiny clearing with log benches around a firepit and space for a couple of tents. They could almost see the bridge from here. "Wait here until we're done," Alunareth whispered. "And stay on guard."

They vanished into the bush and even though Haley could sense where they were and knew where to look, she could barely see them at all. Upon reaching the edge of the path, Alunareth readied his bow and took aim at the nearest Archon, waiting for a clean shot at his eye.

"Keep in mind that they are the last of their species," Samuel whispered.

"Oh." Alunareth lowered his bow and observed them for a moment, determined that the closest Archon was right-handed and decided to target the reptilian's arm instead. "You have restraining disks, right?"

"I do." Samuel put his bolt pistol on high power and aimed for another Archon. The one known as Nokitahm. Their physiology was tough and further enhanced by magick. A full power blast would kill most people, but it would take at least a couple headshots just to knock out an Archon.

Alunareth let his arrow fly and Samuel fired two rounds at Nokitahm's head. Before the second blast landed, he shifted his aim to the first Archon, who was screaming from an arrow in his arm and fired two more shots, knocking him out. Nokitahm was staggered by the blasts but did not go down and the third was already throwing orbs at them. They both ducked back into the foliage, avoiding the attack. They held still, ready to pounce, but the Archons were not foolish enough to follow them in. Having regained his bearings from the pistol bolts, Nokitahm held up his hands while chanting and an orb of fire formed. He threw the fireball into the foliage and there was a flash as flames expanded out in a thirty-foot radius, forcing both Samuel and Alunareth to dive out into the open.

"Oh no!" Haley exclaimed. She didn't know what they did for brush fires here in Atlantis, but being in a cavern, she didn't see how this couldn't become a disaster. Elizabeth stood up. "Can you stop it?" Hayley asked.

"I think so." The young mystic moved toward the burning bushes and trees while reaching out with her energetic senses, feeling the energy of fire. Holding her arms out wide, she curled her fingers and started pulling her hands together. The flames peeled and rolled back, all of them pulling together back into a concentrated orb that was now under Elizabeth's control. She cupped the orb in her hands, turned to Haley and said, "I'll go help Al, and you help Sam."

Haley nodded and Elizabeth charged out from the woods. Just as Haley went to follow, the empath sensed a focused aggression coming right for her. Turning around, she next heard heavy footsteps running, accompanied by the rustling and cracking of the foliage as a large man charging through the brush came into view.

Haley's stomach dropped when she saw the eight-foot-tall humanoid rushing between the trees, his eye fixated on the farmgirl. "Uh-uh." She turned and bolted for the edge of the tree line and came out by the chasm.

To her right was the bridge and an Archon with a wounded arm that was starting to regain consciousness. Further down was Samuel and another Archon engaged in melee while Alunareth was trading mystical blasts with Nokitahm by the edge of the pathway. Elizabeth ran out alongside Alunareth, released the orb and raised her protective field around her and the Elf right before it burst against the Archon, knocking him back twenty feet.

The Archon near the bridge regained his senses, realized that Nokitahm was taking a hit and jumped to his feet. He used a healing spell on his arm and charged at Elizabeth and Alunareth. As they turned to face the charging Archon, Nokitahm stood back up and caught sight of Haley turning left and running along the chasm toward the eastern wall as the large humanoid gave chase.

Looking over her shoulder, Haley reached back to fire a couple of blasts at large man. He winced as the concussive bursts hit but kept charging with little sign of discomfort. Nokitahm joined the chase and he came running up alongside the man, throwing a couple more blasts as he passed.

He reached out, and grabbed Nokitahm by the collar, shouting, "Stay outta my way, Snake!" He effortlessly hurled the reptilian over the edge of the chasm. "She's mine!" With his long arms and incredible strength, he scooped up a large rock, almost a boulder, and hurled it at Haley.

Feeling the sudden dread and terror of Nokitahm and glancing back, Haley saw the incoming missile and strafed to her left as the large stone bounced off the ground right next to her and tumbled ahead, knocking into another boulder. Then she felt a rage boil up from somewhere in the brush. *His aim is really good. So is mine.*

Her potato gun became covered with wisps of blue and purple light. She skidded to a stop with a pivot and released her charged blast. Still holding the red key crystal, her blast came out in the shape of a lion's head, packing double the punch as it hit the Troll square in the chest with a burst. He roared as the concussive burst knocked him, tumbling back ten feet, but Haley was surprised when he hopped right back up, bruised but nowhere near beaten. Haley fired some more shots and was surprised again by how agile this large creature was.

Now that he understood the kind of power Haley was packing into her orbs, he ducked to the side, avoiding the blasts and continued running forward. Haley fired a few more blasts and hit him with a couple before he got too close, and she turned to run, weaving around the many chunks of rock between the woods and this end of the chasm.

But this area of the cavern was not as wide as the others, and she quickly found herself facing the eastern wall. They were now too far away to see the bridge area and there were plenty of large rocks and small boulders there. Haley thought about climbing the wall to escape, but the Troll's aim would allow him to crush her with a rock before she could get out of his range. Haley had to fight.

"Haley, where are you? Are you okay?" Elizabeth's voice called over the comm.

"I'm being chased by Bigfoot!" Haley replied.

She turned and locked eyes with the oncoming threat, figured he'd run right up and try to grab her, but he instead came to a stop about thirty feet away. A grin climbed his cheeks as he reached down and scooped up a boulder. "Dance." He threw the boulder like a fastball at Haley, and she dove to the side, out of the way of the impact, but not the shrapnel. The boulder shattered and bits of rock showered Haley like bullets. Her PJs protected her body, but her face was exposed, and three pieces of stone bounced off the side of Haley's cheek and temple with small splashes of blue and purple light. She held her left hand up to her face when she felt the intense sting of the welts.

A roaring laughter erupted from the man. "Can you dodge them all?" He chuckled as he scooped another boulder up in each hand.

While he was picking them up, Haley focused her energy and healed, but another boulder was flying at her, and she threw up her protective sphere. The cavern wall to her back and the incredible momentum of a speeding boulder in front, Haley's field took the full force as it was crushed between the literal rock and hard place. She felt the intensity of the impact squeeze her barrier, then boulder dropped to the ground, but that drained much of her energy.

He looked at Hailey, who was apparently still fine, with astonishment. "How are you still…" His mirth was gone as he furrowed his brow, winding up for another throw. After holding up to that hit, he now saw her as a true threat.

Diving to the side, Haley conjured her helmet before the incoming boulder shattered against the wall. She may be protected from the shrapnel, but more rocks were being hurled at her as she started scanning. He was too durable for her regular blasts to do much, even with the red gem, but that's about all she could do until her energy built back up. She dodged two more boulders as the PJs and helmet protected her from the shrapnel, but one mistake could cost her dearly. Information was then displayed on the inside of her face shield:

SPECIES: TROLL (HOMO TROGLODYTAM)

KNOWN FOR THEIR INCREDIBLE STREGNTH AND DURABILITY, TROLLS ARE A HIGH-LEVEL PHYSICAL THREAT. ALTHOUGH AS INTELLIGENT AS OTHER SPECIES, THEY ARE OFTEN CONSIDERED STUPID OR SIMPLE, LIKELY DUE TO THEIR RELIANCE ON PHYSICAL STREGNTH TO SOLVE MOST PROBLEMS. USE EXTREME CAUTION.

Haley fired some shots at the Troll, which merely shuddered him a bit. He threw another. She dodged, fired back and caught him in the knee, which managed to make him wince. Still, firing at him seemed basically useless and another boulder came flying, so she fired at the boulder. Her blast hit, the concussive burst released, and the force was enough to counter some of the boulder's momentum, causing it to drop to the ground and tumble to a stop by her feet. Haley looked at the Troll, dismissed her helmet and smirked.

"How many can you throw before your arm gets tired?" She immediately felt the Troll's irritation spike, well on its way to becoming anger. *Good.*

The Troll threw more boulders, and kittens flew to meet them in the air. Aiming close to the tops of the boulders, the concussive bursts knocked them to the ground as the Troll seethed. Haley could sense three other people just inside the brush, watching. All three felt as if they were itching to jump in, but one, definitely an Archon, still radiated anger along with some kind of inner conflict and anxiety. She tried to stay aware of, but not distracted by, the three people watching from the woods while she continued to fire blasts at the incoming boulders.

The Troll's arm tired, and his anger spiked: he had had enough. Letting out a roar of frustration, the large man clenched his fists and charged forward.

Too soon. Not all of Haley's energy had returned, so she would have to work with what she had. Sound slowed to a lower pitch, and then all was silent. Haley ran forward, feeling her energy drain as she went. She wouldn't get far before her speed shift ran out, and they would be right on her tail again, so she stopped behind the Troll and popped her claws, taking a swipe at the back of his thighs. Sound returned to her ears as her energy ran out, bringing with it the voice of an agonized Troll screaming out in pain.

"Ow!" The Troll fell over backward, and Haley strafed to the side before he landed on top of her. He thudded to the ground and squirmed. "My legs! My legs!" He looked up to see a blue glow emitting from the end of a potato gun right above his face.

Before Haley fired, she heard the sound of clapping hands as she felt the three people who were hidden in the woods step out from behind the tree line. She looked up at the approaching trio, and her heart sank when she saw, flanked by two Trolls, who it was that clapped. She should have recognized that anger. And now, the intense stare and smug smirk of Ahnk-Hume unnerved Haley to her core.

With intense hatred, the Drakel's eyes bored into Haley's as he strode up to her and the wounded Troll. "Well done," he said as he reached down with his upper right arm, grabbed the Troll by the neck and hoisted him up above his head.

"Hey!" one of the other Trolls shouted.

"Nokitahm wasn't just a dear friend," he turned his gaze from Haley to the other Trolls, and they shrank back, "but my mate." Ahnk-Hume looked up and into the eyes of the choking Troll with a hissing venom for breath. "And you killed him…Like this!" Ahnk-Hume shouted, and with strength just as impressive, he flung the Troll over the edge of the chasm, plummeting toward the magma deep below.

Halfway down, he bounced off the opposing wall, trying and failing to grab at the sheer surface, but there was no handhold to find. He fell the rest of the way down, where his final screams could not be heard by those who were still above.

Ahnk-Hume said, "Now that that score is settled…" he turned to Haley with a wicked sneer. Out of energy and exhausted, Haley was visibly shaking with fear. "Hello, kitten."

Feeling the heat from the chasm behind her, Haley couldn't even take a step back. There was nowhere to run, Kone ruled the world, Elizabeth usurped her opportunity with Dalton and Ahnk-Hume had the upper hand. All seemed like weights of hopelessness on her very spirit, and she didn't want to carry them anymore. *What would Dad do?* She couldn't think of any course of action that would actually help. With tears in her eyes and nothing left to lose, Haley raised her potato gun toward Ahnk-Hume.

"How cute." He said with a chuckle. "I have been thinking about this opportunity since our last encounter." Haley stood there, shaking while holding up her right arm. "What?" Ahnk-Hume asked with mock surpise. "No quippy comments?" He crossed his lower arms while holding out his uppers, palms up with a shrug. "None of your obnoxious movie references?"

"No." Haley fired, and her blasts burst on Ahnk-Hume's protective field while he laughed. She relented and lowered her arm, with nothing left to do. She wondered why the Drakel hadn't already made his move. She felt hatred, conflict and anger all swirling together inside the Archon, and she had no doubt that it was all about to be aimed at her.

"You're packing an unusual amount of punch. It's impressive, but it won't help you here. Before we finish this, tell me something." His wicked grin spread wide, and he asked, "Do you believe in redemption?"

"Huh?" Haley sniffled.

"Do you…believe…in redemption?"

"Uh…yeah?"

"Really? Well, I don't know if I believe in redemption, but I do know what I can do." He leaned down and forward, bringing his face close to Haley's and she shivered in fear when she smelled his breath. His wicked grin disappeared, replaced by an earnest expression. "I can try." In a sudden burst, Ahnk-Hume pivoted, grabbing one Troll's neck with his upper right and punching him in the solar plexus with his lower. At the same time, he reached out and grabbed the other Troll's wrist with his lower left and his neck with the upper. He pulled on the Troll to his right, making him stumble forward, and the Drakel let go. Between Ahnk-Hume's tail and the falling Troll, Haley had to jump down the ledge, pop her claws and cling to the sheer wall.

The remaining Troll, having better leverage, struggled back against Ahnk-Hume. He dug in his heels and pushed the Drakle, causing Ahnk-Hume's foot to slip. The Troll gave another shove, but Ahnk-Hume, instead of attacking, grabbed on with all four hands. "Whoa!" The Troll started pulling Ahnk-Hume back before Ahnk-Hume pulled him over the edge. "Okay, can we talk about a truce?"

Deep inside, Ahnk-Hume still wanted to revel in Haley's agony, craving the euphoric sensations of power through pain. But he didn't want to be that anymore. He knew himself, knew he would eventually continue as the horrific thing he had been. Self-loathing and disgust washed over him, and he knew there was a way to avoid that. He turned his head away from the struggling Troll and looked down at Haley as she clung to the side of the chasm. Oh, how he hated her!

He knew he was wrong to do so, that it should be the other way around, but he still held contempt in his heart for the farmgirl. Yet he couldn't help but respect and admire her for what she had already done and what he knew she would continue to do. An inferior being; yet even though she had no hive, she had the ability to connect with those around her.

Perhaps there truly is more to Terrans than even I realized. Perhaps she and her kind can break the cycle. Haley looked up from her perch at Ahnk-Hume and the Troll, both teetering on the edge in a strange life-or-death tug-o-war, confused by this strange turn of events and saw something different in Ahnk-Hume's eyes. It was respect.

He looked down at her and said, "Don't let them become what we were. Break the cycle! Free my species from corruption! Fair well, Haley Starr," and he tightened his grip on the Troll, pulling with all his strength.

"No, no, no…" The Troll pulled back with everything he had, but even he could not match the strength of Ahnk-Hume. "Noooooo!"

They went over the edge and dropped straight down. Haley watched in disbelief as Ahnk-Hume didn't even try to use his wings while they plunged down toward the magma. She felt the Troll's terror and fear. Heard his screams. She felt Ahnk-Hume's anger, conflict and hate. Two lives, one jumble of harsh emotions becoming smaller as they fell further away from the empath. Then she felt it. A shift in Ahnk-Hume as he began to radiate something powerful that she never thought she'd sense from the Drakel.

Peace.

Then nothing. Haley hung there for a moment, stunned. She had no idea what she should be feeling. *Ahnk-Hume's gone.* The farmgirl couldn't believe what had just happened in front of her. With a faraway stare, though she wasn't looking at anything, Haley had trouble processing these events for a moment.

Should I feel bad for him? Did he just die on purpose to save me? She blew out a confused sigh, then her eyes popped open wide. "Peace…He felt peace."

Considering that, Haley felt her moral rise as she became less disheartened and furrowed her brow in determination.

"If Ahnk-Hume can do something good and find peace, then maybe things aren't as hopeless as I thought." New hope invigorated her, and, with a smile, she said, "We're gonna win! We're gon…we." Her eyes popped wide again as she darted up to the ledge while engaging her comm. "Beth?!" Haley was back to the cavern floor in an instant and began to sprint back toward the bridge. "Beth?!"

"Hang on!" Elizabeth responded with a grunt. A couple of seconds later, her voice returned. "Are you okay?"

"Yeah, you?"

"Yeah."

Sensing relief and calm coming from the others, Haley slowed to a jog. "Beth…Ahnk-Hume is…dead."

"Really?"

Haley responded with a long slow, "Yeah."

Hearing the tone in Haley's voice, she asked, "Why do you sound sad about it." As soon as she asked, a possibility dropped into her mind, and she added, "Did you…do it?"

"No…No, I didn't. But I'm not happy about it either." As much as the unexpected sacrifice had Haley befuddled, there was something else weighing heavy on her mind. Before Elizabeth could ask another question, she said, "We need to finish this, Beth. But first, we gotta talk."

CHAPTER 24
Chill Out

Jogging alongside the chasm, Haley could now see the bridge. Getting closer, the foliage that was obstructing her view was less dense and receding back from the chasm as she neared the path, and she could start to see the rest of her party, along with two Archons lying on the ground, dead. Haley slowed her pace as she approached and saw that the Dwarves had rejoined them. Balgar was removing his climber's pick from one Archon's chest.

"Hey." Elizabeth stepped forward to greet Haley, seeing the steeled look upon her friend's face. It was similar to an expression she had seen Haley make many times, especially when she was close to completing a video game, but something about her face was different this time. It somehow carried more weight. "What happened?" she asked as everybody gathered to hear Haley's answer."

"I still can't believe it, but Ahnk-Hume died saving me from some Trolls."

Elizabeth stared at Haley dumbfounded. "That…doesn't make sense." Nobody else said anything, but instead all bore similar dumbfounded expressions at the strange news.

With a shrug, Haley started to say, "I don't get it either. He said something about breaking the cycle of corruption for his species, but we need to ta…" Then her eyes snapped open as she sensed the approach of another from the south. And due to a past empathic entanglement, she was able to recognize who. "Sabrina's coming."

"From Churgen?" Samuel asked.

"Yeah. She's still a few minutes away."

"Then we should get moving and meet her on the way," Samuel said, then turned and looked at the bodies on the ground with a sigh. The group moved them to the side of the path and laid them on their backs. Alunareth had to close one Archon's eyes before he stood up to take his leave.

Though they met here as enemies, the Alfan culture respects life much like the Hunters and still shows respect to the fallen. Especially now that here before him were the last two bodies of an entire species. They tried their best to take the reptilians alive but were hit with a nasty spell just as the Dwarves showed up with the element of surprise and finished them quickly.

The party made their way across the bridge, and Elizabeth walked alongside Haley. "Hey. What do we need to talk about?"

"Not now," Haley replied with a huff. "Not in front of everyone else."

"Okay? How far away is Sabrina?" Elizabeth asked, not only because she wanted to know, but also because she rarely felt this kind of tension from Haley and since they couldn't address it now, she would rather focus on something else.

"Close."

"How close?"

"Look beside you," Haley answered while keeping her eyes straight ahead.

"Ha! You're funny," Elizabeth's sarcastic tone had a bit of a snipe to it until she actually turned to look. "Oh! You are here!"

"Hello, girls," Sabrina said with what was almost a warm expression, but she had already heard the tension between them before arriving.

"Hi," Elizabeth said.

Though truly glad to see her, the most Haley mustered at that moment was a monotone "Hello," delivered while still looking straight ahead.

"Good to see you," Samuel called back from the head of the pack. "Where's Jake?"

Returning Samuel's greeting with a nod, Sabrina answered, "Back in Meelyhn. He broke his ankle, but he'll be okay."

Balgar's head snapped toward Sabrina. "Really?! That man moves through caves as well as any Dwarf. How'd that happen?"

"He did it, saving my life from a giant lizard."

"A giant lizard?!" Rudge exclaimed. "Glad you both got away with your lives still intact. How big was it?"

"They're about the same size as the icelots." Sabrina's thoughts returned to the rift between Haley and Elizabeth. *This must be addressed before it becomes a real problem.* Her eyes glanced off to the side, then back to the front. *But not now, not with an audience.* "Are you two okay?" she asked, trying to get a better gauge of how they've handled everything they've been through.

Haley shrugged. "We're still alive."

"I heard about Neil. My condolences." She felt a wave of sorrow come from them both at the mention of Neil but was impressed at how well the two eleven-year-old girls were composing themselves, though a visible mist appeared in their eyes.

"Thanks," Elizabeth said. "But the last thing he said to us was to beat Kone and that's what we're gonna do. We already have two of the keys."

"Then the last one is in Churgen. I hope you don't mind the cold."

"We're from Connecticut," Haley flatly stated.

"Understood."

The further south they went, the thinner the foliage became as the temperature was steadily dropping. It was in the upper sixties when they came across the passage up to Meelyhn, which marked the border of Churgen.

"Soon, the cavern will slope down, and most of the light is from the clouds up here," Sabrina informed everyone. "The further down we go, the darker and colder it gets." She walked over to the western wall, where a large duffle bag was placed. She opened it and retrieved the coat from earlier. "It's a thirty-degree slope most of the way down. A lot of it is icy. Jake had set anchors and ropes in the more troublesome spots when we were here earlier, but there are creatures down there. I even saw a saber tooth tiger." She looked at the girls, "A living one," she clarified, remembering the encounter with the reanimated cat carcass from earlier. "Most are natural animals. But the lizards are something else."

"Why do you say that?" asked Alunareth.

"Because I don't sense any feelings within them. There weren't any of them around, but then a wave of mystical energy flowed through, and they started popping up everywhere."

"Like the angry salad men," Haley commented.

"Is that really what we're calling those things?" Samuel asked with a smirk, coaxing a fleeting smile from Haley.

With a shrug, Haley asked, "Got a better name?"

Chuckling, Samuel replied, "No, not yet."

"Are the lizards made of ice chunks, like the bugs we fought earlier?" Elizabeth asked.

"They appear to be flesh and blood, but they're large and very fast. And unlike reptiles that I'm familiar with, they don't mind the cold. But they turn into ice when you kill them."

"Well," Balgar said with a laugh, "We'll see how fast they are when impaled with my climbing pick." He held up his tool, that was designed to double as a weapon. "If it can puncture stone, then it can puncture lizard flesh." A fact he had already demonstrated on one of the Archons.

"I've no doubt," Sabrina replied. "But they are still dangerous, so use caution."

"Of course. I might be a little nuts sometimes," Balgar said with a smile, "but I ain't stupid."

They removed the coats from their packs and donned them, preparing for the descent. Sabrina reached behind her and took hold of her scabbards. With a tug, they separated from their magnetic perch. She set them on the ground and slipped her arms into the coat sleeves. After zipping it closed, she picked up her scabbards and swung them over her shoulders, against her back, where the magnetics of her jumper held them in place.

"Wish I had something like that for my bow, "Alunareth commented as he readjusted his strap to fit overtop his coat. A moment later, he had it set right and slung his bow and quiver across his back. He practiced reaching back for it a couple of times, getting used to the bulkier sleeves of his coat. "At least the bolt pistol is still an easy draw."

"Everybody ready?" Samuel looked at each member of the party, who nodded as he caught their gaze. "Good." He turned to Sabrina. "Anything else we should know before we move?" he asked while putting on a pair of gloves.

"Just that it gets dark, like twilight. So, we need to make it back up here before these clouds go dark, or else we might be in pitch black."

"We've got about three hours," Samuel said. "We better move."

Sabrina led the way with Samuel alongside. Cautiously picking their steps, they descended the steep slope of dirt and stone. The vegetation thinned out quickly, and far fewer birds could be heard. The temperature continued to drop as they descended, and the chill hung in the air like a wet blanket. Ropes were already hanging in the more treacherous areas, thanks to Jake, and it made this passage down far easier than Sabrina's previous trip. Haley had the easiest time since she just used her cling ability to keep her feet from slipping.

"Jake knew right where to put these," Rudge commented while taking hold of another rope at a steeper drop.

Balgar laughed. "He said that spelunking was his passion and that becoming a geologist was incidental."

"Well, the man appreciates stone for what it is. I gotta respect that."

"Yes, he does!" Balgar replied. "He has the heart of a Dwarf."

Down at the front of the pack, Sabrina and Samuel got a few more yards ahead of everybody for a discrete conversation.

"I need a few moments alone with the girls," Sabrina told him. "There is a problem between them, and it needs to be settled before we run into more trouble."

"A problem?" he asked, a little confused. "They seemed to be doing just fine."

"I've gotten to know them a bit over the last week, and Haley is not this…reserved. Elizabeth is acting like her normal self, but Haley is upset with her. I need to find out why, although I suspect it has to do with an Atlantean farm boy."

Considering Sabrina's words, Samuel thought back across the last couple of days and realized that she was right. Haley was more whimsical and would crack a joke here and there. And she still did, even when he found them in Buruum after the death of Neil. But she hasn't done any of that for the past hour. "Ever since we left Freq," Samuel said with a nod.

"We need them to get past this. We can't have them fighting while we're down here."

"How do you want to do this?"

"When we get to the bottom, let me take them aside for a few minutes and hopefully, I can handle it right there." She blew out a sigh, "I hope I know what I'm doing."

"Well, you are good at helping people figure things out."

"If I was helping them select weapons, then yes. But this…this is something I've never had to deal with." Sabrina and Derick had been a couple since they met, and she had no idea how to deal with boy drama. The words of Flashipor weighed on her once more. Having kept most people in her life at arm's length, she now lacked the interpersonal experience to provide adequate counsel but understood that she was still the best one to address it. "Perhaps I do need to get a life."

"Well, you certainly helped me with my emotional problems."

"Yes, but that was a very different circumstance."

"True. But I don't understand what they see in that goofy-looking kid."

"Goofy?" Sabrina replied in surprise. "What do you mean, goofy. He's a handsome young man."

Samuel shrugged with a bit of a chuckle. "If you say so. But I know what a handsome guy looks like." He flashed a smile and said, "I do have a mirror, you know."

"At least you never lost your confidence," she replied in a deadpan manner.

"Well, when a lady like Fiona is into me, why would I think otherwise?"

"Who's Fiona?"

"My girlfriend. Alunareth's sister."

"Samuel!" Sabrina beamed. She began speaking at a normal volume, "That's fantastic! Congratulations." She saw the surprised look on his face and asked, "What?"

"I'm just not used to seeing you smile like that. You're usually all business."

"True, but this is good news! We can all use some of that right now." She made her way past a slick patch of ice. "And I can't wait to meet her. I have to make sure she's good enough." She paused and tilted her head back, listening.

"What?!" came Alunareth's voice, exactly what she was waiting for.

Sabrina looked back at Samuel with a straight face, "And you say that I have no sense of humor," bringing a laugh out of Samuel. "But still, you're my protégé, and I need to look out for you."

Alunareth stated, "I assure you that my sister is an honorable woman."

"Al…first, you wanted to kill me when you found out we were dating, and now you're defending the choice? I'm touched."

"Just treat her right, or I'll touch you with my knuckles."

"Now you sound more like a Dwarf than an Elf."

"That's what we call personal growth," Balgar called from the back with a grin as his brother chuckled.

"Mostly pine trees now," Elizabeth said as they continued their descent. "I wonder how far before they can't grow."

"Don't know," Haley shrugged.

"I wonder why it's so cold," Balgar said.

"Yeah," Rudge added. "It shouldn't be freezing down here. It should even be getting hot depending on how close we are to the magma."

Sabrina looked up at the others, "Jake said the same thing."

They neared the bottom, and as Sabrina said, it was like twilight, but the ice reflected the light further south into the cavern as it leveled out, yet it shouldn't be enough for them to see. The dark and frozen terrain before them had an unnatural glow, presenting the landscape in dim, dark blues.

Haley would have thought that the place was oddly beautiful if it wasn't for the unnatural chill that hung in the air. The kind that was felt in the spine rather than the skin. The cavern opened in width as it leveled out, and the length continued south. The western wall became further away, opening the land up to many conifers and a few other varieties of vegetation. The ground was uneven in most places, with rocks jutting up between patches of dirt and ice.

Haley was surprised to see the trees and plants, not because of the cold but due to the lack of light. For just a moment, she forgot her boy problems and took in the sight, unsure of how to feel. Some of the scenes before her would have been fitting for a postcard, while at the same time, the energy that hung in the cavern like an uncomfortable humidity was a constant reminder that this was a cursed place with an energy that everyone could sense.

On the other side of the cavern, the crack between their path and the western wall had widened, and now was a narrow chasm running the length of Churgen that plunged down to the dark unknown.

Sabrina's eyes scanned the area, looking for a spot that was far enough away for the girls to have some privacy but close enough for the others to respond if something happened.

Samuel turned to face the others, who gathered around as Sabrina determined the best place on the western side of the path. "We're going to stay here for now while Sabrina takes the girls for a couple moments of privacy."

"This way," Sabrina said with a wave of the hand. The girls followed as the others quietly conversed while waiting at the path. The walking wasn't too troublesome, a few slick patches here and there, but it was mostly bare rocks and dirt. She led them behind some larger boulders jutting up from the ground by a large leafless tree.

The tree, Haley noticed, was encased in a thin layer of ice, and it was this ice from which the dark glow of Churgen came. She swung her head around, looking for any more ice. A patch on the ground, another tree, every bit of ice she saw emitted this glow. But her attention was drawn from that by a feeling of anxiety from Sabrina. Haley looked at her, the confusion clear on her face.

With their view blocked, Sabrina said, "Bathroom break now. We might not get another opportunity for a while." After they all did what they had to do, the girls started to walk back. "Not yet."

Haley and Elizabeth turned back to Sabrina, wondering what this was about.

"There…there's an issue between you two right now and you need to be united in a time like this. What happened?"

Haley blew out a long sigh as she hung her head forward. Elizabeth turned and looked at Haley, who lifted her head. Though not an empath, Elizabeth could still feel the anger before she even saw Haley's face. Haley's blue eyes drilled into the hazel of Elizabeth's and the farmer looked as if she were about to explode.

"What?" Elizabeth asked, still having no idea what was wrong.

Haley's face turned red, and her eyes became rimmed with mist. "You took him from me!" she shouted.

"What do you mean?" Elizabeth asked, confused and holding her hands up, palms out.

"You need to keep your voices lower," Sabrina reminded.

"I was trying to talk to him, and when I did, you walked up and took over. I grew the plant, and you stole my harvest!"

"But…but I thought you were my wing."

"Wing…wha?"

"You know," she made air-finger quotes, "wingman."

"Uh…no." Haley was now the one who looked confused.

"A friend who helps you try to…get a date," Elizabeth awkwardly explained. Haley still looked confused, so Elizabeth continued. "I was trying to think of something to say to him before he left with Balgar and Rudge, but I was so nervous that I couldn't think of anything. I knew you could feel how nervous I was, and you suddenly stopped him. I thought you were trying to help me.

Haley stood there for a moment, stunned. "I had no idea you were nervous."

"What?! How could you not? I even thought I was gonna throw up."

"I…I didn't know."

Elizabeth's jaw dropped. "How did *you* not feel that?"

"Because I was so nervous that I could've puked too. I was trying to think of something to say to him. I didn't realize that it wasn't all mine, and when I managed to say something, you came over and…" A couple of tears ran down her cheek. "I'm sorry I didn't know, but if you were in my spot, what would it have looked like to you?"

"I…I would have been so angry that it'd make me sick…oh." With a mist now in her own eyes, Elizabeth looked at Haley and said, "I'm sorry. I never meant to do that to you."

Haley and Elizabeth stared quietly at each other for a moment, then stepped together for an embrace with teary I'm-sorry's being said by both.

Sabrina breathed a sigh of relief. The girls resolved it on their own, and the Hunter felt like she had dodged a metaphorical bullet. The girls released their hug, and Sabrina asked, "Are you both on the same page again?"

The girls looked at each other, then back to Sabrina. "Yeah," they said together.

"Good. We need to get back to the others and finish this."

They began making their way back when both Haley and Sabrina gasped. A sudden spike of emotion came from the direction they were heading, but it was so much in a short burst. Invigoration, glee and gratification; a euphoric feeling of being alive, in control and it was nasty.

"What was that?" Haley asked. "It felt…sinister."

"We need to get back now!" Sabrina said.

"Uh-oh," Elizabeth added as they took off running where they could but slowed in the slippery spots. Except for Haley, who used her cling ability to keep running.

"Stay together," Sabrina said, and Haley slowed, allowing the others to catch up.

They returned to the path to see everybody still on their feet, waiting. Except one.

"Where's Balgar?" Sabrina asked.

"He stepped behind the trees for a moment," Rudge said, pointing to an ice-crusted group of trees near the chasm. "He'll be right back."

Sabrina rushed past and toward the trees, which prompted everyone to follow. She got there first and sidled herself alongside the frozen trunk, drew her bolt pistol and carefully began to slink around to the other side but stopped before she disappeared from the others' view.

What Haley felt from Sabrina, the stomach-dropping and a wave of sorrow, put a thought in her head that she did not like. When the others came around to see what Sabrina saw, it confirmed Haley's fears. Lying face down in a pool of blood, Balgar was dead.

CHAPTER 25
Cold Blooded

"Oh, no!" Haley quietly gasped.

"Balgar?!" Rudge bellowed and started to run for his brother.

Sabrina grabbed the hood of his jacket to stop him. "Wait!"

It took every ounce of self-control Rudge had in him at that moment to comply, but he did manage to stop before his charge would have pulled the Hunter off her feet. "What?" the Dvwargarian huffed.

"It looks like a trap," Samuel answered.

Alunareth pointed. "I see drag marks."

"Hold back. And I might need you to cover me," Sabrina added while looking at Samuel and began slowly making her way forward.

As she inched closer, she could tell that Balgar's position was open to many vantage points from the northern slope of Churgun. She paused to inspect her immediate surroundings before continuing with most of her focus up the slope. Reaching out with her empathic senses, the Hunter felt nothing while approaching Balgar's body.

Just as she leaned down and reached for his shoulder, Sabrina felt that strange, euphoric feeling of being alive. Faint for an instant, but then it intensified. Sabrina stood up straight and turned her head to the right, looking up the hill at where the feeling originated. Her eyes scanned the area and noticed a shadowy figure in a tree. And then her eyes widened when the euphoric feeling spiked.

In a snap, Sabrina leaned backward, and the bullet was whistling by her nose before the sound of the rifle's fire reached her ears, and she felt the pressure wave against her face. The few animals in the area, mostly birds, scattered. She bent her legs as the next round sped by just above her head. Her body snapped up straight, and she felt the next round's pressure wave whipping the long braid of her hair as the bullet sped right by where her temple was a split second before.

Flashes of yellow light reflected off the icy trees as Samuel and Alunareth stepped into the area, firing their bolt pistols up in the direction from which the shots came. Alunareth's eyes picked out the figure and fired again. The shadowy figure vanished behind the tree's trunk before the bolt reached its target.

This tree had no ice, which is one of the reasons why it was chosen. The shadow slid down to a lower branch and snaked around to the other side with his rifle to see that the others had gathered around the Dwarf's body. *Perfect,* he thought with a smile. The air felt like it tingled his skin as he took aim at the Elf. He became energized, experiencing the thrill of deciding another's fate. Controlling another life. He got to choose whether someone's heart would take another beat, and that invigoration spiked to a crescendo while he pulled the trigger. The round sped through the air, straight at the Elf's head, but deflected away in a ripple of blue and purple light.

Haley, holding the red crystal, had no problem expanding her protective field to encompass the group. She felt the impact and the drain on her energy when the powerful round was deflected. Two more bullets bounced off her field, one aimed at Sabrina and the other at Samuel. Then she felt the emotion from the gunman fade into nothing.

Rudge turned Balgar onto his back, scooped his arms under his brother's armpits and started dragging him away.

Haley had to move slowly as it took a great deal of focus to maintain her protective field while in motion. They all moved away from the target area as a couple more rounds were fired, and as soon as the landscape offered cover, Haley dropped her field. Balgar's heels dragged on the ground as Rudge pulled him around the group of trees, where they squatted under the cover of the frozen tree.

"Keep watch," Samuel said to Alunareth. He approached Rudge. "Is he still with us?"

"No," the Dwarf answered with more gruffness to his voice and mist in his eyes. "He was…he was stabbed through the back of the skull."

Inspecting the wound, Samuel saw that it was a flat puncture wound right through the base of the skull and into the brain. He recognized the tactic, and Sabrina felt his anxiety rise.

"What is it?" Sabrina asked before Samuel had shown any sign of worry.

Samuel looked at her, his expression grave. "Knife through the back of the skull. A Commando."

Pulling her mayum blade, Sabrina held it up to the wound on the back of Balgar's head. It was the same width.

"This Commando's made a big mistake." Rudge laid Balgar down, crossed his brother's arms over his chest and stood back up. "Because now he'll be dealing with Dwvargarin rage." He looked at Samuel and narrowed his eyes. "And I guarantee he won't survive it."

"I can stop him," Haley said.

"No!" Sabrina snapped. "You're not going anywhere near him. I think I know who it is, and if I'm right, we are in serious trouble."

"He keeps blocking his feelings. Only an empath can do that, but if I touch him, I can break through like I did with…" Haley dropped her head and sighed before looking back at Sabrina with apologetic eyes, "Like I did with you."

"He's not an empath," Sabrina answered. "This is Commando Conrad. A psychopath."

"Oh, no," Samuel groaned.

"Sahmbo has a psychological profile on him, and he's cold. He only feels emotions when he's killing."

"He won't feel anything ever again after today," Rudge vowed.

"Do you know where the temple is?" Samuel asked Sabrina.

"There are statues down near the southern end of the cavern. We didn't find the temple, but it's probably near there."

"You take the girls and head to the temple," Samuel said to Sabrina. "Alunareth, Rudge and I are going hunting."

"Be careful. You know how dangerous Conrad is." She reached out with her right hand and clasped Samuel's shoulder as he grasped hers.

"I will be," Samuel replied.

"Good hunting," she said.

"Good Hunting," he replied.

They released each other's shoulders while Alunareth slipped away to scout the immediate area. Sabrina turned to the girls. "Get ready to move and be very aware of your surroundings. The lizards are now the least of our worries."

Haley looked at the body of Bulgar as a tear slid down her cheek. "We will." She walked up to Rudge and could feel his sorrow, loss and rage, amazed by the self-control he was exercising. Haley wrapped her arms around him, saying, "I'm so sorry. Please, be careful."

"Thanks, kid," he replied with stern but wet eyes. "I will be."

Looking around, Elizabeth asked, "Do we need to stay near some kind of cover?"

"Yes," Sabrina said. "It might slow our progress, but it's better than getting sniped."

Alunareth returned. "Clear."

"Good," Samuel said. "We're going to cross the path." Looking to Sabrina, he continued, "Give us five minutes after that to check the area before you go." He smiled before adding, "Maybe we'll have this handled by the time you come back with the key."

The three crossed the path into the wider areas of Churgen and disappeared from the ladies' view. A few moments later, Samuel's voice was heard on the comm, "Good to go."

"Let's move," Sabrina said. They crossed the path and entered the frozen woods on the other side, turning south to search for the final key.

Rudge moved carefully, trying to stay quiet while Samuel and Alunareth made almost no sound at all. They spread out some but always remained in view of each other.

Alunareth noticed a scuff on the frozen surface of some dirt. His eyes followed it to another scuff. "He went this way."

They began following the trail, which went a bit back up the hill and curved back down. Almost back to the path, Samuel suddenly whispered, "Halt." The other two came to a stop when they heard his voice in their earpieces.

"What is it?" Rudge asked, keeping his voice low.

"A tripwire. And I almost didn't see it," Samuel answered. "Keep your eyes open."

Continuing, it wasn't even two minutes later when Alunareth spotted another trap. "Stop," he exclaimed quietly into his comm. When the others looked to Alunareth, he pointed to a frozen tree. "There's a bomb."

Samuel carefully scanned the area with his eyes, then shifted his position to get a good look at the tree and saw the device. "That's motion activated. Don't go within five feet of it, or it will detonate."

Rudge shook his head. "How do we look around the next bush for one of those things without setting it off?"

The sound of leathery feet slapping against the cold surface was heard, and they looked to the southwest, where a couple of large grayish-white lizards were seen heading in their direction.

"I like a challenge, but this is not what we need right now," Samuel looked to Alunareth. "Can you drop them quietly?"

With a nod, the Alfan readied his bow, knocked and drew an arrow. He waited a few more seconds until the first lizard came to a better position. And Alunareth let the arrow fly. With a slight whoosh, the arrow split through the distance and plunged into the lizard's eye socket. It dropped to the ground and turned into a pile of crushed ice.

The second one dropped an instant later as Alunareth made note of the locations in hopes of retrieving the arrows later.

"So that's where snow cones come from," Samuel said with a smirk, attempting to break some of the anxious tension.

Sabrina's voice was heard in the earbuds. "We encountered a lounge of them and there's a lot more heading to the north, toward you."

"Thanks for the heads up," Alunareth whispered.

Samuel crossed the path first, followed by Rudge and Alunareth, watching the rear. They were now by the chasm, close to where Balgar was found, but with no sign of more boobie traps, they spread out like before, staying within each other's line of sight.

Rudge got close to the edge and peered down into the darkness. *What marvels does the Earth wait to reveal next?* He let out a sigh. *Marvels that Balgar and I were supposed to discover together.* He grasped the handle of Balgar's climbing pick, squeezing it tight and holding it up before him. "I vow that I won't rest until your pick is buried in his…"

Darting out from behind a tree with his sidearm, Conrad kicked Rudge in the back and pivoted while firing a few rounds at Alunareth, who was closest to them. Alunareth ducked behind a tree to avoid the pistol bolts as Rudge tumbled over the edge.

"Rudge!" Alunareth shouted as Samuel opened fire.

Conrad fell back behind the tree for cover as the energy bolts came his way. Samuel and Alunareth kept firing as they moved in, trying to keep him pinned, but the Commando suddenly zipped through the air to a tree limb and then shot southward into another group of trees.

"Grapple harness," Samuel said. "Rudge, are you still with us?" There was no answer on the comm.

"What happened to Rudge?" Sabrina asked.

With a sigh, Alunareth answered, "Conrad knocked him into the chasm and escaped. We're going after him again now."

"Stay sharp and be careful."

Alunareth looked at Samuel, his expression deadly serious. "Let's end this."

"Yes," Samuel replied. "Let's."

"No! No more!" Haley cried. "No more dying. I'm not letting anyone else get killed!"

"Stay focused," Sabrina said. "I know it hurts, but you can't control that. All you can do is finish the mission."

"But it's not fair!" Haley blurted. "He deserved better. And Quinten…" She dropped her head as the tears flooded her cheekbones. "And Neal." She gulped air between a couple of sobs. "Neal," she softly said again as droplets landed on the ground and froze.

Elizabeth was just as much of a mess at that moment but didn't have anything to say. She just stewed at the losses they'd endured on this day, wanting it to finally stop.

"Honor him by exposing Kone's lies to the world," Sabrina said, trying to guide them through the difficult and overwhelming emotions. "And we can do it. You've obtained two of the keys by yourselves. We just have one more and…" The slapping sound of leathery feet was heard. They looked to the west to see more lizards heading their way.

"Where do they keep coming from?" Elizabeth asked in frustration. She drew her sai and was ready to charge them.

"Uh-oh," Haley said, realizing that what she thought was a small pack was just the beginning. As the creatures drew closer, more came out of the dim, frozen forest behind them. "There's gotta be at least fifty of 'em!" Her eyes popped wide as a thought dropped into her head. Haley had a more powerful blast than Elizabeth but tended to run through her energy a bit quicker, especially when she engaged her speed state. "Beth, let's switch crystals."

The first lizards in the wave closed the distance between them and the ladies as Haley and Elizabeth both began to crackle with energetic light. Sabrina set her bolt pistol to full power and took aim with her left while drawing one of her katanas with her right. The lizards continued to advance, and when they got close enough for a clear shot, the ladies opened fire. Haley's bobcat struck one head-on and was followed up by a volley of five blasts.

It kept coming, and she fired again, three more shots before it tumbled to the ground like a pile of crushed ice. Elizabeth's blast hit, and she charged up a second, which finished off the creature. Sabrina fired bolt after bolt at her target, twelve in all, before the beast dropped. She was grateful for the cold environment, which allowed her bolt pistol to cool a bit quicker as she knew that she would be taxing her sidearm to deal with these lizards.

Elizabeth, feeling the vibration of the earth and rocks around her, sensed some smaller stones and reached out with her energy and intentions, and they responded. Three rocks about the size of golf balls broke free of the ice and began flying through the cavern at the young mystic's command. *I hope this works,* she thought as she pushed them with her mind to high speeds.

The rocks zipped toward a lizard like a set of bullets. One stone went clear through the creature's midsection, another through the neck and the third lodged itself in the skull. The lizard started running in circles, flopping weirdly as it went. A single blast finished it, and she mentally pulled the stone from the ice pile and sent it off, with the other two, for the next lizard as it closed in on her.

Only managing to drop one before the lizards reached her, Sabrina snapped into motion, taking the first lizard's head off with a single swing of her new katana as she let go of her bolt pistol, and it snapped back to its cradle. She sliced the next one, and as it dropped into a heap of ice, she launched a grapple anchor onto the side of a large tree fifty feet above the ground.

Haley launched one more shot at the one closest to her, and when it locked eyes with the farmgirl, she jumped into the air and dashed out above the beasts. They turned, tracking Haley's movement, so she dashed again, drawing them away from Elizabeth and Sabrina.

"Haley, what are you doing!?" Sabrina shouted.

Haley went for a third dash, but even though she still had plenty of energy, she just couldn't make it work, and she began to drop. So, she funneled her energy into a pounce, driving down directly on top of one, which instantly turned into a pile of ice, and rebounding back up as a blue wave of light splashed out, shoving back three more. Only two were able to get back up.

At the apex of her rebound, Haley tried again, and this time, she was able to dash, kicking herself back toward the others, but instead of making the second dash, she pounced before getting too close to the others. She slammed down, destroying another lizard and planting her feet into the now cracked ice covering the ground.

Thanks to the gemstone, her energy continued to recover nicely, but she was becoming concerned with channeling too much of it. In the middle of a battle was not the time to stop and take supplements, so she dismissed her potato gun while taking her staff and expanded it.

The stones tore through the lizard in front of Elizabeth as she let out a partially charged blast in its face, dropping it. As it turned into a pile of ice, a realization hit the young mystic. "Duh!" She shouted, slid a sai into her belt and pulled out her lighter.

The blue glow of the spinning staff stood out against the dim background. Haley used the momentum from the spin and swung it across a lizard's face. A concussive burst released on impact, doing visible damage to the beast and the second direct strike took it down. She spun around as two more lizards charged at her, so she held her staff horizontally and pushed it out in front.

The aggressive lizards took the bait, and each took a bite at an end as Haley released another burst of energy through the staff. The concussive bursts blew their jaws off and both dropped into piles. When she spun around again, she was met with the charge of three more.

Elizabeth flicked the lighter and streams of flames were swirling around her arms and torso. The lizards that were charging at her came to a sudden halt and began backing away. "Ah-ha!" She shouted with a laugh.

The mayum katanas were much better suited for dealing with the lizards than her regular swords. Before, her swings would slice part way in, doing some damage, but now, almost every slash was a kill as the new blades carved right through the creatures with ease. She saw three converging on Haley and engaged her grapple harness.

She zipped toward the tree, taking a slash at one more lizard as she moved at an upward angle. She sheathed one sword and was fifteen feet in the air when she disengaged the harness. The Hunter dropped, still moving forward from the momentum while she turned her other blade downward with both hands, plunging it into the back of a lizard next to Haley as she landed. It turned into a pile of ice beneath her feet as the farmgirl launched a bobcat from her hand, down a lizard's throat.

Elizabeth threw orbs of fire, dropping lizards with only three casual shots. The lizards, although they had no sentience, still knew to stay away from the flames and wouldn't go near Elizabeth, and she continued throwing flames while running toward Haley and Sabrina. She noticed that one of those lizards they were fighting with was standing on what Elizabeth believed to be a small boulder.

I hope it's not too big, she thought, and tried to pull it out from under the beast, but it was frozen into the ground. Elizabeth pulled harder, trying to dislodge the rock, but instead, she felt herself pull forward. *Whoa!* She smiled pulled again with everything she had, launching herself forward.

Growls were heard coming from part of the swarm and then a roar. Haley thrust the end of her staff at a lizard, knocking it back as a burst let loose on contact. She was about to make another strike when Elizabeth flew at the lizard, thrusting her flaming sai into its side. It collapsed into a pile as the other beasts started backing away. And not just the ones near Elizabeth, but the entire swarm began moving toward the north as another loud roar was heard. Looking west, they could see the line backing away from a saber tooth tiger surrounded by heaps of ice.

With the lizards retreating to the north, the torn and bloodied tiger stopped his advance and stood, breathing heavily and staring at the receding flood of invaders to his territory. "A giant lounge is heading in your direction," Sabrina said on the comm. Then, the tiger collapsed.

"Oh, no!" Haley shouted an instant before she vanished.

"What the…?" Sabrina's jaw dropped. Before she could complete the expletive, she sensed Haley near the tiger and when she looked, there was the farmgirl, stroking the cat's fur along his cheek, trying to comfort him.

"Oh, yeah," Elizabeth said. "She can move really fast now."

Elizabeth and Sabrina hurried over to Haley and the tiger, who had large gashes down his side and a few on his face. Haley had tears in her eyes as she continued to comfort the dying cat the best she could. She looked up to her arriving companions, "Beth, can you help him?"

"I think so," she said. "Can you keep him calm?"

"I think so," Haley replied.

Sabrina slapped something on Elizabeth's back.

"What was that?"

"Just in case," was all the answer Sabrina gave.

Nervous, Elizabeth slowly approached the Smilodon, knelt and gingerly placed her hands on the cat's side near the most severe wound.

"It's okay," Haley said in a soft voice. "She's a friend."

After taking a deep breath, Elizabeth focused her intentions as she hummed. She could feel her energy move, riding out on the sound of her voice and engulfing the tiger. She transitioned to the ah and the wounds began to knit themselves together. She took another breath and began again, humming and then vocalizing. Haley saw the wounds closing on the tiger's face and felt the relief he was experiencing.

Seeing the job done, Elizabeth fell back onto her butt. "Hoo! That wiped me out." The great cat suddenly hopped to his feet, and Elizabeth flew backward, pulled by an unknown force. Her back slammed into Sabrina, who was braced against a tree with her arm wrapped around a low branch to keep herself in place when she activated the grapple harness. "Oof." Elizabeth took a breath. "Whoa. Thanks…I think."

"He's okay," Haley said as she stood to her feet. "Wow! A real saber-tooth tiger," she said and wrapped her arms around his large neck. The tiger chuffed in response to the hug and gently nuzzled her back. The empath took a step back and smiled. "Such beautiful green eyes. Green like Hayseed's." Looking deep into those green eyes, Haley took a sudden, sharp inhale as the entanglement began.

"What am I feeling from them?" Sabrina asked while she felt excitement building in Elizabeth, who was already wondering what Haley would be able to do next.

Necahual gave everything he had to protect his territory. His claws tore through many a lizard and he carried on through devastating injuries. Haley could feel the fierceness with which Necahual fought and she once again felt the electricity within her building and intensifying. She felt her energy flow to her hands, her claws popped, and the energy concentrated within them. The purple glow of her claws brightened as they began thrumming and crackling with blue light and the energy was begging for release.

Haley spun around, facing a direction where nobody was standing, held up her right hand and swiped it down and across in front of her. Her claws left trails of razor-sharp purple light that shot forward as she swiped her left arm, generating more slashing lines of light. The lines shot forward and sliced clean through the trunk of a tree, a few frozen bushes around it and dissipated ten feet out. The tree shifted and started to fall.

"Uh-oh!" Haley exclaimed as she and Necahual dove out from beneath the falling timber. The ground shuddered with the impact, Haley stood to her feet and looked at the tiger with a nervous chuckle while rubbing the back of her head.

"Uh…sorry about that. Necahual chuffed as he nuzzled Haley one last time, then turned and bound off into the frozen forest. The farmer let out a long slow, "Yeah," and said, "I'd be hungry after healing that much too." She turned to see Elizabeth and Sabrina standing there, jaws dangling. "What?"

CHAPTER 26
At Death's Door

Leaning out to his right, Alunareth could see Peter Conrad standing up against a tree and holding his rifle as he surveyed the area. Alunareth pulled back behind the trunk of the tree and knocked an arrow. The Alfan was standing on a limb almost thirty feet above the ground and had good footing. He leaned back out to take aim, but the Commando was gone. *Harngas,* he thought, an Alfan cuss. "I lost him."

Down on the ground, Samuel stuck his head out from behind a tree and searched the area for any movement. Anything out of place. "Stay up high. I'll find him…or he'll find me." He heard the sudden slapping of feet against the ground nearby. "Some of the lizards are already here."

"Just great. I'll cover you, but I only have eight arrows left. After that, it's all bolt pistol."

Samuel could see three lizards coming his way from the south and knew that many more would soon pour in behind them. He launched a couple of grapple anchors into the trees then, holding the bolt pistol in his right hand, he drew his hunting knife with his left while surveying the area one more time before the lizards reached him. Two crossed Alunareth's line of sight and collapsed into mounds of ice when his arrows pierced their eyes. One charged right for Samuel, but he held his fire, waiting until the last second.

Engaging the grapple harness, he shot upward, and the lizard collided with the tree, Samuel disengaged the harness and dropped, plunging his knife into the lizard when he landed. It transformed into a pile of ice beneath his feet while he looked again to see more lizards heading his way from the south and southeast, but he also noticed a few piles of ice where Alunareth's arrows could not reach. "Found him! To the southeast, back near the path."

"I'm moving now," Alunareth replied as he danced down the tree limbs to the ground.

Making the same effort as Samuel and Alunareth to keep quiet, Conrad had already felled three of the lizards with his blade, but more were bounding over the small hills and charging right for him, and he had no grapple anchors set in the immediate area. With his options for stealth gone, he pulled the sub-machine gun and squeezed the trigger. Nearly one hundred rounds sprayed into the growing lounge, turning all the closest beasts into slushies, but he knew that the gunfire gave away his position and he began scanning the area with his eyes for a viable grapple point while switching the gun's magazine.

Reloading just in time, he sprayed bullets into the next wave of lizards and though the gun made quick work out of the beasts, their numbers were immediately replenished by more of the swarm flowing over the icy hill. He changed the magazine again and moved north as the growing lounge continued to advance.

Mowing down another wave, he still hadn't found a tree that wasn't encased in ice, and now that he was down to his last magazine, the opportunity to be choosy was gone. He sprayed his last magazine into the lizards and launched an anchor to the side of a tree, four feet above a large limb.

As soon as it was attached, he activated the harness and hoisted himself into the air. Pulled tight to the tree by the magnetic grappler, he carefully found just enough footing to stand on the tree limb while searching for another grapple point. Five hundred yards to his west was a tree he couldn't see from his vantage point on the ground, with large limbs and free of ice.

Conrad aimed, raising his shot to compensate for the distance, launched his other anchor and dislodged the first. He paused to assess the situation before moving to the next tree. The lizards were everywhere, but his main concern was the Hunter and Ranger. His eyes searched for his targets, along the frozen forest floor and through the trees. When he saw the shadowy figure moving in another tree, he snapped one end of his handle to his harness and the other magnetically pulled on the anchor, ripping him off the limb and across to the other tree, an instant before the arrow struck the spot where Conrad had stood.

"He just mag-grappled west to another tree."

"I see him," Samuel replied. He was in a tree just to Conrad's north, trying to avoid the lizards. He cranked his bolt pistol to full power and was about to take aim when some of the lizards took notice of him and started up the trunk of the tree.

Conrad noticed the lizards' gathering, looked up and sure enough, saw Samuel on one of the limbs, raising his pistol. He pressed tight against the tree, just out of Samuel's line of sight and readied his rifle. *Only three rounds left.* He looked back to the east, wondering where the Elf could be.

Attaching an anchor to his handle, Samuel launched it to Conrad's tree, twenty feet above the Commando. He sent the mental command into the jumper's harness, and he was pulled across to the other tree. The Hunter found good purchase on the limb beneath his feet and slinked around the trunk to take aim at the Commando on the limb below. But he was gone. "He slipped away again." Samuel sought the best way he could go to get away if he were in the Commando's position. All other trees nearby were encased in ice and would provide poor footing.

No, Samuel thought, *He would need to go back to the ground and keep the tree between me and him to block the line of sight.* His eyes dropped down, and he saw where he could back up and find the cover of more trees. He proceeded with his eyes, following the path that he himself would take. Then, his eyes went to the base of a tree, and he snapped back around to the other side as bark splintered from the rifle round. *Yep, found him.*

Conrad pulled back behind the trunk and slid the bolt. *Two.* He turned and kicked a lizard, releasing his rifle and drawing his mayum blade. With a sudden burst of speed, Conrad darted forward and buried it in the lizard's skull, pulled it back and spun, slashing at another as the first one turned to ice. He now had the attention of more lizards and was again out of options. With his rifle strapped over his shoulder, he drew his bolt pistol and sprang out from behind the tree.

As he expected, Samuel was out there, ready and waiting. The Hunter opened fire as Conrad made it behind the next tree, where there was a patch of bare ground which he used to pivot and dart back out. Samuel had anticipated his sudden reemergence, but on the wrong side of the tree. He fired to the right when Conrad came out on the left, blasting with his pistol.

The Commando engaged his grappler as Samuel slipped behind the tree. The Hunter also engaged his harness, pulling himself back toward the upper limbs as Conrad zipped back to his former perch and launched his other anchor at the underside of an upper limb. He put the handle against the harness near his shoulder and zipped up with his pistol at the ready. Samuel popped back out, aiming at a lower branch and his eyes snapped open wide when he realized that Conrad was hanging right there, pistol in hand.

A flash of yellow light and Samuel tumbled from the tree. He regained enough presence of mind to reactivate his grappler before he hit the ground. The jumpers insulated them well from pistol bolts, but this was at full power and point blank to the torso. Samuel was lucky that his heart didn't stop, but as he was zipping back up, he saw that

Conrad already had that rifle trained on him. Instead of firing, Conrad dropped as Alunareth's last arrow sliced into the tree where the Commando had just been.

Aiming and firing before his feet touched down on the limb, Conrad saw the Elf spin when the round hit his left arm, then pulled back behind the tree. *One. And that bow should no longer be an issue.* He zipped back up and disengaged, setting his feet on the limb where Samuel was before, and sidled around the other side to finish the Hunter. But Samuel wasn't there.

Conrad's first instinct was to return to the other side of the tree, expecting to be fired upon in his current position, but this was a Hunter that he was dealing with and realized the trap. *If I dropped down, where would I want to position myself?* He readied his rifle, chose his footing and moved. He stepped right out, planting his feet with the rifle aimed at a lower limb and fired with a smile. He chose correctly.

Samuel took the hit in the chest and tumbled from his branch. The jumpers were considered bullet-proof, but the rifle round was more than it could take. The round penetrated his left peck and came out the back, collapsing Samuel's lung. The Hunter hit the ground with a thud and laid still.

Conrad didn't get the chance to savor the moment because a barrage of pistol bolts came his way. Conrad pulled back to cover as the injured Ranger started running toward Samuel, trying to get to him before the lizards did.

The Ranger is injured, and Couture is near, if not already dead, he thought with a grin. He leaned back out to see the Elf drag Samuel behind a tree with his good arm and lizards heading toward them.

With only his blade and bolt pistol remaining, he wasn't well equipped to take on another hoard of lizards. Lizards that will probably finish these two off for him. *They won't last long. I'll let them fight with the lizards and verify their status on the way out, but right now, I need to deal with my primary target.*

Two statues stood before them, one on each side of the pathway and they were identical. A thin woman, with long cloths wrapped around her body for clothing, smooth skin on the right side of her face, but it looked aged and withered on the left. All three of them immediately recognized the visage of Hel.

"This is where we were attacked by lizards and had to turn back," Sabrina said. "And we should keep going before more show up."

The girls shuddered, remembering the earlier encounters with Hel. Their eyes continued to linger on the statues as they walked past, heading to the southern end of the cavern. The ice-encased trees were plentiful here and they passed another pair of statues along the path. All three were on edge, with Haley and Sabrina turning their empathic senses outward while Elizabeth did the same with her energetic senses. Though no one's presence was felt, the ladies knew that did not guarantee the Commando's absence. Then, where a third pair of statues stood, the path opened to a large clearing, free of ice, at the cavern's southern wall with two more statues; one on either side of an arched opening carved into the rock.

Haley gulped as she tried to steel her nerves and reminded herself that they had already handled two with success.

"Ready?" Elizabeth asked, also feeling nervous.

Looking in Elizabeth's eyes and taking a deep breath, Haley blew it out as a long, slow, "Yeah." Then, she snapped up straight with a gasp when she felt that gross invigoration coming from behind them. The farmgirl heard the soft crackle of Skilja lighting up as she began to pivot and Elizabeth followed suit. By the time the girls had spun around, Sabrina had snapped away two pistol bolts with her whip. Haley and Elizabeth both raised their protective fields, overlapping them, which created a barrier that Conrad had no means of penetrating by the time the third shot arrived. It hit the field and waves of blue, amber, purple and indigo light rippled out from the point of impact.

Conrad fired a few more shots, seeing the rippling lights and nodded. "How long can you hold that?" he asked with a grin while he lowered the setting on his bolt pistol. On the new setting, he began firing a couple of shots every second, each one blocked by the field, and even though these bolts didn't hit as hard, the lower setting allowed the pistol to regain a charge while he picked away at their energy with two shots every second.

"We can keep this up for a while," Haley said to Sabrina.

"But not forever," Elizabeth added.

"Can you keep it up while moving us to the entrance?"

"Yeah," they both answered.

They moved slowly as they stepped back and their thoughts turned to Samuel and Alunareth, wondering what became of them, but could not dwell on those thoughts with the situation that was before them. Shot after shot continued to peck away at their energy, but they made it to the entrance as the Commando calmly moved with them, maintaining a gap of fifty feet. Sabrina detached her scabbards and removed her coat.

"We're here, now what?" Elizabeth wondered.

Haley felt the nervous sinking in Sabrina's stomach when she answered, "Now, you two do what you came here to do," she said as she placed the scabbards back in place. "I'll handle Commando Conrad." The Hunter gripped Skilja's handle tight.

"But," Haley started.

"But nothing," Sabrina interjected. "You have your job," she lifted her eyes to meet the Commando's, "and I have mine." Drawing her bolt pistol with her left hand, she narrowed her eyes. "Now!"

The fields dropped and Skilja rose, snapping away the next few shots while the girls ran into the entrance of Hel's temple. Sabrina dashed to the side, returning fire at the Commando as a door manifested in the temple entrance.

There were five steps down to the corridor's floor and when their feet touched it was when the door formed, blocking their exit. Taking in the dimly lit sight, they could not tell from where the dark purplish-blue glow came, but it was enough to see the arched ceiling almost two stories above them. The walls were perfectly smooth, except for a series of what the girls thought looked like bunks that lined the entire length of the corridor, two rows on either side. Each one was six and a half feet long, three feet deep and three feet high. The bottom row was three feet above the floor, the top row was nine and each one contained a dead body.

"How much do you wanna bet that they're gonna move?" Haley asked with a roll of her eyes.

Elizabeth lifted her palm into the air and yellow specs floated up and out, adding more illumination to the bleak corridor. She drew her sai and said, "I wish they would already. They're probably going to wait until we're halfway down so they can come at us from both sides. Like the owls did."

"Hmm…" Haley looked down the corridor and said, "Let's wake 'em up early." She lifted her arm, launched a potato and it flew forward to land and skitter across the floor. They both stood there, holding their breath and waiting for a zombie to jump up. Nothing.

Elizabeth furrowed her brow and conjured an orb. "This is taking too long." She threw the orb at the body in the closest cubby, it hit, and the body flailed from the impact, then remained still. "Great," she spat with a roll of the eyes. But then, a gurgle escaped from the body's throat, and it rolled out of the cubby and onto the floor.

"That worked. Good thing zombies are slow," Haley said with a grin and added as she rubbed her hands together, "It's gonna be just like that shooting game at Neil's."

"I suppose you have a song for this, then?"

"Yep! I got just the thing."

Elizabeth shook her head. "No, I was being…" The steady beat began to play from their PJs along with the electric guitar as the upbeat intro to The Bangles' version of Hazy Shade of Winter began. Elizabeth let out a sigh and said, "At least it's a good song."

Haley readied a charged shot as the zombie stood to his feet. She released it and hit the body in the chest. The concussive burst knocked it over, and it fell backward, tumbled and came right back up on its feet. "Huh? Zombies aren't supposed to move like that." The zombie opened its mouth and an other-worldly howl reverberated through the corridor, prompting the others into motion. Then, it sprinted straight for Haley. "Awe, spuds! They're fast! They're fast!" she shouted while unleashing a volley of kittens. "This is *not* like the game! Not until the later levels!"

As Haley's blasts finally put the first one down, Elizabeth was channeling her own blasts through her sai at the others while they were rolling out of the walls. "This is a lot of zombies!"

"Forty-eight! Well, forty-seven now." Haley sent more kittens down the corridor, knocking the closest zombies back, but not down as the pack grew and advanced. "Why are they so tough?"

"Because Hel's a b—"

"Hey!" Haley interrupted as they continued blasting.

"Let's hit 'em with the big blasts," Elizabeth said and began to crackle with energy. Haley did the same, and the zombies closed in. They unleashed their beams together, shoving the horde back and finishing off four more of them in the process. "This is going to take longer than I thought…this isn't meant to beat us; it's meant to wear us down."

"There's probably a huge zombie at the other end," Haley speculated.

As the zombies began their charge again, Elizabeth said, "I got an idea. Hang on." She reached out to the stone all around her and pulled at what was above, lifting herself from the ground. Once up near the ceiling, she wobbled a bit before she tugged hard at the other end, pulling herself forward. Flying overtop the horde, she released to drop down by the other door.

"Whoa!" she blurted as she fell and instinctively pushed at the stone through her feet, causing her to wobble as she slowed her descent. Her feet touched the floor and she turned to face some of the zombies that broke from the pack to follow her.

A flurry of blasts was slowing the horde's advance on Haley, and she managed to take a few more down as she did. A follow up with a bobcat finished off another two. But they were finally upon her, Haley popped her claws, and they began to crackle. Swiping her arms forward, she unleashed the slicing waves of purple light, shredding eight of the zombies before her. "Beth! We gotta slice 'em!"

Channeling energy through her feet, Elizabeth knocked the closest zombies back with a kick, turned and checked the door. There was no handle, latch or any discernable way to open the door. The young mystic wanted to scan the door but had to spin around to deal with the attacking horde. "Slice 'em with what?" She was ill-equipped for this situation, so launched herself back into the air and made her way back to Haley while trying to be mindful of her energy use. While attracting and repelling the stone to keep herself aloft wasn't as energetically expensive as she would have thought, it was still a steady drain, and she was trying to form a new plan.

Haley continued with regular slashes, tearing apart the zombies. More came rushing in, and she waited until the last second to release a pounce through her feet. The wave knocked them back as she rode it up into the air, where she kicked forward toward Elizabeth. The mystic was higher up which prompted Haley to kick one more time in her friend's direction. She shot up at an angle and clung to the wall next to Elizabeth as she realized what she had just done. "I can air-dash upward, too?!"

"I can't keep myself up here much longer," Elizabeth said.

"Come closer." Haley reached out and wrapped an arm around Elizabeth and pulled her in. "At least we can take a break."

"Nobody told them," Elizabeth replied, pointing down to the floor where the zombies started to climb up the wall.

"Lousy zombies!" Haley spat as Elizabeth began blasting, knocking a couple off the wall.

"If we rush back to the other end and get them to group together…" Elizabeth began.

"I can finish them off with one good saber-claw." Haley finished with a smirk. "I'm ready when you are."

"Let's do it!"

They zipped back up the corridor and landed on the floor as the zombies dropped from the wall and began sprinting. Haley's claws crackled as the group closed in and she waited until the last second, unleashing a crisscross off purple slicing light. Most of the zombies collapsed to the floor in pieces as Elizabeth dropped the remaining few with a flurry of bolts. When the last zombie hit the floor, the door blocking access to the temple's main chamber vanished.

Peter wasn't as fast as Sabrina, but pistol bolts move slower than bullets, and with the distance between them, he didn't have much trouble dodging the shots. *The whip has to go first.* He pulled an object from his vest with his left hand and threw it.

The Hunter dodged and snapped away shots when she saw the grenade coming in. Her eyes snapped wide open, and she sprinted to her left as Conrad shifted his aim just ahead of Sabrina's path. She dropped Skilja as she went into a tumble, and the whip recoiled to her hip. Coming up to her feet, she leaped and twisted, doing anything she could to keep moving away from the grenade when the second one landed in front of her.

¡Aye, bandito! The first grenade exploded. She was far enough away from the blast and turned to run back, away from the second as a hail of pistol bolts continued from the sprinting Commando.

She flipped and twisted, avoiding the bolts as Conrad ran alongside and closed the gap between them, firing the pistol with his right hand, the mayum blade in his left. Sabrina drew her mayum blade with her left and a katana with her right while he came right up to her as the other grenade exploded. Kicking with his left foot, Conrad knocked the katana from the Hunter's hand, and it clanked to the ground as he thrust his blade forward.

Sabrina's blade dug into the pistol, rendering it unable to fire as she intercepted the thrust by grabbing just below his wrist and digging her fingers into a pressure point, forcing his hand to open. Conrad's blade dropped to the cavern floor as Sabrina thrust with her blade, only for him to intercept the thrust in a similar manner. He grabbed and twisted the Hunter's wrist as she threw a forward kick. She dropped her blade while he was knocked back, but then he charged forward again before she could draw her Colt.

Fists moved in a blur as the Hunter dodged and deflected. She mixed counters in with her blocks to have most of them deflected and the only blows she was able to land so far were few and glancing. She could tell that he was guarding the nerve points that she would usually target and realized that he understood his opponent. She switched fighting styles and unleashed a barrage of attacks, most of which were again deflected or avoided.

The Hunter switched again and continued to cycle through a variety of styles as the Commando blocked and countered everything that came his way. Though Sabrina was faster, Conrad was able to anticipate and intercept almost everything that she threw at him, while returning with some harsh counters of his own.

She rolled with a punch and positioned herself for a solid hit, but still could not get near a good pressure point and the Commando absorbed the blow with little discomfort, then countered. His fist connected with the right side of her ribcage, and the impact lifted Sabrina off her feet. She tumbled to the ground, rolled and came back to her feet with a grunt, about to pivot and face the Commando, but he grabbed her before she could turn toward him, pulled her by the collar and stepped to the side as he shoved.

Sabrina staggered backward, trying to keep her feet beneath her, when her back slammed into the cavern wall next to Hel's statue to the right of the temple entrance. Conrad scooped up his blade while he ran after her. He held it with both hands, the tip pointed at Sabrina when her hands came up and grabbed his wrists, stopping the blade six inches away from her throat.

Just beyond the chamber entrance was a set of five steps down to the floor. The girls walked in and the first thing they noticed was the other end of the room. The chamber itself was the same gray stone as the corridor but wider with a higher ceiling, which was flat.

There was a giant depiction of Hel's face carved into both the eastern and western walls, the intimidating visage staring down at the floor, but at the southern end was another set of five steps leading up to a seven-foot-tall carving of a skeleton on the wall. And an icy blue gemstone embedded in the sternum. They turned around and as expected, the door reappeared, blocking their exit. That's when they noticed the three large scythes mounted on the northern wall above the doorway.

Turning their attention back to the southern end, the girls stepped down onto the floor and they heard a few feint popping sounds from the skeleton. Tiny pebbles and flakes of rock fell from the wall around the skeleton as it leaned forward.

"Whoa!" Haley exclaimed as Elizabeth said, "Uh-oh."

Extracting its right arm from the wall, the skeleton reached out and held its bony hand open. When the girls heard a shuddering sound behind them, they turned around and looked up, seeing the vibrating scythes on the wall just before the middle one broke free and shot across the room into the skeleton's awaiting grasp as a reddish-orange glow appeared in its eye sockets.

"This isn't a game!" Haley shouted. "It's a horror movie!" She could feel Elizabeth's intimidation as well when the skeleton lunged its left shoulder forward, extracting the other arm, followed by a twist of the hips as it broke its legs free and more flakes around it crumbled to the floor. The skeleton's foot touched the first step, and a black mist began to circle around it, thickening as the skeleton continued to walk down. Once it stood on the floor, it held out its arms and the mist solidified into a hooded cloak, completing the Grim Reaper look. It took the scythe in both hands and began twirling it around, going through a demonstration before it set its foot forward and stopped, holding the scythe pointed toward the girls in a ready stance. Elizabeth had her sai in hand and Haley's potato gun had light rippling across the surface.

The reaper dashed forward, and Haley fired at its legs, but it leaped over the shot and rushed on, twirling the scythe overhead and swinging it down to be intercepted by one of Elizabeth's sai. She thrust the other one forward, only sliding between a couple of rips to pierce nothing. The reaper pulled the scythe back up with a spin as it reversed its grip and swung it in from the other side. Elizabeth hopped over the swing, threw a blast in its face, then leaped back and out of the way as a volley of kittens slammed into the skeleton.

"I know how to deal with you!" Haley bellowed as she popped her claws and charged them up. She ran right for the skeleton, sliced, and the razor-sharp lights of her saber-claws tore through the reaper. Its cloak tattered and lines of purple light could be seen on the bare bones. The light faded and the bones looked unharmed as the cloak reconstituted itself. "Uh-oh."

The reaper swung the scythe from its left and Haley, with the training that she hated so much taking over, stepped inside the swing as she raised her forearm vertical and out to her right, clashing her potato gun against the scythe's beard, where the tang and chine met. She shuddered from the impact but held her ground.

The reaper pulled the chine end back as it thrust the lower end of the snath forward, sweeping Haley's feet and she dropped to the floor as the reaper brought the scythe down with an overhead chop. A chop that was interrupted by Elizabeth as she rushed in and caught the upper snath with the tine of her sai while taking a nasty gash on her forearm from the chine.

Haley jumped up, dismissing her potato gun as she expanded her staff and rushed back in to aid Elizabeth, who had conjured an orb and smacked it into the reaper's face, staggering it a couple of steps. The mystic fell back, and Haley rushed in, crossing her Elven staff with the reaper's scythe. She blocked one strike, then another before thrusting forward with one of her own, a concussive burst of blue light knocking the reaper back on impact.

Elizabeth took the fleeting opportunity to conjure her helmet and scan the skeleton.

SCAN COMPLETE

**IDENTIFIED: MYSTICAL CONSTRUCT:
STRUCTURAL ANALYSIS CONCLUDES THAT
THESE BONES ARE MORE DURABLE THAN
NATURAL BONE. RESISTANT TO SLICING
ATTACKS, REPEATED USE OF BLUNT FORCE
IS THE MOST EFFECTIVE METHOD
OF NEUTRALIZING THE THREAT.
USE EXTREME CAUTION.**

"The scan says that we have to bash him," Elizabeth shouted. "But we're gonna have to do it a lot!"

"Working on it!" Haley shouted as she landed another strike. The reaper countered and sliced Haley's left arm. "Ow! Those aren't supposed to be sharp on the outside!"

"It wasn't made for farming," Elizabeth shouted as she took to the air, raining blasts down upon the reaper. It responded by levitating to meet her, a reddish-orange glow in its eyes. It opened its mouth and spewed orbs down at Haley while flying at Elizabeth and swinging the scythe. She was getting better at moving through the air, but without her feet on solid ground, everything felt wrong. After an awkward block with her sai, the reaper followed up with another twirl and swing, putting a deep slice in Elizabeth's leg. "Ahhhhh!"

Haley strafed away from a reddish-orange glowing orb as it hit the floor next to her. She collapsed the staff, conjured her potato gun and jumped back out of the way of the next while charging. Darting sideways from a third, she was now directly under the reaper, where she aimed straight up and fired. Just as Elizabeth started to fall, the bobcat burst into the reaper's pelvis, knocking it off kilter while Haley held her arms out to catch the falling mystic. She grunted when

Elizabeth fell into her arms and set her on her feet. "Can you heal yourself?"

"I don't know."

"Time to find out," Haley replied as the reaper regained its bearings. Haley crackled with energy and turned toward the reaper while Elizabeth began to hum. A stream of ghostly purple cats encased in a beam of blue shot up at the reaper and it dodged to the side, but Haley swept her arm, following the speedy construct and caught it with the tail-end of the blast. It was knocked off kilter again, but quickly regained its bearings, then dropped back to the floor.

"It worked!" Elizabeth said, ready to go another round.

The reaper dashed forward, spun and hurled the scythe like a discus.

"Whoa!" They both shouted while diving to the sides. The scythe, spinning like a buzzsaw, skipped off the floor rose and hit the southern wall, bounced back out into the chamber and continued to ricochet off the walls as the glow reappeared in the reaper's eye sockets. Opening its mouth, the hood slipped back, and a stream of reddish orange energy spewed forth, and the reaper turned its head following Haley.

She ran to the side while Elizabeth dodged the skipping scythe, but ended up against the southwestern corner as the reaper turned his head directly at the farmgirl. She threw out her field just in time, holding off the remainder of the reaper's plasma, but at a high energetic cost while Elizabeth took a few shots at it. Closing its mouth as the hood covered the head, the reaper reached up and opened its hand, calling the scythe back as Haley dropped her field and launched a volley of kittens. The reaper tried to dart out of the way, but only managed to dodge one while the other four shuddered the skeleton's unnatural bones. It reached its other hand into the air as a second scythe flew into its grasp.

"Are you kidding me!" Haley cried!

The reaper hurled one scythe and charged at the girls with the other. Haley still hadn't healed the cuts on her arms, trying to conserve her energy, so when she dismissed the potato gun and expanded the staff it was painful to clash her weapon against the reaper's.

Elizabeth changed strategy and stopped avoiding the spinning scythe, choosing instead to intercept. She jumped into its path and threw up her field, but the scythe bounced off and kept going. She rushed at it, this time hooking the scythe in the tine of her sai and throwing it to the ground. "Ha!" She turned to start blasting the reaper as it was overwhelming Haley and staggered it back.

Haley released a few kittens from her left hand while collapsing her staff and conjuring her arm cannon, causing the reaper to stagger back further. The reaper reached out, and the scythe on the floor came back. It hurled one against a wall to ricochet across the chamber right before hurling the other, and its eye sockets began to glow once more. The girls were busy dodging when the reaper's plasma sprayed across the chamber. Elizabeth went high and continued to dodge the flying scythes as Haley ducked and darted forward.

The reaper followed Haley, and Elizabeth continued to dodge while charging up an orb. Haley still didn't want to use her speed state because it would wipe out her energy pool and take too long to come back, so she hoped that what she did have left would be enough to hold up to this next blast.

She conjured her helmet for extra protection as she expanded her field right before Elizabeth's charged shot hit the back of the reaper's head. The beam of plasma stopped as the reaper stumbled forward. It reached its arm out as the hood came back up, and the third scythe flew off the wall into his grasp.

"Awe, c'mon!" Elizabeth shouted as she knocked one of the scythes from the air. The reaper recalled it to its hand and threw it again, then took to the air, spewing orbs across the room as Elizabeth dropped back to the floor. The girls danced to avoid all the missiles flying about the chamber as the reaper threw the third scythe and touched down to the floor, the glow appearing in its eyes sockets as the hood dropped and it opened its mouth.

"Nope!" Haley yelled as she ducked a scythe and launched a bobcat into the reaper's face. Staggering back, the reaper levitated again, spewing orbs as it called a scythe to its hand.

Elizabeth knocked down another scythe while on her way up for a direct run on the reaper. Still lacking fine control, she was bested once again, but when she tried to drop down and away, the reaper's free hand darted out, grabbed her by the throat and squeezed while lifting her up, face to face. The hood slipped back, and the glow appeared in its sockets as Elizabeth choked.

Haley knocked down the other scythe with her staff right before she looked up. "No, not happening!" Haley jumped straight up and at the apex, kicked higher with an air-dash. "I beat you…" she shouted and kicked a second time, "…in Castlevania…"

Haley's air dash shoved her between them, knocking Elizabeth out of its grasp while she popped her claws, latching onto the reaper, and her glowing blue eyes bore into the glowing sockets and mouth of the construct.

"…and I can do it here!"

With that, she pounced. In a streak of blue light, the reaper rocketed to the floor under the force of the Falling Starr. Haley's feet slammed to the surface, the energy discharged on impact, and the pressure waves blew the bones across the room, accompanied by a fading black mist that hung in the air as the sternum landed at her feet with a blue gemstone ready to be claimed.

She turned to Elizabeth, who was rubbing her neck while she walked to Haley. "Are you okay?"

"Yeah," the young mystic replied, looking down at the stone. "So, what does it do?"

Haley conjured a work glove on her left hand and picked up the breastbone. "Yuck." She popped a claw and stuck it into the crystal, plucking it out. As soon as it was removed, the sternum and all the bones scattered throughout the chamber turned to dust, and the door disappeared. Holding the gem, Haley focused her energy on healing her arms. The wounds closed, and Haley looked at Elizabeth with a smile, tossing it to her. "Check it out. Try healing yourself."

Elizabeth caught the stone and began to hum, and as the pain in her neck vanished, the young mystic realized that she was only drawing on half the energy that she should need. "Cool!" She looked up at the exit. "Let's get out of here while we can."

He leaned in, pinning her hips to the wall with his knee to prevent her from kicking or sweeping his leg and pressed. She had a tight grip on his wrists but couldn't reach any pressure points with her fingers, and she dared not let go to readjust her grip.

The blade inched forward as a smile formed on the Commando's face, and Sabrina heard the emotions within him begin their deadly tune. "The great Hunter Sabrina Carmen," Conrad teased as he casually pushed the blade closer. "You've earned quite the reputation amongst your peers, but do you know what the Commandos call you?"

He pressed forward another inch. Sabrina grunted, trying to push back, but there was no contest between them when it came to raw strength. His smile widened as his gleeful anticipation soared to a near crescendo. "The Glass Cannon." He pressed forward another inch, savoring the visceral emotions while he could. "Looks like your luck has just run out."

Through the sensors in her collar, the jumper received Sabrina's mental command, snapping a switch into the down position. And her zipper popped. In his heightened state of sensitivity, the visual stimulus was just too good to ignore and when his eyes dropped down, Sabrina felt his press relax enough for her to shove back, releasing her grip with her right and striking his throat.

Conrad gagged and dropped the blade as he staggered back and Sabrina followed up with a left hook to the underside of his jaw, sending what felt like shocks through the Commando's nerves as he stumbled left and in a daze. "I don't rely on luck," Sabrina said as she was about to draw her pistol and end it right there, but she remembered a previous conversation with Haley. She slid the switch up with her finger and rushed forward as the zipper began to close itself.

With a great leap, the Hunter hooked her left leg over Conrad's right shoulder, then wrapped her right leg around the other side of his neck as she went. She clamped down with a scissor grip as her momentum transferred into centrifugal force while she swung her torso around his back, making his head dip forward and to the left. Sabrina twisted her hips, guiding Conrad's head down hard on the rock floor of the cavern.

Her palms touched the floor next as she released her scissor grip and pivoted, tucking her knees in as she twirled and placing her feet to the ground, pulling a restraining disk from her belt as she stood.

"But I sometimes do welcome it," she finished and slapped the disk on the unconscious Commando. The tendrils slid around him, cinched tight and levitated him into an upright position, his feet dangling six inches above the ground. Although Haley wasn't there to ask, Sabrina wondered aloud, "Did that count as cool?"

Activating her comm, she began removing his weapons and tripwires when she called, "Samuel, Alunerath, do you read me?"

"Sabrina," Samuel replied, the pain in his voice evident while bandaging Alunerath's arm. "Conrad's coming your way."

"Conrad is detained."

"Oh, thank God!" he sighed. "But Alunerath's in rough shape. He's lost a lot of blood, and I don't know how much longer he can hold on. We need Elizabeth!"

Opening his eyes as he came back to consciousness, Conrad felt the throbbing in his skull, the tenderness in his jaw and it hurt to swallow. He realized that he was in a restraining disk and turned his head to see Sabrina walking toward her katana. With his arms pinned to his side, he could barely move his hands, which is why the hidden switch was located in between the trousers' layers of fabric on the thigh. He pressed and held the button, and his fatigues released a signal burst that deactivated the disk. He held onto the tendrils, dropped silently to his feet and placed the restraining disk on the ground as he took off in a silent sprint.

"They're in the Temple," Sabrina said as she picked up her katana, twirling it over her shoulder and into the scabbard. "I'm about to try to go in after them and…" Her words turned into a grunt as she was shoved to the wall from behind.

"Sabrina?! What's happening?"

As she spun around, Conrad was already pulling his blade from her belt. She threw her arms up in time to catch his wrists, and he pressed forward. The Hunter felt his emotions begin their song once again, but this time, it thundered with anger and rage.

His lips curled into a snarl, and hatred was in his eyes as he continued to press, saying, "I'm not going to fall for that again, you b…" His last word became a weak cough and some gurgles when a sharp piece of metal stuck out from his chest. He looked down in shock as he dropped the blade, then dropped to his knees, but could fall no further due to the hand that grabbed the right side of his collar. Without letting go, the Dwarf walked around to face Conrad directly with half his face bruised, a few missing teeth and a rage in his eyes beyond the one that was previously in the Commando's.

"Rudge!" Sabrina said in both shock and relief.

"Rudge?" came Samuel's voice over her comm.

Stooping down to scoop up the blade, Rudge looked back into Conrad's eyes, held the blade to the side of his head and said, "This is for my brother." With an easy press, the mayum blade slid in through the skull and pierced the brain. Conrad went limp, but Rudge held him up for a few more seconds, staring at the body of the man who killed Balgar. With a huff, Rudge pulled the blade out and shoved his body over. It collapsed to the ground, and he placed a foot on the dead Commando's hip as he yanked Balgar's pick from the back. He turned to look at the stunned Sabrina and nodded. "You okay?"

"Yes. And glad to see you, but how are you still alive?"

With a shrug, Rudge said, "I'm a Dwarf. I've fallen down worse holes than that."

The shattering of ice was heard as a chunk fell from the side of a nearby tree. Surveying the area, they saw that the ice encasing many of the trees was cracked and glistened with moisture. That's when they both realized the strange chill in the air was gone, and the cavern was warming up.

She nodded and looked to The Temple entrance, "We need to go help…" Her expression shifted, and a slight smile came onto her face, "They're coming." Looking back at Rudge, she said, "We need to get to the others. Alunerath is severely wounded." The temple door vanished, leaving an open archway.

Samuel's voice came onto the comm, "A lounge just broke away from below us, and they're heading your way."

Haley and Elizabeth emerged from the temple as Sabrina said, "And we're about to head yours. Haley and Elizabeth are back."

"Rudge!" both girls shouted, rushing over and leaning down a bit to give the thought-to-be-dead Dvwargarian an enthusiastic hug.

"Glad to see you two, as well," he said with a smile as he wrapped his arms over their shoulders and returned the hug. "But we need to get to the others," he said, releasing the embrace. "Alunerath's critically injured and needs a healing."

"What about your…" Elizabeth began pointing at the bruising on Rudge's face.

"Save it for Alunareth. If you got any juice left after him, then I'll gladly accept your offer."

Elizabeth gave a single nod for a reply. She turned her head and saw what was left of Commando Conrad. Haley sensed her shudder, followed her gaze and had a shudder of her own upon seeing yet another dead body. Friend or foe, it didn't matter. Haley was sick of people being hurt, but also knew the best way to stop all this was to finish the job.

"We have to move," Sabrina said. "Alunareth can't wait."

The feint slapping sounds of lizards' feet were heard and getting louder. Elizabeth turned to Haley and held up two key crystals, "I've got an idea," she said with a smirk.

"What are you two doing?" Sabrina asked as Haley walked up beside her. The lounge was now close, and some could be seen through the trees as they continued to shed their ice.

Haley held up her left hand, showing Sabrina that she held all three key-crystals. She took a preemptive B12 tablet, closed her fingers around the gems and her mouth snapped up into a big toothy grin as her eyes shined with fierce blue light. The farmgirl turned toward the approaching lizards, lifting her potato gun as waves of blue and purple light wisped across its surface. The lizards crowding the path came rushing their way and Haley released the charged blast. A large orb shaped like the head of a tiger flew forward, hitting the first lizard with a devastating concussive burst that took out seven others.

"Yes!" Elizabeth exclaimed with clenched fists.

A stream of kittens poured forth like from a Gatling gun, concussive bursts pulverizing the lizards into slushies and shuddering more ice from the trees. Continuing her stream of fire, Haley began laughing as she sprayed kittens at the lizards while they came out from the woods. She kept laughing until Elizabeth placed her hand on Haley's shoulder and said, "That's enough." Confused, Haley turned to look at Elizabeth, wondering why she had stopped her and saw that the young mystic was popping a B12. She held out her hand with a big smile. "My turn."

CHAPTER 27
How To Fight City Hall

More lizards pulled away from below the tree as a commotion sounded from the south. Reggie was holding Alunerath, who was unconscious and shivering when that commotion came closer. He looked to see Haley and Elizabeth coming into view, blasting and slicing a swath through the lizards like they were nothing, with Sabrina and Rudge right behind them.

"There they are," Haley said while pointing to the tree.

Elizabeth conjured her helmet and scanned, their position immediately highlighted in her visor. She felt the stone and earth below her, focused her energy and pushed it down. She went up and forward, bringing herself to the tree in seconds.

"You can fly now?" Samuel grunted.

"Not exactly," she replied, seeing the wound through the hole in his jumper. But Alunerath was the priority. She could easily see that he was on death's door, and she took another B12, placed her hands on him and began to hum. With the aid of all three stones, her energy flowed forth, bathing the wound with the mystic's intention of regeneration. She continued her song of life as the energy condensed into physical tissue, rebuilding the lost muscle and taking the form of blood cells.

She took a deep breath and began again, pouring her energy into the Alfan, restoring his body. Still shivering, he took a long inhale and opened his eyes, looking around, confused as to where he was. Some clarity came a second later when he remembered passing out while trying to heal Samuel.

"Sam!" he shouted as he sat up and almost tumbled off the tree limb.

Elizabeth grabbed his arm before he fell. "Take it easy." She pulled him up to a sitting position. "You were almost dead." She turned to Samuel as Haley, Sabrina and Rudge worked on the lizards below the tree. "I've got a little left in me." She placed her hands around the bullet wound that Alunareth had been working on when he fainted and began to hum. The relief was almost instant for Samuel. Alunareth restored his lung, and Elizabeth finished sealing the wounds.

"Thank you," Samuel said, now able to speak without grunting.

"So, what's the status on…everything?" Alunareth asked while trying to steady himself. His blood pressure was still too low for him to get up and move.

"Well, for starters, somebody would like to say hi," Samuel answered while pointing to the ground below.

Looking down, Alunareth almost tumbled again from the surprise when Rudge waved up to him and said, "Hi." What tumbled instead was some ice from a nearby tree.

"Is it getting warmer?" Samuel asked.

"Yes," Sabrina answered from below.

"Darker, too," Alunareth added. The bluish-purple glow that bathed the cavern was dimming as the ice from where it originated was melting.

"Then we need to move," the Ranger said and tried to stand to his feet. Elizabeth caught him again as he became light-headed.

Samuel shook his head, "You're in no condition to move yet."

"I'll carry him," Haley said and climbed up the trunk to their limb. She held her right arm out and said, "Just lean over my shoulder." She felt his apprehension at the idea. Alunareth, a full-grown man, was about to be carried down a tree by a petite eleven-year-old girl. The image of his weight being too much for her and them crashing to the ground flashed in his mind, but he reminded himself of her enhanced strength and agreed.

He dangled his legs off the side of the limb and leaned forward over Haley's shoulder, and she began to descend like a roofer carrying a bundle of shingles down a ladder.

"There's something you don't see every day," Rudge commented.

The Tundra, West Antarctica

Bast, Ptah and Artemis all stumbled as the ice broke apart beneath their feet, turning to steam and pulling them into a swirling maelstrom. Apophis laughed hysterically while Lillith and Hel took the opportunity for some easy targets, hurling blasts at the struggling gods. A bolt of lightning struck Apophis from a clear sky, and Cernunnos appeared, extracting the others and changing the whirlpool of steam back into ice with a wave of his hand.

Hel and Lillith turned their attacks on the King of the Wild, but Bast, Ptah and Artemis were back in the fray, allowing Cernunnos to focus on Apophis. The Egyptian God of Chaos tried to warp the reality around them, but Cernunnos, a bit of a trickster in his own right, counteracted Apophis's efforts and began to thrash him with more lightning bolts discharged from his hands.

Out of nowhere, Baphomet appeared and cracked his knuckles across Cernunnos's face. He stumbled back as Baphomet pushed forward, punching him again. As Cernunnos was staggering, Baphomet lunged forward, grabbing him and teleporting them both to another location. With Cernunnos gone, Apophis started to warp everything again as Ares arrived in pursuit of Baphomet.

"You!" Apophis shouted as he discharged a multicolored blast at Ares.

It encircled the God of War in a display of swirling lights and disappeared. Ares charged at Apophis and took a swing, but his fist went right through the Egyptian god. Ares threw a blast of energy in his face, but this, too, phased right through Apophis, who disappeared and reappeared behind Ares.

With a quick pivot and a kick, his foot went right through the laughing Apophis's face like he wasn't even there. Because he wasn't. And neither was Ares. He was instead standing on the icecap of West Antarctica, all by himself, doing battle with one of the most convincing illusions that Apophis had ever cast. Apophis, however, was again making Bastet, Patah and Artemis his playthings as Hel and Lillith continued blasting at the disoriented gods and laughing like it was a yard game at a family cookout.

"Watch this one," Apophis said with a confident grin and discharged another multicolored blast. It flew forward at Ptah but slowed before it reached him, starting to swirl as a vortex as it reversed direction and flew right back at Apophis. "What?!" he shouted while the vortex was engulfing him, and he was suddenly standing in a cavern somewhere beneath the continent. "What is this?" he asked while he glanced around the tight cavern, confused.

"Hi!" a boy's voice said.

Spinning around, Apophis saw the boy, who could not have been more than eight years old, standing next to a boulder. Holding a candy bar, he was barely four feet tall, obese with a red and white horizontally striped T-shirt, sandy-brown unkempt hair, freckles and chocolate smeared around his mouth. Another smear was added when he took the next bite.

"It actually worked!" he said while chewing. "I've been wanting to try that spell." The boy shoved the rest of the chocolate bar in his mouth and threw the wrapper on the cavern floor. "And since you're here, let's play! What do you want to do?"

"Who do you think you are, Little Boy?" Apophis spat with contempt. "Who are you to summon a god?"

"I heard that can be tricky. That's why I summoned you instead of a powerful one."

"What?!" Apophis shouted, unable to believe what he had just heard. "Foolish child! You have no idea the power that looms before you!" he raged.

"But you're not really that powerful. I summoned you, didn't I?" the boy said with a shrug. "I bet you can't actually do anything. You're boring." He crossed his arms and turned his head away, looking disappointed.

Apophis had now forgotten completely about the battle raging on the tundra and began to rage at the child while he was pulling another candy bar out of his pocket. "You are a child, and I am the God of Chaos! You have made the biggest mis…" He felt a tugging from behind. He turned to look, and the boy was standing behind Apophis, holding his shirt tail in one chocolate-smeared hand and the candy bar in the other. "How…" Before he could utter a second word, the boy jumped and shoved the candy bar in his mouth, then disappeared. Apophis gagged and wretched as he spat out what morphed into a bar of soap. "Bleh!" Spinning around and searching the cavern with his eyes, he saw the fat little boy standing off to the side.

"See?" the boy began with a chuckle. "You can't do anything. You're just a joke."

"Arrogant bug! Do you not realize who I am?! I can bend the very reality around you!" Apophis stretched his arms out and closed his fingers. The rock around them cracked, and two large chunks of stone broke away and flew in circles around the Egyptian god. He threw one arm forward, and a chunk flew toward the boy. He threw his other arm forward, and the second chunk followed.

The first chunk reached the boy, and he rippled like a watery image as the boulder disappeared, then it clocked Apophis in the back of the head. He stumbled forward as the second chunk reached the boy and disappeared in the ripple, teleporting right behind Apophis to strike him again, knocking him face-first to the floor.

The boy was suddenly standing in front of him. "So just admit it. You're not that powerful. I won't be mad."

"Won't be mad?" Apophis roared as he teleported off the cavern floor and into an upright position, hovering off the ground. "I'm the one who's mad now! Don't you understand, boy? I can literally break your reality!" He threw both his arms out and the air itself seemed to shatter.

Everything went dark, and all that could be seen was thousands of glass shards circling Apophis in a void. Then all the shards turned sideways, and each one had a tiny little version of the fat boy standing atop it, riding them like surfboards. Laughter erupted all around the God of Chaos as the shards began zipping by and slicing him open. Apophis clapped his hands together, recoalescing the cavern, and he felt a tap on his left shoulder.

When Apophis looked, he felt a tap on his right hand and an energy encircle his wrist. He turned and saw the little boy standing there. The boy waved with a smile as Apophis felt a tap on his other hand. He turned and saw another boy standing there as energy circled around the wrist. Both boys tapped his hands at the same time, and his wrists were forced together behind his back.

"Wha…how?!" he shouted as he levitated, and his body stiffened, leaving him unable to move.

"I made the binding enchantment myself," the boy said with pride. "Do you like it?"

"How is this possible, you little brat?"

The boy, walking toward Apophis, glowed with yellow light and began to morph into his true form. "Impossible is what I do."

"You!" Apophis started to chuckle and then snapped his head forward as much as he could, his face contorting into a rage as he shouted, "Traitor!"

Flashing a wry smile, the man in the black suit quipped, "Flattery will get you nowhere." He reached up and placed his fingertips on Apophis's chest, and reality began to blur as they shifted out of phase with the Second Density.

The barrier prevented them from fully moving into the First or Third Densities, but they still could access the space directly between them, which was a powerful riptide of opposing polarities. Interstellar civilizations refer to this space between densities as the Split, which they used to launch their ships, as if from a railgun, to achieve faster-than-light travel. But this close to a planet, Apophis would be caught in an eddy which, instead of launching him across space, would leave him circling the Earth in an endless superluminal orbit.

With an unnerving grin, Apophis said, "When I get out of this, and I will, I'm going to tell Molech what happened here, and you're as good as dead."

"Oh, I know you will," he replied. "You may be the God of Chaos, but to me," a smug smile spread across his face as he thought how these words would get under Apophis's skin, "You're just predictable."

Trying to squirm and thrash with no success, Apophis screamed, "I'll rip you apart with my bare hands! I'm going to spread your entrails across the Nile! You are a second-rate cheap-trick piece of…"

"Ta-ta," teased the man in the back suit as he tapped Apophis in the sternum, knocking the Egyptian god into the Split, where he would circle the Earth beyond light speed if it weren't for one problem. In an instant, Apophis's face planted into the continental barrier, pinned in place by the overwhelming forces.

The man turned, waving his hand and the narrow cavern rippled and disappeared, revealing the real and much bigger cavern in which they had battled. A brand-new enchantment of his own design, A Room Within a Room presented Apophis with a constructed space that was designed to backfire on anyone who tried to manipulate it. Anyone who wasn't the man in the black suit. *Not a bad trial run, but I can make it better,* he thought with a measure of satisfaction. *The Shatter was a little taxing.*

Meelyhn, Atlantis

No one had ever seen Serge smile this much as he turned the disruption emitter back on and scanned it again. He already knew what the data would say, but he read it anyway as his smile grew bigger, basking in the long-awaited success of a functioning device. Nomad brushed against Serge's leg as an offering of congratulations. The old physicist reached down and gave him a gentle scratch under the chin, then looked up at Manny. "How long have you been holding onto that Flekkle?"

"Years," he replied. "I once had a larger supply but used most of it to make the port returns and a set of beacons. I can't believe that I never thought to use it to make a portable emitter."

"Papi?" Sabrina's voice was heard over his comm.

"¡Mija! Where are you?"

"We're coming back to you but could use a ride. And some food."

Before Manny could answer, Serge leaned out of his shop and shouted to his next-door neighbor, "Rodge! Get the deputy and the rover!" It was less than ten minutes when the vehicle came rolling into view of the weary group, and they were saddened to see them with another body in tow. Rudge had tried to bear the burden of carrying Balgar up by himself but had to accept Haley's help at the nearly vertical inclines. She made multiple trips to those sheer areas, once for Alunareth and again for Balgar.

The Elf was walking, supported by Samuel, as the vehicle came to a stop. A bag of sandwiches was in the vehicle, and Elizabeth sang her healing song, healing Rudge's face from when he landed on the ledge and Sabrina's ribs. The bag was passed around, and everybody ate, ravenous from their earlier activities. The sheriff was already there and waiting when they returned to the village.

As they exited the vehicle, the sheriff greeted them with both congratulations and condolences. "Kone has gone back to Rome and plans to address both densities in a while. Then, he's coming back here." He sighed. "He wants to hear back from the Archons and a Commando. To ensure the capture of all of you."

"He won't be hearing from any of them," Rudge replied.

"He's starting to become…concerned," the sheriff said. "He wanted the Sheriff's Department to just focus on the citizens and leave the man-hunting to the ones that he summoned. But now, he even has us out looking for you." Deputy Karn came walking over and the sheriff asked, "Did you find them yet?"

The deputy looked at the group, then back at the sheriff. "Nope."

"The moment you access the vault, Kone will receive notification," the sheriff explained. "And once he knows, I'll have no way to stall him, which is why I think you should wait until he begins his speech. He's all about optics and can't go running off to an emergency while addressing the world. That would not build confidence."

"When is that?" Samuel asked.

Looking at his watch, the deputy said, "Forty-five minutes."

"Hey, Sheriff. What does the inside of the vault look like?" Elizabeth asked.

"Yeah!" Haley added. "We need a piano ready to drop on his head when he shows up."

"What?" the sheriff quietly asked, confused.

"I mean, something set up as a trap."

"Oh," Gurden replied. "I wasn't familiar with the metaphor."

"It's more literal than metaphor," Sabrina dryly added, remembering when Haley dropped an entire deck on top of her avatar a little over a year ago.

"Anyway," Gurden began, "I've only been in there four times, and they were brief, but the layout is pretty simple."

Fifth Density. Mount Olympus, Olympus

"No," Ra said. "The demons haven't gone there in quite some time. I don't know why they would have started attacking Xibalba now."

Stroking his beard, Zeus considered the change in patterns when a flash of green light ripped him from his thoughts. He looked up to see the source of this interruption. "Tuweltha," he said in a stern tone. "I would like to say that it's good to see you, but this is highly inappropriate!"

"What could be so important that you would cross this boundary?" Ra asked, equally unpleased.

"I'm sorry," Tuweltha said, "but this is an emergency."

"There are channels to go through for that," Zeus reminded.

With a nod, Tuweltha said, "I know. I've tried them, but your bureaucracy is just as stifling as the mortal realm's."

Zeus lifted his hand and pointed at the Elven goddess, but he bit his tongue before he started to shout. He gained a bit of composure before he asked, "What is so dire that you came here?"

"Molech has returned."

With a scoff, Ra said, "This again! Every time something slightly sinister happens, everybody starts ranting about Molech like he's the boogie man."

"He *is* the boogie man," Tuweltha reminded.

"Look," Zeus stated in as calm a manner as he could. "If he ever were to return, we would deal with him immediately. But you cannot come in here like this when…"

"Ares and Artemis are both trapped within his spell," Tuweltha blurted. Zeus paused, and Tuweltha looked at Ra. "As well as Ptah and Bast."

"Where?" Zeus asked.

"Antarctica. In the Second Density. Look and see for yourself."

Both Zeus and Ra had a glow in their eyes as they peered at the continent. "I don't see anything," Ra said.

"Neither do I," said Zeus. "And I've…wait! Ra, look again."

A golden glow appeared in Ra's eyes right before his jaw dropped. "What manner of barrier is this!"

"Even I cannot penetrate this field!" Zeus exclaimed. "Ra, please contact Michael. He's going to want to see this."

Second Density. Rome

With a tailored three-piece suit and shoes so polished that he could see his reflection, Kone was ready to address the First and Second Densities worldwide. A master of spectacle, he made sure to have cameras in position to see the massive crowd below the balcony from where he would speak, with carefully selected angles to make it look even larger, furthering the appearance of support and positivity. News channels across the densities were live and waiting for the Uniralt to take the balcony and speak to the world. Heated arguments took place around the First Density over whether Kone was a savior or a tyrant; arguments that hushed as the Cetatian Uniralt was seen heading out to the railing on their television screens.

The crowd cheered when he stepped out to the railing and waved, wearing a smile that was warm in appearance. As the crowd cheered, Kone felt a vibration in his pocket, and if his phone was vibrating now, it would have been a dire emergency. He pulled it out and gave it a quick glance, his stomach dropping as he saw that his vault was being accessed. *The Hunters.*

He slipped it back in while continuing to stand with an air of confidence. *This shouldn't take too long. I'll deal with them as soon as I finish this speech.* "People of the World!" The cheers faded as he began speaking. "I have met with many people in the First Density over the last week and must say that I am impressed by the level of cooperation that I am seeing. I knew that the Humans have great potential, but now I'm convinced that even I underestimated what you're capable of. I am more confident than ever that our futures will be bright and prosperous as a new day dawns upon our world."

Atlantis City, Atlantis

The sheriff led them down a staircase from the city hall to the top of the ziggurat's southern edge. A narrow room, more like a hallway, that had a single door in the middle of the northern wall that had three impressions across its surface. Haley had the green and blue gems, and Elizabeth had the red one. When they placed them into the impressions, the door shifted an inch inward and slid to the side as a signal went to Kone.

"Okay," Samuel said, "We're on the clock."

They filed through the door, and when Haley stepped through, her eyes were greeted with a large, square room. White stone walls with veins of different colored crystal marbled throughout, just like the rest of the city. Rows of shelves filled the room and held numerous boxes and crates. Most of the contents were boxed, neatly placed and labeled, ready to be taken and used at Kone's discretion.

"This way," Gurden said, and they followed the sheriff to the eastern wall and turned left toward the north. Halfway down the room was a stairwell going down to a larger level. Here, there were two columns to the right of the staircase, directly under the outer wall of the upper level, six altogether. More shelving rows occupied the center mass of the large room, and in one corner was a screen hanging on the wall with a video camera pointed at it.

Gurden noticed Haley looking at the screen and camera. "Sometimes, Kone makes a worldwide broadcast from there. But when his current one ends, he'll be here, so let's hurry. The vault's main terminal is on the next level down."

"How many more levels are there after that?" Elizabeth asked.

"Just the bottom," Gurden answered. "He keeps prototype vehicles down there."

"Like concept cars?" Haley asked.

"That…except military."

Descending the next staircase, they were in an even larger version of the level above, this time with three columns beneath each wall and tapered support beams stretching out across the ceiling to channel the weight of the upper two floors directly to the columns.

"If it wasn't for the veins of crystal," Rudge commented, "I would have thought it to be all one giant piece of stone. Everything is so perfectly flush and tight."

"It was built by the original Atlanteans," Gurden said. "And yes, Dwarves were among them. The main terminal is this way."

This level had computer mainframes along the walls, in which all the information on Atlantis's greatest developments and achievements was stored. The center of the room had no floor, but railings around the square space where one could look down to the prototype vehicles stored in the ziggurat's base level. Sheriff Gurden led them to a terminal and said, "This is it. This is the terminal that Kone uses."

Haley felt the anxious anticipation building inside the sheriff's gut as he knew that they were so close to having everything they needed to expose Kone's lies to the world. And even closer to Kone arriving. The sheriff wondered if he'd even still be alive in the next twenty minutes. Haley and Elizabeth both placed their phones on the terminal, and a holo screen appeared before them.

The PJs began to interact with the Ziggurat's computer system, dealing with some of the most advanced firewalls and security measures on the planet. Luckily, Gus's adaptive programs had become used to dealing with Cetatian computer code, which was derived from Atlantis's ancient system. The com-system recognized the patterns, decrypted more code and began syncing with the Atlantean mainframe.

Sabrina and the others were looking around, trying to find a place to set the incendiary traps for Kone, but there was nowhere viable to put them without risk to the mainframe itself.

The com-systems, Haley's, Elizabeth's and Neil's, were all processing the information separately while communicating with each other, allowing the three PJs to operate as one computer with triple parallel processing, cracking through a few final security features and obtaining access. Haley held up her hand, made a fist and pumped her elbow down. "Yes!"

CHAPTER 28
Kone's Quest

"Okay!" Haley began. "What are we looking for?"

"Anything that will break the world's confidence in Kone," Samuel answered.

"But there's so much here. Hundreds of years' worth of files," Elizabeth commented.

"Could you just copy it all and take it with us?" Alunareth asked and then added, "Before Kone shows up."

"No. There's way too much here for the PJs to carry. I got an idea!" Haley sent a mental command to her com. "I just asked it to give us a summary of what Kone's been doing since as far back as it knows." The holo screen flashed as she finished her sentence and new information was displayed. Haley thought about the camera and screen above them. *He can broadcast to the world from here.* She sent another mental command to her phone, set it back on the terminal and watched the screen with the others.

Second Density. 0033 AD

They were around a bonfire, drinking the wine from the raid and speaking with enthusiasm about what they had done. After listening from the shadows, Tasi walked into the camp and everyone hushed, stunned expressions on their faces.

Five foot eight and muscular with black hair and a thick beard, Shalim was an intimidating sight, standing near the fire and holding Tasi's cantina. His expression was a mixture of confusion and amusement as he asked, "How, in the name of The Lost Kingdom, did you survive?"

Tasi looked directly at Shalim and narrowed his eyes as he pointed at the cantina and calmly stated, "That's mine."

He returned Tasi's gaze with equal intensity and smirked, "Not anymore."

The others all began to chuckle. Even though the two were the same size, Shalim was fourteen years older than Tasi and had much fighting experience. Nobody there would dare challenge him in a physical confrontation.

The group's mirth disappeared in a flash when Tasi waved his hand, releasing a mystical orb of red light and shadow. It shot through the air and into Shalim, knocking him to the ground.

Gasps were heard from the group and one of the men shouted, "Sorcery!" as Tasi walked to Shalim, who had rolled over and pushed himself up to his knees, trying to regain his wind. Tasi grabbed Shalim by the throat and hoisted him back to his feet.

Shalim threw a punch, but Tasi caught it with his left hand and squeezed. Cracking sounds, accompanied by screams of pain were heard as the bones of Shalim's hand were crushed like dried twigs.

Tasi grabbed Shalim's left arm and yanked, dislocating the shoulder. He followed that with a kick to the right knee and, with another sickening crack, Shalim fell to the ground, shouting in agony.

Leaning over, Tasi punched his left thigh, snapping the bone as everyone heard Shalim's continuing cries of pain. With his right, Tasi grabbed the anguished man by the throat once more and lifted him into the air. Regardless of strength, when Tasi held Shalim by the neck at arm's length, he should have toppled over, yet he did not.

Taking the cantina with his left hand, Tasi stated, "That's mine," and then slowly began to squeeze with his right.

Shalim tried to speak but could not. He only managed some chokes that sounded like, "Kone…Kone…"

"Yes, I am," Tasi responded. He looked at the group and his pupils began to glow with red light. "I am Kone. And this is what happens to those who cross me." He tossed Shalim like a ragdoll into the fire. Shalim screamed as he landed on the burning wood, but the next inhalation was flame, burning his lungs and he could scream no more. Neither could he use his broken limbs to get off the searing hot surface. All he could do was silently writhe for what was the longest and last thirty seconds of his life until he finally passed out, never to regain consciousness.

The group all stared at Tasi, stunned and afraid. He looked back to everyone and said, "Continue you celebration this evening, for tomorrow, our work begins."

Under Kone's leadership, the band had a series of victories, but that was just the beginning. It wasn't long before their numbers and resources grew, and Kone began coordinating multiple bands and then continued by challenge states.

Kone's empire grew, and he ruled multiple regions as the years went by, yet the age did not show after he reached full maturity. Every so often, he would make a public display of an agonizing execution to discourage people from opposing his rule.

Under Molech's tutelage, Kone learned a great deal of magick and was also shown the truth of his reality. Molech revealed the other densities to Kone and said, "You must take your rule to these other realms as well. Continue to expand, until the entirety of this sphere is under your control." It took some time, but Kone learned to magickally teleport himself among the densities.

The First Density was populated with people who looked just like the descendants of The Lost Kingdom, except they didn't have a secondary pigment on their backs. The Third Density was primarily inhabited by two species. The Dvwargarians, a shorter species of people averaging four feet tall, who worked well with the stone and earth. They were a strong people who took pride in their beards and had a drive for building and crafting. And the Trolls. Tall, strong and resilient.

Also living in this density were Humans, Alfan and Gnomes. The Fourth Density was ruled by the Alfan, who averaged about five and a half feet in height, had a tendency to be slender of build with elongated ears and had an affinity for nature. There were also some smaller populations of the other species of people here. Everyone in the Fourth, regardless of species, had pointed ears, but none as pronounced as the Alfan.

While the Uniralt's empire expanded further across the Second Density, he influenced some wealthy families in the First. After a couple of generations, Kone had these families, who he referred to as his Illuminati, under his firm control, expanding their wealth and power across the First Density.

Using his guile, Kone sowed the seeds of contention between the Dvargarians and the Alfan. Fanning those sparks of mistrust, they eventually burst into flames of war and the Third and Fourth Densities descended into chaos.

As he conquered nations in the Second Density, Kone would come across a few ancient buildings. Secured structures with relics from the past. Items and information pertaining to the Lost Kingdom, from which legend says his people hailed. After so many discoveries, enough pieces were found that Kone was able to determine the location of the Lost Kingdom. Under the ice of the South Pole, he found Atlantis.

When he gained access to the city proper, Kone was astounded by the architecture. Just like some of the buildings discovered throughout Kone's empire, these buildings seemed to be made from smooth stone, but much bigger and unfamiliar items were everywhere. The ice slowed his progress until Molech cleared it away, and Kone began going through all the buildings once he could access them and he eventually found the key to understanding much of what was before him.

While exploring a building, he entered one of the rooms, the strange glass-like panels in the ceiling illuminated, providing ample light. Kone noticed a red colored light flashing on one of the strange looking desks and went to investigate. He approached the control panel and a sheet of glass on the wall filled with light, presenting in an image of a Human man. Kone watched in wonder as the man began speaking in an unknown tounge. He had never seen anything like this.

Upon showing Molech the discovery, the malicious god smiled, recognizing the language. "It's Atlantean. I haven't heard it spoken since before the flood." He turned back to Kone and said, "I will teach you the language. Learn their crafts. It could be advantageous to your rule."

Learn, Kone did. And he put the lessons to good use. He listened to the man in the video recording, "The planets had fallen out of their alignment and the results were catastrophic. The First Density facility was collapsing all around us when we ported here. Many of us managed to find shelter…" He sighed and then firmed his jaw before continuing. "A great many more did not. There are only a couple thousand of us left. A few Alfan and Dvwargarians are among us, but most of us here are Human. We hope to take what we have left and rebuild our lives and, hopefully, regain contact with the other densities. We have also started the process of recording all our knowledge so, should we fail, the information will remain for future generations to find."

The man continued speaking, giving an instructional on how to operate the control panel. Kone went through the many logs, learning the history of Atlantis and the wonderful technologies they had discovered. Kone saw the age of the man increase as he went through the videos, along with videos from a few other people addressing scientific topics and discoveries. An Elf was in the next video, speaking an older variation of one of the Alfan languages, discussing magickal knowledge. Kone recognized enough to understand what he was saying and learned a few concepts to increase his power.

The next video was the daughter of the man in the first video. "It's becoming the norm, all the children who were born recently have an odd color on their backs and necks. It seems to be harmless to the children, but we have no idea why this happening."

It was a recording from a couple generations later that revealed the reason. A man in one of the logs said, "It's an effect that happens on the epigenetic level, a result of the energy of this density, the same as the pointed ears in the Fourth Density and the thicker hair of the Third, according to our data." He turned and looked at someone off camera, "I hope we can reestablish inter-density travel in our lifetime.

"Yeah, right!?" a woman's voice replied.

Kone watched and read much information, Dwarves giving tutorials on trade skills. Elves delivering lessons in magick and agriculture. Humans discussing electrical principles. The final video recorded was a man's last day as he said, "Venus came too close, and the planetary shock has caused massive devastation! Everything's flooded and the rain is still falling. I don't know if anyone will survive this no matter where in the world they are."

Returning frequently, Kone spent the course of a few years going through the information. He began a selection process, choosing smart and inventive people from the Cetatian population who had few social or familial ties. Kone brought them to Atlantis, having them study the information and apply it to their projects. He began to integrate the tech into the population a little bit at a time, but the people he had brought to the city were never seen by the others again, keeping Atlantis a secret from the rest of the world.

Controlling the information, the people knew only what Kone wanted them to know. He wrote his own version of history and after a few more generations went by, this was the only history that the people of the Second Density knew. Using the legend of Atlantis, the people believed that they were descendants of an aquatic species, and that the Humans of the First Density had at one time enslaved them.

But the ageless Kone had broken the chains of their captors and led the charge to push them back into their own realm. They were also told that the Humans had lost information over the years, had come to believe the Cetatians a myth and now was the time to start preparing to one day take over the First Density, ensuring that the evil Humans could never enslave them again.

As they advanced, Kone had laborers restore the buildings. Since he had the ability to teleport between the densities, The Cetatian leader brought the portgate technology to the other realms, allowing his people to make the trips. When he needed to infiltrate the Humans, Kone selected people who lived in the same corresponding areas and since the buildings and roads were the same, they would know their way around.

The Cetatians placed devices throughout the First Density that emitted frequencies disruptive enough to prevent people from tuning in to their energy fields and learning mysticism, but not disruptive enough to impede one who had already learned. As the Human's technology advanced, this became more effective when Kone integrated these frequencies into broadcast signals.

With the Illuminati answering to him and the technological advantage, Kone manipulated the growth of Human civilization. One generation at a time. Leading them in a direction where they would be willing to give up their freedoms bit by bit. Preparing them for when Kone would one day reveal himself to the Humans as the one with the solutions to their problems.

The fighting between the Alfan and the Dvwargarians continued in the Third Density but a peace treaty was struck in the Fourth. When Kone realized that things had cooled off, he returned to again sow the seeds of contention, but the Alfan had a five-hundred-year lifespan, and the Cetatian leader was recognized by some of the older Elves. They rejected his schemes, so Kone tried to move in with force.

The magick of the Alfan was tested against the technology of the Cetatians, and a vicious battle ensued. The Cetatian people were pushing hard, and victory seemed certain until the Dwarves entered the fray. The combined forces of Elves, Dwarves, and some Humans were too much for the Cetatians to handle, and they were forced back into the Second Density.

To make matters worse, the magick users of the Fourth Density figured out how to teleport to the Third and the fighting there soon ended as well. Kone realized that he would need to focus on the First Density and use the combined might of the Humans and Cetatians to overtake the other two. So, from then on, Kone's primary focus was on the First Density.

"This should already be enough to break his narrative," Rudge commented. "Maybe we should take this and go, while we still can. The world needs to see this."

"They will." Haley sounded so certain in that statement, causing everybody to look her way, wondering what she was thinking. Sensing the curiosity, Haley explained, "Sheriff said that Kone can talk the world from here, so I told it to put all this on the world wide web."

"You mean everything we just saw?" Samuel asked.

Haley shook her head and got her mischievous smirk. "No, I mean everything, everything!" She threw her arms out wide as she finished her sentence. Then the hairs on the back of her, and everybody else's, neck stood up.

"Obnoxious, but futile. I can have that scrubbed from the internet in an hour." Everyone turned in the direction from which the deep voice came to see an unhappy looking Kone standing with his hands clasped behind his back while he faced them directly. He didn't even twitch a muscle when seven bursts of energy shout out from him at the others.

Gurden, Rudge and Samuel were all hit square in the chest, knocking them to the ground. Haley tried to dodge, but the bolt clipped her shoulder, spinning her in a circle as she shuffled her feet, keeping them beneath her.

Elizabeth, Alunareth and Sabrina managed to dodge the bolts completely. Sabrina activated the disruption emitter, drew her bolt pistol with one hand and her Colt in the other. Alunareth drew his pistol as well, Rudge and Samuel jumped back to their feet, while Gurden struggled back to a stand.

"Don't move," Sabrina said. "You're being detained."

This managed to coax a chuckle from Kone. "Do you really believe that?"

"Yes," Gurden grunted as he straightened his posture, trying to muster all the confidence he could. "Kone. You are under arrest for the subjugation of the Atlantean people."

Suppressing his laughter, Kone replied, "I know you're aware of what happened the last time Atlantis attempted a coup. Do you really think this time will be different?" He didn't give anyone a chance to respond before continuing. "Well, you're right. This time will be different." His mouth took the form of an unnerving smile. "Because this time, the consequences will be worse…much worse."

Keeping their pistols trained on Kone, Alunareth, Rudge and Gurden spread out to surround him while Samuel approached with a restraining disk. Sabrina stood herself between Kone and the girls, with both her firearms aimed at Kone's head. The empaths were reading the room, and everybody was tense. Everybody except Kone.

He remained as calm and confident as always. Unconcerned with what may happen next. Samuel slapped the restraining disk on Kone, the tendrils extended out and wrapped around him, cinching tight then lifting him a few inches off the floor. They all seemed to relax as soon as the disk took hold.

"I just have one question," Kone said with his tone as calm as ever. "Does the governor know what you're doing?"

"No," Gurden lied.

"Good. Then I won't have to kill him. I have more pressing matters than overseeing another Atlantean election." Kone stretched his arms out, snapping the metallic tendrils like wet cardboard, and his feet dropped to the floor. Gurden and Samuel fired their bolt pistols and the blasts slammed against Kone like puffs of smoke against a mountain. Haley and Elizabeth watched the others join in, firing upon Kone, but he didn't budge. He stood there, hands again clasped behind his back, as if nothing were happening.

"I felt the signal the instant it came on, but your toy is useless. Disruption emitters aren't powerful enough to shut me down." He looked at Gurden first, lifted his hand as it began to glow, but before he could discharge his blast, yellow light splashed out from his temple accompanied by a sudden and loud bang that left a ringing in everyone's ears as the gunshot reverberated through the ziggurat's interior. Kone looked at the bullet on the floor, then lifted his eyes to glare at Sabrina.

"Turn it off! Turn it off!" Elizabeth shouted.

Sabrina reached for the emitter as Kone took aim, but this time his discharge was interrupted, not by a bullet, but a potato. He looked at Haley just as the signal cut out and a blue glow appeared in her eyes. She launched a bobcat at Kone, who swatted the orb away with a backhand swing; the concussive burst did nothing to budge the Uniralt.

Coming in behind that was an amber and indigo orb, but right before impact, its color shifted to a brilliant white. It hit, Kone staggered back a couple of steps and snapped his angry gaze at the young Paladin. "No!" he shouted as he launched a blast at the girls. They both erected and overlapped their protective fields, stopping the potent blast.

Rudge and Sabrina charged in, drawing swords and pick. Kone swung his arm around, releasing a wave of yellow and red that pushed everyone back, except Haley and Elizabeth, who were both standing within Haley's field while Elizabeth was gathering energy. Kone fired another blast against Haley's field which, as soon as it hit, she dropped, allowing Elizabeth to launch her attack.

A brilliant white beam of flames flowed from the mystic's outstretched palms and blasted Kone back, across the room and into a collum. Her beam continued, keeping him pinned until it ended in a burst of white light and from the place where Kone had been, two men stumbled to the floor.

Side by side, Kone and Molech stood up and looked at each other, then they both looked at Kone's wrists, to the cufflinks that had kept Molech hidden. Now separated from Kone, his energy was no longer masked, and all the other nearby gods could sense him. Before anyone could say a word, Bast appeared, alongside Artemis, who already had an arrow knocked and drawn.

The Huntress did not hesitate, releasing the arrow directly at Molech's heart. Though it did not penetrate Molech's body, it still hit with godly force, shoving him through the collum and the wall, tumbling to the Atlantean streets below. The two goddesses pursued him through the new hole to the outside, from where screams were heard, and the buildings started to shake.

Gurden ran to the hole, looked out and down to the center of the city to see people running in terror. Molech hurled Bast into the building across the street, and the structure began to crumble but suddenly stopped as Bast held the broken structure in place with her will, allowing the mortals to escape. "We need to get the people away from here!" the sheriff shouted.

Kone was about to hit Samuel with a blast when a kitten burst against his head, causing him to stagger, then an amber and indigo orb hit his knees, making him stumble back to the floor. "Go help the people," Haley shouted at the others. "Elizabeth and I've got Kone."

"Sheriff, stay with them." Samuel pointed to the girls and Kone. "We'll protect the people." He turned and leaped out the side of the ziggurat, followed by Rudge and Alunareth.

Sabrina turned to the girls. "We got this," Elizabeth said while drawing her sai. Sabrina nodded and hopped out through the wall.

Kone started to stand, but Haley shot a blast to the floor beside him, just far enough away for the concussive burst to give him a slight shudder, then aimed her arm cannon directly at him. "Stay down."

"No," he calmly replied and began to stand. Haley fired and her kitten burst against Kone's protective field as he straightened up to his full height and brushed off his sleeve. "If you were thinking that my power was solely from Molech," his eyes began to glow with yellow light and a smug smirk spread on his face, "then you have made a grave misjudgment."

He threw his hand forward and unleashed a beam of swirling red and yellow light. Haley threw up her field as Elizabeth dove to the side, throwing an orb in response. Kone stopped his beam to raise his own field of protection right before it hit. Haley continued the press with a volley of kittens as Sheriff Gurden began firing his bolt pistol. Elizabeth came up to her feet and began throwing blasts as well, hoping to wear down his energy before this battle could go much further. But then Kone vanished.

"Where'd he go?" Elizabeth wondered aloud.

Haley suddenly felt the sense of smug superiority behind her and started to spin around only to be hit by Kone's blast. Another blast hit Elizabeth before she could raise her field and both girls tumbled to the floor as a pistol bolt hit Kone from the side.

Kone turned his head to Gurden as the sheriff continued blasting. A yellow light flashed in the Uniralt's eyes, and he threw a blast, knocking Gurden against a mainframe before he crumpled to the floor.

"No!" Haley launched a charged blast while she stood back up and the bobcat landed before Kone could raise his field. The burst shuddered the Uniralt, but did not knock him down.

He disappeared before the next blast came in and the girls immediately raised their fields in anticipation of his next attack, which came from the other side of the room, across the railings. The girls deflected the blasts and dropped their fields, returning the fire. Blasts flew back and forth across the opening to the level below while the combatants dodged side to side.

Kone side-stepped a blast, conjured an orb of red light and threw it toward an adjacent wall, then dodged a couple more blasts while throwing another. The orbs flew out, ricocheted off the walls and kept going. Haley ducked as one flew by, bounced off the wall behind her, down to the floor and up at Elizabeth, who spun to the side, avoiding it. The other came through causing them to dive around, avoiding the red blasts while trying to dodge more of Kone's regular blasts.

"Enough!" Elizabeth growled, and traced the paths of the two red orbs, anticipating where they would come close to each other. She rushed to that spot and found she calculated correctly as one orb flew her way from both sides. She threw up her field right before impact. "Whoa!" she grunted and shuddered as they hit her field, resulting in a deep drain on her energy.

Haley launched another volley at Kone, but he vanished before they got near him. The Uniralt reappeared between them and backhanded Haley. Blue and purple light splashed out from her jaw with the impact, launching her ten feet back. Kone turned and caught Elizabeth's wrist as she was swinging in with her charged sai.

She discharged the blast against Kone's torso, causing him to wince but he pulled Elizabeth in, grabbed her collar with his other hand and threw the young mystic at Haley, who was in the middle of standing back up. They both collapsed to the floor. They tried to jump back up as Kone teleported himself right in front of them. Elizabeth discharged another blast from her sai as Haley dismissed her potato gun while grabbing her staff with one hand and Elizabeth's shoulder with the other. Kone raised his hand and Haley released a pounce.

A wave of blue light rippled out, knocking Kone over as she and Elizabeth rebounded upward. Haley released her grip on Elizabeth and dashed forward, directly above Kone and pounced once again. Her feet pounded down on top of the Cetatian Uniralt; she did not rebound with the energy burst, but instead drove her feet down. The flooring beneath Kone cracked as Haley's impact shoved him into the stone structure, shaking the building itself.

Elizabeth took the opportunity to quickly pop a B12 and then shot a blast at the dazed Kone lying on, and partially in, the floor. Kone jolted from her orb while Haley charged up her staff, then thrust it downward. Kone vanished right before the butt end connected with the broken floor, discharging an energy burst on contact.

Haley was yanked back by her suspenders and tossed. Elizabeth immediately charged in, her sai moving in blurs. Kone's arms raised and moved with fury, blocking and redirecting her strikes. Two millennia of experience gave Kone a comfortable advantage in the skill department, though he was still impressed by the competence that Elizabeth displayed.

It's a real shame that I can't have them work for me.

He anticipated her next movements and went a step ahead, disarming her and striking his fist into her solar plexus. In a splash of amber and indigo, Elizabeth gasped for breath as she flew backward. He pivoted toward the returning Haley as her staff spun with wisps of blue trailing from both ends. Kone dodged the swings and strikes, stepped inside her next swing and jabbed.

The punch caught Haley in the cheekbone, her head snapped back, and she dropped down on her butt in a haze. Kone pulled his leg back for a kick, aimed right at Haley's face, but another blast from Elizabeth, who was still trying to catch her breath, staggered him. Haley hopped back up, a shiner under her left eye and a fierce blue glow in both.

Popping her claws, lines of purple and blue began crackling from her fingers and she shouted, "Raah." She swiped with one arm, and then the other, unleashing razor-sharp lines of purple light on Kone.

Kone roared in surprise and pain. His suit and skin on his back were sliced open but Haley could see the wounds knitting themselves together before her eyes.

Elizabeth launched some more blasts from her sai, but Kone vanished again, and Haley had to quickly raise her field before the blasts hit her. Kone appeared next to Elizabeth and swung, the strike knocking her back as he vanished once more. He appeared behind the young mystic, caught her and then threw her at Haley and was gone again. Now behind the farmgirl, he shoved her into the oncoming Elizabeth. The girls collided and dropped to the ground.

"I have ruled for nearly two-thousand years. Defeated enemies the likes of which would give you nightmares. Do you really think that you two could possibly take me on?" He let the girls detangle themselves and stand back to their feet. "This is my one-time offer. You know that I will retain power. You know that the world is mine to command. Why sacrifice your lives needlessly? Join me. You can still be a force for good. You may not like my methods, but you have seen it yourself. Wars have been stopped, people will prosper and be kept safe in an advancing society. I may be a monster, but in the end, all people will benefit and have access to greater technologies, medicine and advancements in proper philosophies. There's no need for your lives to end here. I'll never task you with things that go against your values. In fact, I have plenty of work that you would already do on your own. You have the means to rescue people who were stuck in a burning building. Would you refuse such a task and let innocent people perish, just because I'm the one asking you to do so?" Kone waited a moment, but when no reply came, he asked again. "Would you?"

"Well…no," Haley said as Elizabeth shook her head.

"Excellent," Kone said, a smile coming to his face. "Then you understand, that while some of my methods you find distasteful, many people can and do have better lives. Can you deny that fact? Look around at the wonders of Atlantis. This could be a reality for the entire world. Isn't that a goal worth striving for?" He didn't wait this time and followed up with, "Isn't it?" letting them know that the question was not rhetorical.

"Uh…no?" Elizabeth said as Haley shrugged.

"You do not think the world having access to the advancements of Atlantis to be a good thing?"

"Not the way you're gonna do it," Elizabeth said.

Kone's eyes shifted to Haley, and she said, "Go kick rocks."

"Unfortunate," Kone said and vanished.

The attacks came fast and furiously as the girls were being knocked around every which way by a constantly teleporting Kone. Haley managed to land one good blow in the ruckus and Elizabeth landed a couple of shots, but they were being worn down and exhausted by the varied attacks, which felt like they were coming from all directions at once. Haley dodged an attack, Kone vanished, then sound began to distort and finally stop as Haley slipped into her speed state. She looked around, Elizabeth was as still as a statue and Haley could see an apparition-like Kone materializing behind her. Haley went to move Elizabeth aside, but when she touched her friend, the young mystic was also brought into the speed state. She blinked her eyes, looked around and tried to speak. "What's happening," The words did not flow on soundwaves, but instead were heard inside Haley's mind.

"Excuse me," Haley replied. Elizabeth heard Haley's words inside her head. "I need to stand there." Elizabeth looked over her shoulder, saw Kone materializing and stepped to the side. Haley removed her hand from her friend's shoulder, and she became still again as the farmgirl took her place before the Uniralt.

Kone materialized and was caught off-guard to see Haley standing right in front of him, with her left arm held across her torso, her right arm underneath it, her right hand held up in a fist and her potato gun barrel, wisping with blue and purple light, pressed under his chin. "I don't like the words, but you get the idea," she said and then released the bobcat.

Bursting at point blank, Kone was knocked off his heels, arching backward to land on his shoulder blades. As soon as he hit the ground, the girls unloaded a barrage of blasts before he could comprehend what was happening. The Uniralt finally gained the presence of mind to raise his field but was becoming energetically exhausted. The field dropped, orbs slammed against him, and he dropped to the floor. Haley took a couple of steps closer and aimed her gun at the motionless dictator.

"Keep watch on him, I'm going to try and heal Sheriff Gurden."

"Okay, Haley replied, not taking her eyes off Kone. He opened his eyes and looked up to see Haley with her arm cannon aimed at his head. "Stay down."

Kone sneered, and let loose an omnidirectional burst of energy, taking Haley by surprise and knocking her back. She fired as she stumbled, Kone rolled out of the way, and was pushed a bit by the burst. He came up to his feet and disappeared, but Haley felt him manifest beneath them, on the bottom level.

"Beth!" Haley called, spinning around to see her helping the sheriff sit up. "He's downstairs!"

"Let's go get him!" she replied but then turned to the sheriff, who was in no condition to get up and move. "Hang on, I can heal you."

"No, I'm okay. Go. Stop him while you've got the chance. Free the world," he said with as much strength as he could muster but grunted and almost passed out.

"We'll be back," Haley said. The girls ran for the stairwell and bounded down to the bottom level.

CHAPTER 29
The Owel's Talons

The red glow in Molech's eyes brightened with the widening of his smile. "It's been quite some time, hasn't it?"

Bast and Artemis stared at the malicious god with contempt and disgust. The atrocities he had orchestrated throughout the millennia stained the god's spirit with the stench of misery and Bast could feel it emanating from him like a radiator stuck on high.

"What?" Molech asked with a smug smirk, "Don't you have anything to say?"

Artemis narrowed her eyes past her drawn bow at Molech. "No." She released. The Olympian arrow sped forward, magickally enhanced by the Goddess of the Hunt, but it stopped in midair right in front of Molech's face before it dropped to the ground. The arrow vanished and reappeared in the knocked position as Artemis drew again, but an arch of deep red lightning blasted her back before she could complete the motion.

Bast let out a bolt of gold energy and threw out a protective field right before Molech returned fire with an intense yellow beam. It hit the goddess's field and Bast managed to hold her ground for a couple of seconds before she was thrown back thirty feet into a building, shattering the lower corner and the structure began to topple. She focused her mind on the structure, holding it still as the mortals rushed to escape.

Molech was still wearing that smug smile on his face as Artemis challenged him again. She dashed in, thrusting with her hunting knife, but the blade did not penetrate, it just sliced his tunic and skipped across his skin. Molech grabbed her by the wrist and Artemis swung with her left fist, connecting to the side of Molech's cheek.

"Argh!" she shouted when her knuckles broke.

Another blast of golden light exploded against Molech's head, yet he did not budge. The glow in his eyes intensified when he released his grip on Artemis's wrist and lifted his arms into the air. Bast and Artemis were yanked upward in sync with his arms, and they remained in sync when he swung his arms down, slamming both women into the road, leaving two distinct craters. The area shook, and people scrambled. One onlooker was so engrossed in the spectacle that he didn't realize the building next to him was cracking. He was suddenly yanked to the side before a chunk of marbled stone landed on his head.

"Whoa, thanks," he said, turning to look at his rescuer, surprised by the presence of an Alfan.

The Great Owel lifted his arms again, pulling the goddesses into the air, when Molech felt a tremendous impact to the right side of his face. He was hit with enough force to be staggered. Bast and Artemis were released, and he turned back toward where the strike had come in time to see Ptah's scepter slam into his face.

Molech was knocked to the ground and Ptah followed with another strike hard enough to release a shockwave. So taken back was Molech by these strikes, so powerful the impacts fueled by Ptah's anger, that Molech was utterly shocked by the craftsman's aggression. But Ptah was facing a far more powerful Molech, enhanced by the suffering of countless innocents from across the ages. And this Molech had just recovered his bearings.

The next swing of the scepter was intercepted by Molech's grasp. He smiled at Ptah, "I never knew you had it in you." Standing up, he yanked the scepter from Ptah's hands and swung it at the Egyptian god when he lunged in to take it back. It hit and the energy Molech should not have been able to channel through the scepter burst against Ptah's face, knocking him through a building while more Atlanteans fled the scene.

Ptah groaned as he stumbled back. Bast and Artemis were still on the ground, and Molech laughed. "Not even Zeus could challenge me right now." He stroked his chin, "I may even be able to stand against the likes of Odin himself." He took a deep breath and released a satisfied sigh. "This really is so much fun," he said, lifting his arms and stretching them out. "It feels good to finally cut loose a little bit, and I would love to keep going for a while, but there are some things that I must tend to." His right hand began to glow with red energy. The intensity increased, and he held it out toward his three adversaries. I'd say goodbye, but honestly, it's good riddance."

The red light intensified for a discharge, and with a cracking sound, his wrist became ensnared by a supple metal. Molech turned to see the source in mid-leap, speeding toward him, and he smirked. Sabrina waited until the last second to channel her energy. Skilja crackled to life and disoriented Molech for an instant before she thrust her katana into his chest, through his heart and out his back. A twisted and convulsing expression on his face made Sabrina think for just a second that she had dealt an effective strike, but that second soon passed, and Molech quickly regained his bearings. The empathic Hunter realized that all she had dealt him was amusement.

His smile returning, Molech chuckled. "This is too cute."

Ptah rushed back in, but with a mere thought, he was thrown back, Skilja was cast off from Molech's wrist and Sabrina was thrown to the ground at the god's feet. He flexed, pushing the sword out from his chest and it dropped to the ground next to Sabrina while Skilja returned to her hip.

Molech tilted his head. "Hunter Sabrina Carmen. So nice to finally meet you in person. A couple of your playmates, good friends of Baphomet, have been going on about you for the past week." He crossed his left arm to prop his elbow and stroked his chin as his smile widened. "I think it's time for you to be reacquainted with one of them."

Grabbing her katana, Sabrina began to rise when Molech snapped his fingers. Next she knew, she was standing in one of the caverns beneath Atlantis. She turned, scanning the barren stone area with her eyes, but spun around when she felt the mystical energies coalesce behind her. A demon suddenly appeared in a flash of red light. Her eyes widened, but her brow remained furrowed when the demon pointed at his own face and sneered, "It took me an entire day to regenerate this eye."

Molech turned back to the three gods on the ground, struggling to their feet when they were all slammed back down. "This is fun, but I've got things to do and…" His words were interrupted by a fist swinging out from a sudden flash of orange light. He flew backward twenty feet and cratered the ground on impact. He shot right back up, hovering a few feet off the ground and laid eyes on the man attached to that fist. "Ares! You would think that the God of War would know better how to pick his battles."

Ares didn't say a word, he just lifted his hands, palms up and twice waved his fingers back, inviting the challenge. Bast, Ptah and Artemis were regaining their footing, and it was now four against one. The odds were still not fair.

A massive beam poured forth from Molech's hands, and Ares's energy coalesced in the form of a shield. He stepped forward to meet the blast and dug in his feet to hold his ground, but the road gave way beneath him, and he started sliding back.

"Ha ha ha ha! And you used to call me weak, Ares." His laughter diminished to a chuckle as vines rose from the ground beneath Molech and wrapped around his body, cinching tight. "You're here too," he muttered. "Good." He threw his arms out, snapping the vines and turned around. Cernunnos was there with his bow and an arrow of white light, knocked and drawn. He released the string, and a bolt of lightning arched into Molech.

Molech reflexively braced himself for what would normally hurt, but at his advanced level of power, it only knocked him back a couple of feet into a headlock from behind. Ares squeezed down, orange flames in his eyes flared as he wrenched his arms, snapping the neck of Molech. Ares let go and Molech dropped like a rag doll.

The five gods gathered around Molech to see him lying stomach down on the ground, his head turned weirdly to the side. A head that suddenly turned all the way around and smiled. "Did you really think it would be that easy?"

He released an energetic shockwave, knocking them all back and destroying the closest building while jumping to his feet. His head still turned the wrong way, Molech walked backward to Ares and said, "You've been a thorn in my side for far too long." He turned his body around, but not his head, putting the alignment back to the right with a sickening crack as he spoke. "You and your pathetic tree-hugger of a friend." He glanced at Cernunnos and scoffed, "You call yourself a god. You're a glorified hippie!"

Somewhere beneath Atlantis

In an instant, Skilja was in Sabrina's right hand, erupting with blue-white and purple arches, and her bolt pistol in her left.

The demon waved his hand, and Sabrina was telekinetically thrown against the cavern wall. "I remember your toy, so I brought one of my own." He held out his hand and flames appeared, began to swirl and extend until he was holding a long whip of hellfire. A sinister smile spread across his face as he approached, and Sabrina struggled to move. The demon came within range and said, "I've tasted your whip, now taste mine!"

Despite her struggles, Sabrina couldn't move her arms and had no way to defend herself. Digging deep for everything she had, the Hunter let go of her pistol, and it slapped against the wall alongside her. She managed to bend her elbow just enough to lift her hand to her beltline. The demon threw his arm forward, and his whip of flame lashed toward the Hunter just as her finger reached the button.

The flaming whip dissipated along with Skilja's electrical arches and Sabrina slid down the wall to land on her feet; her bolt pistol returned to her left hip. The disruption emitter at full power afforded her fifteen minutes to resolve the situation.

"What…How?!"

Sabrina lifted Skilja and gave a rare smile as she toggled the switch with her thumb, accessing the power cell. The blue-white arches returned.

"This will not change the outcome!" the demon bellowed and charged ahead.

Despite magick having been taken off the table, the demon was still a serious physical threat, and Sabrina's bolt pistol was not nearly as powerful as the plasma rifles from their previous encounter. She drew it anyway, and with the setting on high, she opened fire. A hail of blasts hit the demon but caused more irritation than harm. He did not slow his charge.

She lashed out with Skilja, and the demon came to an abrupt stop, raising his arm. He took the hit on his forearm with a wince and charged again when she pulled the whip back. Instead of lashing again, Sabrina dove to the side, tumbled and came back to her feet right before the demon plowed into the wall. It cracked. Bits of rock fell to the floor, and the demon turned to face Sabrina. She fired a few more blasts, but the demon shrugged them off while reaching down for a small boulder. His fingers dug into the rock, which he hoisted above his head with one hand and then hurled it.

Sabrina dove out of the way, and the boulder shattered against the floor. The Hunter threw her arm across her face to protect her eyes from the shrapnel while her bullet-resistant jump suit protected her body.

Lowering her arm, Sabrina saw the demon charging once again. Waiting until he was right there, she dove between his legs, rolled back to her feet and broke into a sprint. The demon turned, lowered his head and charged. Sabrina drew her Colt, aimed and fired her last round. The bullet hit the demon between the eyes. His head stopped moving before his feet, causing him to stand bolt upright and let out a sound that was something between a growl and a groan. The bullet was lodged in the skin, stopped by that thick skull and he dragged a couple of fingers across the injury, dislodging the irritating bullet while black fluid trickled from the wound.

The demon was too resilient to be stopped by her ranged weapons, and Sabrina now knew that the only way to take him down would be up close and personal.

Atlantis City, Atlantis

Ares was climbing back to his feet when Molech threw an orb. He pivoted on the way up for a successful dodge as Cernunnos was also getting back to his feet. A blast of fire from Ares hit Molech but had no effect on The Great Owl; however, it distracted him long enough for Bast to latch on from behind and teleport them miles away to the vast, deserted tundra of East Antarctica.

Cernunnos arrived mere seconds later to see the Egyptian goddess already thrown back to the ground. Molech threw his arm upward, launching Cernunnos straight up into the sky and out of sight when Ares and the others arrived. Holding his right hand in the air, The God of War stretched out his fingers, and flames manifested in his palm. They flared and extended out, forming the Seraph's sword gifted to him by Michael.

A maniacal laugh escaped from Molech. "Do you really think that angel's little toy can bother me right now? I never could dream of outfighting you, but now I don't have to, and you'll…" He spun when he heard a roar from behind. Bast morphed into lioness form as she tackled the malicious god and clamped down on his neck with her jaws. It did not harm him in the slightest but did draw his attention away from Artemis, whose hand was now healed.

Bast disappeared right before the arrow penetrated Molech's neck. He stood up, turned to Artemis and saw her teleport away just as Ares skewered him with the Seraph's sword, pinning him to the ice. Clouds gathered overhead, the continent darkened, and the echos of thunder rumbled across the tundra.

Ares disappeared, and lightning erupted everywhere, strikes covering the surface of West Antarctica, and it all began to converge on Molech. Cernunnos landed on the ground next to him; his ethereal antlers were visible, and the green glow in his eyes flared. He slammed his hands to the ground, and the lightning merged into a giant three-mile-wide bolt of electrical plasma.

And Molech was the lightning rod.

The massive arching cracked the ice cap and ceased, but Molech still stood. Steam rose off his body while he smiled and remanifested his clothing. Cernunnos was slack-jawed with disbelief.

"What do you think you're doing?" Molech asked in a condescending tone. "Thor's lighting couldn't even hurt me right now. Do you really think that your pathetic little firecrackers are going to be any better?" He glanced down, "Speaking of cracks…" Molech gave a kick to the narrow fissure in the ice, and the ground rumbled. Cernunnos's eyes widened in horror when he realized that half the icecap itself was about to slide into the ocean, which would result in worldwide devastation for the second density.

Ares appeared, grabbed Molech and threw him, shouting, "Focus on the ice!" and charged after the Owl. Cernunnos quickly sank into the ice, all the way down to the surface, where he phased out of the moving cap. He placed his palm against the wall of ice; it bonded, and he began to pull, legs pumping out step after step back to the other half of the cap. He phased into the ice, pulling the two halves together and fusing them into one mass.

Atop the tundra, Molech was dispatching his opponents with ease, but another man had appeared a short distance away, observing the conflict. The man in the black suit recognized that trying to overpower the Owl in this state was a fool's errand, but he also understood how it worked. He vanished.

Ares's face slammed down, forming a new crack into the ice hundreds of feet deep. Cernunnos and Artemis were both using their bows with no effect. Ptah leaped in for another strike but was halted in midair before being telekinetically slammed down, cratering the ice.

Winding up for another attack, Bast was about to throw her arm forward when Hel grabbed her wrist from behind. She was yanked backward and heard the Goddess of Death hiss into her ear, "This will be our final dance," and they disappeared in a black mist, far away from the immobilized Ptah.

Atlantis City, Atlantis

Kone appeared on the bottom level of the ziggurat by the northern wall. Between two large partitions was a white egg-shaped pod with an opening large enough for a large man to stand inside and a transparent cover in the up position. Large robotic parts and limbs hung on the partitions and an array of mechanical arms was mounted on the wall behind the pod.

With a sneer, Kone looked over his shoulder at the sound of footsteps coming down the stairs. He made a fist and pounded a button on the partition and a thick glass barrier slid down. Kone stepped into the pod and the transparent cover slid shut. Two clamps extended from the inside of the pod's base, closing onto his calves. Another pair extended from the sides, clamping onto his forearms. The mechanical arms behind the pod went into motion, lifting the pod up, taking the parts and limbs and assembling them around it.

Haley and Elizabeth came running in front of the partition and their jaws dropped when they saw Kone within a large mech being assembled. Standing at twenty feet tall, this mech had just enough room to stand up straight without scraping its head. The housing on the torso and limbs was made of metal and had a gleaming white coat of paint. Kone opened and closed his hands, and the mech did the same. The girls conjured their helmets and scanned.

VEHICLE CLASSIFICATION: ASSULT MECH

PROTOTYPE OF AN ONGOING PROGRAM, THE MAYUM ARMOR PRESENTED A HEAT RETENTION PROBLEM, AND THE COOLANT SYSTEM IS CURRENTLY UNDERGOING A REDESIGN

INTENDED FOR TESTING, THE JOINTS ON THIS UNIT HAD NOT YET BEEN PROPERLY ARMORED.

Kone's voice came through the speakers, "I gave you the chance to…" The speakers squealed, and Kone's voice was replaced by Survivor's Eye of the Tiger.

Glancing at his dashboard readout and realizing that he had lost control of his audio system, Kone snarled through the pod's cover and started to shout, but the girls couldn't hear him. They dismissed their helmets as the barrier retracted, and the mech stepped forward, slamming its fist to the ground.

The girls dove to the side, easily avoiding the clumsy attack, and they unleashed a barrage of blasts at its right elbow. Kone pulled the arm back and held up the mech's left hand as the opened palm discharged a powerful blast while the thermometer on Kone's display was steadily rising.

Elizabeth grunted when she blocked it with her field, the blast packing a harder punch than she had anticipated.

"Over here, Robocop!" Haley shouted when she felt his irritation spike, and Kone turned the mech toward her. Haley unleashed her beam on the mech's right shoulder, spinning it back around toward Elizabeth as the arm ejected from the torso, which at least allowed some more heat to vent.

Crackling with energy, Elizabeth waited until Haley had her shot charged and blasted a stream of flames at the left shoulder as Haley's bobcat burst in the back of the mech's right knee. Haley dove between the legs, coming up alongside Elizabeth as the mech fell backward. The temperature rose too high, the emergency shutdown activated, and the music stopped as Kone teleported out of the mech and right in front of the girls. He grabbed them both by their necks, hoisting the surprised pair off their feet.

Enraged, Kone shouted, "I've had enough of your…" His eyes popped open wide when Elizabeth kicked, and Kone dropped them both as he sank to his knees, a long squeak working its way from his throat while he pressed his hands between his legs and collapsed to his side. Then the girls' beams blasted him against the wall beneath the array of mechanical arms, where he crumpled to the floor, unconscious.

"Uhm…now, what do we do with him?" Haley was scratching her head. "We can't just leave him here, or he'll get away when he wakes up."

"I don't know." Elizabeth looked around the room, hoping to find some solution, when the man in the black suit was suddenly standing before them.

"Hello, young ladies. I was hoping I could use your help." He looked to the side to see Kone slumped against the wall. "Oh, this guy." With a wave of his hand, pieces of the mech stretched out, as supple as ropes, wrapped around the Uniralt and solidified. "He's not going anywhere now and…" The man's eyes fell upon the cufflinks, and he pointed. "Those," he held up his forearms, looking at his sleeves to see that the links were now on his own blazer, "are mine." He looked back down upon Kone, and Haley felt his curiosity rise. "Oo, what have we here?" He reached down to where he felt a unique energy. His hand phased through the mayum bonds into Kone's inner breast pocket and removed a clamshell case. Opening it, he gazed upon the ethereal glowing feather and smiled. "And now, so is this."

"Who are you?" Haley asked.

"Not as important as where we're going." He snapped his fingers.

High above Antarctica

Standing atop the barrier, Michael tilted his head as he noticed a subtle shift. "Did you feel that?"

"Feel what?" Zues asked.

"Something's changed." Michael's eyes widened. "I can get through the barrier!" He looked back at Zues, Ra and Tuweltha, said, "I'll be back," and dropped down. As soon as he was through, what looked like the empty and isolated tundra from above was revealed to be bursting with energy from the battle of immortals and Michael rocketed down to the commotion focusing in on the man he had searched for for so long.

Releasing a circular wave of red light, Molech laughed hysterically at the sight of the people he hated most being flung away from him like mere mortals. But his laughter stopped when he sensed the power coming toward him. He looked up at the horizon, where Michael unleashed a beam of brilliant white light upon the Great Owel.

The beam struck Molech, blasting him back a couple hundred feet, where he rolled to a stop with a groan. Michael rushed in, forming his sword and preparing to strike when Molech raised his arm and halted the Seraph in mid-air.

"No, no, no!" Molech said as he staggered to his feet. "For the first time in centuries I was having fun and you had to show up and make it painful."

His face twisted with contempt as he made a fist and began to squeeze. Michael felt the telekinetic field begin to crush down on him and he struggled to push back against it but he was overwhelmed by the sheer force and began grunting.

Molech suddenly released his grip but did not let Michael move. "Wait, this would be foolish." He looked at Michael with a smug grin. "As much as I would love to obliterate you, you would just manifest a new body within an hour to bother me again. And since you can actually hurt me, this cannot be allowed. And since I cannot actually kill you," his grin widened to a wicked smile, "imprisonment will have to suffice."

He snapped his fingers and Michael shot downward, phasing through the ice, deep where the sunlight could not reach, then stopped unable to move when an image appeared in the darkness, a window to what was happening on the surface. "And you can watch while I rip apart some of your friends," Molech laughed as Ares and the others charged at him again.

Appearing on the ice, the girls saw a battle of gods unfolding before their eyes. Pointing to Molech, the man in the black suit said, "He needs to be stopped."

With a look of shock and confusion, Elizabeth said, "What are we supposed to do against him?"

Placing his palms on his knees, the man stooped down to look Elizabeth directly in the eyes and sternly asked, "Young Lady, are you, or are you not a Paladin?"

The words sank in, and Elizabeth's thoughts went back to when she made Baphomet wince. A strange feeling washed through her head, and she shot a nasty look at the man in the black suit when she realized he was probing her mind, but he just smiled and nodded his head.

"That's right," he said as his smile widened. "You can make him vulnerable."

Elizabeth set her gaze upon The Great Owel, and Haley felt her determination rising. "Let's do this," she said quietly and took a step toward the chaos.

"Wait," Haley said as she turned her back toward Elizabeth and looked at her over the shoulder while lifting the lid to her pack. "I need you to do something first."

Molech was laughing while he smacked around the God of War. He wasn't even trying to block attacks anymore as they were all utterly futile against him. Then he heard a girl's voice shout, "Hey, Bird Brain!"

Already knowing what child would dare address him in such a manner, Molech looked to see Haley crackling with blue and purple energy. Then he noticed the white glow in Elizabeth's eyes right before she fired a bolt from the end of her sai. The blast hit Molech, but he stood there, seemingly unphased. "What is this?" he asked rhetorically. "More mortals too big for their britches?"

A fist crossed his face, and he crumbled to the ground. Molech looked up at Ares while holding his palm to his cheek in disbelief. That hurt. Growling in anger, Molech waved his hand and sent Ares flying. An arrow from Artemis hit him, bounced off and landed on the ground before flashing back to her bow for another flight. A second bolt from Elizabeth hit him, and the next arrow punctured his side.

"Uh!" he shouted, realizing what was happening. With his will, Molech flung the other gods away, then turned toward the Paladin, only to get a face full of Haley's sustained blast. Even that stung!

Somewhere beneath Atlantis

The cavern wall cracked from the impact, and Bast dropped to the floor. Rushing in, Hel threw another blast as Bast morphed into a mountain lion and dodged the attack. She zig-zagged, avoiding the missiles and bounded toward Hel with a slash. Hel ducked as the puma dove by, barely avoiding those wicked claws.

Hel pivoted and grabbed Bast's tail, pulling her back, and Bast teleported. Spinning around again, Hel reached out and grabbed Bast, who was back in her Human form, by the neck and slammed her to the ground. "I know all your tricks," she sneered and dug her nails into Bast's face. "Now to finish what we started. Like before, Hel began running mass amounts of energy into the Egyptian goddess's head, causing her to scream out in pain, but this time, there was no one to help her.

It felt like a root canal to the center of her brain, and she was nearly passing out. Bastet tried to concentrate, tried to counter, but the pain was clouding her focus, and she could do nothing.

"There's no escape," the Goddess of Death hissed with glee. Bast screamed in agony as Hel continued, "And after I kill you, your two little friends are next."

Her words got through to the tortured Bast's mind. Hearing that, the Egyptian goddess found her focus. "No!" she screamed and managed to let out an omnidirectional blast of gold. Hel was flung back, and Bast morphed again. Sitting up, Hel saw the tiger bearing down on her. Bast bit down on Hel's neck, and unlike Molech, Hel was not impervious. The teeth sank in, and Hel started to scream, but Bast clamped down harder and began shaking her head with a vicious growl.

Hel flailed her arms helplessly at first but finally found the presence of mind to discharge a blast right into Bast's ear, disorienting her enough to break her grip. She slipped out and ran, holding her hand to her neck, but was tackled again by the tiger. Once again, Bast bit down on Hel's neck and also began scraping with the claws of her hind legs, tearing open large gashes down Hel's side and hip.

Digging down deep, Hel put everything she had into a blast, knocking the Egyptian goddess away. Bast landed on her feet and spun around to see a cloud of black mist dissipating. She morphed back to her true form and turned, scanning the cave with her eyes.

Snapping and lashing, Sabrina worked with speed and fury, attempting to wear down the advancing demon. He backed away from Skilja's stings and picked up another boulder. The Hunter moved in, and the demon let her, waiting for the next move. She lashed forward, and the demon accepted the hit just so he could drop the boulder atop the extended whip, pinning it to the ground. Sabrina pulled as hard as she could, but Skilja was trapped.

A wicked smile returned to the demon's face, "I told you; this would not change the outcome," and began to advance.

Keeping her eyes on his, Sabrina drew her katanas, which prompted a chuckle from the demon. Being plenty resistant to the blades wielded by the mortals, he came in close, and the Hunter slashed as the demon reached up to catch the edge in his palm. The demon was unfamiliar with mayum so was unpleasantly surprised when the blade sliced through his palm and into his wrist.

The cavern echoed with the demon's roar of pain. His eyes were fixed on the injury and, in his shock, didn't notice the other katana thrusting in for his chest. Sabrina skewered him with her other blade, let go of the handle and drew the fordriva blade, slashing his throat. Black fluid poured down his neck as he stumbled back and fell to the floor.

Sabrina leaped on top of the fallen demon, driving the blade alongside the katana right into his heart. The blade was made with the same minerals that held an Archon in the first density, and with no way for the demon to phase back to his realm, it was deadly. He let out a weak grunt, gasped and then fell dead.

Although not sure if it applied to the demon's physiology, Sabrina checked for a pulse, found none and hoped that confirmed his demise while she retrieved the three blades. After taking a couple seconds to catch her breath, Sabrina turned to the trapped Skilja. She tried to roll the boulder off her whip, but it was too heavy.

So, she took one of her katanas and wedged the tip under the boulder and thought, *I hope this is as unbreakable as they say.* Pulling up on the handle, the sword became a lever, and her struggle paid off when the boulder moved just enough for Skilja to return to her hip. The Hunter walked to a smaller boulder, sat down and rested.

She sat there on the cave floor, leaning her back against the boulder between herself and Bast. Despite the knots in her stomach, Hel tried to retain her presence of mind. She had never seen such ferocity from the Egyptian goddess and believed that Bast would have killed her. So, Hel teleported to escape but was too weak from the battle and only managed to transport herself to the other side of this boulder. Hel remained still and silent, hoping Bast wouldn't realize that she remained in the cave. The Goddess of Death pulled her energy inward and stilled her mind to avoid Bast's senses.

Turning her head to look around the area, Bast believed Hel had retreated and said, "You better hope we don't cross paths again anytime soon." Then, she vanished.

With great caution, Hel lifted her head and looked around the side of the boulder, verifying that Bast was gone. She stood up and grunted from the pain in her side as she tried to remember the last time that she felt this drained. Hel needed to heal herself, and for that, she needed to recover her energy. *There are plenty of mortals strewn about this place*, she thought. *I'll just take one of their lives to restore my own.*

She staggered with the first couple of steps and limped toward the end of the cave. Coming to the end, she saw that a tunnel continued from there. She had to stoop a little, causing more discomfort, but it was only one hundred feet before the tunnel opened into a small cavern.

Once there, she could feel it. Someone had recently passed in this cavern. Hel wasted no time in absorbing the ambient energy left over from the deceased, mending some of her wounds. Hel noticed that she had to strain to do so, and this was not a result of her weakened state.

There was a disruption emitter nearby.

Such an emitter would prevent a mortal from utilizing their energy field, but the signal was nowhere near intense enough to cancel out a god's. Although Hel's weakened state was able to hamper her abilities.

Now able to walk and move without discomfort, Hel continued through the cavern, looking for someone to harvest. Partway through, she found the body of a demon on the ground and saw the gash across his throat. *I wonder who managed to take you*, Hel thought as she touched the body. "Only a moment ago!"

Realizing that whoever slayed the demon must be nearby, Hel moved with haste toward the other end of the cavern, silent as death. She slinked her way around the boulders and rocks to find the demon's bane.

Making her way to the cavern's exit, the hairs on the back of Sabrina's neck stood up when Hel laid her eyes upon the Hunter. "You!" Hel shouted with a bitter rage burning in her gut at the sight of the mortal who embarrassed her.

Sabrina pivoted to see the Goddess of Death hurl dark orbs in her direction. She grabbed the whip, flipping the switch with her thumb, and Skilja crackled to life with blue-white arcs. The length of the whip arched in front of her and snapped away the attack.

Hel ran closer, throwing more bolts, and the Hunter snapped them away, then sent a lash directly at Hel. The goddess reached up, let the end of the whip ensnare her hand, and pulled Skilja from Sabrina's grasp. "You don't learn, do you?" Hel asked in a condescending tone as she went to snap apart the whip.

The goddess yanked the whip taught, but Skilja would not yield.

"Flekkle," Hel spat. "No matter." She threw the whip to the ground, but it immediately slid across the floor, coiling itself as it went and returned to Sabrina's hip. Hel threw more bolts and shards at Sabrina, but the woman who dodged bullets had little trouble avoiding the slower-moving blasts while she made her way toward the exit.

With her prey getting closer to escape, Hel instead threw a blast at the ledge above the exit. The cavern trembled as the rocks broke away and tumbled to the cavern floor, blocking Sabrina's exit. Hel moved in, throwing a barrage of blasts and making the Hunter dance.

On the top of a boulder near the center of the cavern, the man in a black suit appeared. He looked toward the end, where Sabrina was cornered, and shouted, "Hel, stop!"

Hel heard the voice and, without even looking, threw a half-hearted blast at the man while throwing dark shards at Sabrina. The man lifted his arm and blocked Hel's shot with his bare hand as the goddess closed the gap between her and her target.

Sabrina ducked and twisted, avoiding the latest deadly shots while Hel broke into a full sprint as she raised her hands above her head, radiating intense energy.

Sabrina's arm flashed forward, and Hel came to an abrupt stop before she could throw her killing blast. The goddess's eyes widened, and her scowl disappeared when her jaw dropped. Hel lowered her eyes and then her head to see the fordriva blade's handle protruding from her chest.

The Goddess of Death shuddered while a soft squeak escaped from her throat. She staggered and collapsed backward as the man in a black suit ran up and caught Hel in his arms. The fordriva blade was enough to hurt a god, not kill. But between her weakened state and the disruption emitter, it was more than Hel could endure.

The man gently lowered the goddess to the ground, kept her back propped up with his left arm, and placed his right palm on her face. "I'm right here," he said. He took his right hand off her face and placed it near her injury as a yellow glow appeared. The man tried to heal the goddess, but she was so weak and, despite all his magickal talent, was not a healer on the level of someone like Bast or Cernunnos. It could not be done.

Sabrina's empathic senses became overwhelmed by the grief from the man, but what hit her hard was the emptiness within Hel. She looked to the dying goddess and gasped as years of her bitterness echoed through Sabrina. "That's…that's all you've known for so long?"

Hel's eyes moved toward the Hunter as she continued. "All those centuries…millennia of life and all you've known was misery," Sabrina said as, despite her stoic face, her words broke, and tears began to stream down her cheeks. "I wish that weren't so…may you finally know peace."

Hel turned her gaze back to the man as he took her right hand in his. The man again said, "I'm right here." He looked into Hel's eyes and saw life fade away from them as tears began to pour from his. There, in the quiet depths of an isolated cavern, the Goddess of Death herself passed away.

The man, with reverence, laid Hel's body on the cave floor. Sabrina could hear the grief resonating from his heart, and as he slowly rose, that tune of grief transitioned to a chaotic rumble of rage. The man stood up with his head hanging low and his shoulders rolled forward. Sabrina took a few steps back as she could hear the chaotic rumble build to a crescendo, and then, without looking up from the floor, he thrust his arm toward Sabrina while holding his palm out.

Yellow lights began swirling around the Hunter's torso and limbs as she levitated into the air. The man lifted his head and turned toward her, a scowl on his face as he began to curl his fingers. Sabrina felt the pressure start to crush against her, and she grunted as the man watched with a crazed look in his eye.

Those thundering beats of rage that drummed out from the man's heart lost their rhythm and seemed to give way to the slower sounds of melancholy as his face softened. If he were the man he used to be, he would have atomized Sabrina without hesitation. But he was no longer that man. With a heavy sigh, he opened his fingers, and Sabrina gasped for air when the pressure relented. The man lowered his arm, returning Sabrina's feet to the floor. "I saw what happened," he took a deep breath and blew it out, "and I know you had no choice."

The man turned around and leaned over Hel's body. He placed his hand on her cheek for a moment as a tear ran down his and then reached for the handle of the fordriva blade. He extracted the blade from Hel's chest, stood up and held it out before him. It began glowing with yellow energy, then the light dimmed and faded away. The man suddenly looked haggard and worn as he walked to Sabrina, holding the blade out to her, handle first. "Here, you'll need this if Baphomet manages to find you before I kill him." Sabrina cautiously grasped the handle and took the blade.

He returned to Hel's body and reached out to the rubble that blocked Sabrina's exit with his left hand, waved it, and the pile of rocks shifted to the side.

"Now go," the man said with a choked voice. "Go and leave me to mourn my daughter." His eyes dropped down to Hel's corps for an instant and then darted back up. His expression shifted to confusion for the next few seconds as he looked around the cavern, realizing that Sabrina was already gone.

The Tundra, East Antarctica

Although his powers were not diminished, the vulnerability suffered when hit by the Paladin's blasts was something he could not afford while dealing with the likes of Ares. He was about to launch an attack on the young mystic when a lightning bolt from Cernunnos's bow hit him in the back. Molech hit the ground, Ptah was breaking out of the ice, and Artemis was lining up another shot while Ares returned to the fray.

The Olympian arrow hit and bounced harmlessly off Molech, who flung the gods away from him, turned and blocked Elizabeth's incoming blast with a protective field. He fired an intense blast at the girls, and Elizabeth erected a protective field of her own with Haley standing inside the radius. The Paladin's shield held up against the unholy blast, protecting them both. The Owl's beam continued, and the young mystic was starting to feel the drain when the other gods returned, piling on top of their nemesis.

Again, Molech flung the gods away from him to focus on Elizabeth. He turned toward her when Haley was suddenly in front of him. "How many licks does it take…"

She swung her staff, and the end connected against his face, releasing a concussive blast of blue light on impact. The Great Owel raised his hand to deal out some punishment when Haley vanished, and he was hit from above by her pounce.

"…to get to the center…"

She rebounded, and he looked up toward the farmgirl as Elizabeth released a charged blast; a direct hit on Molech's face. He turned his gaze back to the Paladin and was hit with another pounce.

"…of a tootsie-pop?"

Haley did not rebound this time but drove her feet into the malicious god, shoving him chest-deep into the cracking ice. Though she couldn't do much damage, he still found it painful, and she noticed a difference in his energy, a feeling that tugged at the empath. Molech's invulnerability returned, and that odd sensation faded as she dashed back toward Elizabeth while the other gods came, launching another assault before he could attack the Paladin.

They got a few strikes in before it became ineffective, and he launched Ares and Cernunnos far away, over the horizon. He turned his ire toward Ptah and Artemis when Elizabeth's next blast hit him. He slammed the two gods into the ice, knocking them both out before they could capitalize.

As soon as the bolt hit, Haley felt the odd sensation tugging at her. She focused and felt a call. A cry! The power that Molech wields was harvested from the agony of the innocent throughout the centuries and though the spirits of the tortured have long since moved on, echos remained embedded in the energy. Echos that called out for justice. The energy felt almost tangible to her empathic senses, to the point where...*I can use it!*

As soon as she tried, Molech struck Elizabeth with a bolt of red lightning. In a loud crackle, she was zapped and flung back fifteen feet where she dropped to the ice, out cold. The feeling faded as his invulnerability returned. Artemis and Ptah were still unconscious, Ares and Cernunnos had not returned from whatever troubles Molech sent them to and now, Haley had Molech's undivided attention.

His wicked smile on display, he began a causal strut in her direction as she unleashed a volley of kittens. They burst against his chest as he advanced, impervious to her barrage. He stopped five feet in front of her and she charged a shot, holding her arm cannon aimed at his face.

"You have a smart little mouth," he said while looking at his fingernails. He turned his gaze upon her as his eyes became two swirling pools of black and red. "Any final quips before all you can do is scream?"

"Yeah." Though terrified, Haley kept her calm and even managed a mischievous smirk onto her face when she said, "This spud's for you!" and launched a potato.

Careless in his invulnerability, Molech stood there to let the missile hit him, not noticing the white glow around the incoming tuber until it was too late. It broke on his face and Elizabeth's energy released, immediately followed by the burst of a bobcat. Molech stumbled backward and fell as Haley pulled on that energy. Molech felt the pull and jumped back up in a panic, but Haley was already crackling with blue and purple light. She unleashed her sustained beam of blue, filled with the purple ghostly faces of those that Molech had tortured.

They sped forward within the beam, coursing into him and he felt all the agony that he inflicted on those victims compressed into a couple of seconds. An unearthly shriek echoed across the tundra and Ptah began to stir. Molech took a couple of deep breaths, shock and horror on his face from the indescribable pain that just racked his every nerve. He stood up as his invulnerability returned and snapped his head toward Haley.

She launched another potato, but he deflected it before it got close and advanced on the empath, his eyes a mix of fury and fear. Haley launched another, but he would not let this happen again. He walked right up to Haley and reached out to grab her but stopped suddenly when a pair of sai was shoved into his back. Elizabeth had paid attention to the lessons Sabrina had taught her. The sai were both dug into the nerves, paralyzing Molech in place.

The Paladin screamed as she channeled her energy through them and into Molech. He couldn't move but felt Haley tugging at his power. Then he felt another tug from behind and to his left when Cernunnos came flying back, followed by a third to his right as Bast returned.

"No…" Molech could barely whisper. "Don't…"

Elizabeth pulled her sai and dashed away as three beams, one gold, one green and one blue, converged on Molech, all filled with the purple ghostly faces of his past victims. He writhed in his own torment from the triple empathic blast before he collapsed to the ground in shock. With short, sharp breaths and haunted eyes, he somehow managed to force himself back up to his knees when Ares dropped down from the sky, driving the Seraph's flaming sword through the top of his skull and down to the hilt. He ran his energy through the sword and into Molech's body, fire burned from the inside out, flaring with a whoosh, then the flames cleared, and the sword vanished leaving nothing but a charred skeleton that collapsed into a pile of bones on the ice.

The barrier fell and Apophis was shot into motion, circling the Earth several times a second with increasing speed. "Weeeee, he, he, heeeee!"

Michael appeared in a flash of white light as Zeus, Ra and Tuweltha touched down to the tundra.

Looking at the charred remains, Haley asked, "Is he…is he really…?"

"Dead?" Ares looked at the pile of bones then back at the girls. "Yes…it's over. He won't hurt anyone else, ever again."

Haley and Elizabeth were glad that he was gone, but not sure how to feel about taking part in someone's death. Even someone as evil as Molech.

CHAPTER 30
Last Respects

The Astral Plane

With her physical body deceased, Hel stood in an open space. She had refused Yeshua's gift in life, leaving her unable to pass through the Gates of Pearl and rejoin with her soul. Lost, she lingered as lonely spirit with no body, a ghost, looking out across the wide translucent field of grasses. But then she felt something, someone coming near. She recognized her father's presence but became confused when he couldn't sense her. Unable to locate Hel, the man in the black suit could do nothing but assume that she had already moved on and he returned to the other densities.

"But I'm right here!" Hel shouted, astonished that he couldn't sense her.

"I'm sorry," a voice said from behind her. Hel spun around to see Michael standing there. They locked eyes and he continued, "I truly hoped it would not come to this."

"As did I," another voice said.

Hel turned to see Uriel and knew that her fate had finally been sealed. "I'm surprised Odin did not come to see this through for himself," she muttered.

Michael said, "Odin has nothing to do with this."

With a sigh, Uriel said, "It is with a heavy heart that The Lord has sent us to open the gate, but this is a consequence of the choices that you have made." He waved his hand and a gateway of brimstone manifested.

Hel peered into the gate and her face softened. "What about my people?"

"What?" Michael asked.

"My people," she said again, a saddened look upon her face. "Without me, they'll just be lost spirits." Hel turned to face Michael directly with a pleading expression, "Please, find someone to look after them."

After a couple seconds of shock, Michael's expression went from stunned to somber and he slowly nodded saying, "I will." The next words from Hel shocked him just as much as her previous request.

"Thank you." A stoic expression returned to her face. She gave a nod to Uriel and stepped through the gate.

As the gate disappeared, Michael said, "I had no idea that she actually cared for them."

"Neither did I," replied Uriel, just as stunned.

Atlantis City, Atlantis

As Governer Swan finished his private meeting with Vedant and Derek Sahmbo, others were called into the conference room of the Atlantean town hall. Colonel Decker, Admiral Book and President Gregory Hedge with a secret sevice agent entered the room, followed by King Larriforn and King Knelgan as Gurden returned from the morgue with a grieving Sandra. Haley, Elizabeth and the rest of their party were asked to be present for this meeting and with them was Harry, Ryan and Maggie.

The immortals who took part in the battle on the ice cap were also asked to be part of this conversation, but only Bast and Ptah attended while the others were out searching for Baphomet, Lillith and Apophis. When they began, Governor Swan explained how he planned to move forward with presenting the information to the world, which everyone present found to be agreeable, but Haley, usually quiet in such settings, spoke up, "I know exactly who we need to do this right!"

First Density. Newington, Connecticut

"Another early night?" Ian asked Drew before adding, "Hi, Irma." He was still in his restaurant uniform, having just returned home himself.

"Yeah," Drew answered with a dejected sigh. "It's tough to be an investigative reporter when all we can report now is what we're told to write." He and Irma flopped down on the couch together. The typically exuberant Irma looked just as exhausted and other than a wave of the hand to Ian, said nothing. She leaned into Drew as he placed his arm over her shoulders. "Mark seems more downtrodden than ever," Drew went on. "He was thinking about selling several months back, but now he can't even do that. The new government has ordered him to continue and it's not even news anymore. Just an approved narrative." He took his arm back, placed his elbows on his lap and rested his face in his palms, rubbing the temples. "And I thought he was ready to snap before."

"Moral's down at the restaurant too. A couple of people I talked to think that this is a good thing, but most are feeling…" While trying to find the right word, it was suddenly granted by a woman standing in the corner of the room.

"Hopeless."

Drew jumped up from the couch and spun around. Irma looked over her shoulder, and Ian turned his head. "Whoa!" he exclaimed. Then, seeing the woman's beautiful face, smirked and again said, "Whoa…"

"Who are you, and how…" Drew began, then tilted his head with recognition, "Didn't I see you in a coffee shop in Columbia a little over a year ago?"

"Yes, and I'm sorry for the intrusion but this is important. My name is Bast."

"Like the Egyptian goddess," Ian asked.

With a nod, Bast said, "That's me."

"No," Drew said with a shake of his head. "I'm not buying into pagan gods now."

"Nor am I asking you to. I believe you are familiar with Haley and Elizabeth."

"Yes," both Drew and Ian answered.

"They have requested that you make a special report."

A moment later, Drew, Ian and Irma were standing in a conference room where the walls were made of white stone with different colored veins of crystal. And among the people there was the President of the United States. Drew whispered in Irma's ear, "Please don't squeal."

"Mr. Bean," Colonel Decker said while standing from his chair. He smiled. "So glad you could join us."

Televisions, computer monitors, radio stations, everything that could carry a signal throughout the First and Second Densities suddenly broadcasted a feed that originated from Atlantis. "Good morning, afternoon or evening, depending on your location. I'm Drew Bean, reporting live for the CT Update from Atlantis with breaking news! Now, throughout the First Density, Atlantis was considered more myth than history, but here with me is Percival Swan, Governor of Atlantis." Swan stepped in front of the camera beside Drew as he turned to him. "Governor Swan, from what I understand, Atlantis is regarded much the same in the Second Density. Please tell us how this came to be."

"It started nearly six hundred years ago when Kone found the ruins here…" He continued with a brief history of Atlantis's current incarnation, of how people were taken from the population to be part of Kone's personal think tank. "Our people became so well versed in this planet's greatest technology, and from there, began developing new innovations. He paused before adding, "But we could not leave."

Letting out a sigh, he continued, "We had the brightest minds on Earth collaborating on amazing new ideas. But we could not leave. And even though life in Atlantis was by all measures good, we were still prisoners in our own home. Living to this day under the constant threat of Kone's harsh punishments if we ever stepped out of line."

"So, Govenor, what has changed? How is it that you can reveal Atlantis and yourselves to the world now?"

"Atlantis has launched an initiative to remove the tyrant from power." As he said this, Sheriff Gurden and Hunter-Ralt Sahmbo walked Kone in front of the camera for the world to see him gagged and bound in a restraining disk. "And as you can see, it was successful."

The camera began to move backward, and the wider shot now showed Colonel Decker, Admiral Book and President Hedge of the United States, King Larriforn of Tir na nOg and King Knelgan of Steinelv. "As the highest-ranking official involved in Kone's capture, this by Cetatian law makes me the new Uniralt." The entire world was now paying attention, wondering what this could mean for all of them. "And my first decree as Uniralt is to transform the governor's office in Atlantis to that of President. And on behalf of her people, I declare Atlantis to be a free and independent nation."

Cheers erupted in the city and throughout the caverns below with the announcement and were still continuing as he began to speak again. "My second decree as Uniralt is that sovereignty is to be returned to all nations of the First Density, effective immediately." The cheers that erupted from Atlantis were now echoed by most people across the Human realm.

After a moment, his face softened. "Before we continue, there are some people that I must make known to you all." He looked at King

Larriforn, then Alunareth and back to the camera. "Quinten Earrach from Tir na nOg, Fourth Density." He looked at President Hedge and then his eyes settled on the grieving Sandra, "Neil Potman from the United States of America, First Density."

He next turned his gaze to King Knelgan, then to Rudge. "And Balgar Fjallgaard from Steinelv, Third Density. In the last forty-eight hours, these three men have sacrificed their lives in the effort to free us from Kone's tyranny. So now, let's take a moment of silence and remember what they have done for us all." He and everyone present lowered their heads a bit as the quiet moment was broadcast to the world. "Quinten, Neil and Balgar, thank you so much for your ultimate sacrifices. May the world use your gifts wisely and blessings to your loved ones."

He cleared his throat and straightened his tie before continuing, "All of the information that was in the vault's mainframe, now that we can access it, has been shared onto the internet in both the First and Second Densities. He looked at King Larriforn and King Knelgan. All the information will be made available in your realms as well." He wondered if they had an internet-like system in their densities but chose not to ask in the middle of a live broadcast.

"Now, I have one last decree. I am transferring the office of Uniralt and all its powers to Hunter-Ralt Derek Sahmbo." He turned to Derek and shook his hand, "May you lead the Second Density with the same wisdom and principles that you have used to lead the Hunters."

"Thank you," Derek said as he took the podium and faced the camera. "Tomorrow morning, all Podmen are to report to headquarters as we discuss the future of Cetatia. In the meantime, there are to be absolutely no hostilities toward the other densities or their people. We have a long road ahead of us, but it is a road we must travel to make things right. I ask that the rest of the world grant us some time and hopefully, in the very near future, I would like to establish trade relations with the other nations of our planet. The days of Kone's methods are done and we must all remember what he tried to do to our world and how he planned to achieve it, so this can never be allowed to happen again.

"All people of all nations and kingdoms need to be alert and aware of to whom they grant their power. For true power comes through cooperation rather than dictation. A dictatorship controls what is already there and stifles new ideas. Cooperation encourages creativity and innovation, and it is through a combination of cooperation and independent thought that our world will truly advance."

Sahmbo wrapped up a few moments later and Drew came back in front of the camera. "Uniralt Sahmbo and President Swan, thank you for coming on and addressing the world." He turned to look into the camera directly. "With this new shift in the status quo, we may have a brighter future than any of us would have hoped just a few short days ago. As always, we will do what we do best and update you as events unfold. For the CT Update, this has been Drew Bean. And now, back to your regularly scheduled broadcast." He stood there, looking into the camera, waiting.

A girl's voice was heard whispering off screen. "Stop the camera!"

"The controls are different," Elizabeth whispered back. "I'm trying to figure it out."

"Just use the PJs."

"Oh, wait! Here's the bu…" The screen flickered, and the normal programming returned to the networks. Back in Hartford, Connecticut, Mark Zanders leaped from his chair, fists pumping and cheering like a maniac. "Yes! Yes! Yes! Oh buddy, am I giving you a raise!"

Meelyhn, Atlantis

"A real mammoth!" Harry smiled as he watched the majestic creature.

Samuel and Alunareth had climbed into a nearby tree and started tossing peanuts to the pachyderm. "I guess this answers my question," Samuel said with a smile as the mammoth snubbed the legume and walked away. "Did you think they would?"

"No," Alunareth replied while shaking his head with a smile. "Elephants, in general, don't really like peanuts. I don't even know where the idea began. But it did give us an excuse for a closer look." He turned toward Samuel. "So…Hunter-Ralt, huh?"

"*Acting* Hunter-Ralt," Samuel corrected. "At least until Sahmbo can come back and I hope that it's sooner rather than later."

"Well, you've got the best possible advisor for the job."

Samuel nodded in agreement, grateful that Vedant was in his corner.

"What an amazing place," Maggie said to Ryan as they all made their way back to the village.

Sandra sighed but nodded, torn between the raw beauty of Meelyhn and knowing that Atlantis was where her husband died. Upon arriving at the village, Derek and Sabrina were there, waiting for Samuel so they could return to Cetatia and assume their new roles.

"Haley! Elizabeth!" a boy's voice called out. Dalton was jogging down the village's walkway and waving as a few of the other Atlantean kids followed.

"Here we go," Haley muttered.

"Yep," Elizabeth whispered. "Moment of truth."

The children came up to the two girls and Dalton had a big grin on his face. "I'm so glad you're here," he said to them. "There's somebody I really want you to meet!" He turned and took a girl's hand as she stepped forward. She was almost as tall as Dalton, had brown skin with hazel eyes, framed by epicanthal folds. Long, thick, dark wavey hair danced just beneath her shoulders when she moved, revealing the purple on the back of her neck. The rarest secondary pigment that there was. "Joyce, this is them! The girls I was telling you about. Haley, Elizabeth, meet my girlfriend, Joyce."

"Uh…hi," Haley said awkwardly.

Elizabeth nodded with false enthusiasm. "Hey."

"Did he really try to go with you to stop Kone?" Joyce asked with excitement.

Haley nodded. "Yeah, he did." *At least Beth and I won't be having jealousy issues now.* She thought, trying to keep a more positive perspective. After a few moments of talking, they found that they got along well with the Atlantean kids, and the conversation flowed as they began joking, laughing and running around to play. Like children.

Willimantic, Connecticut. First Density. Two days later

Despite the freezing cold, the preacher's words were that of warmth and compassion. He delivered Neil's eulogy with a short sermon about carrying on the memories of our loved ones and how they are always a part of us. Sandra cradled Junior as her tears fell and Maggie placed her right arm around Sandra's back and left hand on the shoulder.

After a moment, Haley took Junior so Sandra could blow her nose as Maggie and Bast continued trying to comfort the grieving widow. Elizabeth took Junior when Haley became empathically overwhelmed by the grief of all in attendance combined with her own. Sabrina leaned into Derek, as she also heard the slow but intense melody of everyone's emotional weight and a few tears managed to escape her eyes.

Neil was laid to rest and the service was coming to a close. Sandra stood up and turned around to see Bast with tears in her eyes and offering another box of tissues. With a cracking voice, Sandra said, "Thank you," took the box and a hug from the goddess.

Somber, Elizabeth and Haley slowly made their way back toward the vehicles with Junior when they felt the energy shift. Maggie and Bast also snapped their heads toward the changing vibration to see seven formally dressed people, five men and two women, who weren't there a moment ago.

A look of surprise on Bast's teary-eyed face, the goddess managed a slight smile and said, "You came!"

"Who are they?" Sandra asked as Haley, Elizabeth and the others approached.

The newcomers walked over to Sandra and one of the men spoke. He was just shy of six feet, had an olive skin tone, dark brown hair and a full beard, neatly groomed. "My name is Ares, and we came to pay our respects to the man who set us free."

He then turned and introduced the others, "My sisters Artemis and Aphrodite. The twins are Enumclaw and Kapoonis, this is Cernunnos, and this is Quetzalcoatl."

Artemis stepped to the front and held up what looked like a folded blanket. "This is for you," she said as she held it by two corners and let the rest unfurl. The fabric opened and revealed itself to be a tapestry bearing Neil's likeness. He was standing tall, with an expression on his face that looked both confident and kind.

Sandra took a deep breath and held it upon seeing the masterfully crafted piece depicting her lost love.

"There's one other just like it," Artemis informed her. "It hangs on the Wall of Heros, back in Olympus."

Releasing her breath with a sob, her voice broke again as she said, "Thank you."

Once Sandra steadied her breathing, Enumclaw pointed to the sky, and everyone looked up. Clouds began to gather, swirling above the cemetery and formed into letters which read, "Thank you Neil." Then lightning began to arch around the clouds, highlighting the words and drawing attention from miles around.

Junior watched the sky from Elizabeth's arms, mesmerized by the display as Haley and Elizabeth shed more tears. Harry put his arm around Haley as Ryan dropped a hand onto Elizabeth's shoulder. It continued for a full minute, then the lightning stopped, and the clouds faded away.

"We will never forget him," Cernunnos said.

With a flick of the wrist, the tapestry refolded itself and Artemis handed it to Sandra. She warmly held the widow's hand for a moment, then stepped away as Aphrodite came to her next, took her hand and looked into her eyes. "Blessings," she said and then stepped aside as the others all followed suit. One by one, they took her hand and offered their condolences. Ares said, "Take your time. Mourn. But then you must continue. Always persevere." He looked over to Junior and smiled, then looked back to Sandra, "He continues on, in the lives of all that he's touched." Ares gave her one last smile, said, "Fairwell," and the seven people disappeared in flashes of light.

Sandra looked at the folded tapestry in her hands and then looked up to Bast and Maggie. They shared a tearful three-way hug and then Sandra turned to Elizabeth. The young mystic held Junior up to his mother, Sandra took him and hugged her little man.

Harry noticed that Haley and Elizabeth were looking up the hill, then they both nodded. He followed their gaze to see two figures standing solemnly beneath a tree. Derrik and Sabrina, hand in hand, returned the girls' nods and then vanished into the woods.

Bast and Ptah, hand in hand, came up to the girls, "We must be going now," Bast said, "but I'll catch up with you in a few days."

Yesh Goldman walked up to the casket and placed a hand on the surface. No one noticed Him speaking, but beyond space and time, where the spirit was rejoined with the soul, Neil heard Yesh say, "Let's go see my dad."

The Split

*Almost…almost…*The binding spell broke, and Apophis reached out with his power, slowing himself from circling the Earth thousands of times a second. Phasing into the Third Density, he tumbled across a landscape and crashed into a mountainside. Laughing. He stood up and stretched.

"Ah, that feels better." He took to the sky, near as high as he could go and looked down upon the globe with a snicker. "That was impressive," he said aloud while thinking about the man in the black suit. "But that will also be the last time you get one over on me." He clenched his fist with determination. "You like to say that impossible is what you do, but I will show you what I can do. I will show you your end. I will utterly defeat you for everyone to see. I will show the world what happens when you cross the God of Chaos!" He lifted his eyes up from the planet to watch the sun sink behind the horizon as he vowed. "I'm coming for you, Loki!"

Manhattan, New York. Second Density. The next day.

Raymon Stith stumbled into his apartment and set the paper bag down on his kitchen counter. Flipping a switch, the lights came on, revealing the grease left over on the counter's surface. The entire apartment was cluttered, and the kitchen could use a good scrub, but Raymon didn't care. He pulled the two bottles of rum out of the bag, set them on the counter and crumpled the paper to throw it at the overflowing trash can, but fell short of his target. He paid no mind to it as he opened a cabinet, pulling out a nearly empty rum bottle, draining it into his throat and replacing it with the full one.

He took the other new bottle, twisted the cap off and took a swig as he stumbled to the living room. He collapsed onto the couch, splashing a little rum as he dropped, then took another swig.

"Ah." He held it in his lap for a moment, sipped again, then looked around. "I forgot to flip the switch," he slurred before setting the bottle on the coffee table and as he struggled to stand, the lights came on. "Thanks…wait, what?" He turned his head toward the light switch and the woman who turned it on was standing there. "Hey…who are you?"

With a wobble, he managed to stand up but continued to sway as Sabrina walked over to him.

"I'm here to talk to you. Do you remember me?

His glazed eyes looked over her face, finding it quite appealing and other than the two dots of fresh scar on her left cheekbone, he would have thought her visage to be perfect. His eyes dropped down, then back up as he slurred. "No…no, I wouldn't forget a woman that looks like you."

"Not woman," Sabrina said. "Try to think back further."

"Yeah…yeah, sure, I remember you." A sloppy smile found its way onto Raymon's face. "For you, I'll remember anything you want me to." He lifted the bottle. "Would you like a trink?"

"No. I need you to remember."

"I remember that I have a few creds left on my account. Are you hungry? I'll take you out for drinks…and to eat and drink." He smiled and added, "I'm really good at the dating scene. Even better later."

Sabrina was trying to get through to Raymon's mind, but in his drunken stupor, could not seem to rip his attention away from the biological imperative. With a sigh and a roll of her eyes, she said, "Well maybe this will jog your memory," as she pulled her bangs to the side, revealing the vertical scar.

Tilting his head, Raymon stood there with a blank stare before he lifted his head up straight and his mouth started to open in a slow-motion expression of surprise as the memory trickled back into his consciousness. "You…you're…"

Hearing his heart's change in tone, Sabrina knew that the memory was finally cutting through the booze. "Yes?"

"Yer that kid that we…Are you here to kill me?" he asked with a rising voice as all the misery that the drink usually suppressed came rushing to the surface and he turned, throwing the bottle against the wall, where it shattered. He held his arms out to the side, as Sabrina felt the waves of nihilism flowing out from the bitter man. "Then do it! Get it over with! I deserve it!" His shouts radiated self-loathing and even Sabrina was shocked at how much of a mess that Raymon had become. "Well? What are you waiting for?!"

"I'm not here to kill you. I'm here to talk to you."

"About what?" he spat.

"I…I was…trying to forgive you."

A strange laugh escaped Raymon's mouth alongside a belch. "I'm the last person who deserves forgiveness." Holding his arms back out to the side, he added, "Now do it!"

The usually stoic Sabrina wore the expression of shock on her face, clear enough for even the drunken Raymon to read. "What? You know what kind of guy I am. You know I'm a piece of…"

Sabrina lifted her hand, "That's enough. If you were still as bad as you say you are, then guilt would not be eating you up inside. But it is. And your life does not have to be this way."

"What do you know about my life?"

"Much. But that's not the point. I've seen people change, and you can too." She looked him in the eye and had to remind herself not to keep her expression neutral. Her eyes softened as she let the earnestness show on her face when she said, "I forgive you."

She turned to leave when he shouted, "No! No, you don't. All I'm doing is killing time 'til time kills me. You're my ticket out!" He lunged at Sabrina, trying to force her to fight back, but his swing never got anywhere near her face before he stumbled to the floor.

I can't believe that this is one of the men who haunted my dreams. She stooped down as he tried to roll onto his back and sit up. "Here are some things that I know about your life. You have no family, no friends, and you don't even know your next-door neighbor's name."

"It's Elroy," Raymon slurred.

"No, it's Elliot. Elliot Novak. There are people all around you. Good people. The type of people that you wish you could be like." Raymon propped himself up on his elbows. "Build rapport, make friends and you'll gain a support system that can help you become who you should be. We are social creatures and deteriorate without that contact. Go talk to them. Get to know them. Get a life." Her eyes wandered to the side, then she stood and turned away.

"Where are you going?"

"To take my own advice," Sabrina answered as she slipped out the window.

Second Density. Location: Unknown

Walking through the room, the Uniralt looked inside the brooding chamber at the large spotted egg being kept warm. "And we know the lineage?"

"Yes, Uniralt. The Archons had kept their mainframe updated with every egg. According to the files, the eggs usually hatch around eighteen months. The first hatch should happen next month."

"And who are the parents?" Sahmbo asked.

"The egg was laid by Nokitahm. Sired by Ahnk-Hume."

First Density. Willimantic, Connecticut. One week later

Hanging up the phone, Sandra let out a long sigh and let herself collapse to a reclining position on the couch. The widow had inherited the ownership and responsibility of Neil's businesses, a position to which she was not accustomed. Thankfully, Problem Solders pretty much ran itself and she had developed a good rapport with the employees over the last few years, but she still needed to pay attention to what was happening and The GamePort's future was uncertain. The arcade, though unprofitable, was a labor of love for Neil, and Sandra didn't want to close down the place for which he was known. The place where he made many friends and touched many lives.

She lifted her head and looked to the living room floor, where Junior played with his blocks. "I miss you, Honey," Sandra whispered while watching Junior place a third block on the stack. A tear in her eye and a slight smile on her face, she picked up her day-planner and double checked her schedule for the next morning. Upon opening the book, she looked at the date and froze.

After staring for almost a full minute, Sandra picked up her cell phone and dialed a number, hoping she would answer.

"Hi," Maggie answered in a cheerful tone.

"Hi, um. Do you have time for Junior and I to come over for a bit?"

"Of course. Is everything okay?" Maggie asked, becoming concerned.

"Yeah, I…I just think I might need a friend right now," Sandra answered with a sniffle.

"Okay," Maggie gently replied. "Come on over. We'll all be here."

"Thanks."

After the car warmed up, Sandra buckled Junior in the car seat and made a quick stop at the convenience store on her way out of town. She drove to the Guerrerios's house in Columbia, and Maggie opened the front door as Sandra was taking Junior out of the car.

"Hi," Sandra said while walking to the house.

"Hi," Maggie replied.

"Could you take Junior for a moment? I need to use the bathroom."

"Absolutely," she answered and smiled at the toddler while reaching out to take him. Maggie took Junior to the living room where Elizabeth brought out some toys and began playing with him. A few moments of playing ticked by but came to a sudden stop when they all heard a scream from the bathroom.

"Keep an eye on Junior," Maggie said to Elizabeth as she and Ryan jumped up and ran toward the bathroom. She knocked on the door and called, "Sandra?" while sobs could be heard from the other side of the door.

Ryan turned around and Maggie said, "I'm coming in." Opening the door, she saw Sandra standing there with streams down her cheeks and what looked like smile. Sandra took a step, leaning forward and Maggie pulled her into a tight hug while she sobbed. A moment later, Maggie lifted her eyes and noticed the positive pregnancy test on the bathroom counter.

Epilogue

Sahmbo implemented changes quickly, tasking all the districts with finding ways to operate independently without heavy reliance on the Cetatian State for instruction. It was difficult at first, considering that, up until now, every move the Podmen made was carefully directed by Kone. Now they had to learn to decide for themselves, as well as take responsibility for the outcomes. Not to the Uniralt, but to their people. The people themselves were no longer subjects of the state but were now constituents, and some of the Podmen resigned, unable to deal with the pressure.

Some districts began having elections and the road was a bumpy one at first, but as six months had passed, the different districts began to find their footing and made trade agreements with one another. As time went on, the counsel of Podmen changed faces, exchanged ideas, and the districts became independent states. Sahmbo also insisted that the individual Cetatian states also communicated with the nations of the world's other densities.

After a year, The Counsel of Podmen were communicating in good fashion, established a quarterly meeting schedule for collaboration and became interdependent. The states were able to function on their own and through cooperation, made each other stronger and more stable.

As the process continued, things finally reached a place where Derek's direct involvement was no longer needed. Having meetings with other nations himself over that year, Derek managed to reach an agreement with many of them, the United States included, that being a Hunter would be viewed as both a private investigator's license as well as a bounty hunter's license. However, they were always required to notify local law enforcement of their presence. This worked out well, and many police departments were thrilled to have a Hunter on a case with them.

Less than two years had gone by, and the world was amazed at how things had changed for the better. Though nothing was perfect, there was much less difficulty in finding ways to cooperate without Kone's manipulations to keep people divided, and the time that Derek was working toward had finally arrived: the time for him to return to the Hunters.

In his final order as the Cetatian ruler, Sahmbo abolished the position of Uniralt, allowing the Cetatian nations to be truly independent.

As for Kone himself, a televised tribunal was held in Atlantis where he was found guilty of crimes against all peoples and sentenced to death, but his health began to fail before that could even happen. Nearly two thousand years of atrocities left a bad energy within him and without Molech's power to extend his life, the former Uniralt began to whither at an alarming rate. Doctors and healers tried to stabilize him so that his formal sentence could be carried out, but there was nothing that they could do. It was only three months after his capture when he passed, but not before an unexpected visit from a maintenance man that somehow entered his cell unseen.

Second Density. Earth, High Orbit. July 2000

The hull was comprised of a tan-colored metal, larger than a cruise liner and rounded at the front, which was wrapped with five rows of viewports, one for each deck. The back was flat, making the vessel reminiscent of giant steam-iron. Standing at the bridge viewport, Flarn Rel looked upon the Earth while stroking his chin in thought. He was the captain of this ship, and his brother Spart was his second-in-command. These two Sabidaran men have never even set foot on Sabido, their ancestorial home world, due to the family business.

For generations, the Rel family had been fugitives in most sectors for piracy and trafficking. Their great-grandfather was the one who had traded a substantial amount of mayum with some slaves to Kone for Flekkle, and the Rels had profited greatly from that deal. They had come again for a meeting with Kone and were utterly surprised to learn of the Uniralt's defeat.

"I suppose I should let the Dracos know that we'll be available sooner than expected," Spart said to his brother, heading to the comms.

Flarn closed his eyes and began to nod, but his eyes shot back open with a smile when he shouted, "Wait!" just before Spart touched the panel. He turned to face his brother with a smile. "Think about the opportunity! Kone has been removed and the power structure is decentralizing, but this means new economies. And with that will come new black markets."

Spart tilted his head, liking where this was going, and his brother continued. "It's the perfect opportunity to establish new contacts and trading deals. While everything is in flux, we can be one of the first to build rapport with both established and budding organizations." His smile grew wider as he went on. "The rest of the galaxy will eventually want to establish relations with this planet, and when they do, our family will already have a monopoly on this world. You have been saying that we need to make long-term plans. I can't think of a better chance than this, and as the Terrans like to say, we are on the ground floor."

The excitement returned to Spart's eyes. "Who was the man from the First Density that Kone kept speaking of."

After a moment of thought, Flarn asked, "You mean the one who lives in Ireland?"

"Yes."

With a snap of the fingers, Flarn said, "Driscoll."

"That's it!"

"Tell the crew to prepare for density shift," Flarn said with eagerness in his eyes. He turned back to the viewport and fixed his stare upon Europe. "It's time to make some new friends."

Omniwatch Data Entry:

Multiversal Cluster 77. Designation: Frequency
Universe 7, Timeline 1-C1-C42
Earth: 2018

"I feel it," Remy said with confusion.

Logan nodded, "Me too. It's right here, but I don't see anything."

"Whoa!" Alexander exclaimed. "That feels weird…and strong."

Also sensing the strange energy, Chuck called Gus over to their spot. Their com-systems were scanning the strange invisible energy, but none of them could make heads or tails of what it was or meant.

Gus approached and immediately sensed it, too, while he looked at the data and tried to understand what was happening.

"Any idea what it could be?" Joseph asked while holding his palms toward the spot, feeling the potent vibes.

"Yes," Gus answered, still looking unsure. "It's an anomaly."

Kenny shot him a look, "Thanks for clearing that up, Genius."

Gus looked up from his phone screen to everybody staring back at him. "I really said that, didn't I?"

"Yeah, you did," Chuck and Logan said in Unison.

After a quick, self-deprecating chuckle, Gus clarified. "It's likely a port anomaly."

"I thought that wasn't possible without another gate or beacon," Joseph mentioned.

"Technologically, no," Gus explained. "But magickally, yes."

"Maybe more of those things that we fought inside the ruins," speculated Remy. "Can you get a bead on its origin?"

"I'm trying…what?!" Gus's face dropped to an expression of astonishment while looking at his screen.

"What is it?" Chuck asked.

Gus looked up to the others. "If I'm understanding this correctly, it's coming from outside our universe."

"Seriously?" Alexander asked with a mix of excitement and wonder.

Logan and Joseph were the first to notice. Logan spun around as he drew his pistol, and the other Marshals followed suit before he had completed the movement to find a woman standing thirty feet away. Even with their attention on the anomaly, how could someone who radiated such power have gotten so close to them without the empaths noticing? The woman was 5'10 and had beautiful dark skin, with black hair tied up into a bun, yellow pupils with specs of green and a purple silk blouse paired with black dress slacks. She bore an expression of calm superiority and seemed very aloof despite the firearms pointing in her direction.

No, Logan thought. *She's not aloof…she's reserved. Guarded.* Joseph was realizing the same thing right before she spoke.

"Those will not be necessary, gentlemen. I am simply guiding my counterpart."

"Counterpart?" Gus asked under his breath.

A spark appeared. A small gold spark that began to spin and grow. They all backed away from the spot as the spinning electrical ball opened at the vortex, slowly growing wider.

The little speakers in the Marshals' collars began to play music that they recognized as The Guess Who's American Woman, and they all shot Logan a look.

Throwing his free palm up toward the others, he said, "It ain't me!"

Looking down at his screen and then back to the widening vortex, Gus said, "It's coming from there…from another set of PJs."

"How can that be?" Chuck asked as the vortex opened completely.

They all looked back to the anomaly to see a woman step through. Wearing coveralls, she was 5'5 with blue eyes and blonde hair, braided back into two long pigtails. An orange and white cat with a similar coat pattern as Scott came trotting out behind her, followed by a taller woman.

This woman was 5'8 with a bit of a tan, hazel eyes, and brown hair that was tied back into a ponytail that hung down between her shoulder blades.

Behind her appeared a third woman who looked identical to the one who showed up just a moment ago, but her demeanor was different. Though she radiated the same kind of energy, her hair hung loose down to the lower back while giving the empaths a sense of friendly warmth. The vortex closed and disappeared.

Lowering his gun, Logan said, "There's no hostility."

"I'm getting the same," Joseph added.

The other Marshals lowered their firearms as well, although Chuck kept his at the ready.

The blonde woman stared at the Marshals with a look of excitement and disbelief. The empaths were picking up a sense of having run into a long-lost friend.

The music was cut off with the sound of a scratching needle. "Marshals?"

"Yeah," Chuck answered. "Who are you?"

A wide smile spread across the woman's face, and she threw her arms out wide, running toward them with a joyful shout. "Marshals!"

Unthreatened but with no idea what to make of this situation, they stood there dumbfounded as this woman charged toward them with open arms. She closed the distance and threw her arms around Remy and Gus. "I've missed you guys so much!" she exclaimed while squeezing with considerable strength. Haley let go, and they gasped for air as she spun toward Chuck and Logan, grabbing them into a hug. "It's so good to see you!"

His voice sounding a bit forced, Chuck said, "Nice to see you too, whoever you are."

"And you're making it difficult to breathe," Logan added.

Haley released her overly enthusiastic embrace with a sheepish grin. "Oh, heh…sorry."

Glossary

Density:

Reality is made of energy. Energy exists as a spectrum, and so, too,
does reality. Multiple realms exist within the same space at the same
time but on different wavelengths. The term dimension is often
incorrectly substituted.

Dimension:

A method of spatial measurement. There are only three.

Flekkle:

Flekkle is a soft metal, similar to gold and lead, but much lighter in
weight. Very rare, little was found in the Second Density, and the only
known sources that remain are in the Third and Fourth Densities.
After being worked, Flekkle is quenched in mystically charged fluid,
making it as supple as leather yet nigh unbreakable. But, if heated to
twice the temperature at which it was worked, it will smelt and return
to its original properties. Allowing the flow of both electrical and

mystical energies, Flekkle even surpasses silver and is the best-known conductor on Earth.

Fordriva:

A mineral that was discovered by the Dwarves, fordriva is disruptive to some forms of magick and cannot be enchanted.

Magic:

The art of making it appear as if something happened when it did not. An illusion. Sleight of hand. A stage performance.

Magick:

Raising and directing energy by way of consciousness to produce a result.

Mayum:

A lightweight metal not found on Earth, mayum is the hardest known substance in the galaxy. Unbreakable, it is a difficult material with which to work. It is a horrible conductor, unaffected by magnets, strenuous to enchant and applying heat only warms the surface. Because of its unique thermal shedding ability, a few wealthier civilizations of the galaxy have had some of their ships' hulls plated with mayum, allowing it to withstand heat from a star. Mayum is worked by bathing it in sonic pulses of a very particular range and intensity while applying heat to make it pliable. As soon as the sonic pulses cease, the mayum sheds its heat and remains solid.

The Split:

Exactly between two densities, the split is where the magnetic energies of the two opposing realms meet. Many space-faring civilizations use this for faster-than-light travel. Inside the split, a ship is accelerated like a missile from a rail gun and being out of phase with physical matter allows for a continuous increase in speed.

The Gods:

Aphrodite/Venus

From: Greek/Roman Pantheon.

She is the Goddess of Love. Daughter of Zeus, sister of Ares, Artemis, and Hermes. Associated with the sea.

Apophis

From: Egyptian Pantheon.

He is the God of Chaos. Associated with death, earthquakes and storms.

Ares/Mars

From: Greek/Roman Pantheon.

He is the God of War. Son of Zeus, brother of Artemis, Hermes, and Venus. Associated with the sword, the pear and golden rams.

Artemis/Diana

From: Greek/Roman Pantheon.

She is the Goddess of the Hunt. Daughter of Zeus, sister of Ares, Hermes and Venus. Associated with the bow and arrow, knives and the deer.

Baphomet

From: An amalgamation.

Not coming from a traditional pantheon, Baphomet has aspects that come from Egypt, the Templars, the imagination of a French magician named Eliphas Levi and pushed into the cultural zeitgeist by Aleister Crowley.

Bastet

From: Egyptian Pantheon.

She is the Goddess of Protection. Daughter of Ra, sister of Sekhmet and wife of Ptah. Associated with the home, fertility, childbirth and cats.

Cernunnos/Herne

From: Celtic Pantheon.

He is the God of the Hunt. Also known as the Greenman, Lord of the Wild, Spirit of the Woods and more. Associated with animals, especially deer, fertility and the oak tree.

Enumclaw

From: Cherokee Pantheon.

He is the God of Lightning. Son of Kanati and Selu, twin brother of Kapoonis. Associated with fire and spears.

Hel

From: Norse Pantheon.

She is the Goddess of Death. Daughter of Loki. She is associated with the dead and wolves.

Hermes/Mercury

From: Greek/Roman Pantheon.

He is the God of Travel. Son of Zeus, brother of Ares, Artemis and Venus. Associated with luck, wealth, thieves and trade.

Kapoonis

From: Cherokee Pantheon.

He is the God of Thunder. Son of Kanati and Selu, twin brother of Enumclaw. Associated with boulders.

Lillith

From: Jewish and Sumerian folklore.

With her name being a possible derivative of a Mesopotamian demon called a lilitu, some research suggests that she was a Sumerian succubus before she was known as a demonic being in Jewish stories who gave birth to incubi and succubi. Known for bringing harm to expecting mothers and her psychopathic delight in crushing the throats of children, especially infants, she has been dubbed the Goddess of Sorrows in this series. She is associated with lust, infanticide and dragons.

Loki

From: Norse Pantheon.

He is the God of Mischief. Father of Fenrir, Hel and Jormungandr. He is associated with birds, chrysoberyl, and potentially fire.

Molech

From: Mesopotamian Pantheon.

He is the God of Human Sacrifice. Although listed here as Mesopotamian, his origins are somewhat murky, and some speculate that his name may not have been in reference to a being but to a sacrificial process. Associated with nothing good.

Odin

From: Norse Pantheon.

He is the God of War and the Dead. He is the father to Baldur, Thor, Vali and others. Associated with wisdom, healing and the dead.

Ptah

From: Egyptian Pantheon.

He is the God of Craftsmen and Labor. Husband to Bastet and Sekhmet (although not Sekhmet in this continuity). Associated with the ankh, the djed, and the bull.

Quetzalcoatl

From: Aztech Pantheon.

He is the God of Wind and Rain. Son of Chimalma and Mixcoatl. Associated with birds, serpents and learning.

Ra

From: Egyptian Pantheon.

He is the God of the Sun. Father to Bastet and Sekhmet. Associated with the falcon.

Raiden/Raijin

From: Japanese Pantheon.

He is the God of Storms. Son of Izanagi and Izanami. Associated with taiko drums and hammers.

Sekhmet

From: Egyptian Pantheon.

She is the Goddess of Lions. Daughter of Ra, sister of Bastet and wife of Ptah (although not in this continuity). Associated with the undead.

Surtr

From: Norse Pantheon.

A Jotunn who resided in Muspelheim, it was prophesized that he and Odin would slay each other in Ragnarok (but in this reality, Odin banished him to Tartarus instead).

Thor

From: Norse Pantheon.

He is the God of Thunder. Son of Jord and Odin. Brother of Baldur, Vali and others. Associated with storms, the oak and protection.

Tuweltha

From: O'salra Pantheon.

She is the Goddess of Nurturing. Daughter of Siobhan and Ulardrad. Sister of Tadhg. Associated with streams, the Alder tree and cultivation.

Zeus

From: Greek Pantheon.

He is the God of Thunder and Sky. Husband of Hera. Father of Ares, Artemis, Hermes and many others. Associated with the eagle, the lightning bolt and the oak tree.

Based on the video game of the same name that has
not yet been made at the time of this publishing.

Special thanks to:

Black Knight.

Christina Adcock.

Connor Cryan-Sasportas.

Logan Cryan-Sasportas.

Garhom.

Geno.

Maryssa Gordon.

Chuck McDonald.

Joshua Stevens.

Sonnet Stevens.

Traci.

TrippySoul.

Yeshua.